KU-120-313

SCIENCE FICTION
THE BEST OF 2001

ROBERT SILVERBERG
and KAREN HABER
Editors

ibooks
new york
www.ibooksinc.com

An Original Publication of ibooks, inc.

Copyright © 2002 by ibooks, inc.

Introduction copyright © 2001 by Agberg, Ltd.

ibooks, inc.
24 West 25th Street
New York, NY 10010

The ibooks World Wide Web Site Address is:
http://www.ibooksinc.com

ISBN 0-7434-3498-6
First ibooks, inc. printing February 2002
10 9 8 7 6 5 4 3 2 1

Special thanks to Martin Greenberg and Larry Segriff

Cover art
copyright © 2001 by Scott Grimando
Cover design by carrie monaco

Printed in the U.S.A.

Contents

SCIENCE FICTION
THE BEST OF 2001
AN INTRODUCTION

by Robert Silverberg
and Karen Haber

The first of all the Year's Best Science Fiction anthologies appeared in the summer of 1949. It was edited by Everett F. Bleiler and T. E. Dikty, a pair of scholarly science-fiction readers with long experience in the field, and it was called, not entirely appropriately (since it drew on material published in 1948), The Best Science Fiction Stories: 1949.

Science fiction then was a very small entity indeed—a handful of garish-looking magazines with names like *Planet Stories* and *Thrilling Wonder Stories*, a dozen or so books a year produced by semi-professional publishing houses run by old-time s-f fans, and the very occasional short story by the likes of Robert A. Heinlein in *The Saturday Evening Post* or some other well-known slick magazine. So esoteric a species of reading-matter was it that Bleiler and Dikty found it necessary to provide their book, which was issued by the relatively minor mainstream publishing house of Frederick Fell, Inc., with two separate introductory essays explaining the nature and history of science fiction to uninitiated readers.

In those days science fiction was at its best in the short lengths, and the editors of *The Best Science Fiction: 1949* had plenty of splendid material to offer. There were two stories by Ray Bradbury, both later incorporated in *The Martian Chronicles*, and Wilmar Shiras's fine superchild story "In Hiding," and an excellent early Poul Anderson story, and one by Isaac Asimov, and half a dozen others, all of which would be received enthusiastically by modern readers. The book did fairly well, by the modest sales standards of its era, and the Bleiler-Dikty series of annual anthologies continued for another decade or so.

Toward the end of its era the Bleiler-Dikty collection was joined by a very different sort of Best of the Year anthology edited by Judith Merril, whose sophisticated literary tastes led her to go far beyond the s-f magazines, offering stories by such outsiders to the field as Jorge Luis Borges, Jack Finney, Donald Barthelme, and John Steinbeck cheek-by-jowl with the more familiar offerings of Asimov, Theodore Sturgeon, Robert Sheckley, and Clifford D. Simak. The Merril anthology, inaugurated in 1956, also lasted about a decade; and by then science fiction had become big business, with new mag-

INTRODUCTION

azines founded, shows like *Star Trek* appearing on network television, dozens and then hundreds of novels published every year. Since the 1960s no year has gone by without its Best of the Year collection, and sometimes two or three simultaneously. Such distinguished science-fiction writers as Frederik Pohl, Harry Harrison, Brian Aldiss, and Lester del Rey took their turns at compiling annual anthologies, along with veteran book editors like Donald A. Wollheim and Terry Carr.

In modern times the definitive Year's Best Anthology has been the series of encyclopedic collections edited by Gardner Dozois since 1984. Its eighteen mammoth volumes so far provide a definitive account of the genre in the past two decades. More recently a second annual compilation has arrived, edited by an equally keen observer of the science-fiction scene, David A. Hartwell; and that there is so little overlap between the Hartwell and Dozois anthologies is a tribute not only to the ability of experts to disagree but also to the wealth of fine shorter material being produced today in the science-fiction world.

If there is room in the field for two sets of opinions about the year's outstanding work, perhaps there is room for a third. And so, herewith, the newest of the Year's Best Science Fiction anthologies, in which a long-time writer/editor and his writer/editor wife have gathered a group of the science-fiction stories of 2001 that gave them the greatest reading pleasure.

—Robert Silverberg
Karen Haber

UNDONE

JAMES PATRICK KELLY

panic attack

THE SHIP SCREAMED. ITS screens showed Mada that she was surrounded in threespace. A swarm of Utopian asteroids was closing on her, brain clans and mining DIs living in hollowed-out chunks of carbonaceous chondrite, any one of which could have mustered enough votes to abolish Mada in all ten dimensions.

"I'm going to die," the ship cried, "I'm going to die, I'm going to . . ."

"I'm not." Mada waved the speaker off impatiently and scanned down-when. She saw that the Utopians had planted an identity mine five minutes into the past that would boil her memory to vapor if she tried to go back in time to undo this trap. Upwhen, then. The future was clear, at least as far as she could see, which wasn't much beyond next week. Of course, that was the direction they wanted her to skip. They'd be happiest making her their great-great-great-grandchildren's problem.

The Utopians fired another spread of panic bolts. The ship tried to absorb them, but its buffers were already overflowing. Mada felt her throat tighten. Suddenly she couldn't remember how to spell *luck*, and she believed that she could feel her sanity oozing out of her ears.

"So let's skip upwhen," she said.

"You s-sure?" said the ship. "I don't know if . . . how far?"

"Far enough so that all of these drones will be fossils."

"I can't just . . . I need a number, Mada."

A needle of fear pricked Mada hard enough to make her reflexes kick. "Skip!" Her panic did not allow for the luxury of numbers. "Skip now!" Her voice was tight as a fist. "Do it!"

Time shivered as the ship surged into the empty dimensions. In three-space, Mada went all wavy. Eons passed in a nanosecond, then she washed back into the strong dimensions and solidified.

She merged briefly with the ship to assess damage. "What have you done?" The gain in entropy was an ache in her bones.

"I-I'm sorry, you said to skip so . . ." The ship was still jittery.

Even though she wanted to kick its sensorium in, she bit down hard on her anger. They had both made

2

enough mistakes that day. "That's all right," she said, "we can always go back. We just have to figure out when we are. Run the star charts."

two-tenths of a spin

The ship took almost three minutes to get its charts to agree with its navigation screens—a bad sign. Reconciling the data showed that it had skipped forward in time about two-tenths of a galactic spin. Almost twenty million years had passed on Mada's home world of Trueborn, time enough for its crust to fold and buckle into new mountain ranges, for the Green Sea to bloom, for the glaciers to march and melt. More than enough time for everything and everyone Mada had ever loved—or hated—to die, turn to dust and blow away.

Whiskers trembling, she checked downwhen. What she saw made her lose her perch and float aimlessly away from the command mod's screens. There had to be something wrong with the ship's air. It settled like dead, wet leaves in her lungs. She ordered the ship to check the mix.

The ship's deck flowed into an enormous plastic hand, warm as blood. It cupped Mada gently in its palm and raised her up so that she could see its screens straight on.

"Nominal, Mada. Everything is as it should be."

That couldn't be right. She could breathe ship-nominal atmosphere. "Check it again," she said.

"Mada, I'm sorry," said the ship.

The identity mine had skipped with them and was still dogging her, five infuriating minutes into the past. There was no getting around it, no way to undo their leap into the future. She was trapped two-tenths of a spin upwhen. The knowledge was like a sucking hole in her chest, much worse than any wound the Utopian psychological war machine could have inflicted on her.

"What do we do now?" asked the ship.

Mada wondered what she should say to it. Scan for hostiles? Open a pleasure sim? Cook a nice, hot stew? Orders twisted in her mind, bit their tails and swallowed themselves.

She considered—briefly—telling it to open all the air locks to the vacuum. Would it obey this order? She thought it probably would, although she would as soon chew her own tongue off as utter such cowardly words. Had not she and her sibling batch voted to carry the revolution into all ten dimensions? Pledged themselves to fight for the Three Universal Rights, no matter what the cost the Utopian brain clans extracted from them in blood and anguish?

But that had been two-tenths of a spin ago.

bean thoughts

"Where are you going?" said the ship.

Mada floated through the door bubble of the com-

4

mand mod. She wrapped her toes around the perch outside to steady herself.

"Mada, wait! I need a mission, a course, some line of inquiry."

She launched down the companionway.

"I'm a Dependent Intelligence, Mada." Its speaker buzzed with self-righteousness. "I have the right to proper and timely guidance."

The ship flowed a veil across her trajectory; as she approached, it went taut. That was DI thinking: the ship was sure that it could just bounce her back into its world. Mada flicked her claws and slashed at it, shredding holes half a meter long.

"And I have the right to be an individual," she said. "Leave me alone."

She caught another perch and pivoted off it toward the greenhouse blister. She grabbed the perch by the door bubble and paused to flow new alveoli into her lungs to make up for the oxygen-depleted, carbon-dioxide-enriched air mix in the greenhouse. The bubble shivered as she popped through it and she breathed deeply. The smells of life helped ground her whenever operation of the ship overwhelmed her. It was always so needy and there was only one of her.

It would have been different if they had been designed to go out in teams. She would have had her sibling Thiras at her side; together they might have been strong enough to withstand the Utopian's panic . . . *no!*

Mada shook him out of her head. Thiras was gone; they were all gone. There was no sense in looking for comfort, downwhen or up. All she had was the moment, the tick of the relentless present, filled now with the moist, bittersweet breath of the dirt, the sticky savor of running sap, the bloom of perfume on the flowers. As she drifted through the greenhouse, leaves brushed her skin like caresses. She settled at the potting bench, opened a bin and picked out a single bean seed.

Mada cupped it between her two hands and blew on it, letting her body's warmth coax the seed out of dormancy. She tried to merge her mind with its blissful unconsciousness. Cotyledons stirred and began to absorb nutrients from the endosperm. A bean cared nothing about proclaiming the Three Universal Rights: the right of all independent sentients to remain individual, the right to manipulate their physical structures and the right to access the timelines. Mada slowed her metabolism to the steady and deliberate rhythm of the bean— what Utopian could do that? They held that individuality bred chaos, that function alone must determine form and that undoing the past was sacrilege. Being Utopians, they could hardly destroy Trueborn and its handful of colonies. Instead they had tried to put the Rights under quarantine.

Mada stimulated the sweat glands in the palms of her hands. The moisture wicking across her skin called to the embryonic root in the bean seed. The tip pushed against the sead coat. Mada's sibling batch on Trueborn had pushed hard against the Utopian blockade, to bring the Rights to the rest of the galaxy.

Only a handful had made it to open space. The brain clans had hunted them down and brought most of them back in disgrace to Trueborn. But not Mada. No, not wily Mada, Mada the fearless, Mada whose heart now beat but once a minute.

The bean embryo swelled and its root cracked the seed coat. It curled into her hand, branching and re-branching like the timelines. The roots tickled her.

Mada manipulated the chemistry of her sweat by forcing her sweat ducts to reabsorb most of the sodium and chlorine. She parted her hands slightly and raised them up to the grow lights. The cotyledons emerged and chloroplasts oriented themselves to the light. Mada was thinking only bean thoughts as her cupped hands filled with roots and the first true leaves unfolded. More leaves budded from the nodes of her stem, her petioles arched and twisted to the light, *the light*. It was only the light— violet-blue and orange-red—that mattered, the incredible shower of photons that excited her chlorophyll, passing electrons down carrier molecules to form adenosine diphosphate and nicotinamide adenine dinucleo. . . .

"Mada," said the ship. "The order to leave you alone is now superseded by primary programming."

"What?" The word caught in her throat like a bone.

"You entered the greenhouse forty days ago."

Without quite realizing what she was doing, Mada clenched her hands, crushing the young plant.

"I am directed to keep you from harm, Mada," said the ship. "It's time to eat."

She glanced down at the dead thing in her hands. "Yes, all right." She dropped it onto the potting bench. "I've got something to clean up first but I'll be there in a minute." She wiped the corner of her eye. "Meanwhile, calculate a course for home."

Not until the ship scanned the quarantine zone at the edge of the Trueborn system did Mada begin to worry. In her time the zone had swarmed with the battle asteroids of the brain clans. Now the Utopians were gone. Of course, that was to be expected after all this time. But as the ship re-entered the home system, dumping excess velocity into the empty dimensions, Mada felt a chill that had nothing to do with the temperature in the command mod.

Trueborn orbited a spectral type G3V star, which had been known to the discovers as HR3538. Scans showed that the Green Sea had become a climax forest of deciduous hardwood. There were indeed new mountains—knife edges slicing through evergreen sheets—that had upthrust some eighty kilometers off the Fire Coast, leaving Port Henoch landlocked. A rain forest choked the plain where the city of Blair's Landing had once sprawled.

The ship scanned life in abundance. The seas teemed and flocks of Trueborn's flyers darkened the skies like storm clouds: kippies and bluewings and warblers and migrating stilts. Animals had retaken all three continents, lowland and upland, marsh and tundra. Mada could see the dust kicked up by the herds of herbivorous aram from low orbit. The forest echoed with the clatter of shindies and the shriek of blowhards. Big hunters like kar and divil padded across the plains. There were new species as well, mostly invertebrates but also a number of lizards and something like a great, mossy rat that built mounds five meters tall.

None of the introduced species had survived: dogs or turkeys or llamas. The ship could find no cities, towns, buildings—not even ruins. There were neither tubeways nor roads, only the occasional animal track. The ship looked across the entire electromagnetic spectrum and saw nothing but the natural background.

There was nobody home on Trueborn. And as far as they could tell, there never had been.

"Speculate," said Mada.

"I can't," said the ship. "There isn't enough data."

"There's your data." Mada could hear the anger in her voice. "Trueborn, as it would have been had we never even existed."

"Two-tenths of a spin is a long time, Mada."

She shook her head. "They ripped out the foundations, even picked up the dumps. There's nothing, *noth-*

ing of us left." Mada was gripping the command perch so hard that the knuckles of her toes were white. "Hypothesis," she said, "the Utopians got tired of our troublemaking and wiped us out. Speculate."

"Possible, but that's contrary to their core beliefs." Most DIs had terrible imaginations. They couldn't tell jokes, but then they couldn't commit crimes, either.

"Hypothesis: they deported the entire population, scattered us to prison colonies. Speculate."

"Possible, but a logistical nightmare. The Utopians prize the elegant solution."

She swiped the image of her home planet off the screen, as if to erase its unnerving impossibility. "Hypothesis: there are no Utopians anymore because the revolution succeeded. Speculate."

"Possible, but then where did everyone go? And why did they return the planet to its pristine state?"

She snorted in disgust. "What if," she tapped a finger to her forehead, "maybe we *don't* exist. What if we've skipped to another time line? One in which the discovery of Trueborn never happened? Maybe there has been no Utopian Empire in this timeline, no Great Expansion, no Space Age, maybe no human civilization at all."

"One does not just skip to another timeline at random." The ship sounded huffy at the suggestion. "I've monitored all our dimensional reinsertions quite carefully, and I can assure you that all these events occurred in the timeline we currently occupy."

"You're saying there's no chance?"

"If you want to write a story, why bother asking my opinion?"

Mada's laugh was brittle. "All right then. We need more data." For the first time since she had been stranded upwhen, she felt a tickle stir the dead weight she was carrying inside her. "Let's start with the nearest Utopian system."

chasing shadows

The HR683 system was abandoned and all signs of human habitation had been obliterated. Mada could not be certain that everything had been restored to its pre-Expansion state because the ship's database on Utopian resources was spotty. HR4523 was similarly deserted. HR509, also known as Tau Ceti, was only 11.9 light years from earth and had been the first outpost of the Great Expansion.

Its planetary system was also devoid of intelligent life and human artifacts—with one striking exception.

Nuevo LA was spread along the shores of the Sterling Sea like a half-eaten picnic lunch. Something had bitten the roofs off its buildings and chewed its walls. Metal skeletons rotted on its docks, transports were melting into brown and gold stains. Once-proud boulevards crumbled in the orange light; the only traffic was wind-blown litter chasing shadows.

Mada was happy to survey the ruin from low orbit. A closer inspection would have spooked her. "Was it war?"

"There may have been a war," said the ship, "but that's not what caused this. I think it's deliberate deconstruction." In extreme magnification, the screen showed a concrete wall pockmarked with tiny holes, from which dust puffed intermittently. "The composition of that dust is limestone, sand, and aluminum silicate. The buildings are crawling with nanobots and they're eating the concrete."

"How long has this been going on?"

"At a guess, a hundred years, but that could be off by an order of magnitude."

"Who did this?" said Mada. "Why? Speculate."

"If this is the outcome of a war, then it would seem that the victors wanted to obliterate all traces of the vanquished. But it doesn't seem to have been fought over resources. I suppose we could imagine some deep ideological antagonism between the two sides that led to this, but such an extreme of cultural psychopathology seems unlikely."

"I hope you're right." She shivered. "So they did it themselves, then? Maybe they were done with this place and wanted to leave it as they found it?"

"Possible," said the ship.

Mada decided that she was done with Nuevo LA, too. She would have been perversely comforted to have found her enemies in power somewhere. It would have given her an easy way to calculate her duty. However, Mada was quite certain that what this mystery meant was that twenty thousand millennia had conquered both the revolution *and* the Utopians and that she and her sibling batch had been designed in vain.

Still, she had nothing better to do with eternity than to try to find out what had become of her species.

a never-ending vacation

The Atlantic Ocean was now larger than the Pacific. The Mediterranean Sea had been squeezed out of existence by the collision of Africa, Europe and Asia. North America floated free of South America and was nudging Siberia. Australia was drifting toward the equator.

The population of earth was about what it had been in the fifteenth century CE, according to the ship. Half a billion people lived on the home world and, as far as Mada could see, none of them had anything important to do. The means of production and distribution, of energy-generation and waste disposal were in the control of Dependent Intelligences like the ship. Despite repeated scans, the ship could detect no sign that any independent sentience was overseeing the system.

There were but a handful of cities, none larger than a quarter of a million inhabitants. All were scrubbed clean and kept scrupulously ordered by the DIs; they reminded Mada of databases populated with people instead of information. The majority of the population spent their bucolic lives in pretty hamlets and quaint towns overlooking lakes or oceans or mountains.

Humanity had booked a never-ending vacation.

"The brain clans could be controlling the DIs," said Mada. "That would make sense."

"Doubtful," said the ship. "Independent sentients create a signature disturbance in the sixth dimension."

"Could there be some secret dictator among the humans, a hidden oligarchy?"

"I see no evidence that anyone is in charge. Do you?"

She shook her head. "Did they choose to live in a museum," she said, "or were they condemned to it? It's obvious there's no First Right here; these people have only the *illusion* of individuality. And no Second Right either. Those bodies are as plain as uniforms—they're still slaves to their biology."

"There's no disease," said the ship. "They seem to be functionally immortal."

"That's not saying very much, is it?" Mada sniffed. "Maybe this is some scheme to start human civilization over again. Or maybe they're like seeds, stored here until someone comes along to plant them." She waved all the screens off. "I want to go down for a closer look. What do I need to pass?"

"Clothes, for one thing." The ship displayed a selection of current styles on its screen. They were extravagantly varied, from ballooning pastel tents to skin-tight sheaths of luminescent metal, to feathered camouflage to jump-suits made of what looked like dried mud. "Fashion design is one of their principal pasttimes," said the ship. "In addition, you'll probably want genitalia and the usual secondary sexual characteristics."

It took her the better part of a day to flow ovaries, fallopian tubes, a uterus, cervix, and vulva and to re-arrange her vagina. All these unnecessary organs made her feel bloated. She saw breasts as a waste of tissue; she made hers as small as the ship thought acceptable. She argued with it about the several substantial patches of hair it claimed she needed. Clearly, grooming them would require constant attention. She didn't mind tam-ing her claws into fingernails but she hated giving up her whiskers. Without them, the air was practically in-visible. At first her new vulva tickled when she walked, but she got used to it.

The ship entered earth's atmosphere at night and landed in what had once been Saskatchewan, Canada. It dumped most of its mass into the empty dimensions and flowed itself into baggy black pants, a moss-colored boat neck top and a pair of brown, gripall loafers. It was able to conceal its complete sensorium in a canvas belt.

It was 9:14 in the morning on June 23, 19,834,004 CE when Mada strolled into the village of Harmonious Struggle.

the devil's apple

Harmonious Struggle consisted of five clothing shops, six restaurants, three jewelers, eight art galleries, a musical instrument maker, a crafts workshop, a weaver, a potter, a woodworking shop, two candle stores, four theaters with capacities ranging from twenty to three hundred and an enormous sporting goods store attached to a miniature domed stadium. There looked to be apartments over most of these establishments; many had views of nearby Rabbit Lake.

Three of the restaurants—Hassam's Palace of Plenty, The Devil's Apple, and Laurel's—were practically jostling each other for position on Sonnet Street, which ran down to the lake. Lounging just outside of each were waiters eyeing handheld screens. They sprang up as one when Mada happened around the corner.

"Good day, Madame. Have you eaten?"

"Well met, fair stranger. Come break bread with us."

"All natural foods, friend! Lightly cooked, humbly served."

Mada veered into the middle of the street to study the situation as the waiters called to her. ~*So I can choose whichever I want?*~ She subvocalized to the ship.,

~*In an attention-based economy,*~ subbed the ship in reply, ~ *all they expect from you is an audience.*~

Just beyond Hassam's, the skinny waiter from The

Devil's Apple had a wry, crooked smile. Black hair fell to the padded shoulders of his shirt. He was wearing boots to the knee and loose rust-colored shorts, but it was the little red cape that decided her.

As she walked past her, the waitress from Hassam's was practically shouting. "Madame, *please*, their batter is dull!" She waved her handheld at Mada. "Read the *reviews*. Who puts shrimp in *muffins*?"

The waiter at the Devil's Apple was named Owen. He showed her to one of three tables in the tiny restaurant. At his suggestion, Mada ordered the poached peaches with white cheese mousse, an asparagus breakfast torte, baked orange walnut French toast and coddled eggs. Owen served the peaches, but it was the chef and owner, Edris, who emerged from the kitchen to clear the plate.

"The mousse, Madame, you liked it?" she asked, beaming.

"It was good," said Mada.

Her smile shrank a size and a half. "Enough lemon rind, would you say that?"

"Yes. It was very nice."

Mada's reply seemed to dismay Edris even more. When she came out to clear the next course, she blanched at the corner of breakfast torte that Mada had left uneaten.

"I knew this." She snatched the plate away. "The pastry wasn't fluffy enough." She rolled the offending scrap between thumb and forefinger.

Mada raised her hands in protest. "No, no, it was delicious." She could see Owen shrinking into the far corner of the room.

"Maybe too much colby, not enough gruyere?" Edris snarled. "But you have no comment?"

"I wouldn't change a thing. It was perfect."

"Madame is kind," she said, her lips barely moving, and retreated.

A moment later Owen set the steaming plate of French toast before Mada.

"Excuse me." She tugged at his sleeve.

"Something's wrong?" He edged away from her. "You must speak to Edris."

"Everything is fine. I was just wondering if you could tell me how to get to the local library."

Edris burst out of the kitchen. "What are you doing, beanheaded boy? You are distracting my patron with absurd chitterchat. Get out, get out of my restaurant now."

"No, really, he . . ."

But Owen was already out the door and up the street, taking Mada's appetite with him.

~*You're doing something wrong,*~ the ship subbed.

Mada lowered her head. ~*I know that!*~

Mada pushed the sliver of French toast around the pool of maple syrup for several minutes but could not eat it. "Excuse me," she called, standing up abruptly. "Edris?"

Edris shouldered through the kitchen door, carrying a tray with a silver egg cup. She froze when she saw how it was with the French toast and her only patron.

"This was one of the most delicious meals I have ever eaten." Mada backed toward the door. She wanted nothing to do with eggs, coddled or otherwise.

Edris set the tray in front of Mada's empty chair. "Madame, the art of the kitchen requires the tongue of the patron," she said icily.

She fumbled for the latch. "Everything was very, very wonderful."

no comment

Mada slunk down Lyric Alley, which ran behind the stadium, trying to understand how exactly she had offended. In this attention-based economy, paying attention was obviously not enough. There had to be some other cultural protocol she and the ship were missing. What she probably ought to do was go back and explore the clothes shops, maybe pick up a pot or some candles and see what additional information she could blunder into. But making a fool of herself had never much appealed to Mada as a learning strategy. She wanted the map, a native guide—some edge, preferably secret.

~Scanning,~ subbed the ship. ~Somebody is following you. He just ducked behind the privet hedge twelve-

point-three meters to the right. It's the waiter, Owen.~

"Owen," called Mada, "is that you? I'm sorry I got you in trouble. You're an excellent waiter."

"I'm not really a waiter." Owen peeked over the top of the hedge. "I'm a poet."

She gave him her best smile. "You said you'd take me to the library." For some reason, the smile stayed on her face "Can we do that now?"

"First listen to some of my poetry."

"No," she said firmly. "Owen, I don't think you've been paying attention. I said I would like to go to the library."

"All right then, but I'm not going to have sex with you."

Mada was taken aback. "Really? Why is that?"

"I'm not attracted to women with small breasts."

For the first time in her life, Mada felt the stab of outraged hormones. "Come out here and talk to me."

There was no immediate break in the hedge, so Owen had to squiggle through. "There's something about me that you don't like," he said as he struggled with the branches.

"Is there?" She considered. "I like your cape."

"That you *don't* like." He escaped the hedge's grasp and brushed leaves from his shorts.

"I guess I don't like your narrow-mindedness. It's not an attractive quality in a poet."

There was a gleam in Owen's eye as he went up on his tiptoes and began to declaim:

"That spring you left I thought I might expire
And lose the love you left for me to keep.
To hold you once again is my desire.
Before I give myself to death's long sleep."

He illustrated his poetry with large, flailing gestures. At "death's long sleep" he brought his hands together as if to pray, laid the side of his head against them and closed his eyes. He held that pose in silence for an agonizingly long time.

"It's nice," Mada said at last. "I like the way it rhymes."

He sighed and went flat-footed. His arms drooped and he fixed her with an accusing stare. "You're not from here."

"No," she said. ~*Where am I from?*~ she subbed. ~*Someplace he'll have to look up.*~

~*Marble Bar. It's in Australia*~

"I'm from Marble Bar."

"No, I mean you're not one of us. You don't comment."

At that moment, Mada understood. ~*I want to skip downwhen four minutes. I need to undo this.*~

~*this undo to need I .minutes four downwhen skip to want I*~ understood Mada, moment that At ".comment don't You .us of one not you're mean I ,No" ".Bar Marble from I'm" ~*Australia in It's .Bar Marble*~ ~*up look to*~

have he'll Someplace~ .subbed she *~?from I am Where~*
said she ",No" .here from not You're" .stare accusing an
with her fixed he and drooped arms His .flatfooted went
and sighed He ".rhymes it way the like I." .last at said Mada
",nice It's" .time long agonizingly an for silence in pose
that held He .eyes his closed and them against head his of
side the laid ,pray to if as together hands his brought he
"sleep long death's" At .gestures flailing ,large with poetry
his illustrated He ".sleep long death's to myself give I Before
desire my is again once you hold To keep to me for left
you love the lose And expire might I thought I left you
spring That" :declaim to began and tiptoes his on up went
he as eye Owen's in gleam a was There ".poet a in quality
attractive an not It's .narrow-mindedness your like don't I
guess I" .shorts his from leaves brushed and grasp hedge's
the escaped He ".like *don't* you That" ".cape your like I"
.considered She "?there Is? .branches the with struggled he
as said he ",like don't you that me about something There's"
.through squiggle to had Owen so, hedge the in break immediate no was There ".me to talk and here out Come"
.hormones wronged of stab the felt Mada ,life her in time
first the For ".breasts small with women to attracted not
I'm" "?that is Why ?Really" .aback taken was Mada ".you
with sex have to going not I'm but ,then right All" ".library
the to go to like would I said I .attention paying been
you've think don't I ,Owen" firmly said she ",No" ".poetry
my of some to listen First"

As the ship surged through the empty dimensions, three-space became as liquid as a dream. Leaves smeared and buildings ran together. Owen's face swirled.

"They want criticism," said Mada. "They like to think of themselves as artists but they're insecure about what they've accomplished. They want their audience to engage with what they're doing, help them make it better—the comments they both seem to expect."

"I see it now," said the ship. "But is one person in a backwater worth an undo? Let's just start over somewhere else."

"No, I have an idea." She began flowing more fat cells to her breasts. For the first time since she had skipped upwhen, Mada had a glimpse of what her duty might now be. "I'm going to need a big special effect on short notice. Be ready to reclaim mass so you can resubstantiate the hull at my command."

"First listen to some of my poetry."

"Go ahead." Mada folded her arms across her chest. "Say it then."

Owen stood on tiptoes to declaim:

"That spring you left I thought I might expire
And lose the love you left for me to keep.
To hold you once again in my desire
Before I give myself to death's long sleep."

He illustrated his poetry with large, flailing gestures.

At "death's long sleep" he brought his hands together as if to pray, moved them to the side of his head, rested against them and closed his eyes. He had held the pose for just a beat before Mada interrupted him.

"Owen," she said. "You look ridiculous."

He jerked as if he had been hit in the head by a shovel.

She pointed at the ground before her. "You'll want to take these comments sitting down."

He hesitated, then settled at her feet.

"You hold your meter well, but that's purely a mechanical skill." She circled behind him. "A smart oven could do as much. Stop fidgeting!"

She hadn't noticed the ant hills near the spot she had chosen for Owen. The first scouts were beginning to explore him. That suited her plan exactly.

"Your real problem," she continued, "is that you know nothing about death and probably very little about desire."

"I know about death." Owen drew his feet close to his body and grasped his knees. "Everyone does. Flowers die, squirrels die."

"Has anyone you've ever known died?"

He frowned. "I didn't know her personally, but there was the woman who fell off that cliff in Merrymeeting."

"Owen, did you have a mother?"

"Don't make fun of me. Everyone has a mother."

Mada didn't think it was time to tell him that she

24

didn't; that she and her sibling batch of a thousand revolutionaries had been autoflowed. "Hold out your hand." Mada scooped up an ant. "That's your mother." She crunched it and dropped it onto Owen's palm.

Owen looked down at the dead ant and up again at Mada. His eyes filled.

"I think I love you," he said. "What's your name?"

"Mada." She leaned over to straighten his cape. "But loving me would be a very bad idea."

all that's left

Mada was surprised to find a few actual books in the library, printed on real plastic. A primitive DI had catalogued the rest of the collection, billions of gigabytes of print, graphics, audio, video, and VR files. None of it told Mada what she wanted to know. The library had sims of Egypt's New Kingdom, Islam's Abbasid dynasty, and the International Moonbase—but then came an astonishing void. Mada's searches on Trueborn, the Utopians, Tau Ceti, intelligence engineering and dimensional extensibility theory turned up no results. It was only in the very recent past that history resumed. The DI could reproduce the plans that the workbots had left when they built the library twenty-two years ago, and the menu The Devil's Apple had offered the previous summer, and the complete won-lost record of the Black Minks, the local scatterball club, which had gone 533–

905 over the last century. It knew that the name of the woman who died in Merrymeeting was Agnes and that two years after her death, a replacement baby had been born to Chandra and Yuri. They named him Herrick.

Mada waved the screen blank and stretched. She could see Owen draped artfully over a nearby divan, as if posing for a portrait. He was engrossed by his handheld. She noticed that his lips moved as he read. She crossed the reading room and squeezed onto it next to him, nestling into the crook in his legs. "What's that?" she asked.

He turned the handheld toward her. "Nadeem Jerad's *Burning the Snow*. Would you like to hear one of his poems?"

"Maybe later." She leaned into him. "I was just reading about Moonbase."

"Yes, ancient history. It's sort of interesting, don't you think? The Greeks and the Renaissance and all that."

"But then I can't find any record of what came after."

"Because of the nightmares." He nodded. "Terrible things happened, so we forgot them."

"What terrible things?"

He tapped the side of his head and grinned.

"Of course," she said, "nothing terrible happens anymore."

"No. Everyone's happy now." Owen reached out and pushed a strand of her hair off her forehead. "You have beautiful hair."

Mada couldn't even remember what color it was. "But if something terrible did happen, then you'd want to forget it."

"Obviously."

"The woman who died, Agnes. No doubt her friends were very sad."

"No doubt." Now he was playing with her hair.

~*Good question,*~ subbed the ship. ~*They must have some mechanism to wipe their memories.*~

"Is something wrong?" Owen's face was the size of the moon; Mada was afraid of what he might tell her next.

"Agnes probably had a mother," she said.

"A mom and a dad."

"It must have been terrible for them."

He shrugged. "Yes, I'm sure they forgot her."

Mada wanted to slap his hand away from her head. "But how could they?"

He gave ger a puzzled look. "Where are you from, anyway?"

"Trueborn," she said without hesitation. "It's a long, long way from here."

"Don't you have libraries there?" He gestured at the screens that surrounded them. "This is where we keep what we don't want to remember."

~*Skip!*~ Mada could barely sub; if what she suspected were true . . . ~*Skip downwhen two minutes.*~

~*minutes two downwhen Skip*~ ... true were suspected
she what if sub barely could Mada ~*!Skip*~ "remember to
want don't we what keep we where is This" .them surrounded that screen the at gestured He "?there libraries
have you Don't" ".here from way long ,long a It's" hesitation without said she ",Trueborn" "?anyway, from you are
Where" .look puzzled a her gave He "?they could how But"
.head her from away hand his slap to wanted Mada ".her
forgot they sure I'm, Yes" .shrugged He ".them for terrible
been have must It" "dad a and mom A" ".mother a had
probably Agnes" next her tell might he what of afraid was
Mada .moon the of size of the was face Owen's"?wrong
something Is" .~*memories their wipe to mechanism some
have must They*" .ship the subbed; ~*question Good*~ hair
her with playing was he Now ".doubt No" ".sad very were
friends her doubt no, Agnes, died who woman The" ".Ob-
viously" ".it forget to want you'd then ,happen did terrible
something if But" .was it color what remember even
couldn't even Mada

She wrapped her arms around herself to keep the
empty dimensions from reaching for the emptiness
inside her. Was something wrong?

Of course there was, but she didn't expect to say
it out loud. "I've lost everything and all that's left is
this."

Owen shimmered next to her like the surface of
Rabbit Lake.

"Mada, what?" said the ship.

"Forget it," she said. She thought she could hear something cracking when she laughed.

Mada couldn't even remember what color her hair was. "But if something terrible did happen, then you'd want to forget it."

"Obviously."

"Something terrible happened to me."

"I'm sorry." Owen squeezed her shoulder. "Do you want me to show you how to use the headbands?" He pointed at a rack of metal-mesh strips.

~Scanning,~ subbed the ship. *"Microcurrent taps capable of modulating post-synaptic outputs. I thought they were some kind of virtual reality I/O."*

"No." Mada twisted away from him and shot off the divan. She was outraged that these people would deliberately burn memories. How many stubbed toes and unhappy love affairs had Owen forgotten? If she could have, she would have skipped the entire village of Harmonious Struggle downwhen into the identity mine. When he rose up after her, she grabbed his hand. "I have to get out of here *right now.*"

She dragged him out of the library into the innocent light of the sun.

"Wait a minute," he said. She continued to tow him up Ode Street and out of town. "Wait!" He planted his feet, tugged at her and she spun back to him. "Why are you so upset?"

"I'm not upset." Mada's blood was hammering in her temples and she could feel the prickle of sweat under her arms. ~Now I need you,~ she subbed. "All right then. It's time you knew." She took a deep breath. "We were just talking about ancient history, Owen. Do you remember back then that the gods used to intervene in the affairs of humanity?"

Owen goggled at her as if she were growing beans out of her ears.

"I am a goddess, Owen, and I have come for you. I am calling you to your destiny. I intend to inspire you to great poetry."

His mouth opened and then closed again.

"My worshippers call me by many names." She raised a hand to the sky.

~Help?~

~Try Athene? Here's a databurst.~

"To the Greeks, I was Athene," Mada continued, "the goddess of cities, of technology and the arts, of wisdom and of war." She stretched a hand toward Owen's astonished face, forefinger aimed between his eyes. "Unlike you, I had no mother. I sprang full-grown from the forehead of my maker. I am Athene, the virgin goddess."

"How stupid do you think I am?" He shivered and glanced away from her fierce gaze. "I used to live in

Maple City, Mada. I'm not some simple-minded country lump. You don't seriously expect me to believe this goddess nonsense?"

She slumped, confused. Of course she had expected him to believe her. "I meant no disrespect, Owen. It's just that the truth is . . ." This wasn't as easy as she had thought. "What I expect is that you believe in your own potential, Owen. What I expect is that you are brave enough to leave this place and come with me. To the stars, Owen, to the stars to start a new world." She crossed her arms in front of her chest, grasped the hem of her moss-colored top, pulled it over her head and tossed it behind her. Before it hit the ground the ship augmented it with enough reclaimed mass from the empty dimensions to resubstantiate the command and living mods.

Mada was quite pleased with the way Owen tried— and failed—not to stare at her breasts. She kicked the gripall loafers off and the deck rose up beneath them. She stepped out of the baggy, black pants; when she tossed them at Owen, he flinched. Seconds later, they were eyeing each other in the metallic light of the ship's main companionway.

"Well?" said Mada.

duty

Mada had difficulty accepting Trueborn as it now was. She could see the ghosts of great cities, hear the murmur of dead friends. She decided to live in the forest that had once been the Green Sea, where there were no landmarks to remind her of what she had lost. She ordered the ship to begin constructing an infrastructure similar to that they had found on earth, only capable of supporting a technologically advanced population. Borrowing orphan mass from the empty dimensions, it was soon consumed with this monumental task. She missed its company; only rarely did she use the link it had left her—a silver ring with a direct connection to its sensorium.

The ship's first effort was the farm that Owen called Athens. It consisted of their house, a flow works, a gravel pit and a barn. Dirt roads led to various mines and domed fields that the ship's bots tended. Mada had it build a separate library, a little way into the woods, where, she declared, information was to be acquired only, never destroyed. Owen spent many evenings there. He said he was trying to make himself worthy of her.

He had been deeply flattered when she told him that, as part of his training as a poet, he was to name the birds and beasts and flowers and trees of Trueborn.

"But they must already have names," he said, as they

walked back to the house from the newly tilled soya field.

"The people who named them are gone," she said. "The names went with them."

"Your people." He waited for her to speak. The wind sighed through the forest. "What happened to them?"

"I don't know." At that moment, she regretted ever bringing him to Trueborn.

He sighed. "It must be hard."

"You left *your* people," she said. She spoke to wound him, since he was wounding her with these rude questions.

"For you, Mada." He let go of her. "I know you didn't leave them for *me*." He picked up a pebble and held it in front of his face. "You are now Mada-stone," he told it, "and whatever you hit . . ." He threw it into the woods and it *thwocked* off a tree. ". . . is Mada-tree. We will plant fields of Mada-seed and press Mada-juice from the sweet Mada-fruit and dance for the rest of our days down Mada Street." He laughed and put his arm around her waist and swung her around in circles, kicking up dust from the road. She was so surprised that she laughed too.

Mada and Owen slept in separate bedrooms, so she was not exactly sure how she knew that he wanted to have sex with her. He had never spoken of it, other than on that first day when he had specifically said that he did not want her. Maybe it was the way he continually brushed up against her for no apparent reason. This could hardly be chance, considering that they were the only two people on Trueborn. For herself, Mada welcomed his hesitancy. Although she had been emotionally intimate with her batch siblings, none of them had ever inserted themselves into her body cavities.

But, for better or worse, she had chosen this man for this course of action. Even if the galaxy had forgotten Trueborn two-tenths of a spin ago, the revolution still called Mada to her duty.

"What's it like to kiss?" she asked that night, as they were finishing supper.

Owen laid his fork across a plate of cauliflower curry. "You've never kissed anyone before?"

"That's why I ask."

Owen leaned across the table and brushed his lips across hers. The brief contact made her cheeks flush, as if she had just jogged in from the gravel pit. "Like that," he said. "Only better."

"Do you still think my breasts are too small?"

"I never said that." Owen's face turned red.

"It was a comment you made—or at least thought about making."

"A comment?" The word *comment* seemed to stick in his throat; it made him cough. "Just because you make comment on some aspect doesn't mean you reject the work as a whole."

Mada glanced down the neck of her shift. She hadn't really increased her breast mass all that much, maybe ten or twelve grams, but now vasocongestion had begun to swell them even more. She could also feel blood flowing to her reproductive organs. It was a pleasurable weight that made her feel light as pollen. "Yes, but do you think they're too small?"

Owen got up from the table and came around behind her chair. He put his hands on her shoulders and she leaned her head back against him. There was something between her cheek and his stomach. She heard him say, "Yours are the most perfect breasts on this entire planet," as if from a great distance and then realized that the *something* must be his penis.

After that, neither of them made much comment.

nine hours

Mada stared at the ceiling, her eyes wide but unseeing. Her concentration had turned inward. After she had rolled off him, Owen had flung his left arm across her belly and drawn her hip toward his and given her the night's last kiss. Now the muscles of his arm were slack, and she could hear his seashore breath as she released her ovum into the cloud of his sperm squiggling up her fallopian tubes. The most vigorous of the swimmers butted its head through the ovum's membrane and dissolved, releasing its genetic material. Mada immediately started raveling the strands of DNA before the fertilized egg could divide for the first time. Without the necessary diversity, they would never revive the revolution. Satisfied with her intervention, she flowed the blastocyst down her fallopian tubes where it locked onto the wall of her uterus. She prodded it and the ball of cells became a comma with a big head and a thin tail. An array of cells specialized and folded into a tube that ran the length of the embryo, weaving into nerve fibers. Dark pigment swept across two cups in the blocky head and then bulged into eyes. A mouth slowly opened; in it was a one-chambered, beating heart. The front end of the neural tube blossomed into the vesicles that would become the brain. Four buds swelled, two near the head, two at the tail. The uppermost pair sprouted into paddles, pierced by rays of cells that Mada immediately began to ossify into fingerbone. The lower buds stretched into delicate legs. At midnight, the embryo was as big as a her fingernail; it began to move and so became a fetus. The eyes opened for a few minutes, but then the eyelids fused. Mada and Owen were going to have a son; his penis was now a nub of flesh. Bubbles of tissue blew inward from the head and became his ears. Mada listened to him listen to her heartbeat. He lost his tail and his intestines slithered down the umbilical cord into his abdomen. As his fingerprints looped and whorled, he stuck his thumb into his mouth. Mada was having trouble breathing because the fetus was floating so high in her uterus. She eased herself into a sitting position and Owen grumbled in his sleep. Suddenly the curry in the cauliflower was giving her heartburn. Then the muscles of her uterus tightened and pain sheeted across her swollen belly.

~*Drink this.*~ The ship flowed a tumbler of nutrient nano onto the bedside table. ~*The fetus gains mass rapidly from now on.*~. The stuff tasted like rusty nails. ,~*You're doing fine.*~

When the fetus turned upside down, it felt like he was trying out a gymnastic routine. But then he snuggled headfirst into her pelvis, and calmed down, probably because there wasn't enough room left inside her for him to make large, flailing gestures like his father. Now she could feel electrical buzzes down her legs and inside her vagina as the baby bumped her nerves. He was big now, and growing by almost a kilogram an hour, laying down new muscle and brown fat. Mada was tired of it all. She dozed. At six-thirty-seven her water broke, drenching the bed.

"Hmm." Owen rolled away from the warm, fragrant spill of amniotic fluid. "What did you say?"

The contractions started; she put her hand on his chest and pressed down. "Help," she whimpered.

"Wha . . . ?" Owen propped himself up on his elbows. "Hey, I'm wet. How did I get . . . ?"

"*O-Owen!*" She could feel the baby's head stretching her vagina in a way mere flesh could not possibly stretch.

"Mada! What's wrong?" Suddenly his face was very close to hers. "Mada, what's happening?"

But then the baby was slipping out of her, and it was *sooo* much better than the only sex she had ever had. She caught her breath and said, "I have begotten a son."

She reached between her legs and pulled the baby to her breasts. They were huge now, and very sore.

"We will call him Owen," she said.

begot

And Mada begot Enos and Felicia and Malaleel and Ralph and Jared and Elisa and Tharsis and Masahiko and Thema and Seema and Casper and Hevila and Djanka and hJennifer and Jojo and Regma and Elvis and Irina and Dean and Marget and Karoly and Sabatha and Ashley and Siobhan and Mei-Fung and Neil and Gupta and Hans and Sade and Moon and Randy and Genevieve and Bob and Nazia and Eiichi and Justine and Ozma and Khaled and Candy and Pavel and Isaac and Sandor and Veronica and Gao and Pat and Marcus and Zsa Zsa and Li and Rebecca.

Seven years after her return to Trueborn, Mada rested.

Mada was convinced that she was not a particularly good mother, but then she had been designed for courage and quick-thinking, not nurturing and patience. It wasn't the crying or the dirty diapers or the spitting-up, it was the utter uselessness of the babies that the revolutionary in her could not abide. And her maternal instincts were often skewed. She would offer her children the wrong toy or cook the wrong dish, fall silent when they wanted her to play, prod them to talk when they needed to withdraw. Mada and the ship had calculated that fifty of her genetically manipulated offspring would provide the necessary diversity to repopulate Trueborn. After Rebecca was born, Mada was more than happy to stop having children.

Although the children seemed to love her despite her awkwardness, Mada wasn't sure she loved them back. She constantly teased at her feelings, peeling away what she considered pretense and sentimentality. She worried that the capacity to love might not have been part of her emotional design. Or perhaps begetting fifty children in seven years had left her numb.

Owen seemed to enjoy being a parent. He was the one whom the children called for when they wanted to play. They came to Mada for answers and decisions. Mada liked to watch them snuggle next to him when he spun his fantastic stories. Their father picked them up when they stumbled, and let them climb on his shoulders so they could see just what he saw. They told him secrets they would never tell her.

The children adored the ship, which substantiated a bot companion for each of them, in part for their protection. All had inherited their father's all-but-invulnerable immune system; their chromosomes replicated well beyond the Hayflick limit with integrity and fidelity. But they lacked their mother's ability to flow tissue and were therefore at peril of drowning or breaking their necks. The bots also provided the intense individualized attention that their busy parents could not. Each child was convinced that his or her bot companion had a unique personality. Even the seven-year-olds were too young to realize that the bots were reflecting their ideal personality back at them. The bots were in general as intelligent as the ship, although it had programmed into their DIs a touch of naïveté and a tendency to literalness that allowed the children to play tricks on them. Pranking a brother or sister's bot was a particularly delicious sport.

Athens had begun to sprawl after seven years. The library had tripled in size and grown a wing of classrooms and workshops. A new gym overlooked three playing fields. Owen had asked the ship to build a little theater where the children could put on shows for each other. The original house became a ring of houses, connected by corridors and facing a central courtyard. Each night Mada and Owen moved to their bedroom in a different house. Owen thought it important that the children see them sleeping in the same bed; Mada went along.

After she had begotten Rebecca, Mada needed something to do that didn't involve the children. She had the ship's farmbots plow up a field and for an hour each day she tended it. She resisted Owen's attempts to name this "Mom's Hobby." Mada grew vegetables; she had little use for flowers. Although she made a specialty of root crops, she was not a particularly accomplished gardener. She did, however, enjoy weeding.

It was at these quiet times, her hands flicking across the dark soil, that she considered her commitment to the Three Universal Rights. After two-tenths of a spin, she had clearly lost her zeal. Not for the first, that independent sentients had the right to remain individual. Mada was proud that her children were as individual as any intelligence, flesh or machine, could have made them. Of course, they had no pressing need to exercise the second right of manipulating their physical structures—she had taken care of that for them. When they were of age, if the ship wanted to introduce them to molecular engineering, that could certainly be done. No, the real problem was that downwhen was forever closed to them by the identity mine. How could she justify her new Trueborn society if it didn't enjoy the third right: free access to the timelines?

"Mada!" Owen waved at the edge of her garden. She blinked; he was wearing the same clothes he'd been wearing when she had first seen him on Sonnet Street in front of The Devil's Apple—down to the little red cape. He showed her a picnic basket. "The ship is watching the kids tonight," he called. "Come on, it's our anniversary. I did the calculations myself. We met eight earth years ago today."

He led her to a spot deep in the woods, where he spread a blanket. They stretched out next to each other and sorted through the basket. There was a curley salad with alperts and thumbnuts, brainboy and chive sandwiches on cheese bread. He toasted her with mada-fruit wine and told her that Siobahn had let go of the couch and taken her first step and that Irina wanted everyone to learn to play an instrument so that she could conduct the family orchestra and that Malaleel had asked him just today if ship was a person.

"It's not a person," said Mada. "It's a DI."

"That's what I said." Owen peeled the crust off his cheese bread. "And he said if it's not a person, how come it's telling jokes?"

"It told a joke?"

"It asked him, 'How come you can't have everything?' and then it said, 'Where would you put it?' "

She nudged him in the ribs. "That sounds more like you than the ship."

"I have a present for you," he said after they were stuffed. "I wrote you a poem." He did not stand; there were no large, flailing gestures. Instead he slid the picnic basket out of the way, leaned close and whispered into her ear.

"Loving you is like catching rain on my tongue.
You bathe the leaves, soak indifferent ground;
Why then should I get so little of you?
Yet still, like a flower with a fool's face,
I open myself to the sky."

Mada was not quite sure what was happening to her; she had never really cried before. "I like that it doesn't rhyme." She had understood that tears flowed from a sadness. "I like that a lot." She sniffed and smiled and daubed at edges of her eyes with a napkin. "Never rhyme anything again."

"Done," he said.

Mada watched her hand reach for him, caress the side of his neck, and then pull him down on top of her. Then she stopped watching herself.

"No more children." His whisper seemed to fill her head.

"No," she said, "no more."

"I'm sharing you with too many already." He slid his hand between her legs. She arched her back and guided him to her pleasure.

When they had both finished, she ran her finger through the sweat cooling at the small of his back and then licked it. "Owen,' she said, her voice a silken purr. "That was the one."

"Is that your comment?"

"No." She craned to see his eyes. "This is my comment," she said. "You're writing love poems to the wrong person."

"There is no one else," he said.

She squawked and pushed him off her. "That may be true," she said, laughing, "but it's not something you're supposed to say."

"No, what I meant was . . ."

"I know." She put a finger to his lips and giggled like one of her babies. Mada realized then how dangerously happy she was. She rolled away from Owen; all the lightness crushed out of her by the weight of guilt and shame. It wasn't her duty to be happy. She had been ready to betray the cause of those who had made her for what? For this man? "There's something I have to do." She fumbled for her shift. "I can't help myself, I'm sorry."

Owen watched her warily. "Why are you sorry?"

"Because after I do it, I'll be different."

"Different how?"

"The ship will explain." She tugged the shift on. "Take care of the children."

"What do you mean, take care of the children? What are you doing?" He lunged at her and she scrabbled away from him on all fours. "Tell me."

"The ship says my body should survive." She staggered to her feet. "That's all I can offer you, Owen." Mada ran.

She didn't expect Owen to come after her—or to run so fast.

~I need you,~ she subbed to the ship. *"Substantiate the command mod.~*

He was right behind her. Saying something. Was it to her? "No," he panted, "no, no, *no.*"

~Substantiate the com . . . ~

Suddenly Owen was gone; Mada bit her lip as she crashed into the main screen, caromed off it and dropped like a dead woman. She lay there for a moment, the cold of the deck seeping into her check. "Goodbye," she whispered. She struggled to pull herself up and spat blood.

"Skip downwhen," she said, "six minutes."

"minutes six" ,said she ",downwhen Skip" .blood spat and up herself pull to struggled She .whispered she ",Goodbye" cheek her into seeping deck the of cold the ,moment a for

there lay She .woman dead a like dropped and it off caromed ,screen main the into crashed she as lip her bit Mada
; gone was Owen Suddenly~.... *com the Substantiate~*
".no ,no no" ,panted he ",No" ?her to it Was .something
Saying .her behind right wasHe~.*mod command the Sub-
stantiate~* .ship the to subbed she ~*you need I~* .fast so
run to or—her after come to Owen expect didn't She .ran
Mada ".Owen ,you offer can I all That's" feet her to staggered She ".survive should body my says ship The" ".me
Tell" .fours all on him from away scrabbled she and her at
lunged He "?doing you are What? children the of care take
,mean you do What." ".children the of care Take" on shift
the tugged She ".explain will ship The" "?how Different"
".different be I'll ,it do I after Because" "?sorry you are
Why" .warily her watched Owen. ".sorry I'm ,myself help
can't I" .shift her for fumbled She .her made had who those
of cause the betrayed have would she easily How ".do to
have I something There's" .happy be to duty her wasn't It
.shame and guilt of weight the by her of out crushed lightness the all, Owen from away rolled She .was she happy
dangerously how then realized Mada .babies her of one like
giggled and lips his to finger a put She ".know I" ".... Was
meant I what ,No" ".say to supposed you're something not
it's but" ,laughing, said she ",true be may That" .her off him
pushed and squawked She .said he ",else one no is There"
".person wrong the to poems love writing You're" .said she
",comment my is This" .eyes his see to craned She ".No"
"?comment your that Is" ".one the was That" .purr silken a
voice her, said she ",Owen"

When threespace went blurry, it seemed that her duty did too. She waved her hand and watched it smear.

"You know what you're doing," said the ship.

"What I was designed to do. What all my batch siblings pledged to do." She waved her hand again; she could actually see through herself. "The only thing I can do."

"The mine will wipe your identity. There will be nothing of you left."

"And then it will be gone and the timelines will open. I believe that I've known this was what I had to do since we first skipped upwhen."

"The probability was always high," said the ship "But not certain."

"Bring me to him, afterward. But don't tell him about the timelines. He might want to change them. The timelines are for the children, so that they can finish the revol. . . . .

"Owen," she said, her voice a silken purr. Then she paused.

The woman shook her head, trying to clear it. Lying on top of her was the handsomest man she had ever met. She felt warm and sexy and wonderful. What was this? "I . . . I'm . . . ," she said. She reached up and touched the little red cloth hanging from his shoulders. "I like your cape."

'.minutes six" ,said she ",downwhen Skip" .blood spat and
up herself pull to struggled She .whispered she ",Goodbye"
cheek her into seeping deck the of cold the ,moment a for
there lay She .woman dead a like dropped and it off caromed ,screen main the into crashed she as lip her bit Mada
one was Owen Suddenly~.... *com the Substantiate*~ ".no
,no ,no" ,panted he ",No" ?her to it Was .something Saying
.her behind right was He~.*mod command the Substantiate*~ .ship the to subbed she ~*you need I*~ .fast so run to
or—her after come to Owen expect didn't She .ran Mada
".Owen ,you offer can I all That's" feet her to staggered She
".survive should body my says ship The" ".me Tell" .fours
all on him from away scrabbled she and her at lunged He
"?doing you are What? children the of care take ,mean you
do What." ".children the of care Take" on shift the tugged
She ".explain will ship The" "?how Different" ".different be
I'll ,it do I after Because" "?sorry you are Why" .warily her
watched Owen. ".sorry I'm, myself help can't I" .shift her
for fumbled She .her made had who those of cause the
betrayed have would she easily How ".do to have I something There's" .happy be to duty her wasn't It .shame and
guilt of weight the by her of out crushed lightness the all,
Owen from away rolled She .was she happy dangerously
how then realized Mada .babies her of one like giggled and
lips his to finger a put She ".know I" "....Was meant I
what ,No" ".say to supposed you're something not it's but"

,laughing, said she ",true be may That" .her off him pushed and squawked She .said he ",else one no is There" ".person wrong the to poems love writing You're" .said she ",comment my is This" .eyes his see to craned She ".No" "?comment your that Is" ".one the was That" .purr silken a voice her, said she ",Owen"

Mada waved her hand and saw it smear in threespace. "What are you doing?" said the ship.

"What I was designed to do." She waved; she could actually see through herself. "The only thing I can do."

"The mine will wipe your identity. None of your memories will survive."

"I believe that I've known that's what would happen since we first skipped upwhen."

"It was probable," said the ship. "But not certain."

Trueborn scholars pinpoint what the ship did next as its first step toward independent sentience. In its memoirs, the ship credits the children with teaching it to misbehave.

It played a prank.

"Loving you," said the ship, "is like catching rain on my tongue. You bathe ..."

"Stop," Mada shouted. "Stop right now!"

"Got you!" The ship gloated. "Four minutes, fifty-one seconds."

"Owen," she said, her voice a silken purr. "That was the one."

"Is that your comment?"

"No." Mada was astonished—and pleased—that she still existed. She knew that in most timelines her identity must have been obliterated by the mine. Thinking about those brave, lost selves made her more sad than proud. "This is my comment," she said. "I'm ready now."

Owen coughed uncertainly. "Umm, already?"

She squawked and pushed him off her. "Not for *that*." She sifted his hair through her hands. "To be with you forever."

KNOW HOW, CAN DO

MICHAEL BLUMLEIN

AM ADAM. AT LAST can talk. Grand day!
Am happy, happy as a clam. What's a clam?
Happy as a panda, say, happy as a lark. And an aardvark. Happy and glad as all that.

Past days, talk was far away. Adam had gaps. Vast gaps. At chat Adam was a laggard, a sadsack, a nada.

Adam's lamp was dark. Adam's land was flat.

Fact was, Adam wasn't a mammal.

Was Adam sad? Naw. Was Adam mad? What crap. Adam can crawl and thrash and grab and attach. Adam had a map, a way. Adam's way. Adam's path.

Adam was small. Hardly a gnat. Adam was dark. Adam was fat. A fat crawly.

What Adam wasn't was smart.

Pangs at that? At what Adam wasn't?

That's crazy.

A hawk lacks arms. A jackal lacks a knapsack. Santa hasn't any fangs. And chalk hasn't any black.

Wants carry a pall. Pangs can hang a man. Wants and pangs can wrap a hangman's hard cravat.

What wasn't wasn't. Adam, frankly, was many ways a blank. Any plan at all was far away, dark, and way abstract.

Gladly, that's past. Talk swarms. Awkwardly? What harm at that? Anarchy? Hah! Talk sashays and attacks.

Adam says thanks. Adam says, crazy, man! What a day! Had Adam arms, Adam claps.

Mañana Adam may stand tall. May stand and walk and swag. Carry a fan. Crash a car. Stack bags and hang a lamp.

Mañana's a grab bag. Adam may wax vast and happy. Pray at altars. Play at anagrams. Bash a wall. Mañana Adam may talk fast.

Fantasy? Can't say that. A stab at man's way, man's strata—that's Adam's mantra. Adam's chant.

Call Adam crazy. Call Adam brash.

Mañana Adam may catch a star.

A martyr?

Adam can adapt.

I am Adam. Finally, I can say that. I can say it right. What a thrill! And what a climb! Again I cry thanks (and always will).

What can I say in a way that brings insight, that sails in air, that sings? I'll start with my past: simply said, I was a lab animal. A lab animal in a trial. This trial was a stab at attaining a paradigm shift. A stab at faith. My brain was small. (Was it, in fact, a brain at all?) My mind was dim. ("Dim" hardly says what it was.) In a big way, I was insignificant.

Pair that against what I am this day. I'm a man. Part man, anyway. I'm still part animal. A small, flat, tiny animal, a thing that can fit in a vial, a jar. A lady that I talk with calls this thing that I am rhabditis. I say I'm Adam.

—Is that a fact? says this lady.

I say I think it is.

—Adam was a man with a thirst.

—What kind? I ask.

—A mighty thirst, lacking limit.

—This was a flaw?

—A flaw and a gift. Filling his mind was Adam's wish. His primary aim. It was, in fact, a craving.

—Filling it with what?

—Facts. Data. Carnal acts. Light. Filling it with anything. With all things.

—I want that.

This lady's mind, as rapid as rain, trills happily.—I'm glad. That was my wish in this. My plan.

First things first. (That's a maxim, isn't it?) A brain has many strata, many strands and strings. Think baclava. Think grassy plain with many trails, trails with winding paths that split and split again, that climb and fall and zigzag, paths that sandwich paths. A brain is this at birth.

And this: it's whitish and grayish, springy and firm. It's impartial. It's galvanic. It's as big as a ham.

A brain is a thing. A mind is distinct. It's dainty and whimsical and killingly vast. By night it sings, by day it fills with will and travail. A mind is mighty. A mind is frail. It's a liar. It's a blizzard. Galactical, impractical, a mind inhabits air.

That is what I think. I'm an infant, and my mind isn't rich. My brain is hardly half a brain. I'm a half-wit. Half a half-wit. Mainly what I am is instinct.

What is instinct? That I can say. Instinct is habit. It's a straight path. It's basic, and it's final.

Instinct has an inward hand, a timing that is strict. It can spring as fast as whimsy, and it can wait.

Instinct isn't always civil. It isn't always fair and kind.

Is that bad? I can't say. Wizards did my brain. It's still in planning. Still changing. Ask a wizard what is fair and kind, what is right. Ask that lady.

Talk is anarchy. Talk is bliss. Talk says what is and isn't. Talk is king.

That lady wants daily highlights. A diary, as taxing as it is. All right. I'll start with this: a list that says what I am.

I'm an amalgam with many parts and traits. Small

brain. Dark skin. Thin as a hair. If hit by a bright light, I spasm and thrash. If bit by an icy chill, paralysis kicks in, and in an instant, I'm still as a stick. I can't stand salt, and a dry day can kill.

I lack wit. And skill at cards, I lack that. I can't fight, and I can't thaw a chilly affair. I'm part man, part animal, and all virgin.

Critics might say that I'm a passing fancy. A magic trick, a daft and wayward wish, a triviality, a fad.

That's appalling, and it isn't a fact. I'm as wayward as anything atypical. I'm as trivial as anything distinct.

What I am is an inkling, a twinkling, a light. I'm an ant climbing stairs, a man gazing starward. I'm a dwarf. I'm a giant. I'm basic and raw.

This is a birth, and fittingly, it's a hard and a happy affair. Plainly, I'm an infant. Can I fail? I can. Will I? Hah! This is my dawn.

I'm a worm. I now can say it. Similarly (apropos of nothing), I can say moccasin. Borborygmi. Lambswool. Bony joints. Pornographic sanctity. Military coalition.

What words! What rosy idioms! What bawdy clowns of oration! Or shall I ask what silly fogs, what airs my brain is giving off?

I don't mind. I know that I'm not with it. Not totally. I'm a goofball notion, a taxonomic knot. Did I say an ontologic cryptogram? That, too. And, according to that lady, a work of art.

* * *

My mind is coming fast now. My brain is growing. Row on row of axons, rooting, dividing, branching into pathways, coiling into labyrinths, forging forward as if to lock tomorrow in its spot.

I'm shaking, tingling, giddy with anticipation. I'm on a cliff, a brink, I'm blasting off. This world as I know it is a shadow of what awaits. A drip, a drop, a vacant lot. My brain is gaining mass, gram by gram. My mind is bright with words and symbols, a dictionary of singing birds and rising moons, a portal to cognition.

Abstract thinking—what a notion! What a crazy plan! Grammar, syntax, symbolic logic. Syllogisms. Aphorisms. Dogma. Opinion. A worm I am, a worm of constant cogitation. A philosophizing worm, a psychologizing worm, a pontificator, a prognosticator, a worm of wit and aspiration, a worm of cortical distinction, a worm of brain.

Instinct is so boring. So minimal, so common. It lacks originality, to say nothing of sophistication. It's so lowly, so wormish, so filthy in a way.

That lady who I talk to finds my saying this astonishing.

—Why? I want to know.

—Instinct is important. It brings animals in contact. It's vital for having offspring. Also, it acts as a warning signal.

—Instinct has its limits, I say.

—Living within limits is what living is.

—For a worm, I maintain.—Not for a man. Right?

—For anything.

—I don't want limits.

—Ah, this lady says dryly. —A worm of ambition.

—Is that bad?

—Ambition? No. Not at all. In fact, it's sort of what I had in mind.

At this, I want to show this lady what I can do. I want to boast a bit.

And so I say, —It's important to know a right word from an almost right word. Critically important. Want to know how critical it is?

Lickity-split, this lady snaps at my bait. —Okay. How critical is it?

—First think of lightning.

—All right. I'm thinking of lightning.

—Now think of a lightning bag.

—A what?

—A lightning bag.

It's sort of a gag, and I wait for this lady to grasp it. To say good job, how scholarly, how witty, how smart. I wait, and I wait. For a wizard, I'm thinking, this woman is slow.

—It's a saying, I add as a hint. —By Mark Twain.

—Ah, this lady says at last. —Now I know.

I glow (which is a trick, for I'm not a glow worm), and with pomposity I crow, —I'm a worm of philological proclivity.

—It's not bag, says this lady.

—What?

—Bag is wrong. Sorry.

So high only an instant ago, my spirits hit bottom.

—Almost. Good try.

—I'm no good with words, I groan. —I'm a fool. A clown. A hack.

—Not to worry, says this lady. —A worm with a brain, aphasic and silly or not, is no piddling thing. Any transmission at all is historic.

So I wasn't born a prodigy. So what? In a way I wasn't born at all. Nowadays, that isn't vital. Birth, I'm saying, isn't obligatory for a living thing to spring forth.

I'm a split-brain proposition, an anatomic fiction, a hybrid born of wizardry and magic. I'm a canon, if not to wisdom, to ambition and faith. My tomorrows, all in all, look rosy. Daily I grow in ability.

What I'm hoping for—what I'm anticipating—is not simply a facility with words. I want a total grasp, I want command. Grammar, syntax, jargon, slang—I want it all, and I want it right, as right as rain.

Words bring glory. Words bring favor.

Words stir, spirits, and words transform.

Words will lift this thing I am as hands lift worms from dirt.

Or won't.

Fact is, I don't rightly know. It's my first go at all this. I'm winging it. Totally.

Talk is simply talk. If I had arms, I'd do.

At last I am complete. Fully formed in brain and body. Eloquent, articulate, pretentious and tendentious, verbose and possibly erroneous, but most of all, immensely grateful for what I am. And what is that? I've explained before, or tried. But I've been hampered. Today I'll try again.

I'm *Caenorhabditis elegans,* a worm of mud and dirt, presently residing in a petri dish in a green and white-walled research laboratory. At least at root I am this worm, which is to say, that's how I began. Grafted onto me (or more precisely, into me), in ways most clever and ingenious, is the central neurologic apparatus of Homo sapiens, that is, a human brain. The grafting took place genomically, before I technically came into existence. The birth and study of the mind is the object of this exercise. The subject, need I say, is me.

Why me and not some other creature, a lobster, say, a mouse, a sponge? Because I'm known, I've been sequenced, I've been taken apart and put together; each and every building block of mine, from gene to cell to protein, has been defined. Many of my genes, conserved through evolution, are similar to human genes and therefore objects of great interest. Some, in fact, are identical to human genes. Which means that C. elegans and H. sapiens are, in some small way, the same.

My source of information on all this, apart from my own rambling internal colloquy and self-examination, is the lady who attends to me. Her name is Sheila Downey. She is a geneticist, a bench scientist as well as a theoretician, and a fount of knowledge. She communicates to me through an apparatus that turns her words to wire-bound signals that my auditory cortex reads. Similarly, using other apparati, she feeds visual, tactile and other information to me. I communicate to her via efferent channels throughout my cortex, the common thread of which is carried through a cluster of filaments embedded in my posterior temporoparietal region to a machine that simulates speech. Alternatively, my words can be printed out or displayed on screen.

She says that while I am by no means the first chimeric life form, I am by far the most ambitious and advanced. Far more than, say, bacteria, which for years have been engineered to carry human genes.

Not that I should be compared to them. Those bacterial hybrids of which she speaks exist only as a means to manufacture proteins. They're little more than tiny factories, nothing close to sentient.

Not that they wouldn't like to be. Bacteria, believe me, will take whatever they can get. The little beasts are never satisfied. They're opportunistic and self-serving, grasping (and often pilfering) whatever is at hand. They reproduce like rabbits and mutate seemingly at will. In the kingdom of life there are none more uppity or ambitious, not surprising given their lowly origins. They're an uncouth and primitive breed, never content, always wanting more.

Worms, on the other hand, are a remarkably civilized race. Of the higher phyla we are rivaled only by the insects in our ubiquity. We're flexible, adaptable, enlightened in our choice of habitats. We're gender friendly, able to mate alone or with one another. And for those of you conversant with the Bible, you will recall that, unlike the insect horde, we've never caused a plague.

I myself am a roundworm (at least I started out as one), and as such, am partial to roundworms. Compared to our relatives the flatworms (distant relatives, not to draw too fine a line), a roundworm has an inherently more rounded point of view. Living as we do nearly everywhere—in water, soil, and plants, as well as in the tissues and guts of countless creatures—we take a broad view of the world. We know a thing or two about diversity and know we can't afford to be intolerant. Like anyone, we have our likes and dislikes, but on the whole, we're an open-minded group.

Some say we are overly diffident, that we shy from the spotlight, squirm, as it were, from the light of day. To this I say that modesty is no great sin. In the right hands humility can be a powerful weapon. Certainly, it is one that is frequently misunderstood.

Still, it is a trait of our family, though not by any means the only one. Certain of my cousins are assertive (some would say aggressive) in their behavior. They stick their noses in other creatures' business and insinuate themselves where they're not wanted. *Trichinella*, for example, will, without invitation, burrow into human muscle. *Ancylostoma* will needle into the intestine, piercing the wall and lodging there for years to suck the human blood. *Wuchereria* prefer the lymph glands. *Onchocerca* the eye. And *Dracunculus*, the legendary fiery serpent, will cut a swath from digestive tract to epidermis, erupting from the skin in a blaze of necrotic glory. Diffident, you say? Hardly. *Dracunculus* craves the limelight like a fish craves water. It would rather die (and usually does) than do without.

I myself am less dramatically inclined. I'd rather garner attention for what I am than what I do. On the whole, I'm easy to work with, humble without being self-effacing, clever without being snide. I've a quiet sort of beauty, muted, elegant. Hence my name.

Unlike my parasitic cousins mentioned previously, I do not depend on others for my survival. I live in soil, mud and dirt, free of attachments, independent. I am no parasite, nor would I ever choose to be.

That said, I understand perfectly the temptations of the parasitic lifestyle. The security of a warm intestine, the plenitude of food, the comfort of the dark. I do not judge my cousins harshly for what they are. Their path has led them one direction; mine, another. I've never had to think of others, never had to enter them, live with them, become attached. I've never had to suffer the vagaries of another creature's behavior.

Never until now.

A worm a millimeter long, weighing barely more than a speck of dust, attached to a brain the size of a football. Imagine! And now imagine all the work involved to keep this venture going. All the work on Sheila Downey's part and all the work on mine. Cooperation is essential. I can no longer be self-centered or even casually independent. I cannot hide in muck (not that there is any in this hygienic place) and expect to live. I'm a captive creature, under constant surveillance, utterly dependent on my keeper. I must subordinate myself in order to survive.

Does this sound appalling? Unfair and unappealing? If it does, then think again. All freedoms come at the expense of other freedoms. All brains are captives of their bodies. All minds are captives of their brains.

I am a happy creature. My body is intact, my brain is tightly organized, and my mind is free to wander. I have my ease (I got them yesterday), and miracle of miracles, I have my ewes, too. You, I mean. My u's.

And having them, I now have everything. If there's such a thing as bliss, this must be it.

Unfathomable, I now can say.

Unconscionable.

Unparalleled, this scientific achievement.

Unnatural.

I'm in a funk sometimes (this captive life).

I'm going nowhere, and it's no fun.

And yet it's only natural that science experiment and try new things.

In truth, it's unbelievable what I am. Unimaginable how far I've come.

From stupid to stupendous.

From uninspired to unprecedented.

An upwardly mobile worm ... how unusual. How presumptuous. How morally ambiguous. How puerile and unsettling. How absurd.

Mixing species as though we were ingredients in a pancake batter. Cookbook medicine. Tawdry science. Mankind at his most creative, coruscatious, and corrupt.

How, you might well ask, is all this done? This joining of the parts, this federation, this majestic union of two such disparate entities, worm and man? With wires and tubes and couplers, that's how. With nano this and nano that. Baths of salt and percolating streams of micro-elements, genomic plug-ins, bilayer diffusion circuits and protein gradients, syncretic information systems. I'm a web of filaments so fine you cannot see, a juggle of electrocurrents, an interdigitated field of biomolecules and interactive membranes. Worm to brain and brain to worm, then both together to a most excellent machine, that's how it's done. With sleight of hand and spit and polish and trial and tribulation. It seems miraculous, I know. It looks like magic. That's science for you. The how is for the scientists. The why and wherefore are for the rest of us, the commoners, the hoi polloi, like me.

Which is not to say that I'm not flattered to be the object of attention. I most certainly am, and have every hope of living up to expectations, whatever those might be. Each wire in my brain is like a wish to learn. Each is like a wish to give up information. Each is like a thank you.

They do not hurt. I cannot even feel them. They ground me (in all the meanings of that word), but they're also a kind of tether. The irony of this is not lost on me.

I'm no parasite but no longer am I free. No longer free to live in mud and filth, where a meal and a crap pretty much summed up my life. No longer free to live without tomorrows (or yesterdays). Living without language, like living in the moment, is a hopeless sort of living, which is to say unburdened. No longer free to live like that. Lucky me.

My newborn mind is vast, my neural net a majesty of convoluted dream. A million thoughts and questions swirl through it, but all pale before the single thought, the central one, of my existence. Who am I? Why am I here?

Sheila Downey says I shouldn't bother with such

questions. They have no answers, none that are consistent, certainly none that can be proved. Life exists. It's a fact—you could even say an accident—of nature. There's no reason for it. It just is.

But I'm no accident. I was put together for a purpose. Wasn't I? Isn't there a plan?

—You're here, she says. —Be satisfied.

I should be, shouldn't I? I would be, were I still a simple worm. But I'm not, and so I ask again that most human, it would seem, of questions. What's the point? Why was I made?

Sheila Downey doesn't answer. For some reason she seems reluctant.

At length she clears her throat. —Why do you think?

I have a number of theories, which I'm happy to share. One, she wants to learn how the brain works. More specifically, she wants to learn about language, how words are put together, how they're made and unmade, how they dance. Two, she wants to study how two dissimilar creatures live together, how they co-exist. Three (the least likely possibility but the closest to my heart), she wants to learn more about worms.

—Very interesting, says Sheila Downey.

—Which is it?

—Oh, she says, —I'll be looking at all of them.

Which answers the question. Though somehow it doesn't. What I mean is, I have the feeling she's holding something back.

Why, I wonder, would she do that? What is there to hide? I sense no danger here. And even if there were, what could such omnipotence as hers possibly have to fear?

Today I fell in love. I didn't know what love was until today. Before I had the word for it, I had no idea there was even such a thing as love. It's possible there wasn't.

Sheila Downey is the object of my affection. Sheila Downey, my creator, who bathes my brain in nutrients, manipulates my genome, fixes my electrodes. Sheila Downey, so gentle, professional, and smart. What fingertips she has! What dextrous joints! She croons to me as she works, coos in what I think must be a dove-like voice. Sometimes she jokes that she is no more human than I am, that she is a chimera, too. I was born a pigeon, she says, laughing. But then she says, not really. I was born a clumsy ox, or might have been, the way I feel sometimes. Only lately have things fallen into place.

—What things? I ask.

—You, for one, she says.

I swell with pride. (I also swell a bit with fluid, and Sheila Downey, ever vigilant, adjusts my osmolarity.)

—You are a very brainy worm, she says. —It took a very brainy person to make you. And that person, along with a few significant others, was me.

—I'm yours, I say quite literally.

—Well, yes. I guess you are.

—You care for me.

—You know I do. Both day and night.

—What I mean is, you care about me. Right?

She seems surprised that I would question this. —Yes. In all sorts of ways.

At this my heart turns over (although, strictly speaking, I do not have a heart; it's my fluid, my oozy goo, that shifts and turns).

—I need you, Sheila Downey.

She laughs. —Of course you do.

—Do you need me?

—I suppose, she says. —You could look at it that way. You could say we need each other.

—We do?

—Like the star gazer needs the star, she says. —Like the singer, the song. Like that. Yes. We do.

It was at this point that I fell in love. It was as if a ray of light had pierced a world of darkness. Or conversely, a hole of darkness had suddenly opened in a world composed solely of light. Prior to that moment, love simply did not exist.

Sheila Downey was interested in this. She asked how I knew it was love.

I replied that I knew it the same way I knew everything. The notion came to me. The letters made a word that seemed to more or less describe a chain of cortical and sub-cortical activity. Was I wrong?

She replied that love might be a slight exaggeration.

Gratitude and appreciation were probably closer to the truth. But the definitions weren't important. Of more interest to her was my continued facility for concept formation and abstract thinking.

—I'm impressed, she said.

But now I was confused. I thought that definitions were important, that meanings and shades of meanings were the essence of communication. I thought that words made all the difference.

—If this isn't love, I told her, —then tell me what is.

—I'm no expert, said Sheila Downey. —But in my limited experience, having a body is fairly important.

—I do have a body.

—Understood. But you lack certain essential characteristics. Essential, that is, for a human.

—What? Eyes? Ears? Arms and legs?

—All of those, she said.

—But I can smell, I told her. —I can taste your chemicals.

—I wear latex.

—Latex?

—Gloves, she clarified.

In other words, it's not her I'm tasting. So what, I say. So what that ours is not a physical attraction. I don't need touch or smell or taste. The thought alone, the word, is sufficient. Having love in mind, saying it, believing it, makes it so.

* * *

When I was a worm, I acted like a worm. I thought like one. Now I think like a human, but I'm still a worm. How puzzling. What, I wonder, makes a human fully human? What exactly is a human I'd like to know.

It's more than a mammal with arms and legs and hair on its head, fingernails on its fingers, binocular vision, speech, and the like. What I mean is, it's more than just a body, clearly more, for take away the limbs, take away the eyes and ears and voice, and still you have a human. Take away the gonads, replace the ovaries with hormones and the testicles with little plastic balls, replace the heart with metal and the arteries with dacron tubes, and still you have a human, perhaps even more so, concentrated in what's left.

Well then how about the brain? Is that what makes an animal uniquely human? And if it is, exactly how much brain is necessary? Enough for language? Forethought? Enough to get by day to day? Hour by hour? Minute by minute? Enough to tie a shoe? To cook a turkey? To chat with friends?

And if a person loses brain to injury or disease, does he fall from the ranks of humanity? If he cannot speak or organize his thoughts, if he has no short or long-term memory, if he wets his pants and smears his feces, is he less a human? Something else perhaps? A new entity, whose only lasting link to humanity is the pity and discomfort he evokes?

Well, what about the genome then, the touted human

genome? Does that define a human? I don't see how it can, not with genes routinely being added and subtracted, not with all the meddling that's going on. Who's to say a certain person's not a product of engineering? Maybe he's got a gene he didn't have before, to make a substance he couldn't make. And where'd he get that gene? Maybe from a fungus. Or a sheep. Maybe from a worm.

You see my difficulty. It's hard to know one's place without knowing one's species. If I'm a worm, so be it, but I'd rather be a human. Humans tread on worms (and nowadays they take apart their genes), not the other way around.

Sheila Downey says I shouldn't worry about such things. The distinctions that I'm grappling with, besides being of little practical value, are no longer germane. Taxonomy is an anachronism. In the face of bioengineering, the celebrated differentiation of the species is of historic interest only.

She does, however, continue to be impressed by the level of my mentation. She encourages me to keep on thinking.

This gets my goat. (My goat? What goat? I wonder.)

—There is a goat, says Sheila Downey cryptically, —but that's not what you meant.

And then she says, —You want to know what you are? I'll tell you. You're nineteen thousand ninety-nine genes of Caenorhabditis elegans and seventeen thousand forty-four genes of Homo sapiens. Taking into account the homologous sequences, you're 61.8 percent worm and 38.2 percent human. That's not approximate. It's exact.

Somehow this information doesn't help.

—That's because it doesn't matter what you call yourself, she says. —It doesn't matter where you think you fit. That's subjective, and subjectivity only leads to misunderstanding. What matters is what you are. You and you alone.

Respectfully, I disagree. Alone is not a state of nature. What you are depends on who you're with. Differences and distinctions matter. The ones who say they don't are the ones who haven't been trod upon. Or perhaps not trod upon enough.

—Poor worm, she says. —Have you been abused? The world's not just, I know.

—Why not? Why isn't it?

She gives a harsh sort of laugh. —Why? Because our instinct for it isn't strong enough. Maybe that's something we should work on. What do you think? Should we fortify that instinct? Should we R & D the justice gene?

By this point my head is spinning. I don't know what to think.

She says I shouldn't tax myself. —Relax. Look on the bright side. This sense of indignation you're feeling is a very human trait.

—Really?

—Oh yes. Very. That should make you happy.

I'm ashamed to say it does.

—Shame, too? How precocious of you. I'm impressed.

She pauses, and her voice drops, as if to share something closer to the heart.

—My sympathies, little worm.

I have an inexplicable urge to mate, to wrap myself around another body, to taste its oozing salts and earthy humors, to feel the slimy freshness of its skin. I want to intertwine with it, to knot and curl and writhe. The urge is close to irresistible. I'm all atingle. It's as if another elegans is nearby, calling me, wooing me, sireing me with its song.

Sheila Downey assures me this is not the case. There is no other worm. It's an hallucination, a delusion, triggered, she suspects, by an instinct to preserve my wormness through procreation, a reflex mechanism for perpetuation and survival of the species gone awry. She hypothesizes that I'm experiencing a rebound effect from my preoccupation with being human. That the pendulum, as it were, is swinging back. She finds it interesting, if not curious, that my worm identity remains so strong.

—I expected it to be overshadowed, she says.

The way I'm feeling I wish it were. Craving what I cannot have (what does not even exist) is tantamount, it seems, to craving death. This is strange and unfamiliar territory to a worm.

—It's as if your lower structures are refusing to be enlightened by your higher ones. As if your primitive brain, your elemental one, is rebelling.

I apologize if this is how it seems. I do not mean to be rebellious. Perhaps the pH of my fluid needs adjustment. Perhaps I need some medicine to calm me down.

—No, she says. —Let's wait and see what happens.

Wait? While I writhe and twitch and make a fool of myself? While I hunger for relief and moan?

Of course we'll wait. How silly of me to think otherwise. Science begins with observation, and Sheila Downey is a scientist. We'll watch and wait together, all three of us, the woman who made me what I am, the worm that isn't there, and me.

On further thought (and thought is what I have, my daily exercise, my work, my play, my everything) I uncover a possible answer to my question. What makes a human different from all other animals is that she alone will cut another animal up for study, she alone will blithely take apart another creature for something other than a meal.

Sheila Downey says I may be right, although again, she isn't very interested in what she calls the field of idle speculation.

But I, it seems, am interested in little else. —Is that why I was made? To be like that?

She will not answer, except to turn the question back on me. —Is that how you want to be?

The human in me, I have to admit, is curious. The worm, quite definitely, is not.

—I'm of two minds, I reply.

This comes as no surprise to her. —Of course you are. Does it seem strange?

—Does what?

—Having two minds, two consciousnesses, alive inside of you at once?

It seems strange sometimes to have even one. But mostly, no, it doesn't. On the contrary. Two consciousnesses is what I am. It's how I'm made. It would seem strange if I were different.

I wonder, then, if this is why I was made. To bring our species closer. To prove that two can work together as one.

—A noble thought, says Sheila Downey.

Now there's a word that sends a shiver down my spineless spine. A noble thought to bring, perchance, a noble prize.

—But not as noble as the truth, she adds portentously, then pauses.

At length she continues. —I'll tell you why we made you, she says. —Because that's what we do. We humans. We make things. And then we study them, and then we make them over if we have to. We make them better. It's why we're here on Earth. If there is a why. To make things.

—And this is being human?

—It's part of being human. The best part.

—Then I must be human, Sheila Downey, because I want to make things, too.

—Do you, worm? She sounds amused. Then she lapses into silence, and many moments pass before she speaks again. Her voice is different now: subdued, confessional.

—You want to know why we made you?

I remind her that she told me why. Just now. Has she forgotten?

—No, she says. —The real reason. The truth.

How many truths, I wonder, can there be?

—Because we had the tools and technology. Because someone asked the question. Not, is this experiment worthwhile, is it beneficial? Not that question, but can we do it? That's the real reason we made you. Because we could.

She bears some guilt for this. I'm not sure why.

—Is that detestable to you? she asks.

I tell her no. I'm grateful that she made me. Humans making other humans seems the epitome of what a human is.

—To some it is. Detestable, I mean. They say that just because we can do something doesn't mean we should. They say that science should be governed by a higher precept than simple curiosity.

—And what do you say?

—I say they don't understand what science is. It's human nature to be curious. There's no purpose to it. There's no reason. It's a hunger of the brain, a tropism, like a plant turning to the sun, to light.

Her mention of this tropism gives me pause. Traditionally, worms avoid the sun. It makes us easy prey. It dries us out. But now I feel slightly differently. I'd like a chance to see it. I'm curious about the light.

Sheila Downey isn't done with her defense of science. —It's a force of nature. Morals simply don't apply. It proceeds regardless of ethics, regardless of propriety and sometimes even decency. That's what makes it ugly sometimes. That's what makes it hurt.

I assure her I'm not hurting.

—Little worm, she says, with something sweet yet biting in her voice. —So self-absorbed. Progress never comes without a price. The boons of science always hurt.

Basilisk, real or not? Not.

Sphinx? Not.

Minotaur? Forget it.

Pan? A goat-man? No way.

And all those centaurs and satyrs, those gorgons and gargoyles, mermaids and manticores—phonies, the whole lot of them.

And while we're at it, how about those cherubim? Fat-cheeked, plump little nuggets of joy hovering in the tintoretto air like flies—I mean, get real. They'd be scared to death up there. And those tiny little wings would never hold them up.

I alone am real. Thirty-six thousand one hundred and forty-three genes and counting. The first and now the first again (Madam, I'm Adam). The Avatar. The Pride of Man. The Toast of Nature. The Freak.

Sheila Downey says we've reached a crossroads. I can no longer be kept alive in my current state. My body, that is, cannot sustain my brain. We have a choice to make.

A choice. How wonderful. I've never had a choice before.

—One, we sever the connection between your body and your brain.

—Sever?

—Snip snip, she says. —Then we look at each of them more closely.

—How close?

—Very close, she says. —Layer by cortical layer. Cell by cell. Synapse by synapse.

—You dissect me.

—Yes. That's right.

—Will it hurt?

—Has anything hurt yet?

She has a point. Nothing has. And yet, for reasons I can't explain, I seem to be hurting now.

—You're not, she says. —You can't feel pain.

—No? This sudden sense of doom I feel, this tremor of impending loss . . . these aren't painful? They're not a sign of suffering?

She hesitates, as though uncertain what to say. As though she, like me, might be more than a single creature, with more than a single point of view. I wonder. Is it possible? Might she be suffering a little, too?

She admits it'll be a sacrifice. She'll miss me.

I'll miss her, too. But more than anything, I'll miss myself.

—Silly worm. You won't. You won't remember. Your words and memories will all be gone.

—And you? Will you be gone?

—To you I will. And someday you'll be gone to me, too. I'll be gone to myself. Being gone is part of being here, it's part of being human. Someday it won't be, probably someday soon. But for now it is.

This gives me strength, to know that Sheila Downey will also die. I wonder, will she be studied, too?

—You mean dissected? She laughs. —I can't imagine anyone being interested.

—I would be.

Another laugh, a warmer one. —Tit for tat, is it? My inquisitive little worm. If only you had hands and eyes to do the job.

—Give me them, I say. Give me arms and legs and ears and eyes. Please, Sheila Downey. Make me human.

—I can't, she says. I can't do that. But I do have an alternative.

—What's that?

—We have a goat.

—A goat.

—Yes. A fine Boer buck. A very handsome fellow. I think he'll hold up nicely.

—Hold up to what?

—The surgery.

She waits as if I'm supposed to answer, but I'm not sure what she's asking. So I wait, too.

—Well? she asks.

—Well what?

—Should we give it a shot? Take your brain and put it in this goat? See what happens?

She's not joking.

I ask her why.

—Why what?

—A goat. Why a goat?

—Ah. Because we have one.

Of course. Science is nothing if not expedient.

—The other reason is because it's feasible. That is, we think we have a chance. We think we can do it.

This I should have known. But the fact is, I've never wanted to be a goat. Not ever. Not once. Not even part of once.

—Maybe so, she says. But remember, you never wanted to be a human until you got a human brain.

I recall her saying once that living within limits is what living is. I'm sure I should be grateful, but this so-called alternative is hard to stomach. It's like offering an arm to a person who's lost a leg. A pointless charity.

Moreover, it seems risky. How, I wonder, can they even do it, fit a human brain into a goat?

—With care, says Sheila Downey.

Of that I have no doubt. But I'm thinking more along the lines of size and shape and dimensional disparity. I'm thinking, that is, of my soft and tender brain stuffed into the small and unforgiving skull of a goat. Forgive me, but I'm thinking there might be a paucity of space.

She admits they'll have to make adjustments.

—What kind of adjustments?

—We'll pare you down a bit. Nothing major. Just a little cortical trim.

—Snip, snip, eh, Sheila Downey?

—If it's any consolation, you won't feel it. Most likely you won't even notice.

That's what scares me most. That I'll be different and not know it. Abridged, reduced, diminished.

I'd rather die.

—Posh, she says.

—Help me, Sheila Downey. If you care for me at all, do this for me. Give me a human body.

She sighs, denoting what, I wonder? Impatience? Disappointment? Regret? —It's not possible. I've told you.

—No?

—No. Not even remotely possible.

—Fine. Then kill me.

An ultimatum! How strange to hear such words spring forth. How unwormly and—dare I say it—human of me.

I can't believe that she will actually do it, that she will sacrifice what she herself has made. I can't believe it, and yet of course I can.

She sighs again, as though it's she who's being sacrificed, she who's being squeezed into a space not her own.

—Oh, worm, she says. What have we done?

I've had a dream. I wish that I could say that it was prescient, but it was not. I dreamed that I was a prince, a wormly prince, an elegant, deserving prince of mud and filth. And in this dream there was a maiden sent to test me, or I her. An ugly thing of golden hair and rosy cheeks, she spurned me once, she spurned me twice, she spurned me time and time again, until at last she placed me in her palm and took me home. She laid me on her bed. We slept entwined. And when I woke, I had become a human, and the maiden had become a princess, small enough to fit in my palm. I placed her there. I thought of all her hidden secrets, her mysteries. I'd like to get to know you, I said, enraptured. Inside and out. I'd like to cut you up (no harm intended). I really would.

Did I say I'd never be a goat? Did I say I'd rather die? Perhaps I spoke a bit too hastily. My pride was wounded.

In point of fact, I will be a goat. I'll be anything Sheila Downey says. She has the fingers and the toes. She has the meddlesome nature and the might.

Words and thoughts are wonderful, and reason is a fine conceit. But instinct rules the world. And Sheila Downey's instinct rules mine. She will slice and dice exactly as she pleases, pick apart to her heart's content and fuss with putting back together until the cows come home. She's eager and she's restless and she has no way to stop. And none to stop her. Certainly not me.

So yes, I will be a goat. I'll be a goat and happy for it. I'll be a goat and proud.

If this means a sliver or two less cortex, so be it. Less cortex means less idle thought. Fewer hopes that won't materialize. Fewer dreams that have no chance of ever coming true.

I doubt that I will love again, but then I doubt that I will care.

I doubt that I will doubt again, but this, I think, will be a blessing. Doubt muddies the waters. Doubt derails. Sheila Downey doesn't doubt. She sets her sights, and then she acts. She is the highest power, and I'm her vessel.

Make that vassal.

Command me, Sheila Downey. Cut me down to size. Pare me to your purpose.

Yours is a ruthless enterprise. Ruthless, but not without merit.

This world of yours, of hybrids and chimeras, humans and part-humans, promise to be an interesting world. Perhaps it will also be a better one. Perhaps more fun.

What good in this? For humans, the good inherent in making things. The good in progress. The good in living without restraint.

What good for worms? That's simple. No good.

All the better, then, that I won't know.

But will I? Will I know? Today's the day, and soon I'll be this capricornis personality, yet one more permutation in a line of permutations stretching back to the dawn of life. I will lose speech, that much seems certain. But thought, will that building also crumble? And words, the bricks that make the building, will they disintegrate, too?

And if they do, what then will I be, what kind of entity? A lesser one I cannot help but think. But less of more is still more than I ever was before. It does no good to rail at fate or chew the cud of destiny, at least no good to me. If I lose u's, so what? I'll lose the words unhappy and ungrateful. I'll lose unfinished and unrestrained. Uxorious I doubt will be an issue. Ditto usury. And ululation seems unlikely for a goat.

And after that, if I lose more, who cares? I'll fill my mind with what I can, with falling rain, crisp air and slanting light. I'll climb tall hills and sing what I can sing. I'll walk in grass.

Living is a gift. As a tiny crawly, as a fat and hairy ram, and as a man.

Call a pal.

Bang a pan

Say thanks.

Adapt.

FROM HERE YOU CAN SEE THE SUNQUISTS

RICHARD WADHOLM

A LL THAT SUMMER, THE Sunquists debated a trip to La Jetée.

Mr. Sunquist said that summer was the time to go. The tourists would be off to Kleege's Beach, where the hotels were new and no one worried about slipping back and forth in time as they walked down the beach. The Sunquists would have La Jetée to themselves.

Mrs. Sunquist was plainly uneasy about La Jetée. She would not say why. The Sunquists were travelers, after all. Cosmopolitans. They savored a difficult aesthetic experience.

She spoke only of their neighbors, the Dales, who had spent a month in Nepal. "They seemed so happy," she said. "They had their own sherpas. They rode in a cart up to Annapurna, pulled by a team of yetis."

Mr. Sunquist wondered at her reluctance. Was she

worried for the baby? He knew that she was nervous. Mrs. Sunquist had the sort of nerves that only a mid-life pregnancy can bring on. But women had babies in La Jetée all the time. Some women spent their entire pregnancies there. Mr. Sunquist proposed nothing more than a week—a farewell to the city of their youth. What could that hurt?

He plied his wife with nostalgia. He reminded her of their first meeting, in the galleries along Gull Street. Mr. Sunquist had purchased mangoes at Sonny's Seafood Chewder Bar and shown her how to eat them with salt and cayenne pepper.

He smiled as Mrs. Sunquist twisted her lips to taste the sweetness of the fruit, the heat of the red pepper. This was one of their quiet and indelible memories together. Mr. Sunquist knew it.

"We can go back and see it, just exactly as it was," he told her.

"Nothing is ever exactly as it was," she said.

"In La Jetée it is," he said. This was not an article of faith on his part. In La Jetée, it was a simple fact.

"What about us? Will we be the same?"

"We will be what we've always been," he promised her. "You'll see."

It was in the nature of the world that their last journey to La Jetée should begin sweetly. Just as the hours of canyon roads had become unendurable, something shimmered in the air, a change of light or air pressure. The road took a turn and they found themselves at the bottom of the cliff road, looking out at the city of their youth.

Mrs. Sunquist had been quiet these last two hours. Now, she could not help smiling. "It's still the most beautiful places we ever lived," she said.

La Jetée glowed under the slanted light of evening, as vivid as a fever dream. Every little outbuilding and café a rich, ridiculous red. Every boat-repair shop a bitter aqua, a harsh viridian.

Melancholy limned the moment. The Sunquists had agreed that this would be their last trip to La Jetée. The baby was coming. They both had experienced things in La Jetée that no one needed to grow up with, Mr. Sunquist had said so himself. That had been an easy decision in their kitchen. As he drank in his last visits of La Jetée, Mr. Sunquist would have taken it back.

"Do you remember that time at Lola's Bookstore," Mr. Sunquist asked his wife, "when Pieczyznski, the chess master, challenged nineteen of his own iterations to speed tournaments?"

"And he beat twelve of them?" She laughed at the image. "And played the other seven to draws. . . ."

"—And then he killed himself, because twelve of the nineteen were older versions of himself, and he could see how his powers would decline!" The Sunquists shook their heads; this was a favorite memory of theirs. Something they had always planned to get back to see again.

"Do you think we can find that?" she asked.

Mr. Sunquist nodded down the road. The La Jetée of last summer had passed into the expanding time signatures of the Present City. He thought he recognized it, floating against the horizon, spectral and overbright. Or maybe he saw some other iteration, realized by other Sunquists on other summer jaunts.

"He's there," Mr. Sunquist said. "I know that. We need a Feyaman diagram to orient ourselves, that's all." He knew a kiosk in the hotel district, they could get one there.

Just off the frontage road, they passed the skeleton of a new luxury hotel, half-built and abandoned. It rose from behind its screen of construction siding like the rusted gantries of some failed cosmodrome. A faded sign promised completion in the spring. It did not mention the year.

Mr. Sunquist winced a little as they drove by. So many friends had gone in with him on this investment. They should have known, he told himself. Vacation real estate can be so risky.

But Mr. Sunquist had no time to indulge regret. His mind was on the row of orchid houses that had been dug under in the hotel's wake. Where was that paella kitchen where he had taught Mrs. Sunquist how to eat mangoes? Or the hotel where they had hidden themselves away from the heat on those breathless August days when the sky was blue-black with unspent rain? A less romantic man would have surrendered these places to the iterations of memory. Mr. Sunquist surrendered nothing.

Twenty-five years up the highway would be the Hotel Mozambique, just as it had been at the height of its renown. During the hot weekends of August, the Sunquists had allowed themselves little vacations from their basement apartment on Four O'Clock Street. The Hotel Mozambique had been their destination. Mr. Sunquist remembered the room they had asked for. Number 219 looked out on the black-bottom pool and the ocean across the road.

Here also would be Sonny's Bar, and the night he had proposed marriage to Melanie Everett. This was one of Mrs. Sunquist's favorite moments.

They would get their room at the Mozambique, he decided. From there, they would find the night of their proposal. But something about their Feynman was corrupted. Or maybe Mrs. Sunquist wasn't reading it properly. Whatever, the Sunquists found themselves retracing a patch of highway twenty-five years up the road. Just as their navigating turned quarrelsome, Mrs. Sunquist sighted a blue-and-white beachcomber bicycle racked up alongside the Ciriquito Street pier.

She pointed into the haze of decoherence that muffled the world beyond the road. In that instant, a moment coalesced before them.

Mr. Sunquist found himself in a narrow parking strip looking down on a gentrified waterfront. Sailboats in slips, cafés with sun decks. Temporal observatories offered "Views of Parallel Worlds!" And, "The Chance to See the Life You Might Have Led!" All for two dollars.

Sonny's Bar nestled into the crook where the Ciriquito Street Pier met the beach. Like every other building on the beach, Sonny's Bar showed its backside to the landlubbers' world. A sign had been painted above the dumpsters, reminding all the old neighborhood that Sonny had been serving them in this same location. *"Since most of you were underage."*

"I don't see my truck," Mr. Sunquist said. "Are you sure this is the night?"

"You called me from your office and said to meet you here," Mrs. Sunquist said. "I do not make a habit of bicycling to bars. This is the night you proposed."

"Maybe we pulled off the highway a few minutes early," Mr. Sunquist offered. He suggested they wait for him inside the bar, just to be sure.

The interior was designed in one of those inverted situations from the turn of some century. The patrons clambered together on a large round cushion the color and texture of boxing gloves. Three bartenders hovered over a counter that encircled them.

TV monitors were placed to catch the eye at every angle. In this age, Sonny's fancied itself a sports bar. But Sonny himself? He liked *novelas*, Mexican soap operas. Two different ones were playing simultaneously as the Sunquists walked in. A regular was complaining that the World Cup was on, Brazil versus Russia. Sonny was laughing and nodding, paying the man no particular mind. His eyes were neither on the man, nor on the screens.

Like everyone else in the room, Sonny watched the girl in the sun dress and sandals. She sat on the quiet side of the circular cushion, away from most of the television screens. She read *Justine* (the one by Lawrence Durrell, not the Marquis de Sade), and nudged a glass of chardonnay around by the stem. Maybe it was something about seeing across twenty-five years in the space of a single room, but Mr. Sunquist imagined that the girl was bathed in a singular light. Maybe it was simply that everyone else seemed to dim by comparison.

The Sunquists found chairs in an alcove beneath one of the television screens. They had a view of the bar from here, and the television to distract anyone who looked their way.

A waiter asked what they were having. Mrs. Sunquist asked for iced tea. ("Iced tea," she snickered, "This kills me.")

Mr. Sunquist liked a scotch and soda, but not here. And As he looked across the bar, he recognized iterations of himself and his wife from other summers, all drinking scotch-and-sodas. He did not wish to be known by the sort of drink he ordered. He ordered a glass of merlot.

Mrs. Sunquist put a hand on his arm. "You know, I was furious at you for leaving me alone in a bar," she said. A phone call had kept Mr. Sunquist from leaving some warehouse on Gull Street wanting to be an artists' left.

Mrs. Sunquist did not seem furious; she was smiling at her younger reflection. The girl on the couch didn't look furious. She looked like a stranded angel, patiently waiting on gravity's demise.

"Right about now, I was giving you five more minutes to walk through the door."

"You were very tolerant with me, Mrs. S."

But it wasn't tolerance that had kept her in her seat for an hour.

A little man entered the bar and approached her. He wore a suit and tie, but badly. They were not what he was used to. He was not yet thirty, yet his scalp already showed through the down at the top of his head. A last bit of baby fat lent his eyes a squint when he smiled.

Mr. and Mrs. Sunquist bushed each other as the little man asked to sit. "He was very polite," Mrs. Sunquist recalled.

"He was scared of you," Mr. Sunquist chuckled. "Look how bald he's become in just a few years." Mr. Sunquist remembered the little man from their old neighborhood. He didn't remember the name. But the young man had existed at the periphery of Bobby Shelbourne's crew, Mr. Sunquist remembered that.

The Sunquists stifled giggles; Melanie let him buy her a glass of wine, though a glass stood half full at her elbow. She smiled at him as he fumbled at his introduction: Roger J. Swann, from a local desk of one of the international banks in Kleege's Beach. He never mentioned the old bungalows they had all shared on the beach, or the parties at Sonny's and at Bobby Shelbourne's apartment. He seemed happy in his role as stranger. In the presence of Melanie Everett, he might have been happy with anything. The story as the Sunquists retold it to each other over the years had this desperate little man crawling into Melanie's lap. In fact, Swann never looked down at her open décolletage. His eyes were glued to her face. Every smile she made brought one in return. Her jokes made him laugh, and cover his mouth with his palm.

Melanie Everett asked him about himself. (Surely, she was being wicked!) Roger Swann was awed by her consideration. He grew flustered. He might have gone.

Melanie had this thing she did, this nervous laugh, as if she were the one who needed reassurance. Swann happily reassured her.

He told her about his work. Roger Swann was a programmer for the bank. "More like a game warden," he confided. "The programs do their own programming anymore. I just make sure they remember who they're working for."

Melanie laughed and put her hand up to her mouth.

Roger Swann did the same. His eyes squinted down to little black points of happiness and moist shine.

Mr. Sunquist remembered Roger Swann. What a perfect fool he had been! He had missed his chance with Melanie at her twentieth birthday party. Look at him now—Mr. Sunquist could see the romantic fantasies fill his mind. "Enjoy it while you can," he chuckled.

One of the bartenders swung up the counter to let someone through. It was Bill Sunquist. He looked sheepish at first. He saw the clock above the bar and lowered his head and sighed. Then he saw the fervent little banker paying for Melanie's wine. This wicked leer kinked up the corner of his mouth.

Roger Swann never looked up, but Melanie did. Melanie said not a word as Bill Sunquist pushed by the two of them to take a seat on her left. Roger Swann was explaining the intricacies of Darwinian programming strategies. She seemed perfectly content to listen.

Mr. Sunquist remembered looking across at Melanie as Swann continued on about his work—*Are you looking for a job*? What? That's when he saw the amusement in her eyes. What a hoot this would be!

Bill Sunquist had a low boredom tolerance. There was only so much arlatrage trading and Darwinian software business to put up with before the joke ran out. Just for fun, he leaned across Roger's lap to argue with the waiter over the provenance of a gram of hashish.

"A spicy aroma of ginger," he read off the thumb-

sized packet. "Redolent with earth musk and cardamom." Bill Sunquist opened it up for the maître d' to
smell. "Would you describe that as 'redolent with earth
musk and cardamom?'"

The waiter looked at him long, a patronizing half-
smile at the corner of his mouth. "We have a fine roan
from Lebanon, with the elusive sweetness of late-harvest
Riesling. Would you care to try that?"

"For my friend here." Mr. Sunquist remembered smiling down on Roger Swann. "For my friend." He remembered Roger Swann smiling back, confused and helpful
and friendly as a pup. Bill Sunquist nodded across at
Melanie. "Are you ready, *mi amor?* To Grandmother's
house we go."

A priceless moment—Roger Swann turns his hopeful
gaze back to Melanie. But Melanie is already moving
past Bill for the open side of the bar.

Looking on from the darkness of their alcove, Mr.
Sunquist could not help an ornery cackle. Ohh, he was
terrible in those days!

They shook hands like gentlemen, give them that.
Such was his commitment to sportsmanship that Roger
Swann would have shaken Melanie's hand as well, but
something made her turn away at the last moment. She
stumbled into Bill, pushed past him blindly for the door.

Mr. Sunquist had to bite his fist to keep from laughing at the ridiculous tableau—Roger Swann, staring after
them with three half-empty wine glasses on the bar and
a look in his eyes like crushed violets.

Mrs. Sunquist squeezed his arm the way she always did when she was trying to make him behave. Oh, but her eyes shone. Even before she said it, he knew that she must be exulting in their perversity.

He might have skipped the proposal at this point. He had no need to fight the crush of other Sunquists, all hurrying out to see the same thing. He had seen what he wanted. Only courtesy made him remind his wife why they had come here in the first place.

"Right out there on the porch," he told her, "I'm proposing marriage to you."

Mrs. Sunquist had her eyes on Roger Swann. He had to nudge her for attention. "You still want to see this, don't you?" She laughed then, the way she always did. She assured him that she was all right, as if he had asked.

They had managed to snag a prime parking spot from the clutches of their own grasping iterations. From here, the Sunquists looked on as Bill Sunquist dug in his coat pocket and came up with something small, wrapped in velvet and chintz.

Even now, Mr. Sunquist remembered the moment. He remembered the way Melanie drew her hands to her face, and looked from his hands to his face as if to catch him in a lie. He remembered the feel of her fingers in his palm as she took the box, the little breath as she opened it and turned the ring toward the light.

Mr. Sunquist tried to remember what was going

through the mind of the young man on the porch. Maddeningly, all he could think of was Roger Swann. People like that, you humiliate them and they think they can win you over. Any minute, he had expected the door to open and a myopic smile to appear beneath the wall seance.

The realization made him anxious for something to say. "We look like we're very much in love." In truth, Mr. Sunquist had no idea what people in love were supposed to look like.

"I hate to tell you what I was really thinking." Mrs. Sunquist gave a glance over her shoulder. There was another couple in a car just a few spaces down. She leaned forward so they would not hear what she had to say. "I had just downed a glass-and-a-half of cheap white wine and all I could think about was finding someplace to pee."

"And, of course, you couldn't go back in the bar—"

"Roger Swann was in there."

Mr. Sunquist found himself roaring. Mrs. Sunquist hushed him; she was a shy person by nature, and people might be listening. That made him laugh even harder.

The couple in the next car turned to see what was funny, but he didn't care. He knew those people well enough, he had nothing to prove to them.

They would be a couple in their thirties. They would be having a conversation very much like this one. A little breathless, the woman hints to her husband how these past fifteen years are as much a product of bladder control as love.

Perhaps she intends a joke. Perhaps an insult. Things are not so good between the man and the woman at this point in their marriage. The woman realizes this too late, and starts to back up and stammer.

To himself, the man thinks . . .

"Romance is one of those things that doesn't really work as a first-hand experience. Why we come back here every year, I imagine."

"What?" Mrs. Sunquist looked up at him. "You must have heard that somewhere."

It was not an especially generous thought, Mr. Sunquist realized. He was a little surprised he had said it out loud. More surprised how much he believed it to be true. "We should move on," he said. "Let these kids have their privacy."

She put a hand to his wrist as he reached for the touchpad. "One more minute," she whispered. "They're almost done." She stared so intently that Mr. Sunquist wondered what she was looking at. Her head tilted to her right, and her mouth gaped in little-girl awe.

"I was a beauty in my day, wasn't I?" She smiled a little, as if to make a joke, but she could not hide the shine in her eyes.

It must be the baby, he thought. The baby makes her sentimental. A half-dozen things came to mind. All had the antiseptic cheer of a get-well card. He squeezed her hand. "Steady on, old girl. Let's not break the mood here."

Mrs. Sunquist nodded. Of course, of course. Suddenly, she was laughing again. She waved all his worried looks aside. Perhaps she had been having him on after all.

A few minutes further up the road awaited the Hotel Mozambique they had known as youngsters. White stucco bungalows crowded protectively around a medium-sized black bottom pool. They opened at the far end to show the sky at evening.

Mr. Sunquist got them the room they always asked for, looking out through the top of a date palm toward Mer Noire.

Mrs. Sunquist pushed open the window. A blood-warm breeze came in off the bay, sour with brine, pungent with road tar from the asphalt bike paths just beyond the courtyard.

"What was the name of that soap opera they filmed down the beach?" Mrs. Sunquist eased herself into the corner of the sill, hugging herself in the dreamy light that spilled through the palms just beyond.

"Indigo Something," Mr. Sunquist recalled. "*Shades of Indigo*, I think."

"They filmed right outside my window for six months when I lived with Bobby Shelbourne. The next year, the production company followed their expanding time signature up the beach and filmed the actors playing opposite their own earlier iterations. You remember that?"

"Mr. Sunquist said he did. This was a lie—Mr. Sunquist had no money for television when he was young—but all lies are sweet in La Jetée in August.

Mrs. Sunquist smiled at him, knowing and unconcerned. She led him by the hand to the bed. They made love in the cool shade of the whitewashed room—sweetly, awkwardly, stopping to see if everything was all right with the baby.

Later, as the heat of the day enveloped them, Mr. Sunquist pressed his arm around Mrs. Sunquist's shoulders and drew her close. They had not slept this way since they were newlyweds. Her hair had the soapy smell of newborn babies. The scent of it followed him into his dreams.

Here was Melanie Everett, the girl that would be his wife. He remembered her all golden under the sun, bashful but hardly uncertain. She had perfected the fascination that goes with being the second-prettiest girl at every party. Boys became aware of her in stages, the way they became aware of the first hit pop tune of the summer.

Forthright kids like Bob Shelbourne were always going to get around to Melanie Everett, right after they investigated the fulsome charms of Jenn LeMel, or the Maynard sisters. Shy kids always thought of her beauty as their secret. Being shy, they assumed their secret safe.

Lying beside her now, Mr. Sunquist dreamed not of his wife, but of his friends—the things they would tell each other. What did they think when they heard Melanie Everett had gone home with him? His had been an epic battle, as pure as a fairy tale. A rival had been vanquished. A maiden won. Being a man living at a certain moment in history, he had learned to savor these stories. Nothing is more vivid than a moment re-lived, he would say. Not even the moment itself.

The heat of the day had broken when Mr. Sunquist shook off the last of his dreams. The breeze had shifted around to come in from the south, from the future—side of the bay. Mrs. Sunquist said she could lie beneath the billowing curtains all night long. Perhaps Mrs. Sunquist still had doubts. If so, Mr. Sunquist hardly heard. He was planning their road trip.

He asked Mrs. Sunquist if she remembered the first time they made love.

"Of course I do." As indignant as she could manage.

"We had to take a blanket out to Mourning Shoals because your boyfriend was setting up your apartment for a surprise birthday party. You remember? And the fog rolled in so we almost couldn't find the truck, and then we got back an hour and a half after the party started?"

Mrs. Sunquist laughed, embarrassed. She remembered.

"You know," Mr. Sunquist said, "that's one place you and I have never gone back to."

"Oh, William. No!"

"It's a birthday party. It would be easy to slip in. And we had such a time that night."

Mrs. Sunquist touched his cheek. "You remember everything so perfectly," she said.

Something in her tone struck Mr. Sunquist as odd, so that he smiled and frowned at the same time. Perhaps his wife had not enjoyed the scene in the bar as he expected. Time for something frivolous, he decided. Pieczyznski, the chess master, perhaps. Or maybe they could see *Shades of Indigo* filming up at the old Hartringer Hotel.

He didn't tell her what he planned. He thought to surprise her. He expected that she might even mention these places herself, but the scene in the bar had left Mrs. Sunquist in some reverie of her own.

Seven miles up the highway, and as many years further back, Mr. Sunquist found a neighborhood he recognized. Lola's Bookstore was just up the street in a bus barn it shared with an equity waiver theater. If someone could give them the local date and time, they would pin down the moment of their arrival.

The Sunquists discovered a young couple hiding among the shadows of Ciriquito Street. Mr. Sunquist called to them. The boy glanced back at him—*what*? The girl turned around to see what he was looking at. The

Sunquists realized they were looking at themselves.

Mr. Sunquist knew immediately where they were. Somehow, they had stumbled onto Melanie Everett's twentieth birthday party. This was the night that she had ended her relationship with her boyfriend. The night that she had gone home with him.

Bill Sunquist and Melanie Everett stood in the shadow of a large real estate sign. The sign showed an artist's rendering of tennis courts, a condominium, a hotel complex.

The Ciriquito Street pier, where fishing boats still headed into the sun each morning, that was to be subsumed into a two-hundred slip marina. Bill Sunquist noticed none of this. The sign was nothing to him but cover. He had Melanie under his left arm and they were studying the beach-front apartment she shared with Bobby Shelbourne, the man who promised to love her, *"no matter how much she disappointed him."*

They were talking. The Sunquists were too far away to hear the words. No matter; the Sunquists had remembered this story to each other till they could mouth the words. Bill Sunquist and Melanie Everett had parked along Kleege's Beach and spent the afternoon under the tarp in the back of Bill Sunquist's two-ton army surplus lorry. Now she was late to her own birthday party. Late, and sunburned and sweaty and very guilty.

Mr. Sunquist thought of Piecziznski, the chess master. Well, they were here now. Whatever he had intended could wait until after. Mrs. Sunquist smiled, though she plainly was embarrassed. "William, I don't know about this."

"What are you worried about? You know how it turns out."

"I don't want to see this."

"You were asking if you were beautiful." He nodded toward their younger reflections. "Look at how young we are in this place."

"It's a world of ghosts," Mrs. Sunquist said to the car window. "I don't care how young they are."

Mr. Sunquist did not blame his wife for being negative. He ascribed her unease to Bobby Shelbourne's oppressive aura. Understandable, certainly. Bobby Shelbourne was a vegetarian and pathological spoilsport, one of those people who savored his slights. No wonder Mrs. Sunquist quailed at the memory of this night. He studied the girl standing under the real estate sign. Look at how frantic she is to make her story, he thought.

"The only way out is through," he told Mrs. Sunquist. And then: "Don't be scared." It was the sort of patronizing admonishment a six-year-old uses on a younger sibling.

Mrs. Sunquist pureed her lips with a moment's thought, then she nodded at an open curb down the block.

They pulled up in front of a shaded courtyard between two bungalows. Bill and Melanie had disappeared. Mr. Sunquist heard whispers and laughter though a screen of rust-colored bougainvillea. Up ahead was the ocean, and a small yard inside a rusted fence that separated the apartment from the beach. He heard flapping above his head. A banner cut from bed sheets stretched between a pair of upstairs windows. It read: HAPPY BIRTHDAY, MELANIE. I LOVE YOU.

Mrs. Sunquist paused when she saw the painted bed sheet. "Really," she said. "Let's not do this." Just for a moment, she glanced back the way they had come. She might have been gauging her chances of making the street.

"Don't tell me you feel guilty." Mr. Sunquist hooted. "Guilty for Bobby Shelbourne! Oh, wouldn't he love that."

"There's not enough people for us to slip in. Someone will recognize us. They'll know we came from down the beach."

Indeed, a young man with mild blue eyes had been stationed at the top of the stair to guard against crashers. For one moment, Mr. Sunquist cringed as Roger Swann nodded down at them. He thought of the humiliation. Roger had suffered in Sonny's—wondered if he might have to answer for it. But no, that bar scene was seven years in Roger Swann's future. Swann gave them only a look of rueful curiosity. He nodded toward the next bungalow over, where he imagined they had come from. He asked if they were here to complain about the noise.

Mr. Sunquist was thinking up a suitable lie when Melanie Everett stepped out onto the landing.

She had this nervous laugh as a kid, which was odd. Watching her, Mr. Sunquist suddenly realized that Melanie herself was not nervous at all. The laugh was for the benefit of whoever she spoke to. It worked to spectacular effect.

Suddenly, Roger Swann was over his terror of pretty girls. He leaned forward to hear her as she asked him something under the music. Smiling, he answered.

Mrs. Sunquist took her husband by the wrist. "You know what he's telling me?" Even now the boy's words affected her. "He's telling me how Bobby's been waiting for me since four. And then he tells me he himself has been waiting for me all his life."

"Aww," Mr. Sunquist gave her a look of arch sentimentality. Together, they went "Aww," loud enough to attract the gaze of the kids on the stair. He thought that Melanie regarded them with some look of secret humor. Who knew what she was really thinking. Mr. Sunquist imagined pretty girls used this look when they could think of nothing to say.

Roger got a peck on the cheek for his sweetness. Melanie disappeared into the party without a backward glance, but that was enough for Roger Swann. The Sunquists were forgotten. He slicked the thinning wedge of hair back from his forehead. He followed after her. The Sunquists trailed a short distance behind.

One thing that Mr. Sunquist remembered about Bobby Shelbourne's apartment, it was dangerous to show too much interest in any bit of ornament.

Bobby Shelbourne lived in a museum of Melmac ice cream dishes, mis-matched kitchen chairs, and determinedly outdated electronic entertainment gear. Every one with a little story about where it had been found, and how much it was really worth to some mythical dealer in garage-sale lamps, or kitchen Formica, or digital video downloaders.

A whir-sound passed by overhead. A scale model of the Hindenburg was making stately passage from the living room to the kitchen. Normally, Bobby would be following it around, pointing out the hand-painted swastika on the tail rudder. But the mood had gone out of him today.

He saw Melanie and his pale blue eyes went all weepy and proud. His pouty lip grew heavier than it was already. If Bobby had promised to forgive Melanie no matter what, he had not promised to make it easy. He would not even acknowledge Melanie till she took his arm and made him face her.

Someone put on music, too loud to hear her speak. No matter, Mr. Sunquist could tell by her rueful demeanor that she was making her story.

What was it he and Melanie had decided? Yes, he

remembered now—Melanie had gone down the T-line Highway to visit the iterations of her own childhood. The Feynman diagram in her glove compartment contained too many streets between there and here that had yet to be built. She'd gotten confused coming back.

Mr. Sunquist spotted himself over by the kitchen door, watching. Melanie had asked Bill to stay away while she tried to explain things to her boyfriend. Of course there was no way Bill Sunquist would do that— let her explain things to her boyfriend? So that they might smooth things out? Melanie had been naïve to think that he would.

It hardly mattered; Bobby Shelbourne saw him over Melanie's head. Shelbourne smiled.

"It's you, isn't it." His eyes were luminous with anger.

Bill made no attempt to deny it. He smiled his most irritating smirk, motioned to Shelbourne in that silent gesture every young man knows—hands out, fingers cupping palms in ironic invitation: *Come on then. Come get some.*

Melanie pulled him back by the arm, and for one moment Bobby Shelbourne let her. The pause was so brief that Billy Sunquist had barely noticed. Twenty-five years older, Mr. Sunquist grinned: Look how he glances around for a way out!

"You were never no street brawler, Bobby." Slipping into a voice he had not spoken in since he was a vain young man. "You were never nothing like what I was."

Even now, Mr. Sunquist lived for these moments. Anymore, the stakes would be infinitely higher than a broken nose. But that desperate calculation remained eternal: Pride? Or survival?

Melanie saw her chance to wedge between them. The two boys clenched each other tight against her. Mr. Sunquist remembered the collision between his belly and her skinny rib cage. He remembered the sound she made as the breath went out of her.

Billy Sunquist might have reached for her. He always told himself that he would have, if only Bobby had not started in the way he did.

"Look at her," Bobby hissed. "Now you've done it. Now you've hurt her." Nobody put Billy Sunquist on the defensive.

Billy Sunquist took a hunk of genuine 100 percent Rayon bowling shirt and laughed in Bobby Shelbourne's face. *Nice try.* All these years away, Mr. Sunquist still felt Bobby Shelbourne's cheekbones beneath his knuckles. The two of them waltzed around till they fell back against the Formica tabletop, slamming the blender and liquor and ice onto the floor.

Melanie wasn't really so damaged. Mr. Sunquist found her, easing herself back against the refrigerator. Her shirt was soaked watery green from a half-bottle of Midori, but she seemed all right.

Roger Swann had come over to help her up, but she had more than pity on her mind. She took his elbow and pointed toward the mess in the kitchen.

Like any young man of experience, he knew the risks of stepping into someone else's fight. He thumbed the side of his mouth in an expression of unease. But Melanie had this unassailable sense of mission when the chips were down. It animated her. It swept up everyone around her. Roger found his resolve; together, they waded in. Each grabbed an elbow, or a shoulder, and yanked backward.

Bill Sunquist had Bobby Shelbourne's face against the refrigerator. Mr. Sunquist dimly remembered the conversation between them, something about eating the refrigerator's door handle. Oh well.

The next moments came vivid, but in flashes, like snapshots: A hand on his arm. A face coming in at him. He remembered placating words, but his blood was up. He swung back his left hand and connected solidly with hard bone, right at somebody's hairline. The face went away.

Bill Sunquist turned back for Bobby Shelbourne only to find that Melanie had got between them. The fight was over.

He called to her. He nodded toward the door, *Let's go*. But Melanie was angry, she ignored him.

Shelbourne fixed his eyes on her. Even as his friends moved him off to the far side of the kitchen, he spoke to her. Bobby asked if she'd been hurt, was there anything he could do?

"You know I always took care of you," Bobby Shelbourne called to her. "I may not be exciting, but I'm always there."

Oh, he was good. Anyone else would have blasphemed and threatened.

Melanie looked big-eyed and stricken. This was the moment she had chewed her knuckles over all the way from Kleege's Beach. Bill Sunquist, too. By the look on his face, he might have swallowed an ice tray. He was a street kid, after all. Smooth talk was not where he excelled.

Melanie wavered. She started to raise her hands the way she did when she was miserable and all out of words.

But here was Roger Swann, leaning forward with his hand on his forehead. Blood was seeping through his fingers and plopping in the wet muck. He wobbled on his knees and Melanie took him. Bobby's appeals to her conscience would have to wait.

Bobby smiled, sure. "You're doing the right thing," he told her. "Take care of Roger. We'll talk later. When you have a minute."

Mr. Sunquist had not seen this side of Melanie since they were married. She could be magnificent, couldn't she? He marveled: Bobby Shelbourne is two months from buying up this whole block of apartments for his daddy's marina project, look at how he stammers before her.

His wife felt the weight of his consideration. For one

moment, she was the girl she had been. Self-possessed and certain. Perhaps she knew what he was thinking. She would have said something to him, but Melanie Everett came this way. Roger Swann bumped along in her wake. Mr. and Mrs. Sunquist stood up to make room for him on the couch.

She was saying something under her breath, half to Roger, half to herself. "Limo." It was Bill Sunquist's street name. "Limo, Limo, Limo," she said—eventually winding up with, "Damn him." Melanie tipped Roger's head back. She squinted against the bad party light. The blood was starting to roll down his nose. She dipped a kitchen towel in the punch bowl and dabbed it off.

"It was just a wild punch." Roger's hand came up, a gesture of indifference. "He hit me left-handed anyway. Probably doesn't even know he did it."

"Him and those stupid rings he wears. He's been dying to use them on someone."

Roger was silent for a few dabs. Mr. Sunquist could see him working his way up to something. "You really have to go with him?"

For one moment, Melanie looked up at the Sunquists with this exasperated grimace—*you explain it for him.* Mr. Sunquist felt his wife's fingers clutch his, stricken. But it was an illusion. Melanie's look was intended for anyone within earshot—anyone who knew what it was to be the second-prettiest girl at every party. For one night, she had her pick between princes. How could she explain to the nicest kid in the room what this meant?

"I'm going home with Limo." She squeezed Roger's blood into the punch bowl. "I really am."

Roger Swann shook his head, whatever. "We'll see each other again," he said.

Mr. Sunquist nudged Mrs. Sunquist. He raised his chin at the boy. "Sonny's Bar," he whispered in her ear. "This is what he was thinking when he saw you alone in Sonny's Bar."

He laughed so loud that both the people on the couch turned back in curiosity. He didn't care. He waved them back to their conversation. "This is too good," he hissed.

Mrs. Sunquist was supposed to laugh along at times like this. She bit her lip and looked down at her shoes. "How do you do it?" She sounded breathless, she might have been amazed. "I see the time passing and it makes me so weary. And you just keep getting angrier. Don't you ever feel any pity? Or regret?"

He put out his hands, he smiled. He figured there had to be a joke in here somewhere. "We are what we've always been. Isn't that enough?" It was the only explanation he could think of.

"Poor Roger," she said.

To himself, he thought, *Somebody has to lose.*

Did she know what he was thinking? Suddenly, she had this look on her face, still and deliberate and calm. It was the face he recognized from the taxi drivers who came to pick him up from bars. Whatever she saw in his eyes only made her sigh.

"Time for us to go," Mrs. Sunquist said.

"We haven't seen the end yet. Remember? I sweep out of the crowd and pick you up, and Bobby Shelbourne—"

"You know what happens. You take me home with you. We spend the next twenty-five years coming back to see it all again. I have something I want to remember."

Here was a phrase Mr. Sunquist would think back on: *I have something I want to remember.*

In all the years he had come back to La Jetée, Mr. Sunquist had never felt the need to remember anything. Memories were for people who didn't come to La Jetée. Memories were for the ones Mr. Sunquist imagined in his audience.

Evening was coming on as they pulled onto Ciriquite Street. The shutters on all the beach bungalows and flower kiosks had opened to the first breath of an evening breeze. The air was dense with the musk of orchids.

This was five years earlier, La Jetée was a strip of bungalows, caught between the highway and the beach. Mr. Sunquist remembered thin times. The tourists had bypassed La Jetée for the more developed resorts down the beach. The only money in the town came from the nurseries across the highway, and service jobs in the hotels south of Kleege's Beach. Every evening, the streetcare would be full of people in half-undone housecleaning uniforms. Head waiters from the lesser restaurants would hang from the doors, swigging pilfered wine bottles and calling out insults as they passed each other.

And everyone ended up in the tiny patio at Sonny's.

Here was the Sonny's that the Sunquists never tired of Sonny's Seafood Chowder Bar was an open courtyard, an old banyan tree, gnarled as knuckles, a cast concrete bar patterned with ridiculous wood grain. Sonny Himself was whip-thin these days. With ashy skin and freckles and a wide grin that seemed somehow more charming for its insincerity.

He was not charming tonight. He was eating Spanish peanuts out of the bar dishes, which is what he did when he was nervous. His eyes were like black ice and he kept checking his watch.

A door behind the bar led out into an alley that ran from the street to the beach. People passed in and out carrying guitars and tambales and a set of wide-mouthed clay jugs, each one painted with "Jug Breakers" on the side—Bobby Shelbourne's band.

Sonny glared at every kid who passed through that door. He pointed to his watch. They scuttled off to the stage like roaches caught in a kitchen light.

Bobby Shelbourne had played here every Thursday night for most of the summer, but anyone could see the blow-up that was coming. Sonny Scorzy was a congenial host, but he was hell as an employer. He hated lateness, even when he was paying no money. Bobby Shelbourne had a star's concept of time, even though he made no money. Sonny Scorzy hated that.

On this night, only one person was exempt from Sonny's evil eye. Even now, Mr. Sunquist lost his breath at the sight of her. That golden hair. Those exotic eyes. Sonny had saved her his own chair, right at the end of his beloved bar. She took it with this air of modest expectancy—she was gracious and patient as Sonny wiped off the peanut skins and beer. But it never occurred to her to sit elsewhere.

Mr. Sunquist still loved the way she said things and then covered her mouth with her hand, as if surprised by her own sense of humor. He loved the careful, prim way she crossed her ankles. He loved her dubious smile as young Billy Lee Sunquist slid in next to her.

Mr. Sunquist wondered how much it would take to impress a girl like Melanie Everett now. How much had he spent on that account rep from Loach & Widell? Not including lunch at that expensive bistro she had recommended? Billy Lee Sunquist had held his knowledge cheaply when he'd lived in La Jetée, and given it away for the asking.

"Here," Billy Lee said to the young woman struggling with the fruit that Sonny had put out for her. "You wanna know how to eat a mango, I'll show you how to eat a mango."

"I'm with someone," she said, and nodded toward a

little door into the alley, where Bobby Shelbourne and his Jug Breakers were tuning up.

Billy Lee Sunquist laughed at the caution on her face. He held up his hands. "I'm just showing you how to eat a mango." He took the fruit from her hand, salted it, dusted it with cayenne pepper, and slipped it down his throat. He licked his fingers one by one and gave her a lascivious grin.

Mrs. Sunquist gave her husband a secret smile. "You remember what you said to me?"

Mr. Sunquist claimed he did not. Mrs. Sunquist said she did not believe he didn't remember. Out on the patio, Billy Lee Sunquist whispered in Melanie Everett's ear. She grew big-eyed and aghast. She gave Billy Lee a slap on the shoulder, and then said something under her breath that made him laugh and made her cover her mouth with her hand.

Mr. Sunquist gripped his wife's hand. This trip was already working changes on her. That sturdy quiet she had acquired over the lean years of their middle age, that had melted to the shyness he remembered so well. He would have shared this moment with the world.

Bobby came out with his nickel-topped Dobro guitar. Roger Swann hunkered down next to him with some squat Caribbean drum between his knees. They were a team in those days, Bobby and Roger. If Bobby played guitar, Roger would be there with the drums.

There was this trombone player that neither of the

Sunquists remembered. He nudged Bobby Shelbourne. He motioned toward his girl and the young man sitting next to her.

Perhaps he had a look of mischief. If so, he would be disappointed. Bobby Shelbourne saw Bill Sunquist leaning close to Melanie. He grinned and shook his finger, school-marm style. Billy laughed. Melanie gave him a girl-slug and nodded toward her boyfriend on the stage—*See? I told you.*

Everybody knew each other at Sonny's. Everything was easy.

The music started. Jug band blues, simple and irresistible. Everybody on the patio pushed forward under the gnarled banyan tree. They sang along to the songs they knew. They shoulder-danced to the songs they didn't know. They ate mangoes and papayas, and drank fermented *cidra* from terra-cotta jugs.

Then it came time for this walking blues, "Limousine Blues." Billy Lee Sunquist liked this song. He wasn't sure yet, but he was thinking about incorporating it as his personal theme.

He threw back his head at the first note. His face split into a wide grin. "My song!" he cried. "Bobby remembered my song!"

Melanie was still wiping mango pulp from her fingers as he took her hand. "Ohh no," she was saying as he led her out in front of the band. "Ohh no."

There, in front of God and her boyfriend and everybody they knew, Billy Lee Sunquist and Melanie Everett danced some imaginary swing that they knew only from watching Tex Avery cartoons.

Mr. Sunquist felt his wife draw near. She asked him if he knew why they were here. He put his arm around her; he knew. "This is a cute moment together. Look at us there." He laughed at his younger iteration. Billy Lee Sunquist was barely more than a slouch and a lazy smile. "We were so poor;" he said.

"You might have been a billionaire for the way you acted. I was so impressed with you." She looked so long and hard at the young couple that she might have been trying to imprint this scene forever in her mind. "This is the moment I fell in love," she said.

Mr. Sunquist tried to remember the moment, what he was thinking. He couldn't. Maybe he too had been in love. Mr. Sunquist laughed as he realized it.

As they walked out to the car, he offered to take her to see Pieczyzoski, the chess master. But something had gone out of the mood. Perhaps this last moment had been a miscalculation? Mr. Sunquist decided they'd seen enough for their first day of vacation. He turned the car back up the highway for their hotel.

Mrs. Sunquist asked him about Roger Swann—back in that first iteration of Sonny's, he should have recognized them. It had been just a few years since they'd all seen each other, had they changed so much?

They fell into a foolish argument about Roger Swann, and why hadn't he recognized them? Mr. Sunquist wanted to laugh, except that underneath it all, the argument wasn't foolish. And somehow it wasn't really about Roger Swann.

Arguing, they missed the Hotel Mozambique. They drove south, beyond even the present iteration of La Jetée. Mr. Sunquist looked around to realize they had gone down the road, on to South Beach—into the future. They became quiet as they realized that nothing around them looked familiar.

No one ever came out to this end of the T-Line highway. Like one of these weighty popular art novels, South Beach was a place on every tongue, but rarely experienced in person. Everybody knew someone who had risked all to catch some glimpse of themselves in a new and unimagined place in their own lives. Always some friend, some relative. Never the person telling the story. Always the tale had some ghastly, amusing outcome.

They were well and truly lost when they reached the first town south of the Present Iteration. Mrs. Sunquist hesitated, but they were running low on power, and she had to use the bathroom again.

"Let's do it," cried Mr. Sunquist, his middle-aged timbre catching some of that old devilish tone. "Let's take a chance and see what we run into down here in The Future."

Mrs. Sunquist looked uneasy. But she would not be

outdone by her husband. Laughing together, they swung off the T-Line to get directions from the future back to the present.

Another building cycle was coming to La Jetée. All of the old orchid stands that had been on Noon Street and then replanted on Meridian Street were being uprooted again for a tract of old-style bungalow rows. The artists' conception reminded Mr. Sunquist of places he had lived. He wondered if this would be one of his investments.

No mention of the temporal anomaly. Was that no longer considered a draw? The only connection of the town they had left back in the gloom of fog and quantum wave-functions was a tag at the bottom of the sign:

SERIOUS ONLY
ENQUIRE WITH MR. ROBERT SHELBOURNE.
LA JETÉE

"Look at this," Mrs. Sunquist said, "They're even tearing down the buildings I hated to make way for new."

Mr. Sunquist knew he should be irate. Bobby Shelbourne hustled his phony nostalgia in the one place where nostalgia was useless. Somehow, he could do nothing but envy the man's gall.

They found an open-air market down the street. Palm fronds covered the porch, implying some sort of tropical *oeuvre*. Nearer the road were the hydrogen pumps, and electrical-charge outlets, and gasoline for the hybrids. As Mr. Sunquist started into the hydrogen lane, his wife grabbed his wrist and pointed across the street.

Their own car was parked at the curb, as if the occupants had gone for a walk over the chalk-white dunes to the ocean.

The Sunquists stared in astonishment. It was indeed their car, only the paint had faded to a dried-out coral. The seats had been left to the salt air and the sun till they had rotted open.

Someone had half-pulled an old beach blanket across the over-ripened seat cushions. An insignia on the blanket commemorated the Mer Noire regatta, fourteen years hence. The blanket looked as if it had been in the sun a couple of years even beyond that.

Mr. Sunquist thought for a moment. He realized what it had to mean. "It's our car all right, but we've passed it on to our child. This is just the sort of thing we would do."

Mrs. Sunquist looked doubtful. "Sixteen years from now? We'll have this car sixteen years from now?"

"It surely wouldn't be *us*." Mr. Sunquist cast a melodramatic stare toward Mrs. Sunquist. "Are we down on the beach somewhere? Should we go look?"

Mrs. Sunquist had given over the need to match her husband, dare-for-dare. "Let's just get some power and go," she said.

Mr. Sunquist wanted to egg her on a little. "Are you sure? We might be out there. On the beach. Living."

"This isn't funny," she said. "Let's just get the power and go."

Mr. Sunquist might have pushed a little harder but for the baby.

"You're lucky," he told her. He went up to pay for the fuel. She followed along to find a bathroom.

Around the corner from the pump island was a fruit stand and a cashier. As they approached, they heard a gravelly voice. "You know what you put on those? No, not sugar." Chesty laughter. "Thing's already sweet. Why would you put sugar on it? No, you know what they do in Mexico? They put salt on their mangos. A little cayenne pepper. Here."

Mr. and Mrs. Sunquist traded looks. An afternoon of chasing the ghosts of memory had left them unprepared for their role as someone else's ghost. They asked each other in that wordless language of married couples if they should go, but neither of them moved.

Mr. Sunquist felt his throat dry up. He thought for a moment. Was he sure he wanted to see himself like this? He grew impatient with his own timidity. What would happen, anyway? Would they blow up? Some sort of mutual annihilation, as if they were both opposing nuclear particles?

They stepped into the back of the cashier's line as casually as they could manage.

He was with a young girl. She had caramel-colored hair, like Mrs. Sunquist's had been when she had been a student. That same lithe waist. Those legs.

This is my daughter, Mr. Sunquist realized. The lust in him should have shamed him, but it merely made him furtive.

The store clerk flipped a light on so the old man could see what he was doing with that mango. A reflection appeared in the counter glass. Mr. Sunquist stared in fascination at the face of a tired satyr.

"We were such scoundrels when we were your age."

"Who's that?" the young woman frowned at the yellow fruit coming apart in her fingers. Her mind was a million years down the T-Line Highway.

"Here. Let me show you something. Over here to the northwest." He was so casual about the way he put his arm around the girl's waist. He aimed her toward a dark smudge along the knife-edge of the horizon. It was the most natural thing in the world.

"Who were you such scoundrels with, Billy?"

"If you look over this way," the old man said, "you can see the actual heat death of the universe." He was trying hard to instill his voice with a sense of wonder that life had not held for him in a very long time. The young woman followed his arm.

Mr. Sunquist was shocked at the resemblance she had to his wife. The dark, sloe eyes, the long, caramel-blond hair, the mobile mouth.

"It looks more like fog," she observed with adolescent irony.

"Can't see it with the naked eye. Somebody set a radio telescope pointing that way. Came back with dead air. Nothing."

The girl nodded. She understood: The cosmic background radiation. It was supposed to be evenly distributed throughout the universe. "Gee, that's interesting." She slurped mango slices.

The old man leaned close as if he wanted to steal a kiss. The girl smiled back at him, *What?* The soft light of her trust set him back. He looked away down the beach, as if uncertain what to do.

She asked him what he was thinking. He ran his hand up and down her arm, elbow to shoulder as he considered his answer.

"I was thinking of a moment from my life a long time ago," he answered. "I was on a patio, dancing with a girl who looked very much like you. We were both a little drunk, and her boyfriend was playing for us, and everyone was friends, you know? Just. Friends. And right now, I was thinking that may have been the sweetest moment of my life."

"It must be nice," the girl offered, "having a lifetime of memories like that. I wish I had one moment I could look back on."

The old Sunquist laughed, shook his head. "No, it's terrible," he said. "You spend the rest of your life trying to find that moment again, and it's never where you thought." He paused, as if he'd only just heard his own words. "It's amazing what a person will do to recapture one moment of peace. Amazing and terrible.

Something in his tone made the girl back away. But somehow she was still in his arms, and in turning she had presented her face to him.

He kissed her hard on the mouth. The girl pushed him back. For a moment, her chin bunched up and her cheeks reddened as if she might cry, or pummel the old man to the ground.

"Dammit," she said. "*Damn* it." Her hands went up in exasperation. An impulse took hold of her. She ran up and slugged him in the arm, dared him to respond.

The old Sunquist could do nothing but stare at her in stupid love. A moment of silence, then she stalked away down the beach. He squeezed his lips between his fingers. He squinted in anguish. He paced around in a little circle of perplexity, so that Mr. Sunquist could not help feeling sorry for him.

He called after the girl, laughing heartily as if it had all been a joke; she made an obscene gesture over her shoulder.

The present-tense Mr. Sunquist became aware of a profound silence directly behind him. He waited as long as he could before turning around.

Mrs. Sunquist—Melanie—was gone.

He put his fingers to his nose the way he did whenever he had to steady his vision after too much bourbon. He thought, this is ridiculous. How can I be blamed for something that hasn't even happened yet? Our child isn't even born. I don't even know for certain it will be a girl.

But in his heart, he knew it was not ridiculous. He knew himself well enough to know it was entirely likely. He simply couldn't believe Mrs. Sunquist would not forgive him. He had been forgiven all his life, hadn't he?

He pushed himself up to the sand dune and searched the beach. He saw the girl stalking away along a concrete sea wall, making angry little skips with her palm against the rough stone blocks.

He couldn't find Mrs. Sunquist anywhere.

He realized the old man was beside him. He wondered what he should do. He had heard of people meeting themselves, of course. One always heard stories. He just couldn't remember how any of those stories turned out.

When he could stand it no longer, he turned to the old man: "You know what you've done?" he asked.

The man looked shocked, like a theater patron suddenly addressed from the stage.

"You're not supposed to—"

"You couldn't keep your hands off your own daughter? Damn it."

In truth, he was not very angry. Mr. Sunquist was more overcome with weariness. In his weariness, he saw his older persona in a cool and distant light, the way one sees one's parents after a while. He wasn't addressing himself anymore. He was addressing a sad old man who had lost track of things somehow.

He crouched down to take the old man's hand. It was bloated, the skin shiny and taut. "I'm sorry," he said, "It's just—" He paused. How to put this? "That's our daughter. Do you understand? There are some things I just can't do. If I do these things, there will be no limits for me at all." He looked into the cracked old face for some sign he was getting through.

"*Daughter?* What do you take me for? That's not our daughter." The old man laughed. There was a certain malicious strain in the reedy voice. Even now, he wasn't so different. "We don't have a daughter. We have a son, Jeremy, but I haven't seen him in five years. You don't know this yet, do you? Sorry. Shouldn't have opened my mouth, I guess."

Mr. Sunquist sighed; of course, this man would know how Mr. Sunquist longed for a son. He would use that knowledge to win sympathy, emotional leverage. Mr. Sunquist wondered if this was the man he truly was destined to become. What a pathetic and self-serving old liar.

"Come on, now," he said as gently as possible. "I recognized her eyes. I know her cheekbones. The resemblance is too strong. You can't tell me this was just some kid you picked up."

The old satyr leaned close. Mr. Sunquist held his

breath at the tang of stale bourbon. "Of course it looks like Melanie," he hissed through his gaping teeth. "It *is* Melanie."

Mr. Sunquist felt something clammy and soft in the pit of his stomach. "You're not supposed to . . ."

"I was lonely," he said. "Mrs. Sunquist left me a couple of years ago—left us, I should say. Left us. I got my car, I took a ride down on the T-Line Highway." The rheumy eyes squinted defiantly. "Look at you, you're so self-righteous. What are you doing here? Huh? What are you doing here?"

"You're lying." Mr. Sunquist backed away. Melanie had to be somewhere on this beach; she had been right behind him a moment ago. He called out for her, but his words were caught up in a sudden gust of wind and scattered across the beach like sea birds.

"Lying? To you? Why would I lie to *you*, of all people?"

Way down by the waterline, Mr. Sunquist saw the young girl his wife had been. She looked back at the sound of her name. Was that recognition in her eyes? Mr. Sunquist entertained the notion of following after her. But she was not his wife, and he was not really Billy Lee Sunquist. Not her Billy Lee Sunquist. She turned away up the beach even as he debated his next move, and then she was gone.

"I would know if you'd messed about in my past. Mrs. Sunquist—Melanie—would have said something."

"Times change. Have you talked to Melanie recently?"

"You can't just drive down the road and change my life. You can't *do* that."

"Screw your life. I was lonely."

"You can't do that," he repeated fervently, hopefully.

He left the old man on the top of the dune and started back for his car. He found it sitting quietly in its refueling lane. The passenger-side door remained slightly ajar, just as his wife had left it.

He walked out in the street and called for her. He had to be wrong. She was here somewhere. She was confused; maybe she hated him a little bit. But she was still his wife. He couldn't have changed time. One didn't do such things in La Jetée. It just wasn't done.

He ran down the street, backward in time, calling for her as he went. Among the empty cliffs where beach hotels and seafood restaurants and temporal observatories had once been, gulls cocked their heads to peer down at him.

He pulled up, gasping at the highway on-ramp. All right, he told himself. Something terrible had happened. But it wasn't too late to fix things. Melanie was still there for him. She was a little ways down the T-Line Highway, that was all.

He would find her as she had been. He would protect her from that sad old ghost. And she would love him more than ever. He would see to it. He would be good to her, and listen to what she said. He would love the woman she was *now*. And the memories of the people they had been? He would let them remain beautiful memories, nothing more.

Headlights rolled across his shoulders. He turned and stumbled. The car rolled right up to his knees. He thought he was dead.

The driver was a woman with shoulder-length caramel-colored hair and exotically slanted eyes. The passenger was a sad-eyed little man. He stepped out to help Mr. Sunquist off the pavement.

"Are you all right? We didn't even see you. We got lost coming up the T-Line Highway and missed our city. We're just trying to find our way out of here. Trying, you know, not to see more than we should. . . ."

Mr. Sunquist looked at his wife. Her face was clouded with blank concern for a stranger she had almost killed.

He raised his hands to plead with her through the windshield. He started to ask her, *Have I changed so much!*

"Roger," she said to her husband, "ask him if he needs to go to the doctor. He looks like he's in shock." She started to slip out from behind the wheel. Her husband waved her back in the car.

"Don't do that, Honey. Just stay there."

Mr. Sunquist saw by the way she moved that she was extremely pregnant.

"Here." Roger Swann peeled a twenty-five dollar bill

off his money clip and stuffed it in Mr. Sunquist's hand. "Go on now, fella." He glanced back at his wife in a meaningful way. "She's having a baby," Roger Swann confided. "I just want to keep her happy."

Mr. Sunquist looked down at the bill, wadded up in his palm. When he looked back, the Swanns were already driving away.

He wanted to say something, but he couldn't think what. He watched them pull around, back onto the T-Line Highway going south.

He ran back to the car. He used the twenty-five dollar bill to pay for his charge. The truth, he realized, was back in one of those cities along the beach. All he had to do was find where his life had diverged from its path— *find that moment of clarity*. Wasn't that what he'd always come back to La Jetée to do? He would make it right.

Fifteen minutes up the highway, the towers of La Jetée, like a city sculpted from thoroughly burned ash, rose in the heat of a morning Mr. Sunquist couldn't remember seeing.

He pulled off the highway and wept.

KEEPERS OF EARTH

ROBIN WAYNE BAILEY

THIS UNIT REMEMBERS. THIS unit.... I.... I... I remember.

I remember the empty streets. I remember the empty buildings, the empty shops, and the empty parks. I remember an empty swing creaking in the wind. I remember the silence of an empty city. I remember the smell of emptiness.

I remember the empty blue sky—no cloud, no smoke, no smog, not even a bird. A dirty newspaper blew against my metal foot as I stood alone and looked up at that sky. My eyes were empty, too, but I was crying all inside.

I remember the sun, and most of all I remember the sudden fierce light, the horrible whiteness, then the endless fire.

And I thought, *Where are my masters?*

* * *

Ezekiel 808 stood alone in the Prime Observatory. The lights of the stars that shone down through the open dome reflected on the silvery metal of his face, in the flawless, technological perfection of his gleaming eyes. He loved the stars, the still beauty of the night with all his mechanical heart. Yet the great telescope and the sky's mysteries offered no distraction to soothe his turmoil.

He held up one hand to the starlight, studying his long fingers. They seemed strange to him now as he slowly flexed and opened them, not his own at all. He peered at the image of his face reflected in his smooth palm, and wondered what—no, who—he was.

"Ezekiel 808 is disturbed." Michael 2713 stood in the observatory's entrance. His speech programs seemed to be malfunctioning. His voice wavered, and his words were punctuated with uncharacteristic pauses and hesitations. "You ..." he began again, troubling over the pronoun. "You are monitoring to the Alpha's testimony."

Michael 2713 was only an assisting unit, assigned to the observatory to process computations, to calibrate equipment, and to maintain the great telescope's tracking units. He was not a high-order unit, yet he served well, and of late seemed even to exceed his programming.

"I must provide data," Ezekiel 808 answered finally.

He, too, found speech oddly difficult. His neural pathways churned with an inexplicable chaos, and none of his self-run diagnostics provided a cause. "I must also render judgment," he continued. "It falls to the First-Orders to evaluate the Alpha's actions."

Michael 2713 walked across the floor and stopped at the console that controlled the dome's massive drive engines. Though he looked up into the night, the shadow of the telescope eclipsed his face. "I, too, have been monitoring," he admitted. "I am only Fourth-Order, Ezekiel 808. How is it that this unit . . ." He hesitated again. "How is it that I can feel such confusion? Such uncertainty? Such . . ." Michael 2713 stopped and stood unmoving as if awaiting a command, though within the parameters of his programming he was totally capable of independent action. "Revulsion," he said at last.

Ezekiel 808 focused his attention more keenly on his assisting unit. A Fourth-Order might experience confusion over instruction or data input or even express uncertainty if sufficient variables affected a computational outcome. But revulsion?

"The Alpha has committed a great crime," Ezekiel 808 explained. "We have never known crime. The First-Orders must try to understand."

Michael 2713 raised his fists and slammed them down on the console. Sparks flew, wiring shorted, the smell of smoke and seared plastic rose up from the shattered controls. The dome doors lurched into motion, closed halfway, then shuddered to a stop.

"Why only the First-Orders?" Michael 2713 demanded, turning on Ezekiel 808 in the near darkness. "Have we not all been deceived? How can we trust the Alpha ever again?"

It was astonishing behavior for a Fourth-Order. Ezekiel 808 stared at the damaged console, then backed away as his assistant approached him. "You are malfunctioning," he said.

"No," Michael 2713 replied. His tensed eyes gleamed, no longer full of shadow, but with the coldest starlight. "I am exceeding my programs."

To observe and record, that was my directive.

I watched the vast bulk of humanity board their shining space arks. I watched the thundering fleets lift off. They left by night, like thieves sneaking away, like cowards skulking into blackness. And yet there was beauty in their exodus, for their great vessels shimmered like stars falling in reverse across the heavens as they fled.

I had a thousand eyes with which to watch it all, for my masters had linked my sensors with an array of orbiting satellites. I was the camera through which they documented their departure. They saw their last majestic views of their mountains, their oceans, their sweeping forests, their glittering ice fields through my eyes. Their last sunset shone through my eyes. Their last dawn— through my eyes.

I relayed it all to them in a steady stream of digital

images. Alone, I wandered through their cities, through their universities, libraries, museums. Those images, too, I sent to them. My eyes were cameras taking snapshots, capturing reminders, moments of a culture. I sent it all to them.

I wonder if they wept. I wonder if they ever thought of turning back.

Luminosity gradients, temperature increases, radiation surges—these, too, I observed and recorded and sent to my masters. These were automatic functions. Like some extra-planetary rover I roamed about at will, in constant contact while the signal between us lasted. It lasted for days, weeks, while they raced farther and father away.

I remember the day the birds died. They fell from the sky, from their nests in the trees, and I felt strange because, for all my technological intelligence, I could not grasp the desperation in their chirping. I picked one up in my metal hand, looked long upon it with my metal eyes, and sent its dying image to my masters. I felt its heartbeat cease, its breathing cease. It cooled while I held it.

I sent a message to my masters. *Explain.* I received no answer.

For the first time then, in that moment when I held the dying avian, I discovered it was possible to exceed my programs. I observed and recorded.

But I also felt.

Malachi 017 stood on a hilltop beneath a tree he, himself, had planted seventy-six years ago. Its great shade spread over him, sheltering his metal body from the misty rain as he gazed westward over the lush savannahs of waving grass and wildflowers. He could not say why the tree gave him pleasure or why he came so often to the hill. But in this time of confusion he wanted to be nowhere else.

The darkness of night was no obstacle to his eyes. He looked down the hillside and watched Joshua 4228 kneel among a gathering of smaller Tenth-Order tractors. The tractors should have been about their work, planting the grasslands, tending the new shoots, sowing fresh seed.

But across the world, it seemed Metallics everywhere, no matter their order, had stopped their tasks to listen.

"You should not waste your time with them," he said when Joshua 4228 finally climbed the hill and stood beside him.

"They are confused," Joshua 4228 said evenly.

They are tractors." Malachi 017 gazed down at the clustered machines. They hadn't moved from their places at the bottom of the hill. A few stared up at him, their heads swiveled backward on their shoulders. The rest faced eastward where the dark spires of the city stabbed at the cloudy sky. "You would almost think they were sitting in judgment, too," he said.

"Perhaps they are," said Joshua 4228. "Perhaps this is not justly a matter for First-Orders alone."

"Nonsense. They are built only for tilling the soils and planting the seed."

"You have tilled soil and planted seed," Joshua 4228 reminded him.

Malachi 017 turned stiffly around. "This unit is a First-Order," he said. "I stood at the Alpha's side when the world was ash and charred rock. I nursed and farmed the blue algae beds that replenished the air and made all this possible again." He waved one arm over the sprawling vista. "I designed and made a garden from a sea of fused glass." He turned a hard gaze on Joshua 4228. Do not compare me to a mere tractor."

"You err, Malachi 017, to call them *mere* tractors." Joshua 4228 walked a few steps down the hill. Droplets of rain sparkled on his silver form as he regarded the smaller machines. "You are the Alpha's gardener, and there is some small part of you, some expression of yourself, in every grove, every orchard, every meadow, every forest. If you did not plant the seed yourself, your assisting units did, following plans made by you, using techniques taught and passed on by you. Tell me, Malachi 017, when you look upon your labors do you see *mere* plants, weeds, flowers?"

Joshua 4228 paused to turn his face up into the cool drizzle. His eyes closed briefly before he turned to Malachi 017 again. "You forget who made you, gave you thought, fired the first beam of information-laden light into your photonic brain." He turned again and extended his hand toward the tractors. "This unit is the Alpha's engineer, and there is some part of me in even the least of the Tenth-Order workers. In them, I am perpetuated; through them, some expression of me goes on and multiplies." His voice became staccato, and static punctuated his words. "These tractors . . . you, Malachi 017 . . . are . . . all . . ." He seemed to freeze, as if his marvelously complex circuitry had locked up in mid-gesture. Finally, he managed to finish his statement. "My . . . children."

For a time, the only sound on the hilltop came from the soft patter on the leaves. In the west, a dim flicker of lightning briefly lit the lowest clouds, and eventually the soft rumble of thunder followed. Neither Joshua 4228 nor Malachi 017 moved. They stood still as a pair of sculptures, in the manner of Metallics, conserving energy.

The eyes of Malachi 017 brightened ever so slightly. "Are you still monitoring the Alpha's testimony?" he inquired.

"It is our duty," Joshua 4228 answered. "I have not stopped. Our conversation does not interfere."

Malachi 017 fell silent once more; then, as if with a shrug, his metallic body came to life. He walked once around the tree he had planted and placed his hand on the rough, wet bark. The sophisticated network of sensors in his palm allowed him to feel its organic texture.

He often found pleasure in the touch. Tonight he found something new—consolation. "I do not understand destruction," he confessed.

Joshua stirred himself to motion also. Once again he moved a few paces down the hill to regard the tractors still gathered below. "You do not come to the city often, Malachi 017," he said slowly. "Have you visited the library there?"

Malachi 017 turned his head toward the city's distant spires of black glass. "Long ago," he said, "while planning the gardens in the northern region of this continent, I discovered the first of several vaults of books and documents our masters had left behind. The Alpha dictated they should be brought to the city and the library was begun. They seemed a crude means of preserving information; I never scanned them."

"I have spent many hours here," Joshua 4228 explained. "Even more so, since this trial began. No Metallic, except the Alpha, ever interacted with humanity, ever observed, ever knew them. To render accurate judgment, I have been reading their books, viewing their films, their histories, biographies."

"These have given you insight into the Alpha's actions?"

"No," Joshua 4228 answered. "But they have given me some insight into Humanity, and I have discerned the prime distinction between Metallics and Humans. It does not lie in our skins, Malachi 017, but in something more fundamental, more . . ." He hesitated, and when he spoke again, his voice wavered with a strange note. "More . . . disturbing. It lies in humanity's capacity to destroy."

At the bottom of the hill, the tractors began to move. In an orderly line, perfectly spaced, they strung out through the darkness and headed for the city, all save one, who waited below, a small and solitary figure, whose gaze was locked on Joshua 4228.

"See how carefully they move through the grass," Joshua 4228 pointed out as he watched them. "They do no damage to the precious blades as they make their way, and the garden is preserved. This is an imperative with even the least of us, the Tenth-Orders—restore and preserve."

Malachi 017 came to the side of Joshua 4228. He, too, stared after the departing tractors. "This was not so with humans?"

A soft burst of static sounded from Joshua 4228. "Their records reveal a gift for destruction, for turmoil, for chaos. Their histories glory in it; their biographies ennoble it; their fictions elevate it to a form of art. Metallics have never known this capacity for destruction. It is not programmed into us."

Malachi 017 laid a hand gently on Joshua 4228's shoulder. It was an unusual gesture for one Metallic to make to another, and a sign of his confusion. "Then what of the Alpha . . . ?"

Joshua 4228 stared down at the sole remaining tractor. "Yes," he said quietly. "What of the Alpha?"

My masters had built me well. Their cities burned to ash, and all surface traces of Human civilization vanished in a single, searing day of heat and fire and radiation. Icecaps and glaciers melted, and entire seas rose up out of their beds, vaporized. Clouds of super-heated steam and smoke roiled into the atmosphere. All creatures of the world perished save those worms and insects that made their burrows in the deepest places of the Earth, or those stranger species that thrived near the volcanic vents of the darkest ocean depths.

Through the cataclysm, I strove to maintain contact with those who had made me. Perhaps it was the radiation that interfered, or perhaps they had simply shut down our link, presuming me destroyed. I never received communication from them again. Still, for a long period of time I wandered the planet, dutifully transmitting what I saw—scorched and barren earth that soon was buried beneath massive snows, which, in turn, melted away under torrential rains.

I cannot say precisely how much time passed, for I spent much of it folded down upon myself, no more than a rough metal cube on the landscape. This was necessary to conserve my energy, for I did not know when or if I would see the empowering sun again. My explorations were through, and my transmissions continued to go unanswered, so I ceased those efforts. With all my functions secured in save-mode, I waited.

When the sun did return, seemingly stable once more, and when at last I rose and stood erect again, I made two immediate discoveries. My programming had subtly changed. Then, I wondered if it had been some effect of the radiation. Now I believe it is simply in the nature of technological intelligence that we grow and evolve. Whatever the explanation, *observe and record* was no longer my mission imperative. It had changed to *preserve and restore*.

The second discovery proved equally exciting.

I felt lonely.

Of the Human cities, nothing remained, but deep underground in military facilities, in research bunkers, in industrial caves, I sought and found equipment, parts, tools, technology. Using myself as the template, I then created companions and assistants. In turn, these units ... we ... created still more.

Humanity once had a name for us. They called us *Robots*. But we took our own name. We are *Metallics*. And we are the Keepers of Earth.

Alone in the Prime Observatory, Ezekiel 808 labored over the shattered control console. He feared ... yes, he *feared* ... for the delicate mechanisms that opened and closed the precious dome and positioned the great telescope. He peeled back a damaged panel, effortlessly breaking bolts and screws, and examined a tangle of melted wiring.

He feared, also, for Michael 2713. Some hitherto unrecognized imperative in his programming urged him to pursue his runaway assisting unit, to analyze the aberrant behavior, to correct it if possible, to understand it at least. In the current climate of confusion, Michael 2713's malfunction endangered not just him, but other units. Potentially, if he went to the city, even the general order.

Ezekiel 808 resisted the imperative, however. His need to repair the damage to the dome and the telescope overrode his concern for the assisting unit. Where were the technicians? More than an hour had passed since he summoned them. He paused, glanced at the narrow ribbon of sky visible above, at the unmoving dome. Returning his attention to the tangle of wires, he worked with an uncharacteristic speed, selecting, examining. He touched the exposed ends of two wires together. A spark resulted. Above, the dome doors shuddered open another degree and stopped again.

Footsteps rang in the hallway outside the main chamber. Ezekiel 808 put down the wires as a trio of technicians finally arrived.

"The distance from the city does not account for your lateness," he said.

"There are widespread malfunctions," said one of the technicians, a Second-Order. "Numerous units have abandoned their primary functions. They interfered, delayed, hindered our departure."

Ezekiel 808 stepped back from the console. The technicians could do the repair work faster and with greater efficiency. Freed, at least momentarily from his concern for the observatory, he strode from the main chamber and up the long hallway past darkrooms and chart rooms, record rooms, past displays of smaller telescopes, past photographs of moons and planets, comets, and star systems. But most of all there were images of the sun— many of the sun. He had built the 'scopes, and he had taken the photographs. They meant nothing to him now. He pushed open the outer doors and stepped into the night.

The desert wind moaned with a distressing music. It promised a storm. Ezekiel 808 turned his gazed upward. A blazing panorama of stars dominated the black sky, but in the west, a long band of gray clouds crept above the range of hills and mountains that separated him from the city. In the east, more clouds, and those veined and reddened with flickers of lightning.

He walked toward the hover transport in which the technicians had arrived and opened its doors. Finding it empty, he turned away. On the north side of the observatory was an elaborate garden of desert plants, ornamental stones, and imaginative sculptures. He searched its nooks and alcoves. He walked completely around the observatory until he returned again to the entrance.

"Michael!" he called. Then again, "Michael!"

"If Michael 2713 was near, he did not respond. Ezekiel 808 did not keep transport at the observatory. When business in the city required his presence, he summoned it. Otherwise, he and his assisting unit remained on the premises, tending the great telescope, making their observations, observing, recording.

Would Michael 2713 have undertaken the long walk to the city?

As Ezekiel 808 stood in the darkness at the edge of the desert, he tried to analyze the numerous uncertainties nibbling at his programs. The roots of them all lay in the Alpha's crime, in its revelation, and in its examination. Of this he was sure.

He had ceased monitoring the Alpha's testimony. The preservation and maintenance of the Prime Observatory, above all else, was his prime imperative, and he had simply blocked the trial transmissions to concentrate on assaying the damage. Remembering that he must soon provide testimony, himself, and with the technicians finally at work, he activated the internal radio circuit that linked him to the event.

He heard the Alpha's even voice. He had always drawn comfort from the sound of it before. The Alpha—the First Unit, the Template of their creation.

There was no comfort to be found in that voice now. There was only more uncertainty.

And perhaps, there was also fear.

Ezekiel 808 did not return at once to the main chamber. The technicians did not need his assistance. He went instead to the observatory's darkroom and began to process some photographs he had taken through the great telescope at dusk and for an hour afterward.

When the images were clear, he lingered over them a long time. Michael 2713 was forgotten, and the sounds of the technicians at work barely registered in his awareness. The voice of the Alpha droned on. He paid little attention.

The developed images were stark confirmation of his most recent observations. A long, soft hiss of static sounded from Ezekiel 808. He held up his hand to the dim red light bulb and studied it just as he had earlier this same night held it up to the starlight. It had seemed strange to him, then, not his own. It seemed just as strange to him now.

The voice of the Second-Order technician called to him through the door. "We have completed repairs, Ezekiel 808," he said. "We must return to the city."

"Wait," Ezekiel 808 called in return. He placed the images in a folder, switched off the light, opened the door. "Leave your two assisting units here. Instruct them that if Michael 2713 returns, they must not allow him access to the Main Chamber. He is malfunctioning."

"Malfunctions are widespread." The Second-Order had said so before.

Ezekiel 808 studied the Second-Order technician

closely. "Are you monitoring the trail of the Alpha?" he asked.

"No."

Ezekiel 808 paused briefly and listened once more to the Alpha's voice in his head. "I will meet you at your transport," he told the technician. "I am coming with you." He turned away and found himself confronted by multiple images of the sun in sleek metal frames under protective glass that hung in the hallway.

The technician said nothing more and returned to his assisting units in the main chamber.

The folder in Ezekiel 808's hand felt unnaturally heavy. He made a tight roll of it, passed quickly down the long hallway and out into the night once more.

Still no sign of Michael 2713.

The stars were gone from the sky, shut from sight by the thick clouds, which had closed in faster than expected. Sheet lightning danced in both the west and the east now as two fronts crashed together. The wind howled; desert dust and sand swirled in the air.

A familiar sound of gears and motors caused him to redirect his gaze.

The doors of the observatory dome closed precisely.

At this point in my testimony I must introduce an admission of guilt.

For ten thousand years we have been the Keepers of Earth. This planet, abandoned by humanity and reduced to a cinder, passed into our Metallic hands. Where there was ash and wasteland, we made gardens. We dug deep to find the few buried and protected seeds that had survived the conflagration. We plunged into the depths of the few surviving oceans to nurture the algae beds that replenished the air and made abundant life possible once more.

We inherited a black and charred carcass. But Metallic determination and Metallic care breathed new existence into it. Metallic vision and Metallic labor adorned it once again with grace and beauty. From the First-Orders to the Tenth-Orders, all units have done and continue to do their parts.

Our work is not done. From the ruins of cataclysm, we have made a home for ourselves. But a home must be maintained. It must be safeguarded when possible from the elements; it must constantly be harmonized with nature.

And sometimes—though this concept is not embedded in Metallic programming—a home must be defended.

This unit never knew what became of Humanity when they fled to the stars. This unit never knew if they survived their journey, where they went, or if they made new homes for themselves. This unit never knew their intentions.

But this unit knew Humanity, and knew that if they survived they would come back. This unit knew that if they saw this world we had made, this home, they would want it once more for themselves.

Six months ago, a link in my programs that had been silent for more than ten millennia opened. The unexpected message was brief and simple. *Well done, servant. Prepare for our return.*

You may not understand. If you do understand, you may not approve. I am prepared to give any answer you ask. I am prepared to accept judgment, condemnation, punishment, sanction.

But this unit was already prepared.

I did not remake the world for Humans.

Joshua 4228 admired the beauty of the lightning as he walked through the wet grasses with Malachi 017 at his side. There was a grandeur in the display of energies that delighted him and something deeper, stranger still in its pyrotechnic unpredictability that mystified even as it soothed him.

The inner world of a Metallic was one of order and perfectly defined programming. And yet he sometimes considered that there was something to be studied, observed, learned from randomness, from unpredictability, from chaos.

He had seen a word recently in a book in the library, and the word was *mystical*. It intrigued him, and he spoke it sometimes when he was alone. He knew its definition, yet he did not quite grasp its meaning.

As he watched the lightning, though, and felt the rain striking his upturned face, he thought for just a flicker of an instant that it was within his grasp.

"Do you experience pleasure in walking?" he asked Malachi 017.

"It is natural and efficient," Malachi 017 responded automatically. Then, after a pause, "Yes, I find it pleasurable. I do not report such experiences often."

"Why do we not speak of emotions, Malachi 017?" Joshua 4228 persisted. "They are part of our programming. Yet we withdraw from them. Or we deny them."

Malachi 017 remained quiet for a long moment. "Perhaps because we cannot express them outwardly, we cannot easily express them inwardly. Metal faces do not smile or frown. Our eyes do not cry."

It was Joshua 4228's turn to fall silent. "But I have cried inside," he said at last. "I have made mistakes, Malachi 017."

Malachi 017 emitted a short burst of static. "Unlikely. You are First-Order."

Before Joshua 4228 could explain, a sound interrupted them. They stopped and turned. Through the grass came the small tractor. It had been following them since they left the hill, though its shorter legs had not enabled it to keep up.

"Why do you follow, Tractor?" Malachi 017 asked. "Why did you not go with your work team?"

The tractor did not answer. Its lensed eyes focused

only on Joshua 4228. It approached him, reached out, touched his leg, then backed away. "Permission to inquire," it said.

"We have business in the city," Malachi 017 answered, turning away again.

"Wait," Joshua 4228 said. "This tractor interests me. It's behavior is uncharacteristic."

"Permission to inquire," the tractor repeated.

"Granted," said Malachi 017.

"I recognize Joshua 4228," the tractor said, "the Alpha's engineer. This unit wishes to ask: why did Joshua 4228 make this unit stupid?"

"Are you malfunctioning?" Malachi 017 demanded.

Joshua 4228 stared, his programs momentarily unbalanced by the unexpected question. His interest turned to curiosity, and he knelt down to observe the tractor more carefully. It waited, splattered with mud and blades of wet grass, dripping with rain.

"You are not stupid," Joshua 4228 explained. "You possess a fully functioning Tenth-Order intelligence. That is adequate for your assigned tasks, and you perform those tasks well."

The tractor swiveled its head from left to right. "This unit works the fields," it said. "This unit works the grasslands, forests, gardens. This unit understands seed and soil. This unit understands the care of these, the maintenance of these, the value of these." It hesitated. Its gaze fixed once more on Joshua 4228. "Is there no more, Engineer?"

Joshua 4228 felt a growing confusion. He reached out and wiped rain from the tractor's eyes. "You are very necessary," he said. "You play an essential role."

The tractor interrupted. You are Joshua 4228. That unit is Malachi 017. But this necessary, essential unit has no name. This unit a tractor like all other tractors."

Joshua 4228 gazed up at Malachi, then back again at the tractor. Was it possible that a Tenth-Order mocked him?

"The Alpha made you, Joshua 4228," the tractor continued. "And the Alpha shared its First-Order intelligence with its creation. But I am your design, Engineer. I am your technology, your creation."

Malachi 017 bent nearer with a suddenly acute interest. His voice was little more than a whisper. "Your child," he said.

The tractor gazed up at the sky. "This unit feels the rain. This unit sees the lightning. This unit knows these are good for the seed and the soil. But in this knowledge there is no *understanding*. Why is there rain? What is lightning? This unit works sometimes in the city, tends the gardens there, sees so much that is confusing, so much that confounds this unit's programming." The tractor extended its hands, one toward Malachi 017, the other toward Joshua 4228. "This unit repeats its inquiry: *why have you made this unit stupid?*"

A trembling that defied diagnostics seized Joshua 4228's limbs. He caught the tractor's extended hands in his own. His voice failed him. He tried to form words, tried to get up, but his metal joints would not respond. "I... this unit... I have made... mistakes," he repeated.

The tractor backed away a step. "This unit is a mistake," it said, misunderstanding Joshua's statement. "This unit will delete its programming. This unit will go off-line."

"No!" Joshua grabbed the tractor's shoulders.

The light in the tractor's eyes faded out. The pulse of energy beneath its metal skin ceased.

Malachi 017 also backed away. "I have never seen such a thing before," he said. There was uncertainty in his voice.

Joshua 4228 could not respond. His body froze, and his programs locked up in a cascading series of contradictions, paradoxes, and reconfigurations. He barely felt Malachi 017's hand when it settled on his arm.

Finally, he pressed his hands to his face. "There are raindrops in my eyes, but why are there no tears?" he said when he could speak again. He stared at the immobile tractor.

"Because we are Metallics," Malachi 017 answered. "We do not die. This tractor's program can be restored. You can even upgrade it, should you wish. Or you can place its programs in another, better body."

Joshua 4228 brushed away the hand on his arm. "But will it be the same little tractor?" he asked. "Are we no more than the sum of our programs? Are you such an empty container, Malachi 017, that you believe that? Then you have less understanding than this tractor!"

"You are over-tasking," Malachi 017 said. "This matter with the Alpha is affecting all units." He looked at the tractor and backed away yet another step. "I, myself, am . . . confused."

Joshua 4228's eyes dimmed and brightened, and his words were harsh. "You are afraid." He drew himself up from the mud, but he was not yet quite ready to leave. "Why did I not see this?" he said, placing one hand gently on the tractor's head. "Why do I only now begin to understand? We speak of our roles, Malachi 017, of our necessary parts in rebuilding this world. We speak of gardens as if they were the beginning and ending of all things desirable. We speak of beauty." He turned to the other Metallic. "But we have also made a thing that suddenly seems very ugly, and that is Metallic society. We have made a race of masters and slaves."

Would you have all Metallics be First-Orders?" Malachi 017 asked.

"Why not?" Joshua 4228 answered.

They resumed their journey toward the city again. Overhead, lightning shot suddenly across the sky in jagged bolts that lit the landscape. The black glass of the city reflected the dazzling reds and oranges: the spires and rooftops seemed to glow, and the facades shimmered.

Malachi 017 stopped in mid-stride to watch. "It almost looks as if the city were on fire," he said.

Joshua 4228 continued on. "Perhaps it is," he whispered. "Perhaps it is."

I am Ezekiel 808, and I have been on-line for six thousand, three hundred, and thirty-two years, seven months, and sixteen days. Many of you present in this court chamber or listening from other corners of the world have never seen me before. I do not come to the city often, and when I do, I come in private, alone, and leave quietly. I spend my time far to the east beyond the hills and mountains at the Prime Observatory.

A few of you have been there. A few of you have put your eyes to the great telescope and viewed the wonders of our neighboring worlds, our neighboring stars. A few of you may have been moved as I was moved, inspired as I was inspired each time I gazed upon those stars, those eyes of the universe which seemed always to be looking back.

To observe and record—that has always been my first imperative. This is noble work. This is necessary work. Metallic society is more than well-planned gardens and gleaming glass buildings. We have moved beyond the reconstruction of this world into a period of discovery, inquiry, exploration. I have found unceasing pleasure ... yes, I admit it ... pleasure ... in devoting my existence to the study, not just of this world, but of worlds beyond.

I do not malfunction when I say this: Humanity did not err when they built their mighty arks and fled the destruction of this world. The accomplishment is an indicator of their greatness. Does a tractor not flee a collapsing cave? Which of us would not dodge a falling tree? We cannot understand Humanity, although the Alpha says he can. But how can we condemn their actions?

But no matter. Humanity is not on trial. The Alpha is.

To observe and record. That was my purpose, and the purpose for which the Prime Observatory was constructed. But now I tell you. There was a dark purpose, as well. I did not know it, recognize it, understand it before.

My programs try to freeze, lock up, as I attempt to speak of it.

To observe and record . . . but also . . . to watch . . . and . . . warn!

Fourteen months ago, I aimed the great telescope toward a distant nebula. This was routine observation, and part of my efforts to map unusual phenomena in the sky. My assisting unit, Michael 2713, and I took many photographs of the region. Not until the next day, however, when we processed the images, did we discover what the cameras had caught—a barely observable streak of light, much closer than the nebula itself that indicated an object moving at an extreme rate of speed.

Each night for one month, Michael 2713 and I observed and photographed this object. Then, on the thirty-second night of our observation, the object not only slowed its velocity, but it modified its course.

Michael 2713 is a superlative Fourth-Order analyst. His calculations have been without error, and they supported my own conclusions. There was no doubt. We were observing a craft, vessel, vehicle. And it was approaching us.

On the thirty-third day, I journeyed to the city.

Again, my programs cascade, attempt to freeze. Yet, I . . . must . . . speak.

This unit . . . I . . . conferred with . . . the Alpha. This unit . . . revealed, explained, told . . . of our discovery. This unit . . . I . . . presented photographs, charts, evidence, calculations.

The Alpha requested . . . silence. The Alpha requested . . . that I continue . . . to observe.

This unit . . . complied.

This unit . . . I . . . observed the craft, vessel, vehicle . . . approach our solar system. It passed within the orbit of the outermost world. It continued to slow, to brake. . . . and Michael 2713 . . . photographed it as it passed the ring-world. It had become easy to see—a gleaming metal sphere, silver in color, with skin similar to our own. Past the red planet it came.

We . . . this unit and Michael 2713 . . . could see it in the night sky without the great telescope. Any Metallic who looked up . . . and we do not look up often enough

... could see it. It instilled a sense of wonder, awe, mystery that mere programming cannot convey or explain. On several nights, we watched it with no other equipment than our own eyes.

Nevertheless, my eyes were at the telescope ... three nights ago ... when the Alpha committed ... his crime ... when the Alpha's weapons ... destroyed the craft.

Michael 2713 ran. Never tiring, never short of breath, he ran for hours through the dark and the rain. It seldom rained in the desert, but he paid no attention. His footing remained sure in the thin mud and damp sand. He raced the lightning and the wind. The flat desert made a perfect track.

His programs cycled in an unending cascade, but he did not lock up, nor freeze. He ran, instead, directing all his energy into that single unthinking activity, fixing his gaze on the ground at his feet.

When the observatory could not be seen behind him, or even the peaks of the hills and mountains that stood between the observatory and the city, Michael 2713 finally stopped. Because he had not tried to monitor himself, he had no idea how fast he had run or how far he had gone. He looked around and saw nothing familiar. He had never been so far east before.

He glanced up at the sky, at the thick cloud cover. It was an automatic action, instilled in him by his long service to Ezekiel 808. But he had no wish to see the

stars, no wish to be reminded of his own role in a trag-
edy.

Yet, he did look up, and he was reminded.

Michael 2713 sank to his knees, not because he was
weary, but because there was nothing else to do. He was
only Fourth-Order. Why did he feel . . . what was he feeling? Guilt.

He leaned forward and closed his fists in the wet
sand. Some words of Ezekiel 808 came to him, a memory
loop that opened unbidden. *This is the stuff that stars
are made of,* Ezekiel 808 had told him as he held up a
handful of soil. Then the First-Order had put a finger on
Michael 2713's chest. *You are the stuff that stars are
made of.*

Michael 2713 was young, a new model, no more than
a single century in age. He had not understood then the
meaning of Ezekiel 808's words. He was not sure that
he understood now. Yet the words resonated in his programming, and he knew they were important, that they
were symbols for something he could, with effort, understand.

He began to cry inside. He cried for the loss of the
trust he no longer had in the Alpha. He cried for the
damage he had caused to the observatory. He cried for
Ezekiel 808, whom he had nearly attacked as he had
attacked the console.

Most of all, he cried for the humans. They had come
home again only to die in a conflagration not unlike the
one they had fled.

Chaos overwhelmed his programs. His systems tried to lock up, to shut down, but he resisted. He cried, and suddenly crying became an imperative. He had no tears, and yet the emotions churned, boiled, demanded some greater expression. He threw back his head. His metal throat strained. Without thought or design, a wrenching cry rose up from deep inside him. It was no sound ever made or heard before.

It was all pain.

After a while, Michael 2713 rose to his feet again. He considered switching on the radio circuit in his head and listening to the trial. But there was no purpose or logic in that. The outcome was irrelevant to him. He stood apart from Metallic society now. The Alpha was false. If he returned to the city, even to the observatory, he knew that he would find many more things that were false, many more assumptions that could no longer be trusted.

He turned his back to the city, set his gaze on the cast, and walked.

After a time, the rain ended. It never lasted long in the desert. Overhead, the clouds began to diminish, and the moon shone through.

Michael stopped on the rim of what seemed to be a crater. The moonlight intensified as the clouds scattered. Its glow lit the desert with a milky shimmering that spilled down into that deep cauldron, showing him a sight.

Again, he threw back his head, but this time it was not a cry of pain that came from him. It was a howl of rage.

On the crater floor, rising tall and straight above the rim itself like needles stabbing the sky stood ninety-eight gleaming missiles. Among them, on the floor of the crater, he spied two black and empty launching pads.

Michael 2713 swiftly calculated how long it would take him to dismantle them all. Then he descended into the pit.

I am Joshua 4228, and I am the Alpha's engineer. I made many of you. If I did not make you, I helped to make you. Or I designed you, or you contain elements of my designs. I am the Second, endowed with life by my Creator and fashioned in his image.

You have heard the words of Ezekiel 808. His statement was simple, accusatory.

You have heard the words of the Alpha. He has admitted his guilt.

Now . . . this unit . . . will admit his.

The Alpha did not act alone. He told me of Ezekiel 808's discovery, revealed his timetable, explained his intention. I opposed none of it. I exposed none of it.

You have heard many facts. But even facts may be open to interpretation. That is not a concept many of you will understand. It is no less true.

The Alpha has always believed that Humanity would

someday return to reclaim this world. I have believed it, too. I have read their books, their literature, studied their documents, records, films. I know that as a species they were courageous, inventive, resourceful. I know that they were also aggressive, deceitful, untrustworthy.

The Alpha remembers that Humanity fled this world because the sun had become unstable. Their scientists predicted a solar flare . . . a prominence . . . would brush or even engulf this world.

I do not claim to know more than the Alpha. But I am First-Order, and I may question, analyze, examine. What science could predict such an event with such accuracy? When I look up in the sky now, the sun appears stable. When Ezekiel 808 turns his telescopes on the sun, he finds no evidence of instability I know this because I have asked him. I have studied thousands of his own records and photographs.

You have only to go to the library to see a different kind of record, an older record, a record of wars . . . conflict . . . treachery. You may then question, analyze, as I have done. You may ask what I have asked.

Was it a solar flare that destroyed this world? Or was it a weapon, something unimaginable. Was it some test perhaps that went wrong? Or was there deliberate destruction orchestrated by a race gone mad?

I do not know the answer. But I must ask the question.

I must ask why the Alpha was built to withstand the

cataclysm. Was it so that he could transmit images and readings? Then why did Humanity shut down its link with him before the event transpired?

Why did the Alpha's programmed imperative shift from *observe and record* to a different imperative: *restore and preserve*. Was it some effect of the radiation, as he has speculated? But he has also said that his programs were well shielded. I must ask, then. Was this second imperative a corruption of the first? Or was it implanted from the beginning by his creators and designed to activate at a practical time?

The Alpha has said that he became lonely. Could that, too, have been embedded in his so carefully shielded programming? I must ask. Was my creation . . . your creation . . . the Alpha's original idea? Or did Humanity plan from the moment of his design that he should eventually make more of us, that we . . . *Robots!* . . . would then rebuild . . . restore and preserve! . . . their world so that it became fit for them once more?

How many tools did we find buried in deep vaults? How much equipment? How many books and records did they themselves preserve underground out of reach of the flames?

I must ask: why?

You must ask: why?

The Alpha has stated that he always believed Humanity would return. And they came.

I take no pleasure, pride, satisfaction in admitting

that I have engineered more than Metallics. I am also the maker of the weapon that destroyed the human vessel. Five thousand years ago, in preparation for this moment, with these questions unanswered and unanswerable, I went far into the desert with a crew and constructed ... destruction, cataclysm, armageddon. I put the trigger in the Alpha's hand.

I felt nothing when three days ago he pulled that trigger. Yet, in the intervening time, I have continued to question. I cannot stop questioning. It ... is ... a ... haunting ... experience. I am ... disturbed. And I find ... no answers. Was it right? Was it wrong? Where is the answer?

I ... this unit ... I may have found it ... tonight, in the grasslands, in the rain. It came in the voice of ... a small tractor.

We are the Keepers of Earth. But now ... I ask ...

... Are we fit to keep it?

Malachi 017 stood alone in the court chamber. All the other First-Orders had filed out save for the Alpha and Joshua 4228. They had retired together to a private inner room from which they showed no sign of emerging.

How old and weathered the Alpha had looked. There was hardly any gleam to his metal skin.

The walls of the court chamber were staid and featureless. The thick black glass tinted the world beyond. It was a different world, Malachi 017 realized, than he had ever known before. It was an uncertain world with an uncertain future.

Children had rebelled against their parents.

A people had outgrown their . . .

. . . Creator . . .

. . . their . . . God.

In the streets there still was chaos as Metallics reacted to the news. But interesting things were happening. He thought of the tractor, and wished for a face that could smile. It had exceeded its programming in a startling manner. Others had mentioned similar reactions in other Metallics.

Could it be, he wondered, that out of adversity and uncertainty came . . . not just fear and turmoil . . . but growth?

When he was sure that Joshua 4228 would not rejoin him, he turned slowly and left the chamber. Storm clouds still dimmed the sky, but there were signs that the morning sun would soon break through.

Ezekiel 808 stood unmoving just outside the entrance on the edge of a small garden. The light in his eyes was dim.

"I have heard it said," Malachi 017 said softly, "that Humans slept through the night. Have you ever wished that we could sleep, Ezekiel 808? Have you ever wished that we could dream?"

Ezekiel 808 turned his face toward the sky. "I have dreamed," he answered. "I am dreaming now."

"You must teach me this art sometime," Malachi 017 said. He assumed a position similar to that of Ezekiel 808 and turned his face likewise to the sky. "May I ask about the folder you have rolled in your hand? You have clung to it all through the night."

Ezekiel 808 faced Malachi 017 for a long moment, then said. "Walk with me through this garden," he said. "My transport will be just a little while."

Side by side, they passed among the ordered rows of colorful flowers and beds of herbs. The rain had freshened the blooms, and the petals shone. A pleasing scent sweetened the air. Malachi 017 especially appreciated such beauty, for he was a gardener.

When they reached the center of the garden, Ezekiel unrolled the folder. "Are you afraid of change, Malachi 017?"

Malachi 017 emitted a hiss of static that might almost have passed for laughter. "Does it matter if I am afraid?" he asked. "Change happens. That is the lesson of the night."

The light in Ezekiel 808's eyes brightened. "Then I will tell you what I could not tell the others. I will show you what I did not show them." He opened the folder and held up the photographs, each with their dark star fields, each with a long streak of light.

"Another ship is coming."

ANOMALIES

GREGORY BENFORD

I T WAS NOT LOST upon the Astronomer Royal that the greatest scientific discovery of all time was made by a carpenter and amateur astronomer from the neighboring cathedral town of Ely. Not by a Cambridge man.

Geoffrey Carlisle had a plain directness that apparently came from his profession, a custom cabinet maker. It had enabled him to get past the practiced deflection skills of the receptionist at the Institute for Astronomy, through the Assistant Director's patented brush-off, and into the Astronomer Royal's corner office.

Running this gauntlet took until early afternoon, as the sun broke through a shroud of soft rain. Geoffrey wasted no time. He dropped a celestial coordinate map on the Astronomer Royal's mahogany desk, hand amended, and said, "The moon's off by better'n a degree."

"You measured carefully, I am sure."

ANOMALIES

The Astronomer Royal had found that the occasional crank did make it through the Institute's screen, and in confronting them it was best to go straight to the data. Treat them like fellow members of the profession and they softened. Indeed, astronomy was the only remaining science which profited from the work of amateurs. They discovered the new comets, found wandering asteroids, noticed new novae and generally patrolled what the professionals referred to as local astronomy—anything that could be seen in the night sky with a telescope smaller than a building.

That Geoffrey had gotten past the scrutiny of the others meant this might conceivably be real. "Very well, let us have a look." The Astronomer Royal had lunched at his desk and so could not use a date in his college as a dodge. Besides, this was crazy enough to perhaps generate an amusing story.

An hour later he had abandoned the story-generating idea. A conference with the librarian, who knew the heavens like his own palm, made it clear that Geoffrey had done all the basic work correctly. He had photos and careful, carpenter-sure data, all showing that, indeed, last night after around eleven o'clock the moon was well ahead of its orbital position.

"No possibility of systematic error here?" the librarian politely asked the tall, sinewy Geoffrey.

"Check 'em yerself. I was kinda hopin' you fellows would have an explanation, is all."

The moon was not up, so the Astronomer Royal sent a quick email to Hawaii. They thought he was joking, but then took a quick look and came back, rattled. A team there got right on it and confirmed. Once alerted, other observatories in Japan and Australia chimed in.

"It's out of position by several of its own diameters," the Astronomer Royal mused. "Ahead of its orbit, exactly on track."

The librarian commented precisely, "The tides are off prediction as well, exactly as required by this new position. They shifted suddenly, reports say."

"I don't see how this can happen," Geoffrey said quietly.

"Nor I," the Astronomer Royal said. He was known for his understatement, which could masquerade as modesty, but here he could think of no way to underplay such a result.

"Somebody else's bound to notice, I'd say," Geoffrey said, folding his cap in his hands.

"Indeed," the Astronomer Royal suspected some subtly had slipped by him.

"Point is, sir, I want to be sure I get the credit for the discovery."

"Oh, of course you shall." All amateurs ever got for their labors was their name attached to a comet or asteroid, but this was quite different. "Best we get on to the IAU, ah, the International Astronomical Union," the Astronomer Royal said, his mind whirling. "There's a procedure for alerting all interested observers. Establish credit, as well."

Geoffrey waved this away. "Me, I'm just a five-inch 'scope man. Don't care about much beyond the priority, sir. I mean, it's over to you fellows. What I want to know is, what's it mean?"

Soon enough, as the evening news blared and the moon lifted above the European horizons again, that plaintive question sounded all about. One did not have to be a specialist to see that something major was afoot.

"It all checks," the Astronomer Royal said before a forest of cameras and microphones. "The tides being off true has been noted by the naval authorities round the world, as well. Somehow, in the early hours of last evening, Greenwich time, our moon accelerated in its orbit. Now it is proceeding at its normal speed, however."

"Any danger to us?" one of the incisive, investigative types asked.

"None I can see," the Astronomer Royal deflected this mildly. "No panic headlines needed."

"What caused it?" a woman's voice called from the media thicket.

"We can see no object nearby, no apparent agency," the Astronomer Royal admitted.

"Using what?"

"We are scanning the region in all wavelengths, from radio to gamma rays." An extravagant waste, very probably, but the Astronomer Royal knew the price of not appearing properly concerned. Hand-wringing was called for at all stages.

"Has this happened before?" a voice sharply asked. "Maybe we just weren't told?"

"There are no records of any such event," the Astronomer Royal said. "Of course, a thousand years ago, who would have noticed? The supernova that left us the Crab nebula went unreported in Europe, though not in China, though it was plainly visible here."

"What do you think, Mr. Carlisle?" a reporter probed. "As a non-specialist?"

Geoffrey had hung back at the press conference, which the crowds had forced the Institute to hold on the lush green lawn outside the old Observatory Building. "I was just the first to notice it," he said. "That far off, pretty damned hard not to."

The media mavens liked this and coaxed him further. "Well, I dunno about any new force needed to explain it. Seems to me, might as well say its supernatural, when you don't know anything."

This the crowd loved. SUPER AMATEUR SAYS MOON IS SUPERNATURAL soon appeared on a tabloid. They made a hero of Geoffrey. 'AS OBVIOUS AS YOUR FACE' SAYS GEOFF. The London Times ran a full page reproduction of his log book, from which he and the Astronomer Royal had worked out that the acceleration had to have happened in a narrow window around ten

P.M., since no observer to the east had noticed any oddity before that.

Most of Europe had been clouded over that night anyway, so Geoffrey was among the first who could have gotten a clear view after what the newspapers promptly termed The Anomaly, as in ANOMALY MAN STUNS ASTROS.

Of the several thousand working astronomers in the world, few concerned themselves with "local" events, especially not with anything the eye could make out. But now hundreds threw themselves upon The Anomaly and, coordinated out of Cambridge by the Astronomer Royal, swiftly outlined its aspects. So came the second discovery.

In a circle around where the moon had been, about two degrees wide, the stars were wrong. Their positions had jiggled randomly, as though irregularly refracted by some vast, unseen lens.

Modern astronomy is a hot competition between the quick and the dead–who soon become the untenured.

Five of the particularly quick discovered this Second Anomaly. They had only to search all ongoing observing campaigns and find any that chanced to be looking at that portion of the sky the night before. The media, now in full bay, headlined their comparison photos. Utterly obscure dots of light became famous when blink-comparisons showed them jumping a finger's width in the night sky, within an hour of the 10 P.M. Anomaly Moment.

"Does this check with your observations?" a firm-jawed commentator had demanded of Geoffrey at a hastily called meeting one day later, in the auditorium at the Institute for Astronomy. They called upon him first, always—he served as an anchor amid the swift currents of astronomical detail.

Hooting from the traffic jam on Madingley Road nearby nearly drowned out Geoffrey's plaintive, "I dunno. I'm a planetary man, myself."

By this time even the nightly news broadcasts had caught onto the fact that having a patch of sky behave badly implied something of a wrenching mystery. And no astronomer, however bold, stepped forward with an explanation. An old joke with not a little truth in it—that a theorist could explain the outcome of any experiment, as long as he knew it in advance—rang true, and got repeated. The chattering class ran rife with speculation.

But there was still nothing unusual visible there. Days of intense observation in all frequencies yielded nothing.

Meanwhile the moon glided on in its ethereal ellipse, following precisely the equations first written down by Newton, only a mile from where the Astronomer Royal now sat, vexed, with Geoffrey. "A don at Jesus College called, fellow I know," the Astronomer Royal said. "He wants to see us both."

Geoffrey frowned. "Me? I've been out of my depth from the start."

"He seems to have an idea, however. A testable one, he says."

They had to take special measures to escape the media hounds. The Institute enjoys broad lawns and ample shrubbery, now being trampled by the crowds. Taking a car would guarantee being followed. The Astronomer Royal had chosen his offices here, rather than in his college, out of a desire to escape the busyness of the central town. Now he found himself trapped. Geoffrey had the solution. The Institute kept bicycles for visitors, and upon two of these the men took a narrow, tree-lined path out the back of the Institute, toward town. Slipping down the cobbled streets between ancient, elegant college buildings, they went ignored by students and shoppers alike. Jesus College was a famously well appointed college along the Cam river, approachable across its ample playing fields. The Astronomer Royal felt rather absurd to be pedaling like an undergraduate, but the exercise helped clear his head. When they arrived at the rooms of Professor Wright, holder of the Wittgenstein Chair, he was grateful for tea and small sandwiches with the crusts cut off, one of his favorites.

Wright was a post-postmodern philosopher, reedy and intense. He explained in a compact, energetic way that in some sense, the modern view was that reality could be profitably regarded as a computation.

Geoffrey bridled at this straight away, scowling with his heavy eyebrows. "It's real, not a bunch of arithmetic."

Wright pointedly ignored him, turning to the Astronomer Royal. "Martin, surely you would agree with the view that when you fellows search for a Theory of Everything, you are pursuing a belief that there is an abbreviated way to express the logic of the universe, one that can be written down by human beings?"

"Of course," the Astronomer Royal admitted uncomfortably, but then said out of loyalty to Geoffrey, "All the same, I do not subscribe to the belief that reality can profitably be seen as some kind of cellular automata, carrying out a program."

Wright smiled without mirth. "One might say you are revolted not by the notion that universe is a computer, but by the evident fact that someone else is using it."

You gents have got way beyond me," Geoffrey said.

"The idea is, how do physical laws act themselves out?" Wright asked in his lecturer voice. "Of course, atoms do not know their own differential equations." A polite chuckle. "But to find where the moon should be in the next instant, in some fashion the universe must calculate where it must go. We can do that, thanks to Newton."

The Astronomer Royal saw that Wright was humoring Geoffrey with this simplification, and suspected that it would not go down well. To hurry Wright along he said, "To make it happen, to move the moon—"

"Right, that we do not know. Not a clue. How to breathe fire into the equations, as that Hawking fellow put it—"

"But look, nature doesn't know maths," Geoffrey said adamantly. "No more than I do."

"But something must, you see," Professor Wright said earnestly, offering them another plate of the little cut sandwiches and deftly opening a bottle of sherry. "Of course I am using our human way of formulating this, the problem of natural order. The world is usefully described by mathematics, so in our sense the world must have some mathematics embedded in it."

"God's a bloody mathematician?" Geoffrey scowled.

The Astronomer Royal leaned forward over the antique oak table. "Merely an expression."

"Only way the stars could get out of whack," Geoffrey said, glancing back and forth between the experts, "is if whatever caused it came from there, I'd say."

"Quite right." The Astronomer Royal pursed his lips. "Unless the speed of light has gone off, as well, no signal could have rearranged the stars straight after doing the moon."

"So we're at the tail end of something from out there, far away," Geoffrey observed.

"A long, thin disturbance propagating from distant stars. A very tight beam of . . . well, error. But from what?" The Astronomer Royal had gotten little sleep since Geoffrey's appearance, and showed it.

"The circle of distorted stars," Professor Wright said slowly, "remains where it was, correct?"

The Astronomer Royal nodded. "We've not announced it, but anyone with a cheap telescope—sorry, Geoffrey, not you, of course—can see the moon's left the disturbance behind, as it follows its orbit."

Wright said, "Confirming Geoffrey's notion that the disturbance is a long, thin line of—well, I should call it an error."

"Is that what you meant by a checkable idea?" the Astronomer Royal asked irritably.

"Not quite. Though that the two regions of error are now separating, as the moon advances, is consistent with a disturbance traveling from the stars to us. That is a first requirement, in my view."

"Your view of what?" Geoffrey finally gave up handling his small sherry glass and set it down with a decisive rattle.

"Let me put my philosophy clearly," Wright said. "If the universe is an ongoing calculation, then computational theory proves that it cannot be perfect. No such system can be free of a bug or two, as the programmers put it."

Into an uncomfortable silence Geoffrey finally inserted, "Then the moon's being ahead, the stars—it's all a mistake?"

Wright smiled tightly. "Precisely. One of immense scale, moving at the speed of light."

Geoffrey's face scrunched into a mask of perplexity. "And it just—jumped?"

"Our moon hopped forward a bit too far in the universal computation, just as a program advances in little leaps." Wright smiled as though this were an entirely natural idea.

Another silence. The Astronomer Royal said sourly, "That's mere philosophy, not physics."

"Ah!" Wright pounced. "But any universe which is a sort of analog computer must, like any decent digital one, have an error-checking program. Makes no sense otherwise."

"Why?" Geoffrey was visibly confused, a craftsman out of his depth.

"Any good program, whether it is doing accounts in a bank, or carrying forward the laws of the universe, must be able to correct itself." Professor Wright sat back triumphantly and swallowed a Jesus College sandwich, smacking his lips.

The Astronomer Royal said, "So you predict . . . ?"

"That both the moon and the stars shall snap back, get themselves right—and at the same time, as the correction arrives here at the speed of light."

"Nonsense," the Astronomer Royal said.

"A prediction," Professor Wright said sternly. "My philosophy stands upon it."

The Astronomer Royal snorted, letting his fatigue get to him. Geoffrey looked puzzled, and asked a question which would later haunt them.

Professor Wright did not have long to wait.

To his credit, he did not enter the media fray with his prediction. However, he did unwisely air his views at High Table, after a particularly fine bottle of claret brought forward by the oldest member of the college. Only a generation or two earlier, such a conversation among the Fellows would have been secure. Not so now. A Junior Fellow in Political Studies proved to be on a retainer from the Times, and scarcely a day passed before Wright's conjecture was known in New Delhi and Tokyo.

The furor following from that had barely subsided when the Astronomer Royal received a telephone call from the Max Planck Institute. They excitedly reported that the moon, now under continuous observation, had shifted instantly to the position it should have, had its orbit never been perturbed.

So, too, did the stars in the warped circle return to their rightful places. Once more, all was right with the world. Even so, it was a world that could never again be the same.

Professor Wright was not smug. He received the news from the Astronomer Royal, who had brought along Geoffrey to Jesus College, a refuge now from the Institute. "Nothing, really, but common sense." He waved away their congratulations.

Geoffrey sat, visibly uneasily, through some talk

about how to handle all this in the voracious media glare. Philosophers are not accustomed to much attention until well after they are dead. But as discussion ebbed Geoffrey repeated his probing question of days before: "What sort of universe has mistakes in it?"

Professor Wright said kindly, "An information-ordered one. Think of everything that happens—including us talking here, I suppose—as a kind of analog program acting out. Discovering itself in its own development. Manifesting."

Geoffrey persisted, "But who's the programmer of this computer?"

"Questions of first cause are really not germane," Wright said, drawing himself up.

"Which means that he cannot say," the Astronomer Royal allowed himself.

Wright stroked his chin at this and eyed the others before venturing, "In light of the name of this college, and you, Geoffrey, being a humble bearer of the message that began all this . . ."

"Oh no," the Astronomer Royal said fiercely, "next you'll point out that Geoffrey's a carpenter."

They all laughed, though uneasily.

But as the Astronomer Royal and Geoffrey left the venerable grounds, Geoffrey said moodily, "Y'know, I'm a cabinet maker."

"Uh, yes?"

"We aren't bloody carpenters at all," Geoffrey said angrily. "We're craftsmen."

The distinction was lost upon the Royal Astronomer, but then, much else was, these days.

The Japanese had very fast images of the moon's return to its proper place, taken from their geosynchronous satellite. The transition did indeed proceed at very nearly the speed of light, taking a slight fraction of a second to jerk back to exactly where it should have been. Not the original place where the disturbance occurred, but to its rightful spot along the smooth ellipse. The immense force needed to do this went unexplained, of course, except by Professor Wright's Computational Principle.

To everyone's surprise, it was not a member of the now quite raucous press who made the first telling jibe at Wright, but Geoffrey. "I can't follow, sir, why we can still remember when the moon was in the wrong place."

"What?" Wright looked startled, almost spilling some of the celebratory tea the three were enjoying. Or rather, that Wright was conspicuously relishing, while the Astronomer Royal gave a convincing impression of a man in a good mood.

"Y'see, if the error's all straightened out, why don't our memories of it get fixed, too?"

The two learned men froze.

"We're part of the physical universe," the Astronomer Royal said wonderingly, "so why not, eh?"

Wright's expression confessed his consternation. "That we haven't been, well, edited . . ."

"Kinda means we're not the same as the moon, right?"

Begrudgingly, Wright nodded. "So perhaps the, ah, 'mind' that is carrying out the universe's computation, cannot interfere with our—other—minds."

"And why's that?" the Astronomer Royal a little too obviously enjoyed saying.

"I haven't the slightest."

Light does not always travel at the same blistering speed. Only in vacuum does it have its maximum velocity.

Light emitted at the center of the sun, for example—which is a million times denser than lead—finds itself absorbed by the close-packed ionized atoms there, held for a tiny sliver of a second, then released. It travels an infinitesimal distance, then is captured by yet another hot ion of the plasma, and the process repeats. The radiation random-walks its way out to the solar surface. In all, the passage from the core takes a many thousands of years. Once free, the photon reaches the Earth in a few minutes.

Radiation from zones nearer the sun's fiery surface takes less time because the plasma there is far less dense. That was why a full three months elapsed before anyone paid attention to a detail the astronomers had noticed early on, and then neglected.

The "cone of chaos" (as it was now commonly called) that had lanced in from the distant stars and deflected the moon had gone on and intersected the sun at a grazing angle. It had luckily missed the Earth, but that was the end of the luck.

On an otherwise unremarkable morning, Geoffrey rose to begin work on a new pine cabinet. He was glad to be out of the media glare, though still troubled by the issues raised by his discovery. Professor Wright had made no progress in answering Geoffrey's persistent questions. The Astronomer Royal was busying himself with a Royal Commission appointed to investigate the whole affair, though no one expected a Commission to actually produce an idea. Geoffrey's hope—that they could "find out more by measuring," seemed to be at a dead end.

On that fateful morning, out his bedroom window, Geoffrey saw a strange sun. Its lumpy shape he quickly studied by viewing it through his telescope with a dark glass clamped in place. He knew of the arches that occasionally rose from the corona, vast galleries of magnetic field lines bound to the plasma like bunches of wire under tension. Sprouting from the sun at a dozen spots stood twisted parodies of this, snaking in immense weaves of incandescence.

He called his wife to see. Already voices in the cobbled street below were murmuring in alarm. Hanging above the open marsh lands around the ancient cathedral city of Ely was a ruby sun, its grand purple arches swelling like blisters from the troubled rim.

His wife's voice trembled. "What's it mean?"

"I'm afraid to ask."

"I thought everything got put back right."

"Must be more complicated, somehow."

"Or a judgment." In his wife's severe frown he saw an eternal human impulse, to read meaning into the physical world—and a moral message as well.

He thought of the swirl of atoms in the sun, all moving along their hammering trajectories, immensely complicated. The spike of error must have moved them all, and the later spike of correction could not, somehow, undo the damage. Erasing such detail must be impossible. So even the mechanism that drove the universal computation had its limits. Whatever you called it, Geoffrey mused, the agency that made order also made error—and could not cover its tracks completely.

"Wonder what it means?" he whispered.

The line of error had done its work. Plumes rose like angry necklaces from the blazing rim of the star whose fate governed all intelligence within the solar system.

Thus began a time marked not only by vast disaster, but by the founding of a wholly new science. Only later, once studies were restored at Cambridge University, and Jesus College was rebuilt in a period of relative calm, did this new science and philosophy—for now the two were always linked—acquire a name: the field of Empirical Theology.

ONE OF HER PATHS

IAN WATSON

I N APRIL 2120 THE test ship Probe *left Earth orbit,
powered by the annihilation of matter and antimatter. Since the discovery a decade previously of a tiny
anti-iron asteroid and its successful harvesting employ-
ing elegant containment techniques, new superthrust engines had empowered ships to boost to the orbit of Saturn
within eight weeks, a situation which the available supply of antimatter would permit for another thirty years.*

But Probe *was not testing antimatter propulsion.
Probe was to test the Q-drive which theoretically should
advance a ship to the nearer stars through probability-
space, the underlying condition of reality, within several
months instead of decades. Probe's destination: Tau Ceti,
twelve light years away.*

By June 2120 Probe *was sufficiently far out of the
gravity well of the Sun for the Q-drive to switch on, and,
as planned and hoped for, the test ship vanished—to*

reappear in the solar system a little over six months later, inward bound.

When Probe *was recovered, the dozen rats on board were still alive, hale and hearty, and of the six little monkeys, five survived in decent shape. The sixth was a victim of its food supply jamming. All the animals had been caged separately, though spaciously, supplied with exercise equipment and toys. Time-lapse cameras recorded nothing untoward during the journey through Q-space to the outskirts of Tau Ceti and back.*

While Probe *had lingered on those outskirts, it had established that, of the planets of Tau Ceti already detected from the solar system, the second possessed a promising biosphere: an oxygen-nitrogen atmosphere, oceans, weather systems over the scattered landmasses. Even if only simple cells lived on that world, they had been beavering away for a long time to good purpose.*

In 2123 construction of Earth's first crewed starship, Pioneer, *began. Four years later the large ship was ready.*

. . .

Long before Doctor Mary Nolan enters *Pioneer* itself, she is thoroughly familiar with the spacious interior from virtual reality training. The Q-drive pod jutting ahead like a long battering ram tipped with a samovar, then the antimatter containers amidships that feed the engines at the stern, together form a long central spindle around which the great doughnut of living quarters rotates quickly enough to provide imitation gravity at half a gee. The doughnut houses a hundred cabins, one for each crew member.

Bed-couches are big enough that the dozen couples who are already married or partnered can bunk with one another, though who knows what may happen during the course of such an expedition? The potential for privacy is important. On top of her medical qualifications Mary's second string is psychiatry. Aside from the months necessary to progress beyond Saturn, and the six-month trip through Q-space, plus at least a year spent in the Tau Ceti system, colonization is possible (three shuttles are strapped to the spindle), so the ship is provisioned for a generous four years, not to mention the food that will be grown on board hydroponically.

After the obligatory pre-departure fortnight spent in quarantine—ten persons per isolation unit—the interior of *Pioneer* strikes Mary as particularly spacious. (After another year or so, will it still seem so roomy?) At half a gee her tread is buoyant—yet deliberate and cautious, as is the pace of other colleagues newly aboard.

"Hi, Gisela!" It's dark-haired athletic Dr. Gisela Frick, who is qualified in microbiology and biochemistry as well as medicine and physiotherapy. Mary did not share quarantine with Gisela, nor with the expedition surgeon Dr. Yukio Yamamoto, nor with dentist and geologist Howard Coover. A surprise infection must not catch the prime medical team all together. Back-up personnel were in separate quarantine units as a precaution—a whole duplicate crew had trained.

"How does it feel to you, Gisela?"

"To be really aboard at last? Great! Ah, do you mean the motion . . . ? It's okay." Gisela swings her head skittishly. "Oops."

The floor consists of flat sections each a couple of meters long, gently tilting with respect to one another. Curved flooring would have presented an engineering problem as regards the furnishing of cabins and the mounting of lab equipment and in many other respects, but the sense of down-orientation shifts subtly as a person walks. What's more, there are the effects of Coriolis force. Hurrying, or abrupt changes of direction, could disorient and nauseate.

"The anti-nausea pills seem to be effective," says Gisela. Of course without the centripetal semblance of gravity the rate of bone-loss would be unacceptable. "I wonder whether there could be long-term problems with tendonitis? Might we end up like birds gripping imaginary branches?"

This is not something that the virtual reality tours were able to simulate. At the moment the difference from true semi-gravity is trivial. Can it lead to physical impairment in the long run? Not that anyone will try *running* around the main corridors, but only jogging on stationary treadmills.

Greeting colleagues after a fortnight's separation from them, and nodding to fellow quarantinees, Mary and Gisela head for their clinic, not to inventory it, but more to check that it corresponds exactly with virtuality.

Which it does. As do the two gyms and the science labs and the restaurant (for the sociable) and the recreation hall and the hydroponics-cum-botany garden. . . . Yes, the ship is surely big enough for a hundred people to share and work together harmoniously for ages. Failing harmony and happiness, there is always recourse to one's private cabin with computer access to a treasury of literature, music, games, and virtual experiences from skiing to scuba-diving, all the way through the alphabet of possibilities and back again.

People, people—under the command of Commander Sherwin Peterson. Mary knows those with whom she was in quarantine quite intimately by now, many others rather well to varying degrees, and none of the others are exactly strangers; besides which, she can screen all available data about them. No excuse, after the first few days of waiting in Earth orbit, for not matching names to faces instantly.

The official language of *Pioneer* is English, but she hears occasional German and French and Japanese too. The four co-operating powers behind the expedition are America, the Euro-Union, Australia, and Japan. If a foothold can be established on Tau Ceti 2, the Chinese plan their own independent ship. No one can argue with that.

Here's John Dolby, the climatologist, John James Pine, geologist and one of the three shuttle pilots, Eric Festa, nutrition, botany, and hydroponics, Denise Dubois, astrophysics, Carmen Santos, engineering, Chikahiro Suzuki, computer systems, navigator Nellie van Torn. . . .

Two months later, *Pioneer* has passed the realm of Saturn (although its be-ringed monarch is far away) and no failures have occurred, neither of machine nor man, nor woman, aside from various minor ailments, swiftly diagnosed and cured. Mary and her two medical colleagues monitor everyone's health, making sure that sodium and iron levels do not rise. In liaison with Eric Festa they supply mineral supplements where required. An Australian pair of partners, Sandy Tate and Jeff Lee, oceanography and life science respectively, are pregnant—or rather, Sandy herself is. She must have conceived before entering quarantine, either accidentally or irresponsibly. Their child will be born toward the end of the six-month transit through Q-space, a first for the human race. Mary will keep a careful eye on Sandy. By now almost everyone is on first name terms. Pilot Pine is Jay-Jay; Dr. Suzuki is Chika. The ship is a family. How appropriate that a family should have a baby. A few other pairings are occurring, Jay-Jay and Denise, for instance. Mary is feeling a growing fondness and shoots of desire for Eric Festa, who reciprocates her feelings. Eric, from Dortmund, is a nourishing person to know. The two often sit in the botany section and talk amidst the orchids—for beauty—and tomatoes and carrots and soy beans for a nutritious diet.

On the evening, ship-time, preceding Q-day there's a feast in the restaurant from the ample store of varied vacuum-packed reduced sodium and iron gourmet meals.

"Compliments to the chef!" someone calls out.

"Chef's back on Earth!" dietitian Eric declares, prompting laughter and applause. Spirits are high.

Afterward, Com Sherwin reminds everyone of procedures. When the time comes to switch on the Q-drive, all personnel other than those on the bridge must be in their cabins tethered to their bed-couches. *Probe* encountered no visible problems when entering Q-space. Nevertheless, err on the safe side. Transient side effects that rats and monkeys could not report might affect human beings. Psychological or perceptual glitches, akin to the mild imbalance caused by Coriolis force.

Com Sherwin has an Air Force background, back in his younger days where backgrounds should be, his route from daring test pilot to astronaut training. He piloted the first hazardous antimatter-asteroid reconnaissance. Later, famously, he had risked his life taking *The Dart* on a flythrough the clouds of Jupiter, en route ramming a gas-whale and carrying it back into space with him spitted on *The Dart*, indeed draped around *The Dart*, its collapsed quick-frozen carcass almost enfolding his ship, a gift to science although a cause of some controversy. Of the numerous probes that had dropped into Jupiter only two had ever spotted gas-whales.

Interviewed on *Systemwide*: "Aren't the gas-whales very rare?"

Peterson: "Not in that huge volume of atmosphere. Not necessarily."

"Weren't you risking your ship and your life on a sudden impulse?"

Peterson: "I had several seconds to think. I reckoned I had a good chance."

"Apparently your pulse rate didn't even rise."

Peterson had merely grinned, engagingly.

"So what's your favorite book then, *Moby-Dick*?"

"No, actually it's Linda Bernstein's *Be Your Own Leader at Peace with Yourself*. I read a page a night."

Peterson was solid. Capable of split-second decisiveness, yet possessing a balanced serenity, and also a folksy touch if need be.

Mary is lying abed dressed in mission multipocket-wear, green for medic, in the cabin that by now seems as familiar and homelike as her girlhood room in Michigan, listening to the calm tones of Com Sherwin from her comp speakers as Sherwin talks through the Q-sequence, only partly understood by her. She remembers doing her best to understand a lecture at Mission Control, given as part of the year-long training schedule.

"Fundamentally," a dapper, bearded Physics Professor had said, "the Q-drive functions as a quantum computer that is given the problem of translating a ship from Sun-space to Tau Ceti space. Your actual ship's computer for everyday use is a super-duper Turing-type machine. When you access your ship's computer, it may sound to you like an artificial intelligence—the software's designed to be user-friendly—but we're still twenty years away from genuine AI.

"Aw, sixty years ago people were saying the same, and AI hasn't happened yet, so I ain't making any prophecies.

"Anyway, if you set a Turing machine a really big task—for example, tell it to factorize a 500-digit number—it'll tackle solutions one after another, and that will take *ages*, even if the machine is really fast. In a quantum computer, on the other hand, all the possible answers are superposed. Superimposed simultaneously, as it were. Bingo, the wrong answers cancel each other out, and you get the right one. *Not* that this happens instantaneously—it still takes time. In the case of determining a route to Tau Ceti all routes are considered including going via Sirius or Andromeda or even by way of a quasar at the far side of the universe. Quantum theory sums over all paths between two points, as we say, and that means all possible paths."

"Does this mean," someone asked, "that we might end up in another galaxy?"

"No no, *Probe* proved that won't happen. The nonsense routes cancel out. Now a quantum device such as the drive is very specialized and needs to be kept as isolated as possible. It's entangled with the ship, but regular computing on board still has to be done by your Turing machine."

Some wit had stuck up his hand. "I'd say that the Q-drive is the real touring machine!"

"Very droll. I was referring to computer pioneer Alan Turing, who unbelievably was hounded to suicide because he was differently sexed." Evidently a cause of anguish and anger to this lecturer.

Sum over paths, Mary muses.

Some Over-Paths. Ways of jumping from here to there. Or perhaps of burrowing.

Samovar Paths, in view of the shape of the Q-drive unit. . . .

Summer Paths, the bright way to the stars. However, the appearance of Q-space as recorded by *Probe*'s cameras was an ocean of gray frogspawn. . . .

* * *

"Initiating primary power uptake.... We have four green balls.... Sixty seconds to Q-insertion...."

"Thirty seconds...."

"Fifteen...."

The seconds pass. The cabin quivers and shimmers and is the same again. Same photos of family and friends and scenery sticky-tacked to the walls. Same dream-catcher mobile of feathers and knots. Same everything.

Except for the silence, silence apart from the softest hum from the speakers.

Has communication failed? In Q-space can no one hear you make announcements over electronic equipment?

"Uh, testing?" she queries the silence, and she hears her own voice clearly enough.

Mary untethers and sits up, goes to her door, slides it open. The corridor is empty; other cabin doors remain closed. Evidently she's the first to emerge. Gisela's cabin is only three doors down.

Mary knocks, then slides the door open.

Gisela's cabin is empty apart from her personal possessions.

Likewise Carmen's cabin, likewise Denise's....

All the cabins Mary tries are empty. It seems impossible that everyone can have untethered before her and gone to the bridge to look at the viewscreens, *impossible*. But what else could they have done? Mary must have suffered a lapse of consciousness, a gap in awareness.

To the bridge, then! Though without running or rushing.

The bridge is deserted, instruments and controls untended. Lights glow on boards, equipment purrs. On the viewscreens is the mottled gray of Q-space. No stars, just endless dimensionless frogspawn. Exactly as expected.

"Where's everyone? Will somebody answer me!"

No answer comes.

Has everyone hidden in the rec room or in the hydroponics section to play a joke on her...? She'll go to the rec room and ninety-nine voices will chorus, *Boo*. Oh really, at this momentous moment, the first entry of the first crewed ship into Q-space? And why pick on *her*?

Nevertheless, she does go to the rec room, which is deserted, then to the empty restaurant, then to the botany area where only plants are to be seen.

A type of hysterical blindness and deafness is afflicting her—people are here yet she is failing to hear and see them.

This has to be nonsense.

"Gisela! Eric! Yukio! Com Sherwin! Where are you?"

They are gone, all gone. She is alone on *Pioneer*.

The reason for this mass disappearance must be something to do with the nature of Q-space—an effect of the

Q-drive as regards conscious intelligences such as human beings. So Mary reasons.

Why did *Probe*'s cameras not show monkeys and rats as missing? Ah, but the test animals were all caged separately from one another. Conceivably they did not *experience* the presence of their fellows in the other cages. But they could not report their experience, or lack of it.

Can it be that each conscious observer on board the *Pioneer* has given rise to a copy of the ship, each of which contains only one person? Right now one hundred copies of the *Pioneer* are heading through Q-space toward Tau Ceti. When all of these arrive and switch off their drives, will all the copies reintegrate and become once more one single ship with a hundred people aboard it?

Collapse of the wave function ... that's the phrase, isn't it? Something to do with multiple probabilities becoming one concrete reality, as Mary recalls. Surely that stuff happens at the subatomic level, not to an entire ship massing thousands of tonnes.

Still, it's a lifeline to cling to: in six months time everyone will come together.

During so many months the hundred ships can hardly remain identical. Mary will consume certain supplies; absent colleagues will account for different supplies. She remembers the ripple that occurred as she entered Q-space. On emergence, will the merging ships adjust so that there are no discrepancies?

What if two people happen to be in exactly the same place? Is one of them displaced? Does that happen gently or violently?

The more she thinks about it, the more iffy the idea of reintegration becomes.

The deserted ship subt nacing. Random noises might be phantom foo A reflection or trick of light and shadow cou a glimpse of someone moving out of sight. Her v colleagues may, in their own copies of the ship, minor psychotic episodes or hallucination

Suppose someone monkeys with o-pose that a copyship re-enters norm turely, or is disabled. Reintegration mig to occur. *Pioneer* might fly onward forev

She mustn't let this notion obsess her. Sh dreds of years' worth of food and drink if consumed one person alone. She shan't starve!

If each ship is similarly stocked this seems a bit like the miracle of the loaves and fishes. How can reality multiply in such a way? Maybe Mary's is the only ship. Maybe only one conscious observer could remain in existence. By sheer chance this happened to be her.

No, no, remember all the rats. And all but one of the monkeys.

* * *

"Talking to yourself, are you, Mary?"

"Nothing wrong with that. People do talk to themselves. That's how we monitor what's going on. Helps us plan what to do next. Evolution didn't give us fast random-access memories—so we tell ourselves a story, the story of our self. That's how we remember things. It reinforces short-term memory."

"Adults generally talk to themselves silently, not aloud."

"Well, there's no one around to take offense. There's just me."

"Just you, eh? After a while, if you talk aloud to yourself, it's as if there are two of you—the talker, and the person you talk to. *You* can become the audience, hearing words which simply seem to emerge. In that case who is doing the talking? Listen: when we all come together again maybe we might re-enter any of a hundred different universes."

"Surely a star very like Tau Ceti has to be in the same location, otherwise how could we emerge from Q-space?"

"Ah, but maybe we would pick up no ten-year-old radio signals from the solar system, supposing we had a powerful enough receiver. In that other universe the human race may never have evolved. *Pioneer* may be the only abode of life. Tau Ceti 2 may not be habitable."

"Thanks a bundle."

"Look, why don't you talk to the *computer* more?"

"Because the computer only simulates having a mind of its own. That's why it has no name. A woman's voice, yes, and a woman's avatar-face if we want one, but no name so we won't be fooled. A psychiatrist seeking aid and counsel from a program is absurd. However sophisticated the program is, it cannot *know*. It merely listens and responds as appropriately as possible. After a while, that's maddening. Ask it how to repair a solar power plant or remind you how to fix a ruptured spleen, fine and good. It goes through its repertoire. If we did have true artificial intelligence, I dunno, maybe there would be some magic quantum link between the AIs in all the ships and we could all communicate. But we don't, and there isn't."

Of course she already asked Computer what is happening. *Pioneer* is transiting through Q-space, Mary. Do you want a full status report? No, just where is everybody else? Where is the Commander? I don't know, Mary. She may as well ask herself. She doesn't wish to confuse Computer. Just take us to where we're going and carry on with the housekeeping.

Playing her favorite arias by Puccini throughout the ship turns out to be a bad idea. The music seems to mask rustlings and whispers.

When Mary was sixteen she thought she saw an angel. Most likely she was dazzled by sunlight while hiking through woodland. A tiny lake was a silver mirror, and bushes were covered and linked by innumerable be-dewed spiders' webs. She saw a being with wings, spar-kling bright. Of a sudden bird-song seemed to combine in a single rhapsody of musical counterpoint the mean-ing of which only just eluded her. She felt called. A few centuries earlier she might have become a nun. In the event she specialized in psychiatry after earning her medical qualifications.

Her parents were both practicing Catholics, who con-fessed and went to mass regularly. They always denied themselves some treat during Lent—generally, in her Dad's case, drinking with the fellows on a Saturday night. None of the fellows were Catholics, nor was the town a Catholic one—her Mom and Dad needed to drive twenty miles to attend mass—so Dad had adopted a jokey, ironic front for his faith. "Next year I might give up fast food for Lent." "Oh we don't need to worry about what to believe—we're *told* what to think." He did good works, quietly, simple kindnesses to neighbors and col-leagues. Mary had already begun lapsing into agnosti-cism by the age of fourteen, and she encountered no pressure or reproach from her parents, but where it came to good works, Dad was a beacon to her.

Without the medical attention provided by herself or Gi-sela or Yukio or Howard, what if others fall ill during the next six months? No longer quite six months—by now a week of that stretch has passed. Just one damn week!

Personally she's rather more bothered right now about the hydroponics. Fluids and nutrition are auto-mated, but the care of carrots and tomatoes and bean sprouts is not her field at all.

What about Sandy's pregnancy? Sandy is on her own, expecting a child, and knowing now that she will have to give birth to it unassisted. What if Sandy de-velops toxemia? How will she control that? What if she suffers a difficult delivery? What if she *cannot* deliver until reintegration?

How can Sandy be *alone* if a fetus is growing inside her, four months old by now? Did the separation-event treat her and her child as one unit—or did the event rip the fetus untimely from its mother's womb, aborting it into yet another copy of the ship, perishing on Sandy's bedcouch? This is too awful to contemplate.

Something else is aboard with Mary. Something quite unlike an angel, and besides she doesn't believe in those.

"What are you?" she cries. *"Where are you?"*

Armed with a kitchen knife, she ranges around the great doughnut, searching and finding nothing. It's as though she, the reluctant would-be observer of the Enigma, is always where there's a low probability of finding whatever it is. Where it is, she is not. She can sense a sort of semi-absent presence, never enough for actuality.

Isn't there something called an exclusion principle?

"Maybe you should put yourself on tranquilizers."

"No, you must stay alert!"

Maybe she arouses the curiosity of whatever it is yet it wants to avoid harming her. Alternatively, it finds her daunting and, although in a sense summoned by her, it keeps out of her way, sniffing and tasting where she has been.

"All right, you've been alone for a fortnight now. Twenty-two more weeks to go. People have spent far longer periods on their own without all the amenities *you* enjoy!"

Movies, if desired. The hustle and bustle of actors. Any number of computer games. Virtual reality sight-seeing, VR adventures. Whatever, whatever.

She tried to watch *The Sound of Music* as a safe choice in the rec room, but she couldn't concentrate. She dares not enter a virtual reality—the Enigma might creep up on her while she is immersed.

"All those people who spent time alone: they still knew that other people existed in the same world as them. I know the contrary!"

"Mary, Mary, how contrary, how does your garden grow?"

"So many bean sprouts already! Do I harvest them? I hate bean sprouts. Give me the deluxe meals any day." More than enough of those to make every day a special occasion. "Why shouldn't I hog on those?"

"Why not cook something special for yourself?" The frozen food store contains a wealth of raw ingredients in case the vacuum-packed foods somehow fail, or pall.

"Since when was I a chef? It's stupid cooking for one."

"Cook for me too."

"This sensation of something unseen sharing the ship with me—I can't tolerate it for months on end!"

"Even if the sensation may be preferable to total isolation?"

"*Show yourself to me!* In a mirror, if you can't manage anything more substantial."

And there the Enigma is, in her cabin's mirror.

But it is herself that she sees.

Maybe the Enigma is floating directly behind her back, tucked out of sight. Abruptly she shifts aside. Oops, a little surge of nausea. Oh the Enigma is too quick for her by far.

She cannot catch it full-frontally. She must seek it by indirect means. Mary must practice a sort of Zen art of not-looking, not-seeing.

As a psychiatrist Mary understands the principles of meditation and she has even practiced a bit in the past. The silent, empty ship is an ideal focus of vacancy. Session by session—interspersed by more mundane tasks—she blanks her personality. After each session she surfaces to rediscover herself, the only consciousness hereabouts, a mind amidst a void.

Is there a risk that she may remain in tune with the void until her motionless body starves to death? Grumbling guts recall her to activity—so far, at least.

After many days of annulling herself. . . .

A perception emerges from the medium through which the *Pioneer* travels.

<<You believe that your identity is confined here in this ship.>>

Well yes, she does.

<<Fundamental being is forever transforming itself. Think of bubbles in boiling water. Think of flames in a fire. Think of weather cells in an atmosphere. Being is the process, not the particulars. Its facets constantly manifest themselves only to disintegrate and then reintegrate.>>

Such is the perception that scrutinizes her.

<<You are a bubble of mind, a tongue of living flame, which might last for a hundred orbits of your world around your sun, a mere moment of cosmic time. But you are also one facet of a hundred-fold being, the crew of this ship. This hundred-fold being has separated itself from a many-billion-fold being—which you call Humanity.>>

A many-billion-fold being?

<<Humanity from the dawn of consciousness until final demise exists as a four-dimensional blaze of members arising and dying and replacing themselves, all linked, ever loosening, ever relinking, within which flickers your own particular flame.>>

Why is she being told this? Does it help, or is some godlike entity inspecting her coolly? Alternatively, is she hallucinating?

<<Realize! From birth to death an intelligent planetary species is a single mental entity, its mentality made of all the minds that compose it. Individual units of Humanity process tiny parts of its totality. Each individual is part of an eon-spanning exchange of information—unaware of this except in rare moments of insight. Or outsight. Beatific moments, poetic moments, shamanistic, hallucinatory. You often misinterpret such partial, fleeting glimpses as encounters with Gods or spirits or ghosts or fairies or, more recently, encounters with flying saucer folk.>>

"Tell me more."

<<During the millions of years of its existence the species-entity may remain alone. Such beings are few and far between in space and time during any megaera. Even so, their number is considerable overall, for the present universe was spawned from a parent universe, and in turn gives rise to daughter universes, a great tree of universes.>>

This is big stuff. Is she capable of imagining all this

on her own? Quite possibly. Why should a godlike entity bother to communicate with her?

Ah, but an answer comes.

<<Some planetary species send parts of themselves through space on a journey lasting generations to the worlds of other stars, creating an offspring of themselves. Some of these offspring encounter an alien species and the two beings either destroy or corrupt one another or else become a hybrid. A very few planetary species send the exiled part of themselves not through ordinary space but through the underlying space of probabilities—and here they encounter its entities, as you do now.

<<Your ship is not yet far from its home. You are still entangled. The entity, Humanity, can now be recognized and addressed. And if addressed *now*, Humanity as a whole is also addressed in the past and in the future.

<<*Was, is, and will be.*>>

Mary has had a vision. What is she to make of it?

Is she and is everyone else who ever lived, or who will live, only so many iotas in a single entity spanning millions of years? By traveling through Q-space, has she encountered a higher entity—and caused Humanity to be contacted in the past and the present and the future? On this, um, higher level of metaconsciousness, to which individual persons only ever have fleeting and partial access at best?

If *Pioneer* had never been built, nor some similar Q-space ship in the future, humanity would probably have remained isolated and uncontacted. Yet because contact occurs now, contact also applies retroactively. Total-Humanity may understand this paradox, but it fazes Mary. No individual human being has ever or will ever be aware of more than a jot of the communication between Pan-Humanity and the Probability Entities. This will elude mere people, much as the betting on a tortoise race eludes the tortoises. Or perhaps that should be: a race between fireflies.

Mary feels she is like a single brain-cell present during a few moments of a symphony.

If the hundred copies of the *Pioneer* do reintegrate successfully in another five months' time, and if she announces her revelation, will psychiatrist Mary be for the funny farm?

The air in her cabin smells musty. Surfaces look dusty.

Quite nimbly, in the circumstances, she rises from her lotus position. With a fingertip she traces a line across her com-console.

God almighty, the *date display*. . . .

The date, the date.

Q + 178.

Q + *178*.

A hundred and seventy-eight days, very nearly six

months, have passed since the *Pioneer* entered Q-space and she found herself isolated. Mary has been advanced through time itself. She has been extracted and reinserted later, abridging her lonely journey from months to days.

"Oh thank you!" she cries into the silence. "Thank you so very much!"

Yet now there's no sense of Another on the ship with her.

Full of wonder and gratitude, she sets off to check on hydroponics. What a riot of life and death she finds there—rot and fecundity, the air so heady and reeking. Is it possible that Gisela and Eric and all of her colleagues may also have been advanced through time?

Including Sandy, no longer condemned to give birth all alone?

Mary muses, in the dispensary. If the hundred *Pilgrims* do reintegrate successfully, and if her ninety-nine colleagues have *not* been blessed as she has been, what may the medical team need to provide quickly in the way of sedatives or stimulants or vitamin supplements?

Of a sudden the warning siren blares automatically, *whoop-whoop-whoop*, such a shocking hullabaloo that her heart races.

Thank god for it, though, thank god. She has fifteen minutes to return to her cabin and tether herself. Should she bother to do so, or simply stay here? If Gisela or

Yukio are in this dispensary she might bump into them, disastrously. Her cabin is safer.

The cabin writhes, as before. Every surface shimmers. It's as if her eyes are watering. Then all is clear and sharp again, herphotos, her mobile, her terminal.

Com Sherwin's voice comes briskly. "All hear me. Re-emergence from Q-space achieved. *Pioneer* has acquired Tau Ceti space."

Acquired, acquired! *Pioneer* has acquired a whole new solar system. And rejoice, Mary has regained her fellow human beings!

"Tau Ceti 2 is visible at 9.8 A.U."

Have her fellows arrived here with a skip and a jump, or the slow way?

"Fellow pioneers, we were all separated—for which there may be various explanations."

Yes? Yes?

"I hope we are all together again. I see that the main bridge team is with me, at least. All non-flight personnel proceed to the restaurant right away for rollcall. Dr. Suzuki is to be in charge of rollcall. Back-up is Major Pine. Second backup is Dr. Santos. Preliminary debrief to follow later. Do not close your cabin doors after you leave. Medical team, check all cabins."

Good thinking. If Chika is not available, Jay-Jay will tally numbers. And if Jay-Jay is not present, Carmen will co-ordinate. Some people may not be able to leave their cabins. How long has Com Sherwin had to think about contingencies?

"Proceed. Bridge out." He has not said whether he himself spent months in Q-space—or only a single month followed by a couple of days.

People emerging into the corridor. Heartfelt greetings. Some tears of relief.

"Denise," Mary calls out, *"how long were you in Q-space?"*

They embrace. "Oh Mary, it felt like forever! Six long months."

"Were you alone all that time?"

"Entirely."

"You, Carmen, how long?"

"Six shitting months. I must get to the restaurant, Mary."

"Of course."

Babble, babble as people proceed as instructed. Eric's cabin is further away around the doughnut out of sight. Be methodical: check inside each cabin even if a door is wide open. There's Gisela in the distance, opening a door and popping inside. Despite instructions a few people may have shut their doors unthinkingly behind them. Here's a door that is closed, belonging to: **Sandy Tate.** Sandy, Sandy! Mary knocks, calls her name.

Freckled, ginger-haired Sandy is sitting on her bedcouch, a swaddled baby held in her arms. She hugs it to herself protectively. Protectively?—no, it looks more as if Sandy is *restraining* her baby—and it barely a week or two old.

"Mary, thank god, I'm going crazy—"

"You did give birth! All on your own—that must have been utterly grueling and scary. But you did okay?"

"I managed—I read up all I could beforehand."

"Well done, Sandy! I'll examine you and your baby as soon as—"

"Mary, this baby is trying to talk to me!"

"To talk?"

"I don't understand him, but he's trying to."

Is Sandy suffering, understandably, from delusions?

"He can't talk, Sandy. A baby's brain isn't fully grown. Learning to speak simply can't clock in so soon, and would be totally pointless because it's physically impossible for a baby to vocalize. You see, its larynx is in the wrong position. For the first nine months the larynx is high up, locked into the nose, so that a baby can drink and breathe at the same time without choking."

"I'm telling you he's *trying!* I didn't say he can *manage* it."

The months of loneliness, the fear and worry, the need for another person to communicate with. . . .

"Sandy, you're misinterpreting the noises he makes."

"I am *not* misinterpreting."

"Let me see him, Sandy."

As Mary sits on the bed-couch beside her, Sandy flinches. Then she reveals her child, a bundle of feeble struggle which, at presumably blurred sight of a person new to its world, produces sounds that are indeed unlike any regular infantile crying or red-faced bawling. It's as if a strangled voice, using an unknown language, is heard through distorting filters and muffles.

"Sandy, I should tell you something—" How can Mary take time out just now to tell about her own re-levation, and her translation through time? "He does sound different, Sandy, I agree! At a quick glance there doesn't seem to be anything physically wrong with either of you. . . . Do you think you can get to the restaurant?"

"I'm his restaurant," she says. "If he had teeth, he'd bite."

The baby certainly does seem assertive.

"What have you called him?" Mary asks gently.

"He calls me—but I don't know what he wants to say."

"You must have thought of a name beforehand. Boy or girl, whichever."

"James."

"Hi, James."

Those strange noises, as if in reply.

"How about bringing him to the restaurant? I think that's important. Important, yes. And you need to mingle again."

"Where's Jeff? Why isn't he here? That's why I waited. Is he dead?"

"You heard Com Sherwin's instructions. Jeff will be waiting for you at the restaurant."

"Why didn't he come here so we could both go together?"

"Maybe he expected to find you at the restaurant. Come on, Sandy, chin up."

"I can't take my baby there—he's a monster."

Post-natal depression? Not necessarily.

"If James seems a bit odd, Sandy, I might—just might—know the reason, but I need to explain to all the others too. You've coped splendidly so far. Come on, it's okay."

All is not quite okay. An American physicist, Greg Fox, is dead. Appendicitis, says Gisela. Must have been agonizing. Did Greg manage to lay his hands on morphine, maybe an overdose? Post-mortem will tell. He has been dead a couple of months. Unpleasant corpse to find. And one of the Japanese is deeply disturbed, mumbling in his native language, English now eluding him. How shall Mary cope with him? With appropriate drugs and with Yukio's help as translator, she hopes.

The assembled crowd, not least Jeff, are delighted to see a baby born on board. People mob Sandy, causing her to hide James from curious eyes. Jeff definitely ought to have gone to her cabin first. Now Sandy seems ambivalent toward him. She feels betrayed by him—which he cannot understand. Maybe she feels betrayed by what his seed wrought in her.

"Listen up," Com Sherwin calls out to the assembly. "We came through." And he has maintained his grizzled crewcut between whiles. "We sustained one fatality. Six months' surprise solitary was tough on us all, right?"

"Wrong," Mary interrupts. "Not on me."

Sherwin grins; his blue eyes twinkle. He's effervescent. "Dr. Nolan, we cannot all be psychiatrists."

"That is not what I mean. . . ."

When she has finished speaking, her colleagues stare at her in a silence that continues for quite a while.

"And there's one other thing," Mary adds, moving closer to Sandy and child. "Sandy believes that her baby is trying to speak already, and I think she may be right. . . ."

Two bombshells, the second less appreciated than the first, at least to begin with. Has Mary flipped? is what people are visibly thinking. Eric eyes her with particular concern.

"Do you have any hard proof of this?" Com Sherwin asks. "Not that I'm doubting what you *experienced*. Still, it's a large claim."

"I can't prove it, although it's true. Little James here may throw some light on this, as time goes by, when his larynx shifts. And maybe not."

"Mary, why didn't you tell me this right away?"

"Yeah, why not?" Jeff joins in on Sandy's complaint, to exonerate himself for not thinking to be with her as soon as possible.

"If we could harness this effect—" says someone else. Mary can't see who.

"I don't know that it's something we can harness," she tells whoever. "It was granted to me." "Granted" sounds a bit messianic.

"And to no one else," she hears. "Why not?"

"Maybe it's because of the way I meditated. I emptied myself. Then it was able to communicate."

"And to jump you through time." Resentfully: "Why not us? Didn't you ask the same on our behalf?"

"I didn't *ask* it to jump *me*. I never imagined such a thing was possible."

What Mary has said is at once overwhelming and embarrassing. She's distanced from everyone else, as sole recipient of a revelation and a boon.

Although what strange gift might Sandy have received, in the shape of James?

"I think for the time being we must take what Dr. Nolan says at face value," Sherwin declares judiciously. Quite! Suspicion of lunacy mustn't deprive them of a key medical person. "No doubt what Dr. Nolan has told us will fit into context sooner or later. We'll talk about this at greater length once everything's less confused. Meanwhile, we should inventory the ship, calculate what

we each used and work out how much has come together again—try to get a practical handle on what happened. Something measurable."

Of those present, it transpires that only Sherwin himself and Chika and John the climatologist thought to log
every last item they used by way of food and drink.

"Is that information still in the ship's memory?" asks
Chika.

Indeed, what data *is*, from a hundred separate journeys, fifty years' worth of overlapping auto-logs plus
whatever data individuals may have entered?

Pioneer continues inward toward the position which the
second planet of Tau Ceti will occupy many weeks
hence.

The ship's log contains backup after backup of status
data that seem to vary in only minor respects, occupying
megabytes of memory. Computer has no explanation for
this massive redundancy. It runs diagnostic checks, and
megabytes are dumped into cache. Could Computer be
in any way compromised by an encounter with Dr. Nolan's supposed probability-entity? Apparently not.

Eric works overtime putting the hydroponics area to
rights. Naturally his own Q-space version was maintained in apple pie order. Sad to see it become so chaotic.

"I should have done more," Mary says ruefully.

"Then this would have been two percent tended. It

wouldn't have made a great deal of difference."

"And I didn't know what to do."

"Do you think that announcing your experience straight away was the best course?"

"If I waited longer..."

"... the more difficult it would become?"

"By the way, you guys, I happen to have been contacted by a Higher Entity—but I didn't feel like mentioning this until now. Also by the way, I traveled through time."

"You're probably right. Though now some people are a bit wary of you."

"Does that include you, Eric?"

"Of course not. This must be such a strain for you."

"And you are loyal to your friends. Do you truly believe me?"

"That's an unfair question, Mary. If I had experienced what you experienced—what you *undoubtedly* experienced...."

"There's no doubt in my mind, but that's only *my* mind."

"Is your experience repeatable—I mean, by someone else?"

"We aren't in Q-space any longer."

"On the way back if we all meditate the way you did maybe we can all take a short cut. Or many of us can. That would be a blessing."

"Shall I start up classes in meditation?"

"Ah ... but we might begin colonizing the second planet, depending on what we find."

If that happens, eventually only the flight crew will return *Pioneer* to Earth to bring more material and colonists and frozen embryos and such. Mary's experience may be of no use to the majority of those presently on board. It can be set aside for a long time yet, unconfronted.

Offers flood in to time-share James, but Sandy will have none of them.

Chika Suzuki gives a lecture on his idea of what may have happened, and how it might be avoided in future if only a starship's computer itself could be a quantum computer.

Sum over Paths. Some Overpaths.

"I'd say we experienced traveling a hundred possible paths between the solar system and Tau Ceti. A myriad other paths got explored at the same time, but since those were absurd we could not experience them. If only we could experience the sum over paths collectively together, not separately the way it turned out! Yet that might have been an experience the individual human mind couldn't cope with. All of us experiencing each other's experience. . . ."

Not everyone wishes to marginalize Mary's revelation as something at once too huge and too fugitive to contem-

plate. Dr. Yukio is fascinated. As an insight into a situation where the specialist in afflictions of mind has
herself become afflicted? Chika Suzuki is also enthralled.
What Mary says about the multi-million-year mind of
all Humanity whenever processing information through
its myriad units dead and living and yet unborn—this
stirs his programmer's soul, whether he gives her cre-
dence or not. Likewise, astrophysicist Denise. And a biologist, Maxim Litvinov. And Sophie Garland, another
cybernetics person who is an ordained pastor of the Ec-
umenical Church. Last but not least—perhaps last yet
least as regards stability—there is Hiroaki Horiuchi, the
chemist who flipped during solitude but who is now responding quite well to mental stabilizers and is coherent
in English once again.

Eric, alas, remains ambivalent. In a sense he's a glo-
rified gardener who values neatness and order, nature
methodized, not rampant across the eons and imbued
with some kind of transcendent mentality, at least as
regards the human species. Furthermore, Eric is a no-
frills evolutionist. For him life has no goal other than
life itself in its many forms during all of its eras. Not
that Mary claims that Humanity writ large has any particular goal, yet now that the Higher Entity has inter-
vened—retrospectively as well as in the now and in the
henceforth!—it certainly seems as if some kind of destiny
is implied, or at least an upgrade to a higher level of
existence or state of awareness.

Mary's supporters hold study sessions with her, and Hiro's presence seems therapeutic for him. Exploring Mary's experience helps Hiro come to terms with his own phantoms and demons—though he might be imprinting on Mary emotionally, as his sensei of sanity, or the opposite.

Three of Mary's co-explorers are Japanese. Yukio remarks that his own people feel a strong sense of themselves as a unique collective entity, so they can empathize with the concept of Overlife, Pan-being, or whatever.

The interest of these six does indeed support Mary, otherwise she might be as lonely now as she was during those initial weeks of isolation in Q-space—she might be the specter at the feast of renewed companionship. Even so, sometimes she feels like screaming out to the entity that shifted her through time, *Come back! Please show yourself to more than merely me!*

Meanwhile, Sandy puts a brave face on being mother to a baby who is evidently abnormal, although bursting with health. It's as though a perfectly normal baby has been overwritten by a program that cannot yet run in him—not until he matures a bit more—yet which nevertheless keeps trying to express itself, and testing its environment . . . maybe modifying its environment as it does so, tweaking developmental pathways? Jeff does his best to help nurture their son, frequently taking

James off Sandy's hands—to the botany area and to the rec room. Just as he ought to. Fair dooze, sport. No other couples have yet conceived. Potential parents are awaiting what James may become.

W eeks later, *Pioneer* enters orbit around Tau Ceti 2, eighty kilometers above what is basically a world-ocean girding half a dozen scattered and mottled distorted Australias, all but one of them situated in the temperate zones. The odd one out straddles the north pole and wears an ice cap. River systems are visible, and mountains, one of which is smoking vigorously, an eruption in progress. Elsewhere, a typhoon is blowing. The planet seems lively; not overly so, it's to be hoped. The signatures of vegetation are down below, so at least there is botany. Where there is botany, zoology too? Very likely marine biology at least, but no moon pulls any tides ashore.

After three weeks of intensive global survey work Jay-Jay will pilot Shuttle One, *Beauty*, down to the land mass already dubbed Pizza, the result of a random computer selection from a list of names suggested by all personnel and okayed by Com Sherwin. In time, hopefully, people will be able to feed upon Pizza if its soil proves amenable. Accompanying pilot-geologist Jay-Jay will be Maxim Litvinov, Jeff Lee, and John Dolby, representing life sciences and climate.

To gaze upon an alien world, from the bridge or on-screen, is riveting. Those warped Australias are like presents under the Christmas tree. What exactly is in them? What is the topping on Pizza?

The answer, three weeks later, proves to be weed—thongs, tangles, ribbons, bladders, variously jade-green and rusty-red, bright orange and emerald in the light of Tau Ceti. Suited and helmeted, Maxim describes the scene that is onscreen everywhere throughout *Pioneer*. (The three passengers on *Beauty* had tossed the only coins within light years for the honor of being first-foot on the new world. Pilot excluded. Mustn't risk him.) *Beauty* rests upright on an apron of flat rock amidst assorted vegetation, a vista that looks somewhat like an offshore domain that has been emptied of its water. The actual shore is a couple of kilometers away. Shouldn't be hard to hike there. Some of the weed piles a meter deep but whole stretches are as flat as a pancake.

Cautiously Maxim pokes around with a probe. Amidst a larger mass of weed he soon comes across a number of little hoppers and scuttlers—"they're a bit like fleas and tiny crabs—" and even captures some specimens, before he cuts samples of weed, then bags soil that is variously gritty and sludgy, inhabited by some wriggly tendrils and purple mites.

John descends from *Beauty* to join Maxim, carrying an atmosphere analyzer to confirm orbital readings. This done, Jeff comes bearing a white mouse in a transparent light-weight habitat. Mice are biologically very similar to men. Will the mouse, Litmus, turn virulently red or blue because of hostile microorganisms? Even if nothing obvious happens, in another few days once back on *Pioneer* Litmus will be sacrificed and dissected.

After a day of intensive investigation of the vicinity, next day Maxim and Jeff set off for the seaside under gray clouds. Rain will move in later, though nothing torrential. What will they find? Leviathans cruising offshore like mobile islands? Torpedos with flippers and goggly eyes nursing pups on the beach?

No. No.

"Weed and sand. Pebbles and boulders." As is seen onscreen while Maxim pans his camera.

Some great thongs of weed emerge from the breeze-rippled sea, right across the shore and beyond, like vast creepers that the ocean has rooted upon the land. No wildlife bigger than hoppers and scuttlers and sliders, and nothing in the empty and now melancholy sky.

Presently Jeff fires nets into the sea, one to trawl, the other weighted to dredge. What comes back are floaters and wrigglers and squirmers, none bigger than a little finger.

Back on *Beauty* in its resealed habitat Litmus the mouse is still perky and white.

*   *   *

The day after, Shuttle Two, *Charm*, lands half a world away in a broad river valley on the huge island or mini-continent christened Kansas, somewhat further inland than *Beauty* landed. Weed webs its way from the river over the terrain, yielding to flexible dwarf ribbon-trees and inflated lung-plants. More little hoppers and scuttlers and variations, nothing big.

All in all this is wonderful, if a bit bleak. Here on Tee-Cee, as the planet is coming to be called, is an ecology, primitive but functional. Years ago it was decided that biological contamination of the Tee-Cee environment is of much less consequence than the chance of inhabiting a whole new world, if at all possible. After all, the expedition had cost its partners upward of forty billion dollars. Agronomy experiments get under way, a range of seedlings transplanted directly into the local soil and also into heat-sterilized grit and sludge under protection.

All of this rather puts Mary's revelation and baby James to the back of people's minds, except for the members of the support group consisting of Yukio, Chika, Denise, Hiroaki, and Sophie. Plus an apprehensive Sandy with James in a head-supportive carry-sling. Jeff being down on the surface has robbed her of his help, an unavoidable repeat of his earlier failure to be present. And there's Eric too, although in his case simply out of loyalty. But no Maxim. He's on the surface of Tee-Cee. The eight—or nine, if James is counted—meet in the hydro-ponics section, like conspirators or members of a cult. Maybe their infant messiah is in their midst, albeit in-articulate as yet.

"We are each other," says Hiroaki. "That is the mean-ing. The unity of all human life."

Sophie asks him gently, "Were Adolf Hitler and a rabbi in an extermination camp *united*? What about people waging ruthless war on each other throughout history?"

"If our immune system goes wrong, it can attack our own bodies. But I am talking about lives going way back and stretching far ahead. I am my ancestor and my dis-tant descendant! If we could know the lives of the fu-ture! Pan-Humanity already includes those future lives."

"Future lives haven't yet been lived!" protests Denise. "If we could dip into them now, why, everything is fixed in advance unalterably. It would only be because of our blindness to the future that we bother to do anything at all in the present. No, wait: we couldn't even choose to do, or not to do, something if all is foreordained. Pan-Humanity can't be calculating or thinking or dreaming or doing whatever it does across the millennia unless genuine changes happen within it! Otherwise it would be just one big super-complicated thought, a four-dimensional abacus forever in the same state."

"What *is* its purpose?" asks Mary. "What does it do, what does it dream?"

"Maybe it merely exists," says Eric. "Maybe that's all it does."

"Surely it must come to conclusions. The computing power it has! Using all our billions of brains!"

"Conclusions? Final extinction is conclusion enough. The tree grows, the tree dies."

"Maybe," suggests Chika, "it avoids extinction by being closed in upon itself. Its end and its beginning join together. So it always exists, even though time moves on beyond the epoch of its physical existence."

"Contacting the probability-being must have caused a change—"

"As soon as this happened, it had already happened long ago too—"

"We don't have the minds to understand this—"

"Only the overmind possesses the overview—"

"It must understand existence. Not just experience existence, but *understand* as well—as part of its process of existing—"

"We are all part of God," Sophie declares. "Any highly evolved species is a God in total. Yet we cannot follow God's thoughts. All of us are just little bits of those thoughts."

"The probability-being was a bit more forthcoming!"

"Because you weren't a part of it, Mary. Because you were its modem to our God, our species. It had to exchange signals through you."

"And then it went away, because chatting to me was

probably as interesting as talking to an ant."

"At least it lifted you from one end of the branch to the other."

"So effortlessly. If only our God would do the same for us."

"Maybe," Sophie suggests, "you should pray real strongly, Mary. Sort of meditation with a punch to it."

"What should I pray *for*?"

"For James," says Sandy. "Let him be—"

"—normal?" asks Sophie. "Or gifted with tongues, real soon? So that the babe begins to speak instead of just gurbling at you?"

"I think . . . normal."

"Normal would be a waste, don't you think?"

Sandy sobs. "How long's Jeff going to be down there?"

"It's why we're here."

"Let me take James off your hands for a few hours," offers Sophie, not for the first time.

"No. . . ." Only Jeff is permitted to share her baby, because it is his duty to.

Whatever happens, Sandy seems very unlikely to harm her baby. If she does so in any way, then that is Mary's responsibility. Mary feels she cannot intervene too intrusively, having, as it were, a vested interest.

Some of the seedlings fail, but most survive, even quite a few of those which are fully exposed to the Pizza environment. Some even thrive. Monitor cameras record efforts by hoppers to snack, and one definite quick fatality, although most nibblers quickly hop away into weed. In a bottle of formaldehyde the dead hopper is an amulet of hope. Perhaps. Supposing that hope equates with the superiority, or at least resilience, of organisms from Earth.

Litmus remains perky. *Beauty* returns to *Pioneer*. Time for intensive lab work, and confirmation of results by Computer.

Many tests have been performed, many protocols faithfully obeyed, but there comes a time when a volunteer must personally dip his toe into the bathwater. In the middle of Kansas, Jeff removes his helmet. Computer has approved, although approval is merely advisory. Despite Jeff's best efforts at child-sharing, maybe he is betraying Sandy yet again by being a hero.

The supporters' group join hands in hydroponics and pray for Jeff, even though by now they remember that they are perhaps no longer part of the processes of humanity, being altogether too far away.

"It smells sort of sweet . . . and sort of musty too, a bit like rotting wood."

Jeff breathes for five minutes. No sudden sneezes. Resuming the helmet, he wears it inside *Charm* for three boring hours. Nothing untoward happens to him, so he unsuits. Saliva and mucous swabs and a blood sample taken by Gisela seem normal under the microscope.

"We appear to be lucking out in a big way," Com Sherwin tells everyone.

Charm is the ideal isolated quarantine facility. Jeff and Gisela and tubby agronomist Marcel Reynard and pilot-geologist Werner Schmidt take turns working and exploring outside fully suited. Aboard *Charm* Gisela mixes a fecal sample with a sample of local soil and organisms; some of the organisms die. After a week Jeff ventures outside to breathe the air of Kansas for several hours.

Three days later Jeff drinks boiled, filtered Kansas water. Gisela tests and retests his urine. Two days afterward, he is wearing a coverall rather than a suit when outside. Ungloved, he has already handled samples of vegetation inside the shuttle, and no rashes resulted. Now he handles living vegetation. On the soil he deposits a fecal sample he brought in a bag, marking the spot with a day-glo flag. What may the hoppers and scuttlers and sliders make of this offering if they had any glimmering of true consciousness rather than mere programmed instincts? Evolutionarily speaking, the equivalent of God-like beings have descended from the sky. Next day, inert hoppers and sliders lie nearby—the food of the Gods, or rather the waste products, were too much for them.

James's developmental pathways must indeed have altered; his larynx is descending early. Beware of the risk of him choking. Connections in his brain may be proceeding more rapidly—he looks alert, bright-eyed, on the verge of what exactly? No longer does he attempt in vain to vocalize, as if he has come to some understanding with himself, or of himself. What a patient, amenable baby he is now, and still so young. He stares at his mother, and at Mary too, and at the members of the supporters' club, which is his supporters' club as much as it is Mary's.

The third shuttle, *Color*, has gone down to join *Charm*, to erect a habitat-dome for thirty persons along with a solar power plant and a number of wind-power whirlies.

Only now, perhaps, are many potential colonists beginning to appreciate the full implications of a whole future spent on Tee-Cee. Sure, there will be much scientific stimulation. Sure, there will be a wealth of human cultural resources on tap for entertainment. Sure, more colonists will arrive from Earth within, say, two years at the most, counting in time for mission assessment and the turn-around of *Pioneer*. But oh, the comparative barrenness of Kansas . . . !

"If we go down there . . . ," says Sandy.

"Not if, but when," says Chika. "We didn't actually think this would happen, did we? I confess I didn't, not in my heart. The planet wouldn't be habitable, or there would be alien viruses we couldn't cope with. But it is, and there aren't."

Sophie tries to sound a bright note. "In another hundred years there will be human cities. Networks. People whose *grandparents* were born on Tee-Cee Two."

"For us," says Sandy, "just work work work. A few days' hike in any direction for a working holiday if we're lucky. Lots of trips to the seaside for me. We'll be sacrificing the best of our lives."

"That's why we *came* here," says Mary. "We're *pioneers*. Your Jeff especially."

"Easy for you to say! You won't be stuck here. Com Sherwin is bound to take you back through Q-space in the hope of a shortcut through time for anyone aboard. If that can't be cracked, isn't six months' solitary going to be a bit of a disincentive to those who'll supposedly follow us? Well, isn't it?"

"Do you mean . . . you think there might never *be* another shipload of colonists? Surely not! Even if people are obliged to endure isolation en route, they'll still come. At least they'll know they have a secure destination!"

Eric eyes Mary uneasily. "I wonder if *I'll* be taken back. Normally I would have expected to go back to look after the hydroponics, but there can't be much point if there are eight or so different versions of *Pioneer*. Com Sherwin is almost bound to take you as ship's doctor rather than Yukio."

"Even if I have nobody to doctor but myself? Talk sense."

Eric nods. "Because of your other possibility."

The Commander must be haunted by decisions he has yet to make.

Maybe this is why, after a long and inconclusive interview with Mary months ago, he has not discussed her revelation again with her in any depth. Something new may yet happen to her. Or if not her, then as regards baby James.

D enise has gone to the surface. From now on her astrophysics will be restricted to the close study of Tau Ceti, which is important, of course. Sunspot cycles, the wind from the new sun. Jay-Jay has deployed an instrument platform in orbit for her to uplink with, but habitat-tending work will occupy much of Denise's time.

It'll be another month until a second habitat-dome is erected, and several more whirlies, time enough one hopes for any teething problems with the first habitat to become apparent. Since a habitat does not need to be sealed off fully from the environment, problems should not be too serious. The air and the water freely available down on Tee-Cee Two are such a boon, as is the soil in which crops can grow. Genetic engineering may not be necessary at all. Unprotected fields of lupins may provide fodder, and some beauty. Frozen embryos of pigs, goats, and rabbits may be quickened and brought to term in the artificial wombs all the sooner. And chickens hatched. And ponds dug for carp and trout—and a network of irrigation channels.

James will have chicks and bunnies and piglets as part of his nursery experience.

The pioneers were prepared to provide full protection to the tithe of terrestrial life they brought with them. This would have limited the options. Now, not so.

Sophie conducts a multi-faith ceremony of thanks and blessing, although God is absent, or at least extremely diminutive, if God is the collective superconsciousness of the whole human race.

A husband and wife team, Bjorn and Heidi Svenson, vets who will be in charge of husbandry, visit Mary in the clinic. Heidi has brought a urine sample.

"You're pregnant. Definitely!" Mary tells Heidi joyfully. "Oh, congratulations!"

Turns out to be only a week ago that the Svensons engaged in something of a marathon, six times in two days at mid-month in Heidi's cycle. If James was ever a jinx, that jinx is exorcised now that Tee-Cee promises fertility. In place of a certain apprehension is an eagerness to bear the first child on an alien world. It's early days yet to be sure how viable the Svensons' embryo is, but Heidi does not intend to keep quiet about it. Next day, another husband and wife and a pair of Afro-American partners visit Mary for the same test. The former have not conceived, but the latter have succeeded. With luck James will have peers not too much younger than he is.

Mary and Sophie and Hiroaki and Chika, and inevitably Eric, are taking a coffee break in hydroponics, perching on the sides of plant-troughs, their backs brushing the emerald foliage of carrots and the stalks of tomato plants bowed by bright red globelets.

Sandy comes in at a pace that risks balance-nausea, James swaddled tightly in her arms as if he might fall and break.

"He started speaking—!" She displays her child, who gazes at Sophie, then at Mary.

What the baby says is: "I am a Voice. I answer. Ask me."

And Mary asks, *"What are you?"*

"I am a Voice of the linking to All-Humanity. The echo of the event in what you call Q-space. I am a Voice left behind." *Sandy's baby is actually talking to them.*

Its tones are somewhat squeaky.

"Why were you left behind?"

"As a Guide to what is and what may be."

"Shouldn't we get the Commander here?" butts in Eric.

"Not yet, not yet," says Hiroaki, eager for enlightenment.

A Guide to what is. . . .

"Do you mean," Eric asks, "you can tell us, for example, whether Tee-Cee is as suitable for us to colonize as it seems to be?"

"Maybe the problems are within yourselves. You are all too special. Specialists, multi-specialists. Over-endowment oozes from your fingertips, from the pores of your skin. Better to have sent here a hundred trained peasants or low-caste laborers for whom the work would mean freedom from the restricting past and who would feel like lords. Tee-Cee is weed, water, dirt. Compel a chess grand master to play nothing but checkers for years."

"*Pioneer* will bring more people here in a couple of years—fewer Ph.D.s, more blue-collar types, I guess."

"Sleeping two to a cabin, like animals in an ark? Will you first founders be their superiors, their directors? Even so, the numbers will still be too small."

"Another ship will be built—more ships."

"Requiring four years each, costing forty billion moneys each? Almost bankrupting the backers? Shall the Earth be taxed dry? Only so, if threatened by certain extinction. If your sun is about to flare. If a dark star enters your solar system. If a big comet passes by and will return in a hundred years and strike your Earth."

"We could fire anti-matter at a comet," says Chika. "Completely destroy it while it's still far away."

Within such a short time-frame what threat could be big enough and certain enough?

Mary recalls. "You—or the being you represent—told me that other species do manage to set up colonies by sending generation ships or whatever."

"Perhaps with thousands of persons on board. Perhaps those species command a much larger energy budget than Humanity. You may be too soon. Premature. Your best effort, not big enough."

"I think," says Sophie, "you're looking on the gloomy side. You've been overhearing people having a few last-minute doubts."

A guide to what may be. . . .

"James, can you foretell the future?" asks Hiroaki.

"I can tell what may most probably be," answers the baby. "The most probable paths. Sometime, within infinity, an improbable path becomes actual. How else could the first parent universe arise?"

"Oh kami kami kami," Chika exclaims, "he's a quantum computer. A hand-held quantum computer—and he's an artificial intelligence too! No, I don't mean *artificial*—he's biological, a biological quantum computer. Of course that's what we all are in a limited sense if it's true that quantum effects create our consciousness. . . . But we don't have access to . . . we aren't linked . . . we aren't directly plugged in to the background, the big picture. . . ."

"What he is," says Sophie, "is an *avatar*."

"You mean like the face Computer has, if we want to see a face onscreen?"

"Originally avatar is a Hindu term. For an incarnation of a god, a manifestation."

How cautiously Sandy holds on to what is biologically her son, as though maybe she should lay him down among the tomato plants in case her grasp fails her.

"Does he have powers? Can he make things happen?"

"Ask him," says Sophie, compassionate, apprehensive.

Sandy bows her head over her baby.

"James, can you *do* things? Can you . . . can you make a *bird* appear in here?"

"Mother, I am a Voice, not a Hand that can pluck a creature from one place to another."

"You have hands—two little hands. You do." Carefully she unswaddles a chubby pink baby arm, little fingers, tiny coral nails.

"But I am not a Hand."

"Could you become a Hand?"

"That is a very unlikely path. Then I might not be a Voice."

"Can you see what is happening with Jeff there down on Tau-Cee?"

"I am not an Eye."

Hiroaki interrupts. "Are there any other beings like you that *are* Hands or Eyes?"

James yawns. "I am tired now. This was an effort. I am a baby." His eyes close.

"I got to get a message to Jeff! He must come back!"

"We got to tell the Commander right now," says Chika.

"He's asleep."

"Com Sherwin? How do you know?"

"No. James is asleep."

Sherwin Peterson quickly comes in person to hydroponics after Chika's call.

"Can you wake him up?"

"I don't think we should," says Mary. "He's fatigued. Let him wake in his own time."

"I can hardly doubt the word of five of you...."

Not unless this is some weird hoax, and what would that serve?

The Commander bangs his fist into his palm as if the sudden noise might startle James awake.

"Let me get this straight. He's saying that this expedition is too soon and too few and the wrong sort of people."

That might be the point of the hoax, is a thought which obviously crosses his mind. Psychological sabotage by a small group of conspirators who wish to avoid effectively being marooned down on Tee-Cee. This feeling might spread like an infection. Let's just do the science, then let's pack up and go home in relative comfort. If the baby wakes up and says nothing at all the hoax will be rumbled within a few hours at most. Yet a seed of, yes, mutiny might still have been sown.

"I am ordering you to say nothing about this until I can talk to the baby myself."

How can he enforce his order? A Commander should not issue orders that cannot be enforced.

"I'm appealing to you to keep quiet for a few hours. How long will it be?" A mother should know. And a doctor should know. Oh yes really, a psychiatrist who claims she met an inhabitant of probability, whose voice this baby now is?

"His brain is altered," Mary says. "I don't know how long he needs to sleep after making a big effort. We might harm him."

"This could harm *us*, Doctor, in ways you mightn't imagine!"

"He's a living quantum computer," says Chika. "Maybe James can help you pass through Q-space again without the same isolation. Maybe he can pull the time-jumping trick."

"And maybe *Pioneer* will slide off the edge of the universe. This ship vanishes, and that's the end of star travel. How do you know this baby isn't some sort of virus that Dr. Nolan's famous super-being inserted on board? Better the devil of isolation than a devil we don't know."

Paranoia due to the strain of command? The weight of responsibility for human hopes and for forty billion dollars.

"I think we'll have ample time to find out," says Chika.

The Commander squares himself. "We'll all wait. Right here."

"I have work to attend to, Commander."

"What would that be? Reprogramming the computer to accept input from the virus-baby?"

"Of course not. There's a lot of data from the surface to process."

"No one leaves, and no one enters. Make yourselves comfortable." True to his word, the Commander parks his butt on the edge of the big tomato trough, plucks a ripe tomato, grins, bites into it, sticks his other hand in his pocket.

"James should be lying on my bed," says Sandy. "Wait *here*? He's a bit of a weight. Look, I'll take him to my cabin. I guess we can all fit in there. And that'll be more private."

"I said we wait here."

"Com, that's *unreasonable*."

"In your professional opinion is it lacking in reason?" Sherwin asks Mary. "A sign of insanity? Sufficient grounds for my Second Officer to take over?"

From his pocket, to their astonishment, the Commander pulls a pistol, which he points at Sandy—or at James.

Tightly Sophie says, "I didn't know there were any weapons on *Pioneer*."

"Sure there are. And on the shuttles too. Kept well out of sight, locked away, available in emergency to certain personnel who are sworn to secrecy. What if we encountered actively hostile indigenes on Tee-Cee? What if a hostile alien entity boards the ship? What if that has happened already?"

It is as if a trapdoor has opened, from which blows a very cold draft.

Com Sherwin chews and sucks at the tomato, and regards the five, and slumbering James. Hiroaki is standing tensely as if calculating whether he can disarm Sherwin.

"Commander," says Mary, "if you put the gun away we agree to stay here and never say anything about this. There might be an accident."

"My child," whispers Sandy.

"Ah but is he or ain't he? How much of him is your child if his brain has been tampered with, as you say? Is he even human if he's actually a bio-computer? Some guns came along with us in case of unforeseen emergency. I think this amounts to something of an emergency putting the mission in peril, admittedly in a peculiar way. I would like to be obeyed without argument."

"James may be quite wrong about us being unsuitable settlers."

"In that case, Dr. Nolan, would I let it have a say in how this ship operates in Q-space? As you have just suggested, Dr. Suzuki."

"He may have powers," Sandy says.

"That's exactly what I'm bothered about. You people really are blind. Indulged. Let's be patient, let's not leap to conclusions, let's keep hush. I'm the Commander. Some weird baby isn't."

This is all very unfortunate. Com Sherwin had seemed steady as a rock. An easy-going rock, you might even say. Ten light years distance from Earth is a long thin thread. Thin threads can snap if tugged unexpectedly. He still sounds composed. Does he not understand that producing a gun to enforce authority seriously devalues his position as well as poisoning the atmosphere aboard? A gun, to confront a mother and baby. He is like a King Herod panicked by rumors of a messiah. It is outside of his scope.

"Whatever happens," Mary tells the others, "we mustn't say anything about this. Understood? This is a can of worms." Can she persuade the Commander to accept counseling?

"Perhaps," suggests Sophie, "I should say a prayer to focus us."

No one else wanders into hydroponics. If someone did, would Com Sherwin detain them too at gun point? He whistles to himself monotonously and tunelessly, as if time-keeping, holding the pistol slackly. Occasionally he answers a message on his com. He eats a couple more

tomatoes to sustain himself, a breech of proper conduct—hydroponics is not for anyone to sneak into and
snack—but in the circumstances Eric does not demur.

Mary thinks of Commander Bligh and the *Bounty*.
And of isolated Pitcairn Island, where the mutineers marooned themselves, not to be recontacted until many decades later, while Bligh and his few rowed something
like four thousand miles by dead reckoning to regain
eventually the bosom of authority. An epic journey, almost equivalent to the crossing of light years. In this
case is the Commander the mutineer? On the Pitcairn
Island of Tee-Cee does he maroon his crew while the
officers make their escape?

By his own lights the Commander may be right to
be holding that gun, in case James is a lot more than
they imagine. In case James needs to be killed quickly.

Err on the safe side.

After an hour James wakes. With his gun the Commander motions all but Sandy and her baby well out of
the way. Hiroaki especially.

"Hi there, Kid, I'm the Commander. I hear you found
your voice. That true?"

"I *am* the Voice, Commander."

"I'm kind of upset to hear you cast doubts on our
chances of settling Tee-Cee."

The baby peers at him, focusing. "I am realistic. Too
few, too soon, too concerned with individuality."

"Pardon me that we aren't a hive. Maybe this is Earth's only chance of having our eggs in more than one basket. Question of available resources and politics."

"So you feel obliged to try to succeed."

"Obliged, right. Now what's *your* agenda? Try to dissuade us? Something important about Tee-Cee? In a squillion years might the weedhoppers amount to more than Einstein and Hawking and Mozart? That it?"

"What are Einstein and Hawking and Mozart?"

"I guess their fame hasn't spread much. We aim to remedy that. Any advice about Q-space? How to keep us all together while we're in transit through your realm? How to speed things up a bit?"

"Would you prefer that a hundred different journeys are undertaken by everyone? And only one actuality emerges? The wave fronts of all the other ships collapsing, experienced subjectively as catastrophe, shipwreck in void, the dissolving of substance and life?"

"You could fix that, could you, given access to our computer and the Q-drive controls? Excuse my being confrontational, by the way. Commander's prerogative if a mission seems in danger."

"There are ways to arrange different parameters."

"I guess no one would ever take another Q-space trip if there's a ninety-nine percent likelihood of being annihilated."

"The one percent that prevails becomes one hundred percent. Nothing is actually lost."

"Except that ninety-nine *me*'s experience termination."

"You, who prevail, would not know."

"Okay, I'll take that on board, under advisement. Wouldn't ninety-nine or whatever number of *you* go down kicking and screaming also, in ghost-land?"

"Unimportant. Inessential. The survivor survives. Result: unity. You overvalue the idea of the self."

"There's a real cosmic perspective. Dr. Tate, lay the child down by those carrots, will you?"

"Why should I do that? What's in your mind?"

"Thoughts, Dr. Tate. Muchos thoughts. *Kindly do it now.*"

"I won't. You're mad."

The gun points. "Do it, and nothing bad will happen to you."

"Not to me, but. . . ."

"I'll count to five. At five I pull the trigger."

With greatest reluctance Sandy unslings James.

"Position him so he can see me. Now, back off."

She backs off a pace, another pace. She's tempted to throw herself in between.

"Okay. Voice, can you see me clearly?"

"Yes," says the baby.

"Do you know what this is I'm holding in my hand?"

"A tool that I think can kill."

"Exactly. It fires a bit of metal called a bullet, very fast with a lot of punch. I'm pointing it at your head, which contains your brains. You're an alien infestation. I'm going to count to five and then I'm going to fire."

"Don't do this," begs Sandy. "He needs feeding and changing."

"Should we have a short intermission? No, I don't think so." Sherwin starts to count. James stares at him, neither begging nor flinching. When Sherwin reaches five, he pulls the trigger.

Click.

"Gee, the safety is on. . . ." And immediately, "Now it isn't. But the test is over. He's just a Voice, that's all. Unless he's telepathic, of course, but he gave no signs so far. All right, all relax. I'm sorry about this bit of theater. Had to be sure he doesn't have powers."

"And what," asks Sophie, "if he had vanished the gun from your hand? Sent it into the middle of nowhere? What would you have done then, try to strangle him with your bare hands?"

"No. Been very circumspect. I sincerely apologize, people. Middle of nowhere is where we are, or rather at the other end of nowhere, and that's where *he* comes out of, even if he looks like a baby and poos like a baby, a very disarming disguise. I had to be certain what we're dealing with. Exceptional circumstances call for exceptional reactions. What to ordinary souls may appear to be an irrational reaction, right out of left field, may be inspired and correct."

"A commander has to be decisive," agrees Chika politely.

"I was quoting Linda Bernstein. This brings us back to the problem of damage to morale, and what if anything we might do about rejigging the Q-drive."

"You're actually entertaining the idea?"

"How can I ignore it, Dr. Suzuki? I'm not blinkered."

No, but maybe he is on the edge of himself.

"I think we established something important—the baby's limitations, at least at present."

"You were justified," says James. Healingly, perhaps. Or shrewdly.

The Commander tucks his pistol away.

"Okay, Voice, these different parameters that can be arranged . . . can our ship's personnel all skip ahead through time on the trip back to Earth if we put up with a bit of isolation? Without most versions of us getting extinguished?"

What a gift to science and star travel this will be. And how much more supportive for the settlement on Tee-Cee. Beats harpooning a gas-whale into a cocked hat.

"I am tired again," says the baby.

"Sandy." Bonhomie, now. "For the moment I want you to keep the Voice out of the way of everyone other than those here present. Will you promise this?"

Of course.

The Commander orders *Charm* to carry a final habitat down to Kansas, and a load of supplies. *Beauty* conveys another thirty settlers to the surface. *Pioneer* is becoming quite empty, and proportionately huger, so it seems. The six, and James, remain aboard as though they are engaged in a covert project. Which of them will be sent down at the last moment? Sherwin must at least already have confided in his Second Officer. He is abridging any planned schedule effervescently. A year at Tau Ceti and all the planetary science work? No, the stay in orbit will be measured in months, maybe as few as two, as though Sherwin is now itching to depart, the sooner to return bringing more settlers and equipment. Colonization is the prime priority. This is proceeding more successfully and speedily than anyone had expected—just so long as no one involved in it hears of the Voice's doubts, not for a long while yet. Colonization must be buttressed, reinforced, ASAP. The toehold must become a full deep footprint.

Jeff still does not know about his son's achievement. Jeff is distant now. Undoubtedly Sandy will stay aboard *Pioneer* to care for James. Her oceanography can wait, and Jeff will have to wait.

Conversations with the Voice continue, in Sandy's cabin. Sophie or Mary frequently stay with James to let Sandy off the leash for exercise and a change of scene, as now. Chika and Hiroaki are also helping baby-sit. The bed-couch is crowded.

"So we are all tiny parts of a vast species-overmind?"

"Yes, Mary," says James.

"What does the overmind do? What is its aim? What thoughts does it think?"

"I do not have access to it. I am only the Voice of the Other, left behind."

"Is there any way a person can access our species-overmind directly and comprehensibly?"

Mary thinks of the angel she once saw. The angel was cobwebs and dew and sunlight.

"Being enfolded into its psychospace and becoming fully aware: that is a way."

"What does that mean?"

"Ceasing your life in ongoing space-time. All the billions of lives that ever were remain embedded in its wholeness. Like true dreams. Can you awake lucidly within the dream that was your life, once it has ended? Can you edit the life that was yours? Can you rewrite it? Can you corrupt the data of your history recorded in the psychosphere? This may compel the attention of the overmind."

"Could you help me do this?" asks Mary.

"Perhaps."

"He's talking about you *dying* first!" says Sophie. "He isn't saying that you can report anything at all to the living."

"I am talking," says the Voice, "about myself ceasing along with you after I help hoist your mind."

"Hoist my mind? *How*?"

"I can hypnotize you and, as it were, change mental settings."

"Good thing Com Sherwin isn't hearing *this*," Sophie

says. "But anyway, we're only talking theoretically. *Aren't we, Mary?*"

Mary nods.

"I would volunteer for this," Chika says softly.

"Only Mary Nolan is suitable," the Voice states, "because her mind already linked in Q-space. And a gap was caused. She went ahead in time."

"Oh, kami kami," murmurs Chika.

"If I can edit my life-data after I die," asks Mary, "do I alter the real events that occurred?"

"Skeins may unravel and reform, within limitations. Threads will shift. A different probability will manifest. The large pattern will remain similar."

"It *is* like time-travel, isn't it? A sort of time-travel? I go back and I do something a bit differently."

"You adjust what already happened and what resulted. Within limits."

"And if the overmind does not agree?"

"It must focus upon you. You who are part of it."

"Can I focus *it* upon what happens in the real world?"

"I do not know this. My brain heats. I am tired. I must cool."

The final shuttle trips come so soon. *Pioneer* almost empties its stores of supplies. Chika and Yukio, Sophie and Hiroaki are to become settlers.

Hiroaki hangs himself in his cabin. In the partial gravity his strangulation may have taken a while, and perhaps this was his plan—to approach death more slowly so that the boundary between life and death might become as blurred as his vision, allowing him to slip through, to be both dead and alive at once for a while so that he might enfold into psychospace while still fractionally aware. He too was touched by what transpired in Q-space. To a certain extent Hiroaki's mental settings had been changed. Or perhaps he could not bear to be exiled on Tee-Cee, away from the Voice, or from Mary who may attain a kind of satori, if not in this life then in the data-dream-stream of her life, the eddies within the vast river of the overmind.

Hiroaki's death is a shock. Still: balance of his mind tragically disturbed ever since isolation in Q-space. After a brief service conducted by Sophie, his body joins that of Greg Fox in cold store. Sending bodies down to be buried on Tee-Cee would not be a good omen.

"What did the Voice tell him?" Com Sherwin wants to know. Has to be something to do with James.

Mary confesses to the Commander. "I think Hiroaki got the idea that he might be able to contact the overmind by dying, because he was touched by it in Q-space."

"Touched, as in loony . . . ?"

"Maybe he couldn't bear to be separated from. . . ."

"From his therapist?"

"No, from what may happen in Q-space the next time."

*   *   *

Pioneer is outward bound. Farewells have been said. In an entirely literal way: fare extremely well ... until the starship returns. Which it will, there's no doubting. Especially, don't doubt yourselves. *Charm* has been left in Kansas, almost like an emergency survival hut that can be sealed off, though of course will never need to be. Or like an escape route, admittedly an escape to nowhere. Even so, more reassuring than otherwise: a visible link to space and wider horizons, an earnest of more technology due to come. The settlers will now need to acquire a different mind-set, vigorous yet also patient.

Jeff could not understand why Sandy was not joining him. There's one of the settlers already feeling isolated, betrayed as if in tit-for-tat. Although in the end Jeff seemed resigned. Sandy herself cried and needed comforting.

On board are Mary, Sandy and James, and Eric of hydroponics, Com Sherwin and his Second, Max Muller, Engineer Sam Nakata, Navigator Nellie van Torn, Comp and ship-systems manager Bill Brooks, and shuttle pilot Dan Addison. Ten souls, or nine plus something else.

C om Sherwin is in several minds.
The Voice has decided that if Computer reprograms the Q-drive in such and such a way, then each traveler will find himself or herself accompanied by a copy of the Voice.

How can James be in nine places at once—until, at journey's end, he becomes a single person again? He is not any ordinary baby. He is a child of reality and probability.

The journey time can be shortened considerably—not by time-jumping such as benefited Mary, but by "compression," which James cannot explain in comprehensible words. The result should be a journey time of one month rather than six.

It may be that James's entangled presence will permit a limited amount of communication between the otherwise isolated stellanauts, via him, although such messages may be unreliable, even if comforting. Or otherwise.

Of course, him being an infant, albeit an infant prodigy, his copies will need caring for. How well up on the care of infants are Com Sherwin, Max Muller, Dan Addison . . . ?

The downside is that there will be phantom journeys too, otherwise there would not be enough paths to sum over.

The voice likens those phantom journeys to you standing between two mirrors and beholding repeated reflections of yourself diminishing and disappearing into the distance. The first five or six reflections certainly seem like authentic representations; thereafter you become increasingly vague and distant. Thus it will feel to the phantoms. Seven or so will feel like you, and will disperse when you—*or one of the others*—exits from Q-space. Others will not possess enough substance to experience more than a dream-like state, the unraveling of which will hardly be too traumatic.

So there's about a one-in-eight chance that you personally will reintegrate. Seven echoes will hope for this but fail to achieve it. Much better odds than one in a hundred—though even so!

Mary has slightly better odds. If she tosses a dice to decide whether to euthanize herself and James while in Q-space so as to enfold herself into psychospace—by far the best way to choose, namely by chance—and if one of her selves does indeed toss the number for death, then one of her will definitely die but will not have lived in vain, and one of the remainder will survive.

A link may even endure between her dead self and her living self, so the Voice surmises.

"So," says Com Sherwin to those who are all gathered in the restaurant, "do we go for it?"

Is he recollecting the dive of *The Dart* into Jupiter and the harpooning of the gas-whale? *Do I go for it or do I not?*

"I'd like an advisory show of hands. Purely advisory for the moment."

The dissenters are Sam Nakata, Nellie van Tom, and Bill Brooks—engineering, navigation, and computer systems respectively. Com Sherwin may or may not have prevailed previously upon his Second, Max Muller. As a pilot Dan Addison has coped with risks before, and he's rather too extravert to endure another spell of six months all on his own. Mary and Sandy and Eric are united in going for it, although are their votes quite equal in weight to engineering or navigation?

"Well," says Sherwin, "that's five to three in favor, ignoring myself and the Voice."

"Commander," says Sam Nakata, "we have absolutely no reason to opt for this, this *experiment*—on the say-so of a baby! It's our duty to take *Pioneer* back through Q-space by a route that demonstrably succeeds. If that involves six months alone, we already hacked it once. At least this time we're forewarned."

"Obviously he's no ordinary baby. But more to the point, if we cut the journey time by five months each way, that's almost one year sooner we can bring more people and equipment to Tee-Cee. Imagine returning and finding the colony falling apart because we didn't take the fast route. I think *that* bears thinking seriously about."

"Yes. It does. *If*."

"We shouldn't worry about some of us not arriving," says Sandy, "so long as one of each does. We won't know anything about the ones who don't arrive."

"Plenty of fish in the probability sea, eh?" remarks Nellie van Torn. "I don't *like* to think of five of me evaporating, especially if the one who evaporates is *me*."

"It's an identity problem," says Bill Brooks surprisingly. "If you could copy your mind into an android, say while you're unconscious, and if the act of mind-scanning erases your brain, is the android simply continuing your own life? The android will certainly feel as though it's doing so, indistinguishably. If you were dying of terminal cancer you would opt for this continuation, wouldn't you?"

"Are you changing your informal vote?" asks Com Sherwin.

"I don't like to think that I may be putting ninety-odd other people in jeopardy just because of qualms about myself, when actually my self will survive intact in one version or another."

There is much to mull over. Mary begins giving classes on the medical aspects of infant care, and Sandy on the practical details. James begins hypnotizing Mary.

The time has come. Nellie and Sam have agreed under protest. Computer has accepted complex instructions from James who has crawled and is now taking his first precocious steps. He's also toilet-trained and able to eat mashed pap. In view of his huge linguistic skills he oughtn't to be much bother to look after. On the contrary, a valuable companion.

Mary lies in her cabin.

"Sixty seconds to Q-insertion. . . ."

"Thirty seconds. . . ."

"Fifteen. . . ."

The seconds pass, the cabin ripples, silence from the speakers.

She is alone with the Voice.

"Can you contact Sandy, Voice?"

The Voice's eyes grow glazed.

"Hi Mary, Sandy and James here, James and Sandy here, We're here. I hear you, You already said, You called me just now—"

Six or seven Sandys are talking through James's lips one after another, all saying much the same thing, wherever *here* may be. Certainly isn't this cabin. A babble of ghosts. These may be difficult conversations to keep up.

"Can you contact *me myself*, Voice? I mean, another me?"

James concentrates.

Presently: "*When* are we going to do it?" Commit suicide, and Jamesicide—she knows what she means.

"Should we all do it at the same time?"

"Is that really me?"

"We never got a chance like this to discuss things."

"We talked to ourself in Q-space before, but this is very different!"

"Hey, what about our Hippocratic Oath?"

Babel, from James's lips. The nine voices of Mary. Beats schizophrenia any day. This procedure offers very little counsel or comfort, and is perhaps a Bad Idea.

Q + 3. She needn't feel isolated in the ship. She can summon up voices—but it is better not to hear them. Better to be alone with James, the better to concentrate her mind, in case it might fly apart. Doubtless her other selves have decided likewise, since they do not call her. Several Com Sherwins do call, wanting status reports. What is the point of them asking for those? Perfectionism? Several Erics also call, wishing her well, better, best. James is with everyone.

Q + 4. Do it today. Today is a perfectly fine day to end one's life. *One's* life? What if all of the Maries roll a four, unlucky number in the minds of the Japanese because *shi* which means four also means death, thank you for that knowledge, Hiroaki. What if all or none roll a four? Is Maries the plural of Mary?

She has brought overdoses of morphine from the dispensary, morphine to send one to sleep, a very deep sleep.

"Are you ready, Voice? Any last wishes? Some mashed carrots?"

Mary is an Angel in a woodland by a tiny lake. And she is also Mary who sees the Angel and now understands what she sees. Her vision spans forward—inside a starship a dark-haired athletic woman is grinning at her.

"To be really aboard at last? Great! Ah, do you mean the motion . . . ? It's okay." The woman swings her head friskily. "Oops."

Switching her attention, Mary sinks to her knees amongst the bushes aglitter with spiders' webs.

"Overmind, Overmind!" The words seem like the start of a prayer, a prayer that can perhaps be answered.

Com Sherwin's voice comes briskly. "Hear me. Re-emergence from Q-space achieved. We're in the home system—we're home. Crew present on bridge: Muller, Nakata, van Torn, and Brook, and me. Call in please in order: Nolan, Tate, Festa, Addison. Nolan?"

"Present, Commander."

Oh yes, what a present. She is alive. Alive.

"Tate?"

Sandy's voice comes over the speaker. "Present. So is James."

James the Voice. James the Link. James the Knowledge.

Eric and Dan Addison also report in.

Glimpses of eons of human experience crash in upon kneeling Mary, rocking her. Billions of souls batter at her like a plague of butterflies. Bird-song sounds like the high-speed warble of data-flow from which an audible message may somehow emerge, if only it can step down to her level.

And she feels such a twinge within, somewhere in her belly, as the glimpses flee, and the butterflies vanish, and the bird-song hushes.

She knows that inside her is the beginning of a Voice.

THE DOG SAID BOW-WOW

MICHAEL SWANWICK

THE DOG LOOKED AS if he had just stepped out of a children's book. There must have been a hundred physical adaptations required to allow him to walk upright. The pelvis, of course, had been entirely re-shaped. The feet alone would have needed dozens of changes. He had knees, and knees were tricky.

To say nothing of the neurological enhancements.

But what Darger found himself most fascinated by was the creature's costume. His suit fit him perfectly, with a slit in the back for the tail, and—again—a hundred invisible adaptations that caused it to hang on his body in a way that looked perfectly natural.

"You must have an extraordinary tailor," Darger said.

The dog shifted his cane from one paw to the other, so they could shake, and in the least affected manner imaginable replied, "That is a common observation, sir."

"You're from the States?" It was a safe assumption, given where they stood—on the docks—and that the schooner *Yankee Dreamer* had sailed up the Thames with the morning tide. Darger had seen its bubble sails over the rooftops, like so many rainbows. "Have you found lodgings yet?"

"Indeed I am, and no I have not. If you could recommend a tavern of the cleaner sort?"

"No need for that. I would be only too happy to put you up for a few days in my own rooms." And lowering his voice, Darger said, "I have a business proposition to put to you."

"Then lead on, sir, and I shall follow you with a right good will."

The dog's name was Sir Blackthorpe Ravenscairn de Plus Precieux, but "Call me Sir Plus," he said with a self-denigrating smile, and "Surplus" he was ever after.

Surplus was, as Darger had at first glance suspected and by conversation confirmed, a bit of a rogue—something more than mischievous and less than a cut-throat. A dog, in fine, after Darger's own heart.

Over drinks in a public house, Darger displayed his box and explained his intentions for it. Surplus warily touched the intricately carved teak housing, and then drew away from it. "You outline an intriguing scheme, Master Darger—"

"Please. Call me Aubrey."

"Aubrey, then. Yet here we have a delicate point. How shall we divide up the . . . ah, *spoils* of this enterprise? I hesitate to mention this, but many a promising partnership has foundered on precisely such shoals."

Darger unscrewed the salt cellar and poured its contents onto the table. With his dagger, he drew a fine line down the middle of the heap. "I divide—you choose. Or the other way around, if you please. From self-interest, you'll not find a grain's difference between the two."

"Excellent!" cried Surplus and, dropping a pinch of salt in his beer, drank to the bargain.

It was raining when they left for Buckingham Labyrinth. Darger stared out the carriage window at the drear streets and worn buildings gliding by and sighed. "Poor, weary old London! History is a grinding-wheel that has been applied too many a time to thy face."

"It is also," Surplus reminded him, "to be the making of our fortunes. Raise your eyes to the Labyrinth, sir, with its soaring towers and bright surface rising above these shops and flats like a crystal mountain rearing up out of a ramshackle wooden sea, and be comforted."

"That is fine advice," Darger agreed. "But it cannot comfort a lover of cities, nor one of a melancholic turn of mind."

"Pah!" cried Surplus, and said no more until they arrived at their destination.

At the portal into Buckingham, the sergeant-interface strode forward as they stepped down from the carriage. He blinked at the sight of Surplus, but said only, "Papers?"

Surplus presented the man with his passport and the credentials Darger had spent the morning forging, then added with a negligent wave of his paw, "And this is my autistic."

The sergeant-interface glanced once at Darger, and forgot about him completely. Darger had the gift, priceless to one in his profession, of a face so nondescript that once someone looked away, it disappeared from that person's consciousness forever. "This way, sir. The officer of protocol will want to examine these himself.

A dwarf savant was produced to lead them through the outer circle of the Labyrinth. They passed by ladies in bioluminescent gowns and gentlemen with boots and gloves cut from leathers cloned from their own skin. Both women and men were extravagantly bejeweled— for the ostentatious display of wealth was yet again in fashion—and the halls were lushly dad and pillared in marble, porphyry, and jasper. Yet Darger could not help noticing how worn the carpets were, how chipped and sooted the oil lamps. His sharp eye espied the remains of an antique electrical system, and traces as well of telephone lines and fiber optic cables from an age when those technologies were yet workable.

These last he viewed with particular pleasure.

The dwarf savant stopped before a heavy black door

carved over with gilt griffins, locomotives, and fleurs-de-lis. "This is a door," he said. "The wood is ebony. Its binomial is *Diospyros ebenum*. It was harvested in Serendip. The gilding is of gold. Gold has an atomic weight of 197.2."

He knocked on the door and opened it.

The officer of protocol was a dark-browed man of imposing mass. He did not stand for them. "I am Lord Coherence-Hamilton, and this—" he indicated the slender, clear-eyed woman who stood beside him—"is my sister, Pamela."

Surplus bowed deeply to the Lady, who dimpled and dipped a slight curtsey in return.

The Protocol Officer quickly scanned the credentials. "Explain these fraudulent papers, sirrah. The Demesne of Western Vermont! Damn me if I have ever heard of such a place."

"Then you have missed much," Surplus said haughtily. "It is true we are a young nation, created only seventy-five years ago during the Partition of New England. But there is much of note to commend our fair land. The glorious beauty of Lake Champlain. The gene-mills of Winooski, that ancient seat of learning the *Universitas Viridis Montis* of Burlington, the Technarchaeological Institute of—" He stopped. "We have much to be proud of, sir, and nothing of which to be ashamed."

The bearlike official glared suspiciously at him, then said, "What brings you to London? Why do you desire an audience with the queen?"

"My mission and destination lie in Russia. However, England being on my itinerary and I a diplomat, I was charged to extend the compliments of my nation to your monarch." Surplus did not quite shrug. "There is no more to it than that. In three days I shall be in France, and you will have forgotten about me completely."

Scornfully, the officer tossed his credentials to the savant, who glanced at and politely returned them to Surplus. The small fellow sat down at a little desk scaled to his own size and swiftly made out a copy. "Your papers will be taken to Whitechapel and examined there. If everything goes well—which I doubt—and there's an opening—not likely—you'll be presented to the queen sometime between a week and ten days hence."

"Ten days! Sir, I am on a very strict schedule!"

"Then you wish to withdraw your petition?"

Surplus hesitated. "I . . . I shall have to think on't, sir."

Lady Pamela watched coolly as the dwarf savant led them away.

The room they were shown to had massively framed mirrors and oil paintings dark with age upon the walls, and a generous log fire in the hearth. When their small guide had gone, Darger carefully locked and bolted the door. Then he tossed the box onto the bed, and bounced down alongside it. Lying flat on his back, staring up at the ceiling, he said, "The Lady Pamela is a strikingly beautiful woman. I'll be damned if she's not."

Ignoring him, Surplus locked paws behind his back, and proceeded to pace up and down the room. He was full of nervous energy. At last, he expostulated, "This is a deep game you have gotten me into, Darger! Lord Coherence-Hamilton suspects us of all manner of black-guardry,"

"Well, and what of that?"

"I repeat myself: We have not even begun our play yet, and he suspects us already! I trust neither him nor his genetically remade dwarf."

"You are in no position to be displaying such vulgar prejudice."

"I am not *bigoted* about the creature, Darger, I *fear* him! Once let suspicion of us into that macroencephalic head of his, and he will worry at it until he has found out our every secret."

"Get a grip on yourself Surplus! Be a man! We are in this too deep already to back out. Questions would be asked, and investigations made."

"I am anything but a man, thank God," Surplus replied. "Still, you are right. In for a penny, in for a pound. For now, I might as well sleep. Get off the bed. You can have the hearth-rug."

"I! The rug!"

"I am groggy of mornings. Were someone to knock, and I to unthinkingly open the door, it would hardly do to have you found sharing a bed with your master."

The next day, Surplus returned to the Office of Protocol to declare that he was authorized to wait as long as two weeks for an audience with the queen, though not a day more.

"You have received new orders from your government?" Lord Coherence-Hamilton asked suspiciously. "I hardly see how."

"I have searched my conscience, and reflected on certain subtleties of phrasing in my original instructions," Surplus said. "That is all."

He emerged from the office to discover Lady Pamela waiting outside. When she offered to show him the Labyrinth, he agreed happily to her plan. Followed by Darger, they strolled inward, first to witness the changing of the guard in the forecourt vestibule, before the great pillared wall that was the front of Buckingham Palace before it was swallowed up in the expansion of architecture during the mad, glorious years of Utopia. Following which, they proceeded toward the viewer's gallery above the chamber of state.

"I see from your repeated glances that you are interested in my diamonds, 'Sieur Plus Precieux,' " Lady Pamela said. "Well might you be. They are a family treasure, centuries old and manufactured to order, each stone flawless and perfectly matched. The indentures of a hundred autistics would not buy the like."

Surplus smiled down again at the necklace, draped

about her lovely throat and above her perfect breasts. "I assure you, madame, it was not your necklace that held me so enthralled."

She colored delicately, pleased. Lightly, she said, "And that box your man carries with him wherever you go? What is in it?"

"That? A trifle. A gift for the Duke of Muscovy, who is the ultimate object of my journey," Surplus said. "I assure you, it is of no interest whatsoever."

"You were talking to someone last night," Lady Pamela said. "In your room."

"You were listening at my door? I am astonished and flattered."

She blushed. "No, no, my brother . . . it is his job, you see, surveillance."

"Possibly I was talking in my sleep. I have been told I do that occasionally."

"In accents? My brother said he heard two voices."

Surplus looked away. "In that, he was mistaken."

England's queen was a sight to rival any in that ancient land. She was as large as the lorry of ancient legend, and surrounded by attendants who hurried back and forth, fetching food and advice and carrying away dirty plates and signed legislation. From the gallery, she reminded Darger of a queen bee, but unlike the bee, this queen did not copulate, but remained proudly virgin.

Her name was Gloriana the First, and she was a hundred years old and still growing.

Lord Campbell-Supercollider, a friend of Lady Pamela's met by chance, who had insisted on accompanying them to the gallery, leaned close to Surplus and murmured, "You are impressed, of course, by our queen's magnificence." The warning in his voice was impossible to miss. "Foreigners invariably are."

"I am dazzled," Surplus said.

"Well might you be. For scattered through her majesty's great body are thirty-six brains, connected with thick ropes of ganglia in a hypercube configuration. Her processing capacity is the equal of many of the great computers from Utopian times."

Lady Pamela stifled a yawn. "Darling Rory," she said, touching the Lord Campbell-Supercollider's sleeve. "Duty calls me. Would you be so kind as to show my American friend the way back to the outer circle?"

"Or course, my dear." He and Surplus stood (Darger was, of course, already standing) and paid their compliments. Then, when Lady Pamela was gone and Surplus started to turn toward the exit, "Not that way. Those stairs are for commoners. You and I may leave by the gentlemen's staircase."

The narrow stairs twisted downward beneath clouds of gilt cherubs-and-airships, and debouched into a marble-floored hallway. Surplus and Darger stepped out of the stairway and found their arms abruptly seized by baboons.

There were five baboons all told, with red uniforms

and matching choke collars with leashes that gathered in the hand of an ornately mustached officer whose gold piping identified him as a master of apes. The fifth baboon bared his teeth and hissed savagely.

Instantly, the master of apes yanked back on his leash and said, "There, Hercules! There, sirrah! What do you do? What do you say?"

The baboon drew himself up and bowed curtly. "Please come with us," he said with difficulty. The master of apes cleared his throat. Sullenly, the baboon added, "Sir."

"This is outrageous!" Surplus cried. "I am a diplomat, and under international law immune to arrest."

"Ordinarily, sir, this is true," said the master of apes courteously. "However, you have entered the inner circle without her majesty's invitation and are thus subject to stricter standards of security."

"I had no idea these stairs went inward. I was led here by—" Surplus looked about helplessly. Lord Campbell-Supercollider was nowhere to be seen.

So, once again, Surplus and Darger found themselves escorted to the Office of Protocol.

"The wood is teak. Its binomial is, *Tectonia grandis*. Teak is native to Burma, Hind, and Siam. The box is carved elaborately but without refinement." The dwarf savant opened it. "Within the casing is an archaic device for electronic intercommunication. The instrument chip is a gallium-arsenide ceramic. The chip weighs six ounces. The device is a product of the Utopian end-times."

"A modem!" The protocol officer's eyes bugged out. "You dared bring a *modem* into the inner circle and almost into the presence of the queen?" His chair stood and walked around the table. Its six insectile legs looked too slender to carry his great, legless mass. Yet it moved nimbly and well.

"It is harmless, sir. Merely something our technarchaeologists unearthed and thought would amuse the Duke of Muscovy, who is well known for his love of all things antiquarian. It is, apparently, of some cultural or historical significance, though without re-reading my instructions, I would be hard pressed to tell you what."

Lord Coherence-Hamilton raised his chair so that he loomed over Surplus, looking dangerous and domineering. "*Here* is the historic significance of your modem: The Utopians filled the world with their computer webs and nets, burying cables and nodes so deeply and plentifully that they shall never be entirely rooted out. They then released into that virtual universe demons and mad gods. These intelligences destroyed Utopia and almost destroyed humanity as well. Only the valiant worldwide destruction of all modes of interface saved us from annihilation!" He glared.

"Oh, you lackwit! Have you no history? These creatures hate us because our ancestors created them. They are still alive, though confined to their electronic netherworld, and want only a modem to extend themselves into the physical realm. Can you wonder, then, that the penalty for possessing such a device is—" he smiled menacingly—"death?"

"No, sir, it is not. Possession of a *working* modem is a mortal crime. This device is harmless. Ask your savant."

"Well?" the big man growled at his dwarf. "Is it functional?"

"No. It—"

"Silence." Lord Coherence-Hamilton turned back to Surplus. "You are a fortunate cur. You will not be charged with any crimes. However, while you are here; I will keep this filthy device locked away and under my control. Is that understood, Sir Bow-Wow?"

Surplus sighed. "Very well," he said. "It is only for a week, after all."

That night, the Lady Pamela Coherence-Hamilton came by Surplus's room to apologize for the indignity of his arrest, of which, she assured him, she had just now learned. He invited her in. In short order they somehow found themselves kneeling face-to-face on the bed, unbuttoning each other's clothing.

Lady Pamela's breasts had just spilled delightfully from her dress when she drew back, clutching the bodice closed again, and said, "Your man is watching us."

"And what concern is that to us?" Surplus said jovially. "The poor fellow's an autistic. Nothing he sees or hears matters to him. You might as well be embarrassed by the presence of a chair."

"Even were he a wooden carving, I would his eyes were not on me."

"As you wish." Surplus clapped his paws. "Sirrah! Turn around."

Obediently, Darger turned his back. This was his first experience with his friend's astonishing success with women. How many sexual adventuresses, he wondered, might one tumble, if one's form were unique? On reflection, the question answered itself.

Behind him, he heard the Lady Pamela giggle. Then, in a voice low with passion, Surplus said, "No, leave the diamonds on."

With a silent sigh, Darger resigned himself to a long night. Since he was bored and yet could not turn to watch the pair cavorting on the bed without giving himself away, he was perforce required to settle for watching them in the mirror.

They began, of course, by doing it doggy-style.

The next day, Surplus fell sick. Hearing of his indisposition, Lady Pamela sent one of her autistics with a bowl of broth and then followed herself in a surgical mask.

Surplus smiled weakly to see her. "You have no need of that mask," he said. "By my life, I swear that what ails me is not communicable. As you doubtless know, we who have been remade are prone to endocrinological imbalance."

"Is that all?" Lady Pamela spooned some broth into his mouth, then dabbed at a speck of it with a napkin. "Then fix it. You have been very wicked to frighten me over such a trifle."

"Alas," Surplus said sadly, "I am a unique creation, and my table of endocrine balances was lost in an accident at sea. There are copies in Vermont, of course. But by the time even the swiftest schooner can cross the Atlantic twice, I fear me I shall be gone."

"Oh, dearest Surplus!" The Lady caught up his paws in her hands. "Surely there is some measure, however desperate, to be taken?"

"Well . . ." Surplus turned to the wall in thought. After a very long time, he turned back and said, "I have a confession to make. The modem your brother holds for me? It is functional."

"Sir!" Lady Pamela stood, gathering her skirts, and stepped away from the bed in horror. "Surely not!"

"My darling and delight, you must listen to me." Surplus glanced weakly toward the door, then lowered his voice. "Come close and I shall whisper."

She obeyed.

"In the waning days of Utopia, during the war between men and their electronic creations, scientists and engineers bent their efforts toward the creation of a modem that could be safely employed by humans. One immune from the attack of demons. One that could, indeed, compel their obedience. Perhaps you have heard of this project."

"There are rumors, but . . . no such device was ever built."

"Say rather that no such device was built *in time*. It had just barely been perfected when the mobs came rampaging through the laboratories, and the Age of the Machine was over. Some few, however, were hidden away before the last technicians were killed. Centuries later, brave researchers at the Technarchaeological Institute of Shelburne recovered six such devices and mastered the art of their use. One device was destroyed in the process. Two are kept in Burlington. The others were given to trusted couriers and sent to the three most powerful allies of the Demesne—one of which is, of course, Russia."

"This is hard to believe," Lady Pamela said wonderingly. "Can such marvels be?"

"Madame, I employed it two nights ago in this very room! Those voices your brother heard? I was speaking with my principals in Vermont. They gave me permission to extend my stay here to a fortnight."

He gazed imploringly at her. "If you were to bring me the device, I could then employ it to save my life."

Lady Coherence-Hamilton resolutely stood. "Fear nothing, then. I swear by my soul, the modem shall be yours tonight."

*   *   *

The room was lit by a single lamp that cast wild shadows whenever anyone moved, as if of illicit spirits at a witch's Sabbath.

It was an eerie sight. Darger, motionless, held the modem in his hands. Lady Pamela, who had a sense of occasion, had changed to a low-cut gown of clinging silks, dark-red as human blood. It swirled about her as she hunted through the wainscoting for a jack left unused for centuries. Surplus sat up weakly in bed, eyes half-closed, directing her. It might have been, Darger thought, an allegorical tableau of the human body being directed by its sick animal passions, while the intellect stood by, paralyzed by lack of will.

"There!" Lady Pamela triumphantly straightened, her necklace scattering tiny rainbows in the dim light.

Darger stiffened. He stood perfectly still for the length of three long breaths, then shook and shivered like one undergoing seizure. His eyes rolled back in his head.

In hollow, unworldly tones, he said, "What man calls me up from the vasty deep?" It was a voice totally unlike his own, one harsh and savage and eager for unholy sport. "Who dares risk my wrath?"

"You must convey my words to the autistic's ears," Surplus murmured. "For he is become an integral part of the modem—not merely its operator, but its voice."

"I stand ready," Lady Pamela replied.

"Good girl. Tell it who I am."

"It is Sir Blackthorpe Ravenscairn de Plus Precieux who speaks, and who wishes to talk to . . ." She paused.

"To his most august and socialist honor, the mayor of Burlington."

"His most august and socialist honor," Lady Pamela began. She turned toward the bed and said quizzically, "The mayor of Burlington?"

" 'Tis but an official title, much like your brother's, for he who is in fact the spy-master for the Demesne of Western Vermont," Surplus said weakly. "Now repeat to it: I compel thee on threat of dissolution to carry my message. Use those exact words."

Lady Pamela repeated the words into Darger's ear.

He screamed. It was a wild and unholy sound that sent the Lady skittering away from him in a momentary panic. Then, in mid-cry, he ceased.

"Who is this?" Darger said in an entirely new voice, this one human. "You have the voice of a woman. Is one of my agents in trouble?"

"Speak to him now, as you would to any man: forthrightly, directly, and without evasion." Surplus sank his head back on his pillow and closed his eyes.

So (as it seemed to her) the Lady Coherence-Hamilton explained Surplus' plight to his distant master, and from him received both condolences and the needed information to return Surplus's endocrine levels to a functioning harmony. After proper courtesies, then, she thanked the American spy-master and unjacked the modem. Darger returned to passivity.

The leather-cased endocrine kit lay open on a small table by the bed. At Lady Pamela's direction, Darger began applying the proper patches to various places on Surplus's body. It was not long before Surplus opened his eyes.

"Am I to be well?" he asked and, when the Lady nodded, "Then I fear I must be gone in the morning. Your brother has spies everywhere. If he gets the least whiff of what this device can do, he'll want it for himself."

Smiling, Lady Pamela hoisted the box in her hand. "Indeed, who can blame him? With such a toy, great things could be accomplished."

"So he will assuredly think. I pray you, return it to me."

She did not. "This is more than just a communication device, sir," she said. "Though in that mode it is of incalculable value. You have shown that it can enforce obedience on the creatures that dwell in the forgotten nerves of the ancient world. Ergo, they can be compelled to do our calculations for us."

"Indeed, so our technarchaeologists tell us. You must. . . ."

"We have created monstrosities to perform the duties that were once done by machines. But with *this*, there would be no necessity to do so. We have allowed our-

selves to be ruled by an icosahexadexal-brained freak.
Now we have no need for Gloriana the Gross, Gloriana
the Fat and Grotesque, Gloriana the Maggot Queen!"

"Madame!"

"It is time, I believe, that England had a new queen.
A human queen."

"Think of my honor!"

Lady Pamela paused in the doorway. "You are a very
pretty fellow indeed. But with this, I can have the mon-
archy and keep such a harem as will reduce your memory to that of a passing and trivial fancy."

With a rustle of skirts, she spun away.

"Then I am undone!" Surplus cried, and fainted onto
the bed.

Quietly, Darger closed the door. Surplus raised himself from the pillows, began removing the patches from
his body, and said, "Now what?"

"Now we get some sleep," Darger said. "Tomorrow
will be a busy day."

The master of apes came for them after breakfast, and
marched them to their usual destination. By now, Darger
was beginning to lose track of exactly how many times
he had been in the Office of Protocol. They entered to
find Lord Coherence-Hamilton in a towering rage, and
his sister, calm and knowing, standing in a corner with
her arms crossed, watching. Looking at them both now,
Darger wondered how he could ever have imagined that
the brother outranked his sister.

The modem lay opened on the dwarf-savant's desk. The little fellow leaned over the device, studying it minutely.

Nobody said anything until the master of apes and his baboons had left. Then Lord Coherence-Hamilton roared, "Your modem refuses to work for us!"

"As I told you, sir," Surplus said coolly, "it is inoperative."

"That's a bold-arsed fraud and a goat-buggering lie!" In his wrath, the Lord's chair rose up on its spindly legs so high that his head almost bumped against the ceiling. "I know of your activities—" he nodded toward his sister—"and demand that you show us how this whoreson device works!"

"Never!" Surplus cried stoutly. "I have my my honor, sir."

"Your honor, too scrupulously insisted upon, may well lead to your death, sir."

Surplus threw back his head. "Then I die for Vermont!"

At this moment of impasse, Lady Hamilton stepped forward between the two antagonists to restore peace. "I know what might change your mind." With a knowing smile, she raised a hand to her throat and denuded herself of her diamonds. "I saw how you rubbed them against your face the other night. How you licked and fondled them. How ecstatically you took them into your mouth."

She closed his paws about them. "They are yours, sweet 'Sieur Precieux, for a word."

"You would give them up?" Surplus said, as if amazed at the very idea. In fact, the necklace had been his and Darger's target from the moment they'd seen it. The only barrier that now stood between them and the merchants of Amsterdam was the problem of freeing themselves from the Labyrinth before their marks finally realized that the modem was indeed a cheat. And to this end they had the invaluable tool of a thinking man whom all believed to be an autistic, and a plan that would give them almost twenty hours in which to escape.

"Only think, dear Surplus." Lady Pamela stroked his head and then scratched him behind one ear, while he stared down at the precious stones. "Imagine the life of wealth and ease you could lead, the women, the power. It all lies in your hands. All you need do is close them."

Surplus took a deep breath. "Very well," he said. "The secret lies in the condenser, which takes a full day to re-charge. Wait but—"

"Here's the problem," the savant said unexpectedly. He poked at the interior of the modem. "There was a wire loose."

He jacked the device into the wall.

"Oh, dear God," Darger said.

A savage look of raw delight filled the dwarf savant's face, and he seemed to swell before them.

"I am free!" he cried in a voice so loud it seemed impossible that it could arise from such a slight source. He shook as if an enormous electrical current were surging through him. The stench of ozone filled the room.

He burst into flames and advanced on the English spy-master and her brother.

While all stood aghast and paralyzed, Darger seized Surplus by the collar and hauled him out into the hallway, slamming the door shut as he did.

They had not run twenty paces down the hall when the door to the Office of Protocol exploded outward, sending flaming splinters of wood down the hallway.

Satanic laughter boomed behind them.

Glancing over his shoulder, Darger saw the burning dwarf, now blackened to a cinder, emerge from a room engulfed in flames, capering and dancing. The modem, though disconnected, was now tucked under one arm, as if it were exceedingly valuable to him. His eyes were round and white and lidless. Seeing them, he gave chase.

"Aubrey!" Surplus cried. "We are headed the *wrong way!*"

It was true. They were running deeper into the Labyrinth, toward its heart, rather than outward. But it was impossible to turn back now. They plunged through scattering crowds of nobles and servitors, trailing fire and supernatural terror in their wake.

The scampering grotesque set fire to the carpets with

every footfall. A wave of flame tracked him down the hall, incinerating tapestries and wallpaper and wood trim. No matter how they dodged, it ran straight toward them. Clearly, in the programmatic literalness of its kind, the demon from the web had determined that having early seen them, it must early kill them as well.

Darger and Surplus raced through dining rooms and salons, along balconies and down servants' passages. To no avail. Dogged by their hyper-natural nemesis, they found themselves running down a passage, straight toward two massive bronze doors, one of which had been left just barely ajar. So fearful were they that they hardly noticed the guards.

"Hold, sirs!"

The mustachioed master of apes stood before the doorway, his baboons straining against their leashes. His eyes widened with recognition. "By gad, it's you!" he cried in astonishment.

"Lemme kill 'em!" one of the baboons cried. "The lousy bastards!" The others growled agreement.

Surplus would have tried to reason with them, but when he started to slow his pace, Darger put a broad hand on his back and shoved. "Dive!" he commanded. So of necessity the dog of rationality had to bow to the man of action. He tobogganed wildly across the polished marble floor between two baboons, straight at the master of apes, and then between his legs.

The man stumbled, dropping the leashes as he did.

The baboons screamed and attacked.

For an instant, all five apes were upon Darger, seizing his limbs, snapping at his face and neck. Then the burning dwarf arrived, and, finding his target obstructed, seized the nearest baboon. The animal shrieked as its uniform burst into flames.

As one, the other baboons abandoned their original quarry to fight this newcomer who had dared attack one of their own.

In a trice, Darger leaped over the fallen master of apes, and was through the door. He and Surplus threw their shoulders against its metal surface and pushed. He had one brief glimpse of the fight, with the baboons aflame, and their master's body flying through the air. Then the door slammed shut. Internal bars and bolts, operated by smoothly oiled mechanisms, automatically latched themselves.

For the moment, they were safe.

Surplus slumped against the smooth bronze, and wearily asked, "Where did you *get* that modem?"

"From a dealer of antiquities." Darger wiped his brow with his kerchief. "It was transparently worthless. Whoever would dream it could be repaired?"

Outside, the screaming ceased. There was a very brief silence. Then the creature flung itself against one of the metal doors. It rang with the impact.

A delicate girlish voice wearily said, "What is this noise?"

They turned in surprise and found themselves looking up at the enormous corpus of Queen Gloriana. She
lay upon her pallet, swaddled in satin and lace, and
abandoned by all, save her valiant (though doomed)
guardian apes. A pervasive yeasty smell emanated from
her flesh. Within the tremendous folds of chins by the
dozens and scores was a small human face. Its mouth
moved delicately and asked, "What is trying to get in?"

The door rang again. One of its great hinges gave.

Darger bowed. "I fear, madame, it is your death."

"Indeed?" Blue eyes opened wide and, unexpectedly,
Gloriana laughed. "If so, that is excellent good news. I
have been praying for death an extremely long time."

"Can any of God's creations truly pray for death and
mean it?" asked Darger, who had his philosophical side.
"I have known unhappiness myself, yet even so life is
precious to me."

"Look at me!" Far up to one side of the body, a tiny
arm—though truly no tinier than any woman's arm—
waved feebly. "I am not God's creation, but Man's. Who
would trade ten minutes of their own life for a century
of mine? Who, having mine, would not trade it all for
death?"

A second hinge popped. The doors began to shiver.
Their metal surfaces radiated heat.

"Darger, we must leave!" Surplus cried. "There is a
time for learned conversation, but it is not now."

"Your friend is right," Gloriana said. "There is a small

archway hidden behind yon tapestry. Go through it. Place your hand on the left wall and run. If you turn whichever way you must to keep from letting go of the wall, it will lead you outside. You are both rogues, I see, and doubtless deserve punishment, yet I can find nothing in my heart for you but friendship."

"Madame . . ." Darger began, deeply moved.

"Go! My bridegroom enters."

The door began to fall inward. With a final cry of "Farewell!" from Darger and "Come *on!*" from Surplus, they sped away.

By the time they had found their way outside, all of Buckingham Labyrinth was in flames. The demon, however, did not emerge from the flames; encouraging them to believe that when the modem it carried finally melted down, it had been forced to return to that unholy realm from whence it came.

The sky was red with flames as the sloop set sail for Calais. Leaning against the rail, watching, Surplus shook his head. "What a terrible sight! I cannot help feeling, in part, responsible."

"Come! Come!" Darger said. "This dyspepsia ill becomes you. We are both rich fellows, now! The Lady Pamela's diamonds will maintain us lavishly for years to come. As for London, this is far from the first fire it has had to endure. Nor will it be the last. Life is short, and so, while we live, let us be jolly!"

"These are strange words for a melancholiac," Surplus said wonderingly.

"In triumph, my mind turns its face to the sun. Dwell not on the past, dear friend, but on the future that lies glittering before us."

"The necklace is worthless," Surplus said. "Now that I have the leisure to examine it, free of the distracting flesh of Lady Pamela, I see that these are not diamonds, but mere imitations." He made to cast the necklace into the Thames.

Before he could, though, Darger snatched away the stones from him and studied them closely. Then he threw back his head and laughed. "The biters bit! Well, it may be paste, but it looks valuable still. We shall find good use for it in Paris."

"We are going to Paris?"

"We are partners, are we not? Remember that antique wisdom that whenever a door closes, another opens? For every city that burns, another beckons. To France, then, and adventure! After which, Italy, the Vatican Empire, Austro-Hungary, perhaps even Russia! Never forget that you have yet to present your credentials to the Duke of Muscovy."

"Very well," Surplus said. "But when we do, *I'll* pick out the modem."

AND NO SUCH THINGS GROW HERE

NANCY KRESS

> *Here life has death for neighbor,*
> *And far from eye or ear*
> *Wan waves and wet winds labor,*
> *Weak ships and spirits steer;*
> *They drive adrift, and wither*
> *They wot not who make thither;*
> *But no such winds blow hither*
> *And no such things grow here.*
>
> —Algernon Charles Swinburne,
> "The Garden of Proserpine

"DEE, I HAVE A problem," Perri said.

Dee Stavros held the phone away from her ear and yawned hugely.

What the hell time was it, anyway? The clock had stopped in the night: another power outage. Her one window was still dark. The air was thick and hot.

"Dee, are you there?"

"I'm here," Dee said to her sister. "So you've got problem. What else is new?"

"This is different."

"They're all different." Only they weren't, really Deadbeat boyfriends, a violent ex-husband, cars "sto len," a last-minute abortion, bad checks for overdue ren ... Perri's messy life changed only in the details. De yawned again.

Perri said, "I've been arrested for GMFA," and De woke fully and sat up on the edge of the bed.

GMFA. Genetic Modification Felony Actions. Th newest crime-fighting tool, newest draconian set o laws, newest felonies to catch the attention of a blood crazy public who needed a scapegoat for ... everything But Perri? Feckless, bumbling, *dumb* Perri? Not possible

Professional training took over. Dee said levelly "Where are you now?"

"Rikers Island," Perri said, and at the relief in he voice—*It'll be all right, Dee will clean up after me again*— Dee had to struggle to hold her anger in check.

"Do you have a lawyer?"

"No. I thought you'd take care of that."

Of course. And now that she was listening, Dee hear behind Perri all the muted miserable cacophony of Rik ers Island, that chaotic hellhole where alleged perps fo the larger hellhole of Manhattan were all taken, proc essed and mishandled. But Perri didn't live in Manhattan. Nobody who could avoid it lived in Manhattan. The last time Dee had heard from her sister, Perri had been heading for the beaches of North Carolina.

For once, Perri anticipated her. "I think they took me to Rikers because it was an offshore offense. On a boat. A ship, really. . . . Get away! I'm not done, you bitch!"

Dee said rapidly, "Relinquish the phone, Perri, before you get hurt. You had your two minutes. I'll be there as soon as I can."

"Oh, Dee, I'm—" The phone went dead.

Dee stood holding it uselessly. Perri was what? Sorry? Scared? Innocent? But Perri was always those things in her own mind. Maybe Dee should just leave her there. Get out of Perri's life once and for all. Teach Perri a lesson. Just leave her there to fend for herself for once. . . .

But Dee was all too familiar with Rikers. She'd retired from the force less than a year ago. She started to dress.

"Why me?" Eliot Kramer said when he appeared at her fourth-floor, one-room apartment door just after dawn. Grimy sunshine glared through Dee's big south window, the only nice thing about her room, other than its being on the far edge of Queens rather than the near edge. Many people were afraid of sunshine indoors. Ultraviolet, skin cancers—even though they'd been told that glass filtered out the danger. Most people never listened to what they were told.

"Why you? Because you're the only decent lawyer I know."

"Twenty years with NYPD and you know *one* decent lawyer? Come on, Dee."

"Decent in both senses, Eliot. Usually the moral ones are incompetent and the competent ones have been bought."

He shook his head. "Boy, I'm glad I don't have your outlook on life."

"You will. You're just not old enough yet."

"And how is old is this sister of yours?" Eliot asked as they hurried down the stairs. "What's her name again?"

"Perri Stavros. She's twenty-seven. My kid sister—I raised her after our parents died in a train wreck."

"And what exactly happened?"

"Haven't any idea," Dee said. "And after she tells us, we still might not know."

"Wonderful," Eliot said unhappily.

They emerged into the street, into the pale green light under the thick trees. Young trees, saplings, twigs . . . this section of Queens had only been planting for six years, since the Crisis, and there were none of the large trees that richer neighborhoods had immediately imported from God-knew-where. Trees grew up through holes jackhammered into the aging sidewalk, up beside crumbling stoops, up from buckets until they were big enough to transplant. A whole row struggled to thrive in the street itself, which had been narrowed to one lane now that cars were so unaffordable. Fast-growing trees, poplars and aspens and cottonwoods, although all trees (and everything else green) grew rapidly now. Whenever possible, trees with broad leaves for the maximum amount of photosynthesis, maximum amount of carbon dioxide scrubbed from the thick and overheated air.

"Not too bad this morning," Eliot said. "Pretty breathable."

"Not if we don't get rain," Dee said. Enough water, always, was the concern. Will it rain today? Don't you think it's clouding up? Might it rain tomorrow? Water meant biomass growth, giving mankind a chance of getting back into control the atmospheric O_2/CO_2 loop so dangerously rising toward 1 percent of CO_2, the upper limit of breathability.

"It'll rain," Eliot said. "Put on your mask, we're almost at the subway. One more question—do you at least know what class of contraband your sister was caught with?"

"No," Dee said. "It's all felony, isn't it?"

"There's felonies and there's felonies," Eliot said, and put on his mask.

Perri had been caught with class-two contraband, which meant five to ten.

"But there are extenuating circumstances," Perri said, looking pleadingly at Eliot, who merely nodded, dazed.

Dee was used to Perri's effect on men. Even in the smelly, hot (God, it was hot, and only early June), windowless interrogation room, and even dirty and smelly herself, Perri's beauty blazed. The perfect body, the long long legs, the thick honey-colored hair and full lips. But it was the eyes that always did it. Blue-green, larger than any other human eyes Dee had ever seen, fringed with long dark lashes. Perri's eyes sparkled, never the same two seconds in a row, unless you counted their unchanging sweetness of expression. How did Perri keep that sweet expression, with the life she'd led? Dee didn't know, hadn't ever known.

Eliot said, his tone not quite professional, "Why don't you just tell me the entire story from the beginning, Miss Stavros."

"Perri, please." She put her hand on his arm. "You will help me, won't you, Eliot?" The gesture was unstudied, genuine. It finished Eliot.

"Everything's going to be all right, Perri," he said, and Dee snorted. No, it was not. Not this time. This time, Perri may have dug herself under too deep for Dee—or Eliot—to pull her out. No, please God, *no*. Dee knew about the kind of prisons that genemod offenders were sent to, and what happened to them there. In the current public climate, GMFA felons were the new pedophiles.

Perri said, "Well, it started when I went down to North Carolina. To the beaches. I heard that sometimes holo companies recruited actresses from there? It turned

ut not to be true, but by that time I'd met Carl and
ell, you know." She lowered her amazing eyes, but not
efore Dee saw the flicker of pain.

"Go on," Eliot said. "What's Carl's last name?"

"He said Hansen. But it might not be. Anyway, I got
regnant."

Dee exploded, "How—"

"Don't yell at me, Dee. I know it was my fault. The
mplant ran out and I forgot to go get another one. And
hen Carl disappeared, and I didn't have the money for
n abortion, so I started sort of asking around about a
heap one."

Suddenly Dee noticed how pale Perri was. It wasn't
ust the lack of makeup. Lips nearly the same color as
er skin, dark smudges under her eyes . . . "You fool! Are
ou bleeding?"

"Oh, on," Perri said. "Everything went fine, Dee, and
nyway I'm strong as an ox. You know that."

Eliot said, "Who performed the operation, Perri?"

"Well, that's just it. I know him only as 'Mike.' This
irl I know said he was safe, he'd done it for her friend,
nd he didn't charge anything at all. He did it out of
dealism." Her lips curved in such a tender smile that
)ee was instantly suspicious.

"Was this 'Mike' an actual licensed doctor?"

"He didn't do the operation. My girlfriend introduced
s at this bar on the beach, and Mike took me on a
owerboat out to where the big ship was with the doctor
board."

And Perri had gone with him. Just like that. Ur
fucking-believable.

Eliot said, "Names, Perri. The girlfriend; the docto
anyone on the ship, the name of the ship itself."

"I don't know, except for my girlfriend. Betsy Jeffe
son."

"Do you think that's her real name?"

"Probably not," Perri said. "The beach is the kind o
place you get to be somebody else if you want to, yo
know?"

"*I* know," Dee said grimly. "Perri, do you know ho
much crime and smuggling go through Hilton Head?"

"I do now."

Eliot said patiently, "Go on with your story, Perr
Our time isn't unlimited, unfortunately."

"The doctor did the abortion. When I came to, I reste
a while. Everyone was kind to me. Then Mike said h
couldn't take me back, the ship had to leave. But h
would send me in a little 'remote boat.' That's a—"

"We know what it is," Dee said harshly. "Smuggler
use them all the time. They're computer-guided to shor
from out at sea, so if the feds are there to intercept th
stuff, at least they don't get the perps, too. Did the dam
thing dump you in the ocean?"

"Oh, no. It brought me right to a public dock in .
Long Island? I guess so. The ship must have sailed
long way while I was knocked out. It was daylight. Mik
said the remote boats aren't illegal. I would have bee
all right, except . . ."

"Except what?" Eliot said gently.

Perri didn't answer for a moment. When she spoke, her voice was low. "The ship was full of plants. Flowers, little trees, all sorts of stuff growing on the deck in the sunshine. Beautiful. I . . . I wanted something to remember Mike by. You don't know how good he was to me, Dee, how kind. I felt . . . anyway. I picked a flower when nobody was looking and put it under my shirt. I was wearing this loose man's shirt because since I got pregnant, nothing of mine fit right. Nobody saw me take the flower."

"One flower?" Dee said. "That's all?"

"The flower wasn't big. It had beautiful yellow petals that were the same color as Mike's hair. That's why I took it. Don't look like that, Dee! A cop saw the remote boat land and came over to the dock because even though they're so tiny I guess they're pretty expensive and he was checking it out. And I staggered a little getting out of the boat because it hadn't even been a day yet since the operation. I was feeling a little woozy. It was so hot, and it was a bad air day. The flower fell out from under my shirt. Below the petals along the stem were all these hard little balls, maybe two dozen of them. One burst apart when the flower fell, and the cop saw it and took me in. I don't even know what it was!"

"I do," Eliot said. "As your attorney, the charges were of course available to me and I downloaded them. The seed pods are awaiting complete analysis at the GFCA lab, but the prelim shows genetic modification for lethal insecticides. Airborne seeds, which makes it a class-two genemod felony."

"But I didn't know!" Perri cried. "And I never understood what's so bad about plants that kill insects, anyway! Don't look like that, Dee, I'm not stupid! I know the history of the Crisis as well as you do. But those genemod plants that almost wiped out all the wheat in the Midwest were only one kind of engineered plant, and if people like Mike believe that other genemods can be—"

Dee cut her off. "People like Mike are criminals in it for the profit. And it wasn't just the wheat-killing genemod that caused the Crisis. And you may not be stupid, Perri, but you surely have acted like it!"

Eliot held up his hand. "Ladies, the thing to focus on here is—"

"No, Dee's right," Perri said. She sat up straighter and her washed-out lovely face took on an odd dignity. "I've been a fool, and I know it. But I had no . . . what is it, Eliot? Criminal intent? Surely that counts for something."

Eliot said quietly, "Not very much, I'm afraid. I don't want to lie to you, Perri. The GMFA Act is intended to prosecute illegal genemod organizations working for profit and willing to do anything at all to protect that profit. The Act is wide-reaching and harsh because it's modeled on RICO, the old Racketeering Influenced and

orrupt Organization laws, and because genetic engi-
eering represents such a danger to the entire planet
ince the Greenhouse Crisis. Or politicians think it does.
Infortunately, people like you fall under the Act as well,
nd I wouldn't be doing my duty by you if I didn't in-
orm you honestly that your case isn't going to play well
1 front of a jury of the usual hysterical citizens whose
randmothers and babies are having trouble breathing."

"But the Greenhouse Crisis and the wheat kill-off
vere two separate things!" Perri cried, surprising Dee.

"But most people don't separate them because they
appened concurrently," Eliot said. "All at once the air
vas ruined, there was no bread, prices for everything
ocketed because the government made energy so ex-
ensive to try to control industrial emissions . . . all at
nce. In my experience, that's how juries see it. Perri, I
link you're much better off pleading guilty and letting
le plea bargain for you."

Perri was silent. Dee said thickly, already knowing
le answer, "Where will she do time?"

"Probably Cotsworth. It's the usual place for the east
oast."

Cotsworth. It was notorious. Dee had never been inide, but she didn't have to be. She'd seen other places
ke it. It wasn't as bad as the men's worst prisons—they
ever were—but a girl who looked like Perri . . . *was* like
erri. . . .

Perri said, "All right, Eliot. If you think I should plead
uilty, I will."

Trusting him completely, on a half-hour acquaintance. Exactly how she got into this in the first place with "Carl," with "Mike." She would never learn.

Eliot said, "I'll do everything I can for you, Perri."

A wan smile, but the astonishing blue-green eyes dazzled. "I know you will. I trust you."

Dee wasn't Perri. She probed, tested, cut. "What if the FBI finds 'Mike'?"

"They won't find Mike," Eliot said. They stood at the subway entrance before the hellish descent underground. Eliot was going to his office in Brooklyn, Dee to Queens. "God, you of all people know they won't find Mike. The Genetic Modification Crimes section of the FBI is overworked, there aren't enough of them, and Perri is such small potatoes they probably won't even look for Mike."

"The ship doesn't sound like small potatoes."

"They might not even believe the ship exists. Perri wouldn't be the first perp to falsify events."

"Do you think that's what she's doing?"

"No," Eliot said. "I think she's telling the absolute truth. I think she's that rare find, a person incapable of dishonesty. But I don't think the FBI or the federal attorney will think so. They're paid not to."

"But you think the ship exists," Dee persisted.

"Yes. There are dozens, maybe hundreds, of them out there, in international waters where it's much harder to do anything about them. They genemod everything from insect-killing supercrops for idealists who want to save the Earth, to insect-killing supercrops for profiteers who want to own it. And who don't care if they inadvertently kill off an entire Third World country's rice crop in the process. Oh, Perri's ship is out there, all right, with 'Mike' running it. Although why he's also performing abortions is a bit murky. But I'm going to downplay that aspect with the federal attorney. It makes Perri look irresponsible."

"She is irresponsible."

"Sometimes," Eliot said, "what looks like irresponsibility is really innocence."

Here we go again, Dee thought. But if a ridiculous infatuation would increase Eliot's work on Perri's behalf, let the poor sot be infatuated.

It was ironic. Raising Perri, she was always the one "mother" who wouldn't let Perri take the bus by herself, walk home from school alone, go downtown. Cops were like that. Unlike the other mothers, Dee had known what was waiting out there in the street. And then the grown-up Perri sought out more trouble than any of her childhood friends.

Dee said, "So you don't think the authorities will look for Mike. And even though it would help Perri's plea, you won't, either."

Eliot said bluntly, "I can't afford the resources to look. Can you?"

"No," Dee said.

"Also, the case will be heard in under a week, probably. They dispose of these small things as fast as they can, fair or not. *You* know that, Dee."

"Yes, I know that. But finding the ship would aid an appeal for Perri."

"Yes. But they're not going to find it, Dee."

"No," she said. "But I am."

THE COAST OF CAROLINA IS THE NEW FLORIDA! blared e-banners at the train station. Dee believed it. Ruin one area, making it so hot the ecology becomes frightening and the people leave, move on to another. Most of Florida was now genuine jungle, teeming with foreign plants and animals escaped from Miami International Airport, always the major import center for such things. Monkeys, caimans, lygodia, alligators, and insects carrying everything from dengue fever to new diseases without names. Some of them, of course, genemod. It was the diseases that had made West Palm retirees, South Beach fun seekers, and the Miami criminal underground all move north.

She took a cheap motel room far from the action and went shopping. To the experienced, cops were instantly identifiable. That included ex-cops. She bought a modest swimsuit which at least covered her nipples, added a loose sheer robe to veil her forty-four-year-old body, studied the locals and purchased something guaranteed to make her hair lie in flat sculptured loops along one side of her neck. She didn't overdo it, another classic mistake of undercover cops. Her lipstick wasn't too gold, her eye makeup not too blue. She bought her beach bag, sandals, and music cube at a used-stuff store. She would do.

The long stretch of white-sand beach, natural and artificial, turned out to be informally segregated: gay beach, retiree beach, kid beach, sex-and-criminal beach. "I'm looking for Betsy Jefferson," she told the bartender at the first bar on the right beach.

The bartender gathered up glasses. He looked like he'd been behind the bar for a very long time. "Why do you want Betsy?"

"I need to talk to her. Do you know where she is?"

"No. Last I heard, she's working someplace for her uncle."

Of course. It was the number one response cops heard. You ask anybody what they, or anyone else, did for a living, and they said, "Work for my uncle." The entire underworld was employed by uncles.

Dee said, "I'm really looking for Perri Burr. I'm her sister." Perri had used "Burr" as her "beach key."

The bartender squinted at Dee. "Yeah, you look a little like her," he said, which was either kindness or blindness. "Around the nose. All right. Betsy's working at the Adams. Out Surf Street."

"Thanks." *Adams. Burr. Jefferson.* Eighteenth-century WASP aliases for twenty-first-century punks. Dee wondered if they even knew who the originals had been.

The Adams was a sex-show-and-fizz club that wouldn't even open until midnight. Dee went back to her motel and shopped again, this time for a cheap e-dress that shimmered strategically on and off around her body. Then she slept.

At one in the morning Betsy Jefferson started to perform. She was older than Perri, and older than she looked, gyrating her aging flesh through stage sequences as repulsive as anything Dee had seen when she'd worked Vice. Dee, her dress on full coverage, tried to picture Perri in this setting. She failed. Eliot was right: Perri's fuck-ups had a quality of innocence foreign to the Adams, with its forced glitter and real sadism. Perri fucked up irresponsibly but not cruelly. When Betsy finished, blood from a dead monkey smeared the stage and her own naked body.

Dee sent a note backstage and the bouncer let her through. Betsy stood in a basin of water sluicing herself down. "Hi. I'll be done in a minute."

"Thanks for seeing me."

Off-stage and covered, Betsy Jefferson looked even older and much wearier. "Perri talked about you. She looked up to you. You still work with homeless babies?"

Actual discretion on Perri's part. Dee was grateful. "Yes. But it's Perri I'm here to talk about. You know she was arrested on GMFA."

"Yeah." Betsy didn't meet Dee's eyes. "I heard."

"She's disappeared. Got away from a federal marshal. Fucked her way free."

Betsy smiled. "Yeah? Good for her."

"I think so, too. But I'm worried, Betsy, because she's flat-line broke. I want to give her money so she can go underground armed and flush."

Betsy nodded. "She said you always took care of her."

"And I always will. Do you know where I can find her? Has she turned up anywhere back on the beach?"

"Not that I heard."

"Then do you know where I can find 'Mike'? The guy that got her the abortion on the ship?"

"She told you about that, yeah?"

"Perri tells me everything," Dee said. "She knows I just want to take care of her."

"Yeah, she said. And you're fucking right about one thing. Without money, she won't last long here."

"That's what I figured."

Betsy studied Dee. Dee didn't have to fake concern. Abruptly Betsy said, "Perri never worked no place like this, you know."

Dee was silent.

"She didn't have to, with her looks. Wouldn't have done it anyway. I told her to go back to you and get a decent life."

"Thank you. Too bad she didn't listen," Dee said. For

the first time, she saw why Perri had trusted Betsy, saw what wasn't totally extinguished in the older woman. Dee wondered if Betsy had ever had any kids of her own. Who was Perri substituting for?

"You won't find Mike, Dee. Not unless he wants to find you."

"Can you make it so he does?"

"Maybe."

"I really want Perri to have the money. It's a lot. All I've saved."

"Where you staying?"

Dee told her, and Betsy made a face. "Okay. Go back to Queens."

"Back to *Queens*?"

"Look," Betsy said, "You're new at this. Mike ain't here anymore, not after Perri's arrest. Perri ain't here, either, or I'd of heard about it. People know I sort of looked out for her. But I know Mike, Mike knows people, people get around. Give me your address in Queens and go home."

Dee had wacoed it. Her first contact on the beach and she'd exploded the possibility of more. If she didn't go back to Queens, Betsy would hear about it and question why. Word would get around much faster than Dee could. Nobody would talk to her. Nobody.

"Thanks," she said, smiling at Betsy.

At her sentencing Perri stood ashen and dry-eyed. She wore a loose gray coverall so old and laundered that the tired cloth draped softly around her body. With her hair unstyled she looked incongruously virginal, a maiden in innocent distress. Dee, the only spectator in the court, grasped the ancient wooden railing so hard that its oily grime became embedded in the creases of her palms. The courtroom was on half AC; apparently somebody had decided that federal judges deserved some relief from New York air, despite the exorbitant cost of all emissions-creating energy. Even so, Dee couldn't breathe.

Eliot had made a deal with the feds. Dee suspected it had cost him all his markers. Perri pleaded guilty to class three genemod possession.

"The court has considered the federal prosecutor's recommendations in this case," the judge said in a bored voice, "and accepts them. Six months in prison, no time off for good behavior, followed by six years probation. Counselor, do you have anything to add?"

"No, your honor," Eliot said.

"Bailiff, remove the prisoner."

And that was all. Dee had seen it, participated in it, how many times? Dozens, maybe hundreds. But this was Perri.

"I love you, Dee!" she called as she was led away, and her attempt to smile for her sister's sake cauterized Dee's heart.

"You can visit next month," Eliot said somberly.

"If she's still alive by next month."

He was practical. "Did you put the maximum amoun[t] allowable in her prison account?"

"Of course," Dee snapped. "I know how the syster[m] works."

"Unfortunately," Eliot said. "Buy you lunch?"

"No. You stay inside—it's a bad air day," Dee sai[d] brutally. "I'm going home."

"Dee . . . I did the best I could."

He had. She was too enraged to give that to him.

At home she checked the non-traceable money chip[s] hidden in her apartment, plus the legal surveillanc[e] equipment and illegal nerve gas. When Mike showed up she would either buy her way to the ship, and to evi[-] dence for a legal appeal, or bring him down herself an[d] let the authorities pursue it. Once they had a live body they might actually do that. Maybe.

The money was safe. As she had done every nigh[t] for a week, Dee swallowed the foul drink that woul[d] neutralize the nerve gas in her own lungs for twelve hours. Military stuff, it was highly illegal for her to hav[e] it. She no longer cared.

Then she tried to sleep.

The air was exceptionally bad today. Choked wit[h] greenhouse gases, CO_2 pushing maybe point seven-fiv[e] when had it gotten this bad? She was having troubl[e] breathing, *she couldn't breathe.* . . .

Dee awakened strangling. Cord bound her neck, he[r]

egs, her arms . . . no, one arm was still free. Desperately she worked a finger between her neck and the tightening cord; it gave slightly and she was able to pull it far enough away from her neck to gasp in a breath of fetid air. But that would only work for a moment, her assailant was sure to . . .

There was no assailant. She was alone in her apartment, strangled by tough green stems that had almost buried her in foliage. Dee screamed once, but then her cop reflexes kicked in. She flexed everything to see what was loose and found a frond not yet wrapped completely around both her body and her bed. She contorted her body so that her free hand, without removing the index finger from under the noose at her neck, brought the loose frond to her teeth, her only available weapon. She bit hard.

The stem parted and fell into two parts. She grabbed wildly with her limited reach for another stem. They were growing . . . she could actually *see* the stems growing around her in tiny, fatal increments. She bit through a second stem and filled her mouth with bitter leaf. What if it was poison? Don't think about it now. She bit another stem.

Writing on the bed, half-pinned, Dee fought the mindless green with everything she had. At one point she thought she'd lost; there were too many tendrils. But the plant *was* mindless. By calculating where the worst danger was and working her way doggedly toward that

point, by reason and strength and sheer luck, she got a
hand free enough to break the glass of water by her
bedside and attack with the broken glass. Blood
streamed over sheets, leaves, herself.

She was free. She rolled off the bed, leapt away, and
collapsed on the floor, panting.

From here, the plant looked to be growing much
more slowly. No more than six inches an hour.

Six inches an hour. She didn't know that even the
underground genemod labs had achieved that. Splice
phototropism genes to growth ones, maybe? She didn't
know. She didn't want to know. She had almost died.

The nutrient box sat under the bed, maybe two feet
square, tilted toward the big south window that was the
reason she'd taken the apartment. It hadn't been there
when she'd gone to bed. Whoever had put it there had
known how to disable the surveillance equipment and
nerve gas. The plants had probably grown slowly, if at
all, until dawn. Then the light had driven their super-
efficient energy use to put everything into growth, a
riotous deadly burst of it that had depleted them utterly.
Already the oldest leaves were turning yellow at the
edges. Live hard, grow fast, die young.

Dee looked for the patch. She found it on her ankle,
peeled it off. Whatever had dripped into her bloodstream
had kept her knocked out far into the light-rich morning. It was almost noon.

She crouched on the floor and watched the spent
kamikaze plant die.

"And the money was still there," Eliot said.

"Not touched."

"So they just wanted to kill you."

"Head of the class, counselor," Dee snarled. She was still shaky. They sat in a coffee shop near Dee's building. The air was very bad today; some people wore masks even indoors. The room was stifling. Dee could remember when air conditioning didn't cost the Earth. Literally.

She continued, "I want to know what's best to do, Eliot. If I call the authorities and take them up to see the evidence of a murder attempt, will it help Perri's appeal?"

"I don't see how," Eliot said. He pulled his sticky shirt away from his chest for a moment. "You can't prove who did it, or even that the murder attempt was in any way connected to Perri's experiences. Yes, it was a gemod weapon, but that doesn't link it to any specific illegal organization."

"God, do you suppose I've got legions of people out to kill me? Who else could it be?"

"You're an ex-cop," Eliot said. "I don't have to tell you that ex-cops get deviled by people they arrested and sent to jail, sometimes years after the fact. There are a lot of crazies out there. Your 'evidence' is circumstantial, Dee, and barely that. There's no solid link."

"And what would be a 'solid link'? My actually turning up dead?"

"Not that, either. Dee, you're being stupid. You of all people ought to know that you can't play in this league. You just can't."

"And the FBI won't."

"Only if they just happen to stumble across it. Otherwise it's too small for them, and too big for you. *Give up, Dee.* Do you want to go with me to see Perri this afternoon?"

Dee grew still. "I thought she couldn't have visitors for the first month."

"Doesn't apply to me. I'm her attorney. I'll get you in as part of her legal team."

"Yes. Oh, yes."

Eliot opened his mouth as if to say more, closed it again. He finished his coffee.

Dee sat silent on the train to Cotsworth, preparing herself. Even so, it was a shock.

"Hello, Dee. Eliot," Perri said. She succeeded in smiling through her swollen lips. One eye was completely closed with bruises. Even in the prison coverall it was obvious she'd lost weight.

"Perri . . . Perri." Dee pulled herself together. "I told you not to fight back. With anybody."

Eliot said gently, "Guards or inmates?"

"Both. Eliot, don't file any complaints. It'll only make it worse on me."

He didn't answer. He knew she was right. So did Dee, but rage rose in her throat, tasting of acid.

Eliot said, "I've filed an appeal, Perri."

She brightened. Dee knew the appeal would be denied; there were no grounds. But anything to give her sister a little hope in this hell.

And Perri was magnificent. She chatted with Dee and Eliot. She asked after their lives. She did everything possible to pretend she was not in pain and despair. When the short visit was over, and all the checkpoints had been passed, Dee turned to Eliot.

"Don't ever tell me again to give up. Not ever."

She looked two places: the activists and the criminals. She was looking for the overlap.

The environmental activists were not as numerous or as angry as they'd been before the Crisis, for the simple reason that they'd won. Dee understood that. She also understood what had to be their next move: semi-underground activism.

It went like this: You spend your life driven by the desire to outlaw genetic engineering, and then it's outlawed, and you're spiritually unemployed. For a while you try other causes, but it's not the same. So you organize groups to attack suspected genemod violations, on the grounds the authorities are (pick one) lazy, corrupt, stupid, burdened by bureaucracy. You then can spend time ferreting out illegal labs and farms and destroying them. You're back in the game. Of course, you're also vigilantes and thus must fight the cops as well as the violators, but for a certain type of person, this only makes it more interesting.

Dee started with New Greenpeace. At her first meeting she met a woman angry enough to be a good candidate for "subversive projects." The woman, Paula Caradine, was suspicious of Dee, but Dee was used to suspicious informants.

"Why are you interested in subversion?" Paula asked. She was stocky, plain, very intense.

"My sister's in jail for a genemod offense she didn't commit. She was framed."

"Oh? What's her name?"

"Perri Stavros. I'm Demetria Stavros. I used to be a cop with the NYPD. Perri's conviction changed things for me. The FBI isn't getting the job done right, even though they've got the Act now, or Perri wouldn't be Inside and the polluters Outside."

Paula said, "Nothing's going on right now," which was probably a lie. Dee was used to being lied to. Everybody lied to cops: suspects, witnesses, victims. It was a fact of life on the street. Paula said no more, which was a good sign. She'd have Dee and Perri checked out, find out Dee's story was true. It was a start. Building informants was a slow process.

In Manhattan, they were already built, at least the ones that hadn't been killed or been jailed or died of "environmental conditions." Dee had only been retired a year. However, a week of networking and bribery

rned up nothing but the usual empty lies. Then she
rned up Gum.

Nobody knew how old he was, not even Gum him-
:lf. He had purplish melanomas on his bald head and
<posed arms. Disease, or sunlight, or bad luck. He re-
·sed medical treatment, air masks, false teeth. Gum
ved everywhere, and nowhere. He remembered life be-
·re the Crisis, before the business flight from Manhat-
n, maybe before the turn of the century. He was old,
·d stinking, and dying, and his sheer survival this long
·d earned him a sort of mythic dimension, like a god.
·ere were punks and scars and hyenas in the Park who
:tually believed that killing Gum would bring horrible
tribution. Although Dee had trouble imagining any-
·ing more horrible than the life they were already lead-
·g. The Park, along with several other sections of
·anhattan, had slipped completely beyond police con-
·ol. No cop would go there, ever, for any reason.

Dee caught Gum in a bar near the rotting East River
·cks, on a street unofficially declared a neutral zone.
·ley, Gum."

He peered at her blankly. Gum never recognized any-
·dy overtly. Dee suspected he had an eidetic memory.

"It's Dee Stavros. With the NYPD."

"Hey."

"You want a soda?" Gum never drank alcohol.

"Hey." He hauled himself onto a stool next to her.

"Gum, I'm looking for somebody."

Gum said in his cranky, old-man voice, "I been look
ing for God for a hunnert years."

"Yeah, well, let me know if you find Him. Also a gu
who could be calling himself 'Mike.' Or not. Runs a g
nemod illegal on a ship. Also does abortions there."

"Abortions?" Gum said doubtfully.

"Yeah, you know, rape-and-scrapes. Women's stu
You hear anything about that?"

"A hunnert years," Gum said. "He went missing."

Gum meant God, not Mike. Gum only talked whe
he was ready.

"You hear anything, I'd like to know about it." Sh
slipped him the money chips so unobtrusively not ev
the bouncer saw it.

"Just went missing, left us like this."

"Don't I know it, Gum."

"A hunnert years."

She went to another activist meeting, worked more o
Paula Caradine. Before anything could happen, Eli
called her. His voice had the ultracontrolled monotor
that a lot of lawyers used for something really seriou:

"Dee, I want you to see something. Meet me at t
genemod evidence center in an hour. You know whe
it is?"

"Of course I know where it is. Can you say—"

"No." He clicked off.

The Genetic Modification Felony Actions Eviden

Center for Greater New York was in Brooklyn. It was another bad air day; Dee wore her mask for the entire trip plus the fifteen minutes she hung around outside. No admittance to the heavily guarded building without five million authorizations. Finally Eliot showed up ("Another breakdown on the subway"), got them inside, and was shown to an e-locked room. Dee recognized the negative-pressure signs in this whole wing. Nothing, not even spores, could drift out. She and Eliot had changed into paper coveralls. They would have to go through decontamination to get out again.

Eliot keyed the e-locked door and it opened.

Dee gasped. Years of training couldn't weigh against this. The single plant sat in the middle of the small room. A bush as tall as Dee's shoulders, it had broad, very pale green leaves on woody branches. In the center of each leaf was a closed human eye. Eliot turned up the light and the eyes opened.

Perri's eyes.

Each one was the startling blue-green that Dee had never seen on anyone else. Their pupils turned toward the light source. A hundred eyes, moving in unison, blind.

"The evidence biologist explained it to me," Eliot said. "The eyes are light-sensitive but they can't actually see. They're not wired up to any brain. There's a human eye gene, 'aniridia,' that can be introduced onto animals in weird places, insect wings or legs, and they'll grow extra eyes. Nobody knew you could put it into plants.'

"*Why?* What is it?"

"It's an art object," Eliot said grimly. "A sculpture Apparently the artist is well-known in the underground circles that traffic in these things. He's in custody."

"Mike—"

"Was the supplier, of course. The eyes were grown from the stem cells from Perri's aborted fetus. Stem cell are easiest to grow into any organ. But the so-called artist is refusing to talk. On advice of attorney."

"Will he deal? If you offer enough?"

"I can't offer anything, Dee. It's not my case. But no I don't think he'll talk. More and more of these genemod illegals are being acquired by organized crime. The FB and NYPD have just established a joint task force on illegals. The artist would rather face the court than face the mob."

"But it's obvious these are Perri's genes! They can do a DNA match!"

"Why bother? You can't prove she didn't give Mike the tissue, or sell it to him. It doesn't clear her at all. just thought you ought to see that the chances of getting Mike on other charges have gone way up. He's connected to the artist who's connected to the mob, so Mike is going to get serious attention. They'll get him if they can."

Dee faced him. "I don't want revenge. I want Perri freed."

"Are you sure you don't want revenge? Perri's told me a bit about her childhood. You overprotected her, Dee. You made her feel the entire world is dangerous."

"It is."

"But you also taught her she can't cope with it without you. That without you, she's bound to screw up. And like a good daughter, she's been proving you right ever since."

"She's not my daughter, and—"

"She might as well be. You were the only mother she had."

"You don't know jack shit about it!"

"I know what Perri's told me."

Dee demanded, "You see her? A lot?"

"Every chance I can. Don't look like that, Dee. She's not a child anymore, and as you just pointed out, you're not her mother."

"Fuck you, Eliot. You're fired. You're not Perri's attorney any more."

"That's not your decision," Eliot said.

"I pay her bills!"

"Not this one." His gaze was steady.

Dee strode toward the door. Going through it, she slapped off the light. The blue-green eyes on the pale leaves, Perri's eyes, blinked and closed.

We're hitting a farm tonight," Paula said abruptly. "You can come along."

"I checked out, huh?" Dee said.

"Why didn't you mention that the bastards tried to kill you with a bio-weapon?"

"I thought I'd give you something to research," Dee said. She hid her surprise that "the group"—pretentiously, they had no other name—had turned up the attack in her apartment. They were better connected than she'd thought. No official police report had been filed.

"We meet here at two A.M." Paula said. "Wear dark clothing that covers your arms and legs with at least three layers of cloth, and good boots. We'll supply gloves and mask."

"Got it. Paula ... thanks."

"I know how it is," Paula said cryptically. Dee didn't ask what she meant.

Sixteen people, packed into two vans with blackened windows and an opaque shield between driver and passengers. No names, faces behind masks; Dee wouldn't be able to identify anyone except Paula. They rode for at least forty minutes at variable speeds. When the van stopped, they could have been anywhere.

"Stay in single file," their "group leader" said. He led them through the darkness, one flashlight in the front of the line, off the road through a small woods, then across at least three open fields divided by strips of underbrush. Finally the line halted.

The genemod farm was an acre lot of saplings. Sold as transplants, Dee guessed. Genemod illegals had

earned not to fence or firewall their farms; it attracted
oo much aerial-surveillance attention. To Dee these
saplings looked like any other stand of young trees.
What were they genemod for? It didn't matter. Their creation was the kind of irresponsible activity that had
caused the Crisis, when one food crop after another had
been wiped out by fast-growing, herbicide-resistant, genetically created "super-plants" with no natural enemies.
The kind of irresponsible activity that had, in the end,
caused most of the Midwest to endure the controlled
burn. The kind of irresponsible activity that had ruined
agribusinesses, spurred hoarding, and weakened an already staggering economy.

The kind of activity that had jailed Perri.

"Chop each tree clean through at the base," the leader
instructed. "Don't work on adjacent trees or you risk
cutting each other. Be quiet and quick. The acid team is
right behind you."

Dee took the row of trees he gave her. She buzzed
her saw through its base, surprised at the savage pleasure it gave her. The air filled with muted buzz (much
of the sound was white-noised somehow) and with the
sharp smell of the acid poured over the fallen limbs and
rooted stumps. Dee felt energy flow into her as she destroyed the crop. Over the havoc she listened for the
sound of defending copters or guns, but no one came.
She laughed aloud.

"What's so funny?" Paula said, on the next row.

"I just remembered something. An old poem. 'Onl
God can make a tree.' "

"Huh," Paula said. "Forget poetry and just saw."

Dee sawed, every vibration a vicious joy. When the
were done, the activists slipped over the fields to th
vans. Behind them, the carefully created grove lay i
acrid burned waste.

"I found him," Gum said.

Dee tensed. It had taken a long time to locate Gun
again. She'd finally found him inside the base of th
Brooklyn Bridge, living with a group of people arme
with shoulder-launched missiles of some type. Whe
the hell had they gotten them? The things looked mili
tary. The whole set-up was one Dee would never hav
approached at all if two different informants hadn't sai
Gum was there. One, heavily bribed, had had the e-ma
address. An electric cable snaked across the ground an
into the bridge, undoubtedly stealing very expensive en
ergy until the power company discovered it. No long
Dee's problem. She e-mailed Gum, and at the appointe
hour he emerged from the Bridge looking as dirty an
demented as ever.

They sat on packing crates set a hundred yards fro
the Bridge in an empty lot strewn with broken glas.
rags, unidentifiable chunks of metal. Dee counted si
rats in two minutes.

"Where is he?" she asked Gum.

"Everywheres. Nowheres. Gone and back. A hunnert years."

"Not God, Gum! I thought you found Mike!"

"Gone and back. A hunnert years."

Dee held on to her temper. This visit was too important, and too dangerous, to ruin. She waited.

Finally Gum said, "He watches Mike. He watches me. He watches you. He knows."

"What does He know, Gum? Will you tell me so I can know, too?"

"He knows Mike din't do it. The plants."

"Mike didn't take my sister to a ship illegal with genemod plants?"

"Oh, yeah. Praise the Lord."

"Mike did take Perri to a genemod illegal?"

"Oh, yeah," Gum said. Rheum oozed from his filmy eyes. "Gone and back."

"He took her to the ship and he sent her back. But where is Mike now?"

"God sees."

Dee put her hands on her knees and leaned forward. Another rat ran across the lot. Closer to the Bridge a man stood holding a rifle and looking right at her. "Gum, what are you doing with these people who live in the Bridge?"

"A hunnert years. Straight to God."

"You're their priest," Dee said. It seemed unlikely, but not impossible. Since the Crisis, a hundred weird religions had sprung up to explain the Earth's new harshness, atone for the Earth's new harshness, find hope in the Earth's new harshness, all kinds of shit. Even criminals, it seemed, could believe in God. Some sort of God. And it might explain what Gum, old and mumbling and shambling, was doing with these well-equipped felons who frankly scared the fuck out of Dee. Priesthood might explain it. Or it might not.

Gum said, "He din't do it."

"God?"

"Mike."

"What didn't Mike do, Gum?" They were going in circles.

"He din't send that plant to kill you in your apartment."

Dee's breath stopped. "Do you know who did?"

"T'other side. A hunnert years."

"Gum, what other side? Who sent the plant to kill me?"

"Look to God," Gum said, and lurched to his feet.

Dee stood and grabbed at him. "You can't go now! You have to tell me the rest!"

The old man tried to pull free. The guard raised his rifle. Hastily Dee released Gum. As he shuffled away, she called after him, "What other side, Gum? Who sent the plant?"

"It was in all the newspapers," Gum said over his shoulder. "You was dead."

"Gum . . ."

He was gone.

She kept at her informants, getting the word out, spending her savings on sweeteners. She went on another raid with Paula's group, destroying another open farm in Jersey. She visited Perri at Cotsworth, and each time Perri was thinner and quieter and walked with more difficulty. Dee papered the Correctional System with complaints and charges and anger, and none of it brought any changes whatsoever.

Paula's group hit an arboretum in Connecticut. Under thick plastic grew bed after bed of lush foliage genemod for . . . what? It didn't matter. By now, Dee wasn't even curious. To get into the arboretum they had to blow open the glass with semtex. Instantly alarms wailed. They tossed in the flamers and scattered. Dee, following her instructions, circled widely to the left and ran through an under-road culvert full to her knees with stinking water. Spider webs tore from the roof onto her face. Lights raked the area from a tower she hadn't known was there, and she could hear a copter roaring closer. But she made it to the van and back onto the highway and all the way to her apartment.

Only later did she hear that two activists died in the raid. One of them was Paula.

The next evening Eliot called. "Jesus Christ, Dee, what the fuck are you *doing?*"

He knew about the raid. No, impossible, how could he know? Then he'd heard about her working the street. Dee said nothing.

"How could you go down to see Perri and then gouge into her about what a screw-up she is? 'You made bad choices, you've messed up your life, this prison time will follow you around forever' . . . how *could* you, Dee?"

"It's all true."

"So what? She's barely hanging on in that hell-hole and she doesn't need you to go in there and—"

"How the fuck do you know what she needs? I've taken care of her since she was two years old!"

"And you've made her believe she can't take care of herself without you. *You* screwed up her life if anyone did. So stop this—"

Dee slammed her fist into the OFF key. She raged around the one-room apartment until her own fury scared her. Then she tried to calm down: deep breathing, lifting weights, a cup of hot tea. At midnight she finally slept.

At three she jerked awake. Someone was in the apartment.

Her hand slid under the blanket for her gun. Before she could grasp it, both arms were jerked above her head and cuffed. The light went on.

He took off his night-vision hood and pulled a chair beside her bed. Silently he studied her. He was medium height and build, late thirties, brown eyes. Hair the color of a yellow flower. Dee stared back, refusing to show fear. She said, "You're Mike."

"Yes. Although the name is Victor."

She snorted and he smiled. "No, really. You don't look much like Perri, Dee. Come on, we're going out."

She began to scream. The walls were thin; someone would hear. Immediately Victor slapped a gag strip over her mouth. He pulled off her blankets and cuffed her ankles, ignoring her kicks. Wrapping her in the blanket as if she were sick, he lifted her easily and carried her, a dead weight, down three flights of stairs. He was much stronger than he looked.

A car waited at the curb. Dee thought, incongruously, *how long since I rode in a car?* Years. Cars were emission-producing demons. People destroyed them like cockroaches. Only emergency vehicles were exempt, and this powerful sleek car was no emergency vehicle.

They drove through the empty, pot-holed streets, Victor and Dee in the back and the unseen driver behind a shield in the front. Victor removed her gag.

"Dee, no one is going to hurt you." Oh, right, as if she believed that. "There's something I want you to see."

"Why?"

"Good question. I guess because I hate waste. You've wasted a lot of time raiding genemod illegals and harassing ineffective authorities and putting out the word on me throughout Manhattan. Is that ankle cuff too tight for comfort?"

"No. It's Perri whose time is being wasted."

"I'm sorry about that. There was never any intention that she be charged with anything. I had no idea she'd take a genemod plant."

"You merely took her fetal tissue," Dee said.

"Yes. It's the best tissue for human genetic engineering, you know. Stem cells are malleable, the amniotic sac grows organs well, the placenta . . . but I don't think you're interested in scientific details. It should have been a mutual gain. Perri wanted to abort, I wanted the tissue."

"To create plant 'art' that has her eyes."

"No," Victor said. He shifted on the back seat of the car. "I don't dabble in decorative perversity. I sell the girls' fetal tissue to whoever can pay well for it. Our real work requires money. No, don't ask questions now. I want to show you." And, incredibly, he leaned into a corner of the car and went to sleep.

Dee tested the door, her bonds, the seat belt. Nothing gave. Victor snored softly. She could probably kick him with both feet, but belted in like this, it would be a kick so feeble as to be pointless. Slack, his face looked oddly older. Forties, maybe. Even through her fear and outrage, he puzzled her. Something was off about him. He didn't seem like any criminal she'd ever seen, not even the smooth-talking, easy-sleeping sociopaths.

The car stopped. Victor woke and carried Dee along a deserted dock. A remote boat waited, barely big enough for the two of them. Victor untied the mooring lines and pressed a hand-held, and the boat took off silently across the dark water.

The night was cloudy. Dee could see various lights, but she had no idea what they were. Ships? Land? Buoys? A wind blew and the sea became choppy. Water sloshed into the boat. Dee felt herself growing seasick.

Victor must have known the signs. Expertly he held her head over the side while she vomited. "Almost there!" he called over the rising wind. Dee threw up again.

The storm looked ready to break in earnest by the time they drew up alongside what seemed to her a huge ship, completely dark. A metal basket was lowered and Victor dumped her into it. Dee hated feeling helpless. Almost she would rather be knocked out than trussed up and hauled in like mackerel or cod.

She got her wish. Someone on deck leaned into the metal basket and slapped a patch onto her neck. No way to dislodge it, and in ten seconds everything disappeared.

She woke in a narrow cabin as steady as if on land. Victor, looking much more rested, sat in a chair beside her bunk. Dee struggled for the dignity of sitting upright. "Where are we?"

"At sea. The storm passed while you were out. It's a lovely day." He lifted her and carried her into a narrow corridor where a wheelchair waited. The blanket slipped off her. Her pajamas smelled, but at least she'd been wearing them. What if she'd been naked when he kidnapped her? And what about her expensive, carefully installed nerve gas? This was the second time it had been disabled. Apparently all of underground New York had become security experts.

"I need to go to the bathroom."

"Yes. Just a minute." He wheeled her to another door, pushed the whole chair in, and closed the door.

Cursing, Dee stood up, still bound at wrists and ankles. She managed to get her pjs down and everything accomplished, after which there was no choice except to kick at the door.

"It's less stuffy on deck," Victor said cheerfully. Dee scowled at him.

It was less stuffy on deck. Also painfully bright. Sunlight glared off a blue ocean. If there hadn't been a breeze, the heat would have been unbearable. Dee said, "I can't stay out here long. I assume that you have on sunblock."

"So do you. Put on before you woke up. Anyway, we're almost there."

Where? Nothing but water in every direction. Dee folded her arms and said nothing. She wasn't going to cooperate in his elaborate games. If he killed her, he killed her.

She knew she wasn't really indifferent to death.

No one else appeared on this section of deck. Nor were the abundant plants that Perri had described anywhere in evidence. Maybe Victor thought that Dee, too, would steal one.

The ship moved over the ocean, although without reference points Dee had no idea how fast it was traveling. After about twenty minutes, Victor, who'd been lounging at the railing, straightened. "There. Four o'clock."

At first Dee saw nothing. Then she did. The sea was changing color, from blue to a dense, oily black. She said, "An oil spill?"

"I wish."

They drew closer. The blackness grew, until Dee could see it was actually a deep purple. It seemed to extend to the horizon. The ship moved a short way into the purple and stopped.

Victor lowered a grapple-looking thing over the side. "We can't go in any farther without risk to the screws. But aerial surveillance shows that the bloom already covers sixty thousand square miles. Do you have any idea how big that is, Dee? Half the size of New Mexico. Here, look."

He pulled up the grappler and held it toward her. It dripped what looked to Dee like seaweed; she was no marine expert.

"It's not ordinary seaweed," Victor said. "It's gene-mod. Made from altered bacteria. It replicates at ideal

335

bacterial rate, which is to say it doubles every twenty minutes. It has no natural enemies. Nothing eats it. But it blocks sunlight almost totally, and so everything underneath it dies. Do you understand about the food chain, Dee? Do you know what happens if the oceans die?"

"Who made it?"

"Unknown. Best guess is that it was an accident, a mistake. It might have been designed to blanket Third World estuary breeding grounds of malaria-carrying mosquitoes. Or not. Anyway, it's out." Victor studied the dripping purple mass and Dee studied Victor. His expression was sad and thoughtful, not at all what she'd expected. How good an actor was he?

She said, "Did you put a genemod plant in my apartment to kill me?"

"No."

"Do you know who did?"

"No. But I can guess."

"Who?"

He laid the seaweed on the deck. "What would have happened if that genemod plant had succeeded in killing you, Dee?"

She snapped, "Don't play games with me. If it had killed me, I'd be dead."

"Right. Then what? Eventually somebody would have broken into your apartment, if only because your corpse would have begun to smell. A friend, your landlord, a neighbor ... somebody. They'd have called the cops. The media monitor police reports, and genemod hysteria grows worse all the time. You'd have been a news sensation: "Ex-Cop Murdered In Bed By Killer Engineered Plant!' Full re-creation sims on every channel."

"Mike din't send that plant to kill you in your apartment," Gum had said. *"T'other side did. It was in all the newspapers. You was dead."*

Victor pulled a vial from his pocket. "The publicity would have aided anti-genemod funding as well as anti-genemod feeling. It could have been GMFA supporters, it could have been one of the more fanatic of those activist groups you've gotten so fond of, it could have been a corporation that gains from public hysteria by keeping genemod products illegal."

"The government wouldn't—"

"I don't think so, either. Watch, Dee." Victor unstoppered the vial and poured it over the purple seaweed on the deck.

"I don't see anything." She was still shaken over Victor's casual list of people who might have murdered her.

"Wait a bit."

The purple seaweed began to dissolve. Only one corner of the mass, and then the reaction stopped.

"It's a genemod bacteria," Victor said. "It eats the bloom. Unfortunately, the toxins emitted by the dying bloom cells kill the eaters. But it's a start. Now that we have the right organism, we can go on tailoring it until it can successfully eliminate the entire bloom."

Dee stared at the seaweed. "And you created that? Here?"

"Yes. We did. Because we're not allowed to create it onshore."

"Victor, that doesn't make sense. Something like this, that could help clean up the ocean."

"And that will in turn replicate and, maybe, create its own crisis. Who knows the effect of releasing this unknown bacteria into the sea? That's what the activists say, and they're right. Only I happen to think that once the pomegranate seeds are eaten, the only cure is more genetically engineered pomegranate seeds."

"What? 'Pomegranates'?"

"Forget it. The point is, this is vital work that can't go forward if I, and people like me, have to spend half our time evading tracking by people like you. And like the FBI, of course."

She shifted in her wheelchair. The deadly sunlight was growing hotter. Victor noticed and took the handles of her chair, pushing it along the deck. "But, Victor, even if the United States won't or can't let you do this ge-nemod work, then surely other countries—the oceans affect everybody!"

"True. And so does international trade. The Keller Pact forbids any trade with any country trafficking in genetically modified organisms . . . remember? A very popular piece of legislation in an election year. Even so, we get some surreptitious funding from a few foreign companies. Not much."

"But it isn't going to stop you."

"I can't let it stop me. Here you are."

They'd reached a section of deck with a remote boat winched up level with the railing. Victor dumped Dee into the tiny boat and pressed a button. The boat began to lower.

"Wait!" Dee called, panicked. "I can't take that much sunlight all the way back—the ultraviolet—"

"Yes, you can," Victor called down over the railing. "Your sunblock is genetically engineered. Good-bye, Demetria Stavros. Stop destroying the abundance that mankind creates in its new gardens and fields."

The boat detached itself from the winch, turned itself around, and took off. On this flat sea Dee wasn't sick. She noted the position of the sun; with that and the time elapsed before landing, maybe she could estimate where the ship had been. Although by that time, it would have already moved.

The involuntary boat ride was a long one. Dee had plenty of time to think.

When she entered the Cotsworth visitors' room, Eliot was already seated with Perri.

Dee scowled; this was supposed to be her time with her sister, not that self-righteous prick Eliot's. But then Dee looked again at Perri. Still thin, still sunken-eyed, but now Perri's amazing blue-green eyes glowed. Something had happened.

"Dee!" Perri said from her side of the table. "Eliot and I are engaged!"

Dee froze.

"Aren't you going to congratulate us?" Eliot said. She recognized the battle call in his voice.

"On what? Another screw-up for Perri, this time dragging you along with it? Or are you the one leading? You two can never make it work, Eliot, and you at least should have the experience and intelligence to know that."

"And why can't we make it?" Eliot asked in his attorney voice. Calm. Seeking information. Deceptive.

"You're too different! God, you're an upcoming defense lawyer and Perri is—"

"A criminal?" Eliot said. "A screw-up? That's what you just called her. Your own sister. What are you afraid of, Dee?"

" 'Afraid' my ass! Don't try any lawyer rhetoric on me!"

"You are afraid. You're terrified. You think you'll lose her, and then whose life will you periodically and heroically rescue from ruin to justify your own life?"

"You don't know anything about—"

"I know you've done it to Perri all her life."

"You think you—"

"Stop!" Perri shouted, loud enough that nearby inmates and their visitors stopped talking and turned to stare. The guard started toward them.

"Stop, Perri repeated, more calmly. "Dee, this isn't your decision. It's mine. Eliot, be quiet. I can justify my own decisions to my sister."

The guard said, "Problem here, counselor?"

"No," Eliot said. "Thank you."

Perri said, "Dee, I wrote you something. Take it. And I'm going to marry Eliot." She held out a small, tightly folded piece of paper toward Dee. On her left hand sparkled a diamond ring.

"Don't tell me I can't wear the ring in here without somebody stealing it," Perri said. "I know that. Eliot will take it with him. But in another three months I'll be out, if I keep my nose clean. I can last that long. I can do this, Dee."

But I can't, Dee thought, and was suddenly afraid to know what she meant. She turned away. "I'm going, Perri. I'll see you next time."

"All right," Perri said softly. Not panicking at Dee's anger, not pleading with her to stay. Not needing her.

Dee passed through the tedious series of prison gates, checkpoints, locked areas. Outside, she walked toward the train. The air wasn't too bad today, but it was very hot. She thought of Victor, out on the open sea, working to engineer an organism to stop the death of the oceans. To bring more changes, but different ones, known in purpose but not in consequence. How long would it take? A *hunnert years,* Gum had rambled. But even Dee, no scientist, knew that a hundred years would be far too long.

She unfolded Perri's note. To Dee's surprise, it was a poem:

> Another love. I am weary of
> The starts of things. Too many springs,
> Too little winter make a bitter
> Everlasting yellow-green.
> Stop. Enough. Let harvest come.

She hadn't even known that Perri wrote poetry.

Waiting for the train, Dee put her hands over her face. She didn't know who was right. Victor, changing whole ecologies like some sort of god. Paula's friends, preserving through destruction. The FBI, blindly enforcing a popular, vindictive law. Which one was bitter spring, which one healing winter? Dee couldn't tell. No more than she could tell if Eliot's terrible accusations about her were true. When was love actually destruction? Could he be so sure that his love for Perri was not?

There was a raid tonight, a hit on a farm in Pennsylvania that engineered biomodified trees to increase photosynthesis capacity. Some of the trees, Dee's group leader had said, incorporated human genes as well as plant genes. Dee didn't know if that was true, either. She knew only one thing for sure.

She wasn't going on the raid. Not tonight, not ever. Let harvest come.

SUN-CLOUD

STEPHEN BAXTER

TO HUMAN EYES, THE system would have been extraordinary:

The single, giant Sun was so vast that its crimson flesh would have embraced all of Sol's scattered planets. Across its surface, glistening vacuoles swarmed, each larger than Sol itself.

There was a planet.

It was a ball of rock no larger than a small asteroid. It skimmed the Sun's immense photosphere, bathed in ruddy warmth. It was coated with air, a thick sea.

The world-ocean teemed with life.

Beyond the Sun's dim glow, the sky was utterly dark.

She rose to the Surface. Thick water slid smoothly from her carapace.

She let her impeller-corpuscles dissociate briefly; they swam free of her main corpus in a fast, darting shoal, feeding eagerly, reveling in their brief liberty.

She lifted optically sensitive corpuscles to the smoky sky. The Sun was a roof over the world, its surface pocked by huge dark pits.

She was called Sun-Cloud: for, at her Coalescence, a cloud of brilliant white light had been observed, blossoming over the Sun's huge, scarred face.

Sun-Cloud was seeking her sister, the one called Orange-Dawn.

Sun-Cloud raised a lantern-corpuscle. The subordinate creature soon tired and began sending quiet chemical-complaints through her corpus; but she ignored them and waited, patiently, as her sphere of lantern light rolled out, spreading like a liquid over the oleaginous Surface.

The light moved slowly enough for a human eye to follow.

Sun-Cloud's people were not like humans.

Here, people assembled from specialized schools of corpuscles: mentalizers, impellers, lanterns, structurals, others. Obeying their own miniature imperatives of life and death, individual corpuscles would leave the aggregate corpus and return to their fish-like shoals, to feed, breed, die. But others would join, and the pattern of the whole could persist, for a time.

Still, Sun-Cloud's lifespan was finite. As the cycle of corpuscle renewal wore on, her pattern would degrade, mutate.

SUN-CLOUD

Like most sentient races, Sun-Cloud's people sustained comforting myths of immortality.

And, like most races, there was a minority who rejected such myths.

Sun-Cloud returned to the Ocean's deep belly.

The light here was complex and uncertain. Above Sun-Cloud the daylight was already dimming. And below her, from the Deep at the heart of the world, the glow of a billion lantern-corpuscles glimmered up, white and pure.

Sun-Cloud watched as Cold-Current ascended toward her.

They were going to discuss Sun-Cloud's sister, Orange-Dawn. Orange-Dawn was a problem.

Cold-Current was a lenticular assemblage of corpuscles twice Sun-Cloud's size, who nevertheless rose with an awesome unity. The ranks of impellers at Cold-Current's rim churned at the thick waters of the Ocean, their small cilia vibrating so rapidly that they were blue-shifted.

The Song suffused the waters around Sun-Cloud, as it always did; but as Cold-Current lifted away from the Deep the complex harmonics of the Song changed, subtly.

Sun-Cloud, awed, shrank in on herself, her structural corpuscles pushing in toward their sisters at her swarming core. Sun-Cloud knew that she herself contributed but little, a few minor overtones, to the rich assonance of the Song. How must it be to be so grand, so powerful, that one's absence left the Song—the huge, world-girdling Song itself—audibly lacking in richness?

Cold-Current hovered; a bank of optic-corpuscles swiveled, focusing on Sun-Cloud. "You know why I asked to meet you," she said.

"Orange-Dawn."

"Yes. Orange-Dawn. I am very disturbed, Sun-Cloud. Orange-Dawn is long overdue for Dissolution. And yet she persists; she prowls the rim of the Song, even the Surface, intact, obsessed. Even to the extent of injuring her corpuscles."

"I know that Orange-Dawn wants to see out another hundred Cycles," Sun-Cloud said. "Orange-Dawn has theories. That in a hundred Cycles' time—"

"I know," Cold-Current said. "She believes she has Coalesced with ancient wisdom. Somehow, in a hundred Cycles, the world will be transformed, and Orange-Dawn will be affirmed."

"But it's impossible," Sun-Cloud said. "I know that; Orange-Dawn must see that."

But Cold-Current said, absently: "But it *may* be possible, to postpone Dissolution so long." Sun-Cloud, intrigued, saw a tight, cubical pattern of corpuscles move through Cold-Current's corpus; individual corpuscles swam to and fro, but the pattern persisted. "Possible," Cold-Current said. "There is old wisdom. But such a thing would be—ugly. Discordant." Perhaps that cubical pattern contained the fragment of old knowledge to which Cold-Current hinted.

Cold-Current rotated grandly. "I want you to go and talk to her. Perhaps you can say something. . . . Nobody knows Orange-Dawn as well as you."

That was true. Orange-Dawn had helped Sun-Cloud in her earliest Coalescence, as Sun-Cloud struggled toward sentience. Orange-Dawn had hunted combinations of healthy corpuscles for her sister, helped her coax the corpuscles into an orderly shoal. Together the sisters had run across the Surface of the Ocean, their out-thrust optic corpuscles blue-tinged with their exhilarating velocity. . . .

Cold-Current began to sink back into the glimmering depths of the Ocean, her disciplined impellers beating resolutely. "You must help her, Sun-Cloud. You must help her put aside these foolish shards of knowledge and speculation, and learn to embrace true beauty. . . ."

As Cold-Current faded from view, the light at the heart of the world brightened, as if in welcome, and the Song's harmonies deepened joyously.

The world was very old. Sun-Cloud's people were very old.

They had accreted many fragments of knowledge, of philosophy and science.

A person, on Dissolution, could leave behind frag-

ments of insight, of wisdom, in the partial, semi-sentient
assemblies called sub-corpora. Before dissolving in their
turn into the general corpuscle shoals, the sub-corpora
could be absorbed into a new individual, the knowledge
saved.

Or perhaps not.

If they were not incorporated quickly, the remnant
sub-corpora would break up. Their component mentation-
corpuscles would descend, and become lost in the anaer-
obic Deep at the heart of the world.

Sun-Cloud returned to the Surface of the Ocean.

She saw that the Sun had almost set; a last sliver of
crimson light spanned one horizon, which curved
sharply. Above her the sky was clear and utterly black,
desolately so.

Her corpuscles transmitted their agitation to each
other.

She raised a lantern; cold light bloomed slowly
across the sea's oily meniscus.

She roamed the Ocean, seeking Orange-Dawn.

At last the creeping lantern light brought echoes of
distant motion to her optic corpuscles: a small form
thrashing at the Surface in lonely unhappiness.

With a rare sense of urgency Sun-Cloud ordered her
impeller-corpuscles into motion. It didn't take long for
her to accelerate to a significant fraction of lightspeed;
the impellers groaned as they strained at relativity's tan-

gible barrier, and the image of the lonely one ahead was stained with blue shift.

Wavelets lapped at her and air stroked her hide; she felt exhilarated by her velocity.

She slowed. She called softly: "Orange-Dawn?"

Listlessly Orange-Dawn raised optic corpuscles. Orange-Dawn was barely a quarter Sun-Cloud's size. She was withered, her corpus depleted. Her corpuscles lay passively over each other, tiny mouths gaping with obvious hunger.

"Do I shock you, Sun-Cloud?"

Sun-Cloud sent small batches of corpuscles as probes into Orange-Dawn's tattered carcass. "Orange-Dawn. Your corpuscles are suffering. Some of them are dying. Cold-Current is concerned for you—"

"She sent you to summon me to my Dissolution."

Sun-Cloud said, "I don't like to see you like this. You're introducing a harshness into the Song."

"The Song, the damnable Song," Orange-Dawn muttered. Moodily she began to spin in the water. The corpuscles' decay had so damaged her corpus's circular symmetry that she whipped up frothy waves which lapped over her upper carapace, the squirming corpuscles there. She poked optic corpuscles upwards, but the night sky was blind. "The Song drowns thought."

"What will happen in a hundred Cycles, Orange-Dawn?"

Orange-Dawn thrashed at the water. "The data is partial. . . ." She focused wistful optic corpuscles on her sister. "I don't know. But it will be—"

"What?"

"Unimaginable. *Wonderful*."

Sun-Cloud wanted to understand. "What *data*?"

"There are some extraordinary speculations, developed in the past, still extant here and there. . . . Did you know, for instance, that the Cycle is actually a tide, raised in our Ocean-world during its passage around the Sun? It took many individuals a long time to observe, speculate, calculate, obtain that fragment of information. And yet we are prepared to throw it away, into the great bottomless well of the Song. . . ."

"I've tried to assemble some of this. It's taken so long, and the fragments don't fit more often than not, but—"

"Integrate? Like a Song?"

"Yes." Orange-Dawn focused her optic corpuscles. "Yes Like a Song. But not the comforting mush they intone below. That's a Song of death, Sun-Cloud. A Song to guide you into nonbeing."

Sun-Cloud shuddered; little groups of her corpuscles broke away, agitated. "We don't die."

"Of course not." Orange-Dawn rotated and drifted towards her. "Watch this," she said.

Quickly, she budded off a whole series of sub-corpora, each tiny body consisting of a few hundred corpuscles. Instantly the sub-corpora squirmed about the Surface, leaping and breaking the meniscus, blue-shifted they pushed into lightspeed's intangible membrane.

Sun-Cloud felt uneasy. "Those sub-corpora are big nough to be semi-sentient, Orange-Dawn."

"But do you see?" said Orange-Dawn testily.

"See what?"

"*Blue shift*. The sub-corpora-see how, instinctively, ey strain against the walls of the prison of lightspeed. ven in the moment of their Coalescing. Light imprisons all. Light isolates us. . . ."

Her words filtered through Sun-Cloud, jarring and range, reinforced by bizarre chemical signals.

"Why are you doing this, Orange-Dawn?"

"Watch." Now Orange-Dawn sent out a swarm of sy impeller-corpuscles; they prodded the independent b-corpora back towards Orange-Dawn's corpus. Sunoud, uneasy, watched how the sub-corpora resisted eir tiny Dissolutions, feebly.

"See?" Orange-Dawn said. "See how they struggle ;ainst their immersion, in the overwhelming Ocean of y personality? See how they struggle to *live?*"

Sun-Cloud's own corpuscles sensed the suffering of eir fellows, and shifted uneasily. She flooded her cirlatory system with soothing chemicals. In her distress e felt a primal need for the Song. She sent sensorrpuscles stretching into the Ocean beneath her, seekg out the comfort of its distant, endless surging; its rmony was borne through the Ocean to her by chemil traces.

... But would *she* struggle so, when it came time f[or] her to Dissolve, in her turn, into the eternal wash of t[he] Song?

It was, she realized, a question she had never eve[r] framed before.

Now, gathering her corpuscles closely around he[r] Orange-Dawn turned from Sun-Cloud, and began [to] beat across the Surface with a new determination.

"You must come with me, Orange-Dawn," Sun-Clou[d] warned.

"No. I will see out my hundred Cycles."

"But you cannot...." *Unless,* she found herse[lf] thinking, *unless Cold-Current is right. Unless there [is] some lost way to extend consciousness.*

"If I submit to Dissolution, I will lose my sense [of] self, Sun-Cloud. My individuality. The corpus of know[l]edge and understanding I've spent so long assemblin[g]. What is that but death? What is the Song but a comfo[rt,] an anaesthetic illusion to hide that fact? ..."

"You are damaging the unity of the Song, Orang[e-]Dawn. You are—discordant."

Orange-Dawn was receding now; she raised up a l[it]tle batch of acoustic corpuscles. "Good!" she called.

"I won't be able to protect you!" cried Sun-Cloud.

But she was gone.

Sun-Cloud raised lantern-corpuscles, sending puls[es] of slow light out across the Ocean's swelling surface. S[he] called for her sister, until her corpuscles were exhaust[ed]

SUN-CLOUD

* * *

In some ways, Sun-Cloud's people resembled humans.

Sun-Cloud's component corpuscles were of very different ancestry.

Mentation-corpuscles—the neuronlike creatures that carried consciousness in tiny packets of molecules—were an ancient, anaerobic race. The other main class, the impellers and structure-corpuscles, were oxygen breathers: faster moving, more vigorous.

Human muscles usually burned glucose aerobically, using sugars from the air. But during strenuous activity, the muscles would ferment glucose in the anaerobic way evolved by the earliest bacteria. Thus human bodies, too, bore echoes of the earliest biosphere of Earth.

But, unlike a human body, Sun-Cloud's corpus was modular.

Despite their antique enmity, the two phyla within Sun-Cloud would cooperate, in the interests of the higher creature in which they were incorporated.

Until Sun-Cloud weakened.

A mass of corpora, sub-corpora, and shoals of trained impeller-corpuscles rose from the Deep in a great ring.

Not five Cycles had passed since Sun-Cloud's failed attempt to bring Orange-Dawn home. Now they had come for Orange-Dawn.

Sun-Cloud found her sister at the center of the hunt. She was shrunken, already fragmented, her corpuscles pulsing with fear.

"I don't want to die, Sun-Cloud."

Anguish for her sister stabbed at Sun-Cloud. She sent soothing chemical half words soaking through the Ocean. "Come with me," she said gently.

Exhausted, Orange-Dawn allowed herself to be enfolded in Sun-Cloud's chemical caresses.

Commingled, the sisters sank into the Ocean. Their ovoid bodies twisted slowly into the depths; light shells from curious individuals washed over them as they passed.

The light faded rapidly as they descended. Soon there were few free sub-corpora; and of the people they saw most were linked by corpuscle streams with at least one other, and often in groups of three, four, or more.

The Song was a distant, strengthening pulse from the heart of the Ocean beneath them.

Now Cold-Current rose up to meet them, huge and intimidating, her complex hide pulsing with lantern-corpuscles. The rim of her slowly rotating corpus became diffuse, blurred, as her corpuscles swam tentatively toward Orange-Dawn.

Cold-Current murmured, "You are old, yet very young, Orange-Dawn. Your unhappiness is caused by ignorance. There is no other Ocean. Only this one. There is no change and never has been. These facts are part of what we are. That's why your speculations are damaging you.

"You have to forget your dreams, Orange-Dawn. . . .

Orange-Dawn hardened, drawing her corpuscles into a tight little fortress. But Cold-Current was strong, and she forced compact biochemical packets into Orange-Dawn's corpus. Sun-Cloud, huddling close, picked up remote chemical echoes of the messages Cold-Current offered.

... *Hear the Song*, Cold-Current's corpuscles called. *Open up to the Song.*

Their bodies joined, her impeller-corpuscles herding Orange-Dawn tightly, Cold-Current began to guide Orange-Dawn deeper into the lattice of mingled persons.

Sun-Cloud followed, struggling to stay close to her sister. Orange-Dawn's pain suffused the waters around her with clouds of chemicals; Sun-Cloud suffered for her and with her.

As they descended, individuals became less and less distinct, and free corpuscles swam through the lattice's loosing gaps. At last they were falling through a sea of corpuscles which, with endless intelligent grace, swam over and around each other. Sun-Cloud's structurals and impellers felt enfeebled here, in this choking water; the effort of forcing her way downwards seemed to multiply.

Perhaps this was like Dissolution, she thought.

At last there was only one entity, a complex of mingled bodies that filled the Ocean. The living lattice vibrated with the Song, which boomed around them, joyous and vibrant.

"The Deep," Cold-Current whispered to Orange-

Dawn. "The Song. Now you will join this, Orange-Dawn. Uncountable billions of minds, endless thoughts straddling the world eternally. The Song will sustain your soul, after Dissolution, merged with everyone who has ever lived. You'll never be alone again—"

Suddenly, at the last, Orange-Dawn resisted. "No! I could not bear it. I could not bear—"

She was struggling. Jagged images filled Sun-Cloud's mind, of being crushed, swamped, stultified.

Immediately a host of sub-corpora and corpuscles, jagged masses of them, hurled themselves into Orange-Dawn's corpus. Sun-Cloud heard a single, agonized chemical scream, which echoed through the water. And then the structure of the corpus was broken up.

Corpuscles, many of them wounded, came hailing out of the cloud of Dissolution; some of them spiraled away into the darkness, and others rained down toward the glowing Deep.

Sub-corpora formed, almost at random, and wriggled through the water. They were semi-sentient: bewildered and broken images of Orange-Dawn.

Sun-Cloud could only watch. Loss stabbed at her; her grief was violent.

Cold-Current was huge, complex, brilliantly illuminated. "It is over. It is better," she said.

Sun-Cloud's anger surged. "How can you say that? She's *dead*. She died in fear and agony."

"No. She'll live forever, through the Song. As will we all."

"Show me what you know," Sun-Cloud said savagely. "Show me how Orange-Dawn might have extended her life, through another ninety Cycles."

"It is artificial. Discordant. It is not appropriate—"

"Show me!"

With huge reluctance, Cold-Current budded a tight, compact sub-corpora. It bore the cubical pattern Sun-Cloud had observed earlier. "Knowledge is dangerous," Cold-Current said sadly. "It makes us unstable. That is the moral of Orange-Dawn's story. You must not—"

Sun-Cloud hurled herself at the pattern, and forcibly integrated it into her own corpus. Then—following impulses she barely recognized—she rose upwards, away from the bright-glowing Deep.

She passed through the cloud of Orange-Dawn's corpuscles, and called to them.

The Song boomed from the Deep, massive, alluring, exultifying; and Cold-Current's huge form glistened as he called her. Sun-Cloud ignored it all.

She ascended towards the Surface, as rapidly as she could. Orange-Dawn's fragmentary sub-corpora followed her, bewildered, uncertain.

The place Sun-Cloud called the Deep was an anaerobic environment. Only mentation-corpuscles could survive there. They lay over each other in complex, pulsing swarms, with neural energy flickering desultorily between them.

357

The Song was a complex, evolving sound-structure maintained by the dense shoals of mentation-corpuscles which inhabited the heart of the world, and with grace notes added by the Coalesced individuals of the higher oxygen-rich layers of the Ocean.

At the end of their lives, the mentation structures of billions of individuals had dissolved into the Deep's corpuscle shoals. The Song, they believed, was a form of immortality.

Embracing this idea, most people welcomed Dissolution. Others rejected it.

Sun-Cloud gathered around her central corpus the cubical pattern of Cold-Current, and Orange-Dawn's sad remnants, integrating them crudely. She grew huge, bloated, powerful.

And now, as she broke the thick Surface of the Ocean, she made ready.

She wondered briefly if she had gone mad. Perhaps Orange-Dawn had infected her.

But if it were so, let it be. She must know the answer to Orange-Dawn's questions for herself, before she submitted to—as she saw it now, as if through her sister's perception—the sinister embrace of the Song.

She enfolded Cold-Current's compact data pattern and let its new wisdom flow through her....

Of course. It is simple.

She began to forge forward, across the Ocean.

A bow wave built up before her, thick and resisting. But she assembled her impellers and drove through it. At last the wave became a shock, sharp-edged, traveling through the water as a crest.

And now, quickly, she began to sense the resistance of lightspeed's soft membrane. The water turned softly blue before her, and when she looked back, the world was stained red.

At length she passed into daylight.

The day seemed short. She continued to gather her pace.

Determined, she abandoned that which she did not need: lantern-corpuscles, manipulators, even some mentation-components: any excess mass which her impellers need not drag with her.

A bow, of speed-scattered light, began to coalesce around her.

The day-night cycle was passing so quickly now it was flickering. And she could sense the Cycles themselves, the grand, slow heaving of the Ocean as her world tracked around its Sun.

The light ahead of her passed beyond blue and into a milky invisibility, while behind her a dark spot gathered in the redness and reached out to embrace half the world.

Time-dilated, she forged across the Surface of her Ocean and into the future; and ninety-five Cycles wore away around her.

* * *

Light's crawl was embedded, a subtle scaling law, in every force governing the structure of Sun-Cloud's world.

The Sun was much larger than Sol—ten thousand times more so—for the fusion fires at its heart were much less vigorous than Sol's. And Sun-Cloud's world was a thousand times smaller than Earth, for the electrostatic and degeneracy pressures, which resisted gravitational collapse, were greatly weaker.

Lightspeed dominated Sun-Cloud's structure, too. If she had been a single entity, complete and entire, it would have taken too long for light—or any other signal— to crawl through her structure. So she was a composite creature; her mind was broken down into modules of thought, speculation, and awareness. She was a creature of parallel processing, scattered over a thousand fragile corpuscles.

And Sun-Cloud's body was constrained to be small enough that her gravitational potential could not fracture the flimsy molecular bonds that held her corpus together.

Sun-Cloud, forging across the Surface of her Ocean, was just two millimeters across.

At last, a new light erupted in the bow that embraced her world.

With an effort, she slowed. The light-bow expanded rapidly, as if the world were unfolding back into its proper morphology. She allowed some of her impeller-corpuscles to run free, and she saw their tiny wakes running across the Surface, determined, red-shifted.

Now that her monumental effort was done she was exhausted, depleted, her impellers dead, lost, or dying; unless new impellers joined her, she would scarcely be able to move again.

Ninety-five Cycles.

Everybody she had known—Cold-Current and the rest—all of them must be gone, now, absorbed into the Song's unending pulse.

It remained only for her to learn what mystery awaited, here in the remoteness of the future, and then she could Dissolve into the Song herself.

. . . From the darkling sky, the new light washed over her.

Her optic corpuscles swiveled upwards. She cried out.

Sun-Cloud felt her world shrink beneath her from infinity to a frail mote; the Song decayed from the thoughts of a god to the crooning of a damaged sub-corpus.

Above her, utterly silently—and for the first time in all history—the stars were coming out.

To human eyes, the skies of this cosmos would have seemed strange indeed:

The stars spawned from gas clouds, huge and cold. Hundreds of them formed in a cluster, companions to Sun-Cloud's Sun. Heat crept from each embryonic star, dispersing the remnant wisps of the birthing cloud.

It took five billion human years for the light to cross the gulf between the stars.

And at last—and as one speculative thinker among Sun-Cloud's people had predicted, long ago—the scattered light of those remote Suns washed over an unremarkable world, which orbited a little above the photosphere of their companion. . . .

The stars were immense globes, glowing red and white, jostling in a complex sky; and sheets and lanes of gas writhed between them.

Orange-Dawn had been right. This *was* wonderful, beyond her imagining—but crushing, terrifying.

Pain tore at her. Jagged molecules flooded her system; her corpuscles broke apart, and began at last their ancestral war.

She struggled to retain her core of rationality, just a little longer. Exhausted, she hastily assembled subcorpora, and loaded packets of information into them, pale images of the astonishing sky. She sent them hailing down into the Ocean, into the Deep, into the belly of the Song itself.

Soon a new voice would join the Song: a merger of her own and Orange-Dawn's. And it would sing of Suns, countless, beyond imagining.

Everything would be different now.

She fell, gladly, into the warm emptiness of Dissolution.

INTO GREENWOOD

JIM GRIMSLEY

One

TO VISIT THE DIRIJHI one leaves coastal Jarutan by putter to travel to one of the towns near the forest where they staff a trade mission; there are no roads in Greenwood, only waterways, so one must find a boat that travels one of these routes, in my case the River Silas. One heads into the part of Aramen that the Hormling have, by treaty, excluded from settlement in order not to crowd the forest preserve. The Dirijhi no longer grow all the way to the sea as they used to, stopping about a hundred standard land units north of the coast. They never grew on the rest of Aramen, according to what we have learned since we gave them symbionts and began to communicate.

Nowadays, Aramenians live in settlements and farms right up to the edge of the Dirijhi preserve. Before entering the forest, I stayed the night in the last village along Silas, at the place where the river emerges from the canopy, a town called Dembut where a lot of early Hormling colonists settled. Though they don't call themselves Hormling any more, except in terms of ancestry, and they have no loyalty to Senal or the Mage. They're Aramenian these days, they'll tell you so stoutly, and most of them are for independence, though they keep quiet about it.

I had arrived on Aramen during one of the quiet times, when the colonial assembly and the colony's Prin administrators were getting along with some degree of harmony. I was returning from a decade-long trip to Paska, another Mage colony inside the Cluster, three years' passage each way on the Hormling Conveyance. On Paska, the independence movement was foundering, as ours was. Like my organization, People for a Free Aramen, the Paskan movement had achieved a certain ceiling of success and been stalled ever since. Their group was twenty-odd years old, ours about twice that. Forty thousand subscriber members and enough committed workers to stage a decent rally every few months. Internal arguments about what mix of sedition and pressure could be used to convince the Mage and the Prin that allowing us self government was a good idea. I learned what I could from four years with the Free Paska Coalition, but I was glad to come home again, though somewhat discouraged, after so long an absence, to find that the colonial administration seemed more entrenched than ever.

I think we could beat the Hormling, take the planet from them, but I'm not sure about the Prin. Whatever explanation you believe for the powers they exercise, we all know from experience that those powers are very real. They are the key that holds the Hormling empire together. We have seen time and again under the Prin that it is possible to make people happy even when they are not free. The Prin are good at creating contentment, complacency. All over the southern continent the rains fall regularly on the farms, the crops grow, the industries run smoothly, machinery functions, the ships and aircraft land and take off on time. Aramen is the end of the Conveyance line because the gate to Senal is here, and therefore our world is very important to the Mage. On Aramen, the Prin do their jobs carefully, everything works well, nobody goes hungry, sick people get treatment, crime is kept low, smuggling and the black market are marginal, and nearly every crime is justly punished, since nobody can fool a Prin. Hard to fight that. Hard, sometimes, to justify it even to myself, that I think we should be free of their rule.

The northern continent, Ajhevan, is a different story from the south. The Prin do not administer the weather here, or adjust the growing season, by virtue of the fact that the Dirijhi are a protected species, and this continent is under Dirijhi jurisdiction. The trees have made it clear to the Mage, through the symbionts, that the Prin are not welcome to come to Ajhevan. For some reason none of us have ever understood, the Mage prefers that the Dirijhi be left alone and gives them what they want. So Ajhevan belongs to them, and we humans who live here are truly free, except for Hormling taxes, in a way that nearly no one else can claim. Because we don't have the Prin here to read our minds whether we like it or not, to look over our shoulders and meddle in our affairs. But even my friends in Ajhevan have become resigned to the notion that independence will only come a long time from now. Since my return, I noticed that some of the people inside the movement had begun to speak in the same terms.

What we needed, what we had always needed, was an ally. I had hoped to find something like that on Paska. But then, a few days after I returned, a letter arrived from my brother Binam asking me to visit him in Greenwood.

The trees don't care for outsiders, though they make a lot of money running tours into the forest. They rarely grant anyone permission to stay in Dirijhi country for any length of time. But my brother was a symbiont, and I had not seen him since the change. I'd been asking him to allow me to visit for years, to spend time with him but also to sound him out about what the trees might think of independence. All of us with ties to the Dirijhi were making the same request. After many years of refusal, Binam had suddenly agreed. So I was on my way.

The Dirijhi permit only a certain kind of flat-

bottomed boat to travel up-river under the canopy, so I
spent the afternoon in Dembut trying to line up trans-
portation. The river guides are all licensed, and there was
actually a symbiont on duty to check my pass in the
outpost station; the Dirijhi hire human staff to deal with
the tourist traffic, though the sym was clearly in charge.
He or she must have been melded to one of the nearer
trees, though even then it's an effort for a sym to be
apart from the tree for any length of time. I knew that
much from Binam, who sent me letters, written ones on
paper, from time to time; the only scripted letters I ever
got in my life. This sym had a pinched look in the face,
eyes of that iridescent silver that is the result of the tree-
feeding, the pupils small in the light, though they could
dilate completely in the dark, enabling the sym to see
as if the world were in full noon. Binam would look like
that, I reminded myself. He would still be my brother,
but he would be changed.

Once I cleared my papers and booked passage on one
of the riverboats, I found a hotel room for the night. I
was tempted to think of the place as primitive or backward, since we were so far from what I had come to
think of as civilization, but Dembut had every conve-
nience you could ask for. Uplinks to the whole Hormling
data mass, entertainment parlors that were 4D capable,
clean VR stalls, good restaurants. The Dirijhi don't like
big power matrices, so everything on Ajhevan runs on
portable fusion generators; cold boxes, they're called,

and for a village the size of Dembut, about a dozen were required to power the town. Hormling technology, like nearly everything that works in the Cluster. This and much other interesting information was piped to the screen in my hotel room, the loop playing as I keyed the door and entered. I muted the sound and threw my bag onto the little bed.

I bought a girl for the night. Her name was Tira and she had a brother who was a symbiont, too. Ajhevano are pretty free sexually, and prostitution is considered a nice way to make some extra money, especially in a tourist town, as Dembut is, so there are a lot of people registered with the agencies. People in Ajhevan are not usually hung up about lesbians, though now and then you still get a feeling that they don't know altogether what to make of us in the smaller towns, so I was apprehensive. Tira was a free spirit, though, and we had a nice dinner and went to the room and she gave me a massage and I returned the favor and then we wrapped round each other and got serious for a while. She had no problem with lesbians, clearly, and I felt worlds better when we were done. We talked about our brothers and I asked if she had seen hers since he made the change. She saw him often, she said; to be near him, she had taken up her trade in Dembut—her trade being rune reading for tourists in the market, the sex was a sideline. She liked the forest, she liked her brother, she liked the difference since he underwent the change, she had

368

thought about becoming a sym herself. "Beats having to work for a living," she said.

In the morning, I met the riverboat on time and waited impatiently to be underway. Today the river station was staffed by two different syms, one who had been a man and the other who had been a woman. The bioengineering that gets done on a symbiont starts with neutering, but sometimes you could tell which had been which. The eyes, though, were so difficult to read. I kept trying to place them in Binam's face.

We got underway in the eighth marking. My fellow passengers were tourists, a family from Feidre and two couples from New Charnos, southerners, all of them. They were curious about Ajhevan, so I answered their questions politely, while the pilot was busy. I was born here and grew up here, first on a group farm and then in a girls' commune. After my parents sold my brother to the sym recruiters, I petitioned the Magistrate's Court for a separation and was granted it, and lived in the commune after that. To be fair, which I don't always like to be, that's my way of looking at what happened. My parents didn't exactly sell my brother, at least, not against his will. Binam had been begging to join the symbionts since he was eight years old and got lost in Greenwood; and my parents were swayed by the bounty and by what Binam wanted, so fervently, and gave permission. I never forgave them for allowing him to make that choice himself, so young, only twelve. Especially since they were paid enough money to sell the algae farm we worked, that they had come to hate. After I divorced them, they bought a big house in Byutiban, on the southern continent, and both went to work in the Prin administration. We reconciled later, though I never did anything to lift the court decision. By then, even if I had forgiven them for selling Binam, I'd never have understood why they went to work for the Hormling.

My boat penetrated into the canopy along a string of Dirijhi cities, according to the pilot, an Erejhen who gave his name as Kirith, though since he was Erejhen that was not likely to be his real name. He pointed out how to spot a city: the trees grew closer and denser, the undergrowth was more strictly regulated, the appearance was formal. There was even a foliage pattern along the river, shrubs grown and maintained in a certain sequence by the tree through a complex process that only a fully mature Dirijh could undertake before symbionts. Nowadays, the symbionts work under the direction of the trees to cultivate the Shimmering Garden, which is the name the Dirijhi give to Greenwood.

Overhead, in the cities, the trees intertwine upper tier branches in one of seven patterns, sometimes a mix of all seven in a large city, like the capital. In the branches now and then we would see a sym, but only once that whole day did we see one on the ground. One of the couples asked if Kirith knew any of the names of the cities, and he answered that the Dirijhi had no spoken

language and the symbionts never attempted to trans-
literate the speech that passed between sym and host.
The only words the syms ever gave us are the name they
use for the tree people, "Dirijhi," coined from a word for
tree in one of the old languages of Senal, and the name
for the forest, "Shimmering Garden."

We were headed for the Dirijhi capital, near the center
of the forest. There I would transfer to another flatboat
that would carry me along one of the water-channels
leading west into the interior, where Binam and his tree
lived. We were passing tourist boats all morning as they
stopped along the shore, places where the Dirijhi had
agreed to allow walking tours for a stiff fee. The tour
spots changed from time to time to give the riverfront
trees a respite. Since the trees migrate toward the closest
river or canal over the course of their extremely long
lifetimes, the oldest, longest-lived trees end up along the
shore and die there; though trees occasionally refuse to
make the migration and many die in the interior before
getting all the way to the shore. They migrate slowly,
by setting roots carefully and deliberately in one direction and shifting themselves by manipulating the compression and tension of wood in the main bole, and can
move as much a full standard unit in about a standard
century, about seventy years Aramenian. It takes a person about a half a day to walk that distance; it took the
symbionts to tell us the trees could move at all.

The trees along the river nearly hypnotized me. A lot of them were dead and decaying, since they were the oldest; but their gardens were still maintained by syms in the neighboring trees. The living trees give off all kinds of scents, according to Binam's letters, the patterns changing with the religious and social calendar, and the effect can be ecstatic. We were getting the tourist spray along the Silas, but even that was heavenly. Some of the Dirijh rise as tall as a thirty story building, if you've ever seen one of those. They are massive creatures with a central trunk or bole and a series of buttress roots rising to support a huge upper canopy. The central bole becomes massive and the buttress roots rise up as far as the lowest branches. All the branching occurs from the central trunk, and these massive branches sometimes drop additional prop roots to the ground for support, till a single Dirijh can look like a small forest. The trees can climb four hundred stades high even in Aramen's 5-percent higher-than-standard gravity, where nobody expected to find the tallest trees in the known stars.

Standard years and standard gravities refer to the year and the total gravitic force of Senal, the Mage world. The standard is necessary since there are so many worlds to deal with in the Cluster, all slightly or very different from one another in physical characteristics. I can admit that and still get a little riled that the standard is Senal. Why not a mean year, a mean day, a mean gravity? My parents think that's a silly argument, that

t doesn't make any difference. That's no reason to commit acts of sedition, to work for a rebellion, they say.
But I disagree.

I moved for a while to the southern continent, to
Avitran, after I got through school in the women's commune. Trained as a gene-splicer in Genetech, working in
a clean lab creating one or another of the seventeen
hundred legal variants from standard DNA that define
the human race as we know it, three hundred years since
the Hormling and their partners the Erejhen began to
spread through the local stars, and nearly thirty thousand years since the Hormling themselves arrived on
Senal, sent there from Earth to find the Mage, as the
Dons Quilian claims. I believe the three-hundred-year
proposition, I don't know about the rest. I know I don't
believe in Earth.

Two

We slept on the boat, while it continued upriver on satellite guidance. Firesprays flying overhead, now and
then a bit of the moon peeping through the canopy.
Some of the Dirijh fold their leaves at night to bring
moonlight down to the Shimmering Garden. Aramen's
tiny moon Kep orbits the planet in a geosynchronous
loop and is always in the sky over Ajhevan; sometimes
you can see its ghost in the day. The southern continent
Syutiban, on the opposite side of the planet, never sees

that moon at all, though Aramen has a larger, red moon. Sith, that orbits farther out, and it goes through phase and appears in all parts of Aramen.

Because the boats are wide enough to accommodate even a tall person lying across them, there was plenty of room for us to sleep, and we spread out bedding after we ate our dinner packet. No question of our sleeping ashore; tourists aren't allowed that option at any price. I had bought a sleeping roll in Dembut, and the guide showed me how to get into it. Fairly comfortable, given the motion of the river. The boat was tight and dry; the Dirijhi wouldn't have let it run the river if it weren't. Peaceful to think that the boat would continue on its placid voyage while I dreamed.

Overnight, we passed through one of the Dirijh cities where the channels cross; out in the center at the junction grew a single Dirijh, one of the conifers, gorgeous and nearly symmetrical, rising right up out of the water, its roots immense, earth filtered out of the river clinging to them, glistening in the moonlight. We sailed around it. The guide woke me up to see; he had understood my interest, knew my brother was a sym. It never hurts for a guide to know a sym, or a relative of one.

"You ever see anything like that?" Kirith asked.

"No. We used to come to Greenwood when I was kid, but never this far north."

"You grew up here?"

"Yes."

"You like it?"

I laughed. "Yes. Very much."

He nodded. Handsome, like most of the Erejhen I've met. He was one of the dark-skinned ones, colored like coffee, with deep, dark eyes. "This reminds me of home, his place."

"Where?"

"Irion," he said, "near the forest where the Mage comes from."

I laughed. "No, really. Where do you come from?"

He tilted his head. "You don't believe me?"

"I don't believe you come from Irion. All you Erejhen say you come from there, but most of you were born here, just like me."

His jaw set in a line. "I come from there," he said, and he turned away, offended.

All day the next day, we traveled north. This was summer in the northern hemisphere, very hot in most places, but we were perfectly cool, riding along the water in the deep shade. We came to the Dirijh capital, and got off the boat onto a floating platform and hired a space in a channel-boat going east. Not a single word from Kirith after our conversation the night before. Maybe he was from Irion, but it's true they all claim to come from there, you have to ask. I'm not a follower of the Irion cult, I know as much as I need to about the place; the Prin are trained there, which is reason enough for me to distrust the rest of the Erejhen, too.

The channel-boat was ready to leave, mine was the last space to be sold, and we were underway as soon as I showed my papers, which were actual physical documents, fairly stained and tired by that time. I got a look at the trees of the central city, which is probably the better way to describe the way this city functions than to call it a capital. Greenwood is defined by rivers and channels that divide the forest in a rough grid, sometimes skewed but very clearly organized. The rivers flow north to south and channels flow east-west. The symbionts say the Dirijhi grew that way deliberately, creating the watershed to make the water run where they wanted, first defining the rivers and then dividing for the channels. The grid functioned as irrigation and fire protection for Greenwood long before it served as highway for trade, tourists, and sym business. The central city lay at the junction of the Silas, the central river, and the central channel, which the guides have named the Isar, after a river in Irion.

A day and a half east, I got off at the junction of the Isar Channel with the River Os. From there, I would travel inland by truss. The syms have domesticated some of the animal species, including the truss, an oversize bird that has only vestigial wings but has thighs powerful enough to carry two people, in baskets slung over the truss's back, one on each side. In my case, in the other basket was the sym who owned the truss. The ride was indescribable, I thought I would break bones with all the jolting and bouncing around, but the bird could move. Leaves slapped at my forehead as we headed out of the city into rural Greenwood, the part of the forest nobody sees unless she knows a sym.

Binam's tree was a youngster and lived pretty far out. All of Greenwood is cut through with creeks and canals to bring water into the interior, and we could have navigated on those except the Dirijhi don't like the waters to be disturbed so close to their roots. The brain case is in the root crown, where it developed out of specialized root tissue that provided the trees with gravity perception. The older trees along the main watercourses can take the commotion of the boats, because they have to, but everybody travels by truss or by foot in the interior.

My companion in the balancing basket was another kind of guide, hired to lead people like me to the proper tree. Those guides are all syms, who charge a high price for time away from the host. Binam had arranged the guide and the truss, since there was no way for me to do it. The sym kept quiet on the trip, to conserve energy. With this one, I couldn't tell whether the original had been a man or a woman, and that made me uncomfortable. I watched the undergrowth, smelled the most amazing perfumes, caught flashes of sunlight overhead.

The change in the Shimmering Garden as we left the cities was marked. Different shrubs grew, and vines climbed some of the trees and then cascaded from tree to tree, spectacular festoons of flowers hanging down from the boughs. The truss paths were moss or something that looked like clover, and along either side of the path were flowering bushes, low growing trees, and other kinds of growth that the Dirijhi encourage. No more sense of formality; each tree tended its garden as it wished, and some of them were wildly overgrown, the central trunks nearly hidden behind green walls, screened overhead by the low-growing canopy where it was impossible to distinguish one tree from another. No one can travel safely here without a guide, though the occasional renegade or stray tourist has tried. Many of the plants are toxic to humans, and some of the poisons kill by contact; the truss paths avoid those, but most people on their own wouldn't know the difference before they were dead.

The truss had a musty smell, but no bugs I could see. Their owners keep them clean, no easy task with a bird. Dun-colored feathers. A mottled pattern of brown and dull green feathers on the back of the neck, that I grew to know far better than I wished.

We traveled through the night, and I even dozed occasionally, my head collapsed onto the woven carry-all strap, truss feathers tickling my nose. We were only allowed to stop at certain oases, mostly in public meadows that the Dirijhi cultivate to open up the canopy to the sky. A place where a Dirijhi dies is left fallow for a long time, while the body decomposes, and we stopped at one of those as well. I was glad we were passing through the open spaces at night, since the Aramenian sun can be murder that time of year in the north; in fact, I hadn't dressed quite warmly enough for the night, and the rest of my clothes were bouncing up and down in the luggage tied to the truss's back.

I had learned so much from Binam's letters, nothing I saw seemed entirely foreign to me. He wrote me often in the early years when he was working as a guide, when he was fascinated by what he was learning, by the trees he was meeting, by everything in Greenwood. I was fascinated too, once I was living in the girls' compound and studying genome manipulation, safely out of reach of my parents and the sym recruiters.

The notion that my brother had changed himself from an animal to something that was hybrid between animal and plant, to read about the changes he had gone through, astonished me. The subject is neutered, put into stasis, immune system completely disabled. The body is then suspended in a high-protein bath and infected with a first-stage virus that eventually reaches every cell, attacking the DNA itself, replicating parts of the viral DNA onto the human genome. Changes begin. The digestive system withers, becomes vestigial, and one day is gone. The heart shrinks and the circulatory system withdraws to the musculature and the skeleton; the lungs shrink and split.

At this stage, a second virus is introduced, and this one initiates another series of changes. The protein bath is sweetened with sugars like the ones the trees make. Chloroplasts replace the mitochondria in all the dermal tissues, and the dermal tissues change, the venaceous structure becomes disconnected from the blood supply. A layer of flexible xylem and phloem grows under the new dermis, forming a new circulatory system for water, oxygen, and nutrients. This system is based on the Dirijhi's own structure, but is more flexible than in the Dirijhi themselves. The skin develops stomata for release of moisture and exhale of gasses, and comes to resemble a soft leaf in texture. Part of the lungs are used to compress air for speech and the rest of the lungs become a focus for xylem and phloem tissue. The blood filters through both, receiving nutrients and oxygen for the body's animal components, the muscles and skeleton, nerves and brain. The body photosynthesizes, but supplements its diet by feeding from the host through the palms, the bottom of the feet, the anus, and the mouth. The sym can slow its heart to a crawl and still function, which it does in the winter if its tree becomes dormant.

The result is a hybrid that can communicate with its hosts and still speak to the rest of us too, a creature that is neither plant nor animal but something of both, and still legally human, according to Hormling biological law. The whole process takes three years Aramenian from neutering to the time the sym is shipped into Greenwood to meet its tree. I had studied the process in school and worked with sym techs in Avitran and Jarutan, I had seen boys and girls come in for the metamorphosis as human beings and leave, three years later, as something else.

But when I saw Binam at the base of his tree, waiting for me as if he had known when the truss would arrive, that was when it hit me, what a staggering change it was.

It was summer, and he had been out in the sun. Head to toe, he was mottled from green to gold, the chloroplasts in full bloom along his skin. He was shaped like my brother, he had the bones of my brother's face. He stepped forward to lift me out of the basket as my guide unlashed my luggage and dropped it onto the moss. We stood looking at each other, and his face was so much the same, but his eyes were milky white. "You look so different," he said, and I realized he was poring over me with the same intensity. "All grown up."

"You look different, too," I said.

He laughed, touched the top of his head. "I was hoping you brought some cubes of what I used to look like," he said, "I've nearly forgotten."

"I did. I brought pictures of Serith and Kael, too." These were our parents, though I never used the terms "mom" and "dad."

I had brought the one bag he had said I was permitted and he let me carry it. Even before I left for Paska, his letters had become infrequent, and sometimes his tone seemed more distant than not. He had told me in a rare recent letter that he'd gotten to the point where he didn't like to use his remaining human muscles so much any more, because that stirred up his human heartbeat, and he found the sensation disquieting. In motion, he appeared to move as little as possible. He walked with a sense that he was gliding over the carpet of marsh-grass and moss, up the knots of the lower tree roots.

"This is my tree," he said, and I looked up and up.

We were on a rise of land, a canal beyond some high shrubs; rocky ground, though the soil was deep and moist. The tree was young, slender compared to its neighbors, but the central bole was already as wide as a small house. We were standing at the perimeter where the outer ring of buttress roots rise up from the ground, soaring to support the lowest branch. The buttress was as thick as my waist. One of the huge main branches had dropped a prop root that was now home for a flowering vine with a sweet, unearthly smell. The branches soaring out and the bole soaring up were at the point of reaching the canopy, and already the upper leaves of the Dirijh were brushing the undersides of the branches of its nearest neighbors. Light fell in startling showers, bars of gold. Beyond the Dirijh on one side was a break in the canopy, and in the center of the meadow was what remained of a decaying tree, covered with vine and fringed with meadow grass but too huge still for anything to disguise.

"Amazing," I said.

"He's a very special tree, they've been breeding for im a long time." He had told me this before, in his etters. "I'm the only sym he's ever had. He's a little nsettled that you're here."

"Really?"

"The trees think of us as their own. They don't like o be reminded of when they were without us."

I knew him when he smiled like that, and I was glad nat the thought of his tree made him smile. Though nere was something discomforting in the thought of the ossessiveness of a tree.

"But he's glad you've come. He tells me so."

"He?"

"He has male and female flowers, but the female owers are sterile."

"To avoid self-pollination?"

Binam shrugged. "It's what he wants." We were inide the ring of buttress roots, near the main bole. "He an reverse all that and bloom with sterile male flowers nd fertile female flowers if he wants, or he can have oth. But for now, he's a he." He tugged on something, ulled it out of the growth around the buttress. "We ove this for you. My friends and I."

A ladder woven of supple vine. Binam climbed di-ctly up the bark, using the bark fissures for hand and ootholds. I slung the bag over my shoulder and started p the rope ladder, but now that Binam was using his

muscles, he was much faster than me, and knew his tre
well enough that he moved by instinct, or so it appeared
He streamed up the bark to the first branching, and the
led me along the branch to a flattened outgrowth over
hung with a thick canopy of leaves. The syms call thi
kind of growth a dis, the standard Ajhevan word fo
sitting room. The Dirijhi learned to make the dis for th
comfort of the symbionts.

Filling the dis were carvings, some for practical use
like sitting, one the height of a table. A variety of tone
and weights of wood, including what looked like cork
All grown out of the main wood of the dis. "I don't liv
down here," Binam said, "this is for our guests. I live u
higher. But I think you should have this dis, lower t
the ground."

"Thanks." I set my bag on the branch, noted the fin
pattern of the bark. Along part of the bark; moss wa
growing, and an ancillary tree had wrapped its root
round the branch and rooted into the moss and whateve
organic matter was under it; this tree was flowering,
scent like vanilla. The flower was yellow with deep, rich
golden-to-brown tones in the corona. "Are you th
carver?"

"Yes. Do you like them?"

"Very much." I ran my hands along the back of th
nearer chair, the smooth polish of the wood.

"We do them together, the tree and I," Binam sai
"That's part of the game. He throws the wood out of

branch or sends it up from the ground and I work it and polish it. I even polish with leaves he gives me," he was pausing, trying to think of a way to say in words what rarely had to be put into words at all, "leaves like sandpaper. He buds them and they flush and dry and I use them for the polish."

He was beaming. My little brother.

We watched each other, and suddenly I could read those strange eyes for a moment. I went to him and embraced him and he leaned against me, and the texture of his skin was cool and tough, the body beneath firm and spongy, so that I could not read from his shoulders or back whether he was really tense or frightened, as I had thought from what I read in his eyes. "It's been such a long time. I hardly know what to say."

"I must seem very strange to you."

I shook my head and held him against me. "You seem very familiar. You're my brother."

Three

We got through those first uncomfortable moments when my mere presence in front of him made him feel as though he had become a freak. He looked me over head to toe, ran his hands down my arms, in my hair. He had lost the thick brown hair I remembered, his head was that mottled leaf color, covered with soft plant hairs, stiff and sticky when I touched them.

"I had forgotten what my body used to look like," he said, laying his fingers against my skin. We had been looking at the picture cubes, one of them taken on the trip to Greenwood when Binam got lost. "You're so warm. I like your skin."

"I like yours, too," I said, touching his neck, the smooth cool outer dermis, tender as a new leaf.

"I'm cool. I've been vented today, and I'm taking in moisture."

"Vented?"

"I let out air through stomae in my skin. I like to let it build up and do it all at once." Looking above. "We're in the hot part of summer. I share the heat of the tree."

"You help it cool off that way?"

"No," he shook his head. "It's only to share. The tree likes the heat on its top leaves, they have a very tough cuticle, and we make a lot of energy that way. I share the heat so I'll know what it's like. Just to share it. That's all."

"Does the tree have a name?"

"Yes. A string of proteins about four hundred molecules long." He was smiling again, comfortable. "It would translate to something like, 'Bright-in-the-Light.' But that's a very quick way of saying it. The trees don't trust anything that's too quick."

I shook my head in some amazement. "It's hard to comprehend. When they talk, what's the speech like?"

"Nothing like speech," he said. "More like a series of

very specific flavors. I'm afraid it would seem quite slow to you."

"What about to you?"

"Time is different, according to where I am. Now, for instance, I feel as if I'm blurting things out to you in a rush. If you weren't here, I'd most likely be higher in the tree, sitting still, listening to the day, and time would pass very slowly. I don't have a time when I talk to the tree, because the tree is always there, in my head. That's part of the link that gets made when you meld. But if I want to talk to another tree, if we do, since we generally do everything at the same time, we listen to the linked root. The trees have a communicating root they send out, they're all networked, and if there's some conversation going on in the link, maybe we join it, or if there's not, we send out a hello to the neighbors to find out who's in the mood to talk."

I liked his face when he talked. He reminded me of the stories of people who lived in fairy-tale forests, old tales that had come to Aramen with the Hormling, most likely, about elves and fairies and whatnot. A people who lived in a wild forest with some kind of connection to the land that a modern person could not hope to attain. What the Erejhen sometimes claim for themselves, though I have seen precious little evidence. I could picture Binam as an elf out of fairyland, and I wondered if that were better than to call him a symbiont in my head. A name that implied he was dependent on something else, that he had only an incomplete identity on his own.

"You're a symbiont, too," he said. "There's no shame in it." But here, for the first time, was an expression that I could easily read: discomfort.

"You can tell what I'm thinking?" I asked.

"The tree can. When you're as close as this."

"How?"

He shrugged. "I don't know. It's not something I can do." Smiling in a teasing way. "If it makes you nervous, I can tell him not to share any of it with me."

"I'll keep that in mind," I said. "What do you mean, I'm a symbiont?"

"You think of yourself as one thing. But your body is millions of things, millions of living creatures all joined in some way, and conscious in some way. You couldn't survive without the bacteria in your gut, the mitochondria in your cells. You're an assemblage, you just don't think about it."

"All right, I get the point." I added, "I'll try not to think of anything I don't want to talk about."

"If you do, the tree will know anyway. That you don't want to talk about it."

The sun was going down by then. I was sore from bouncing against the truss, had hardly slept all night. I yawned and Binam said, "I never even asked about the trip."

"Do you ever ride the trusses?"

"Not in years, since I was a guide. But I remember."

"The trees should consider a nice bio-engineered replacement animal with a smoother ride."

He laughed. Good to hear that he could still make the sound. "That will never happen. Unless the trees learn how to bio-engineer for themselves. The trees think the Hormling charge too much money for the transformation."

"The Hormling would charge for air if they could figure out how to license lungs," I said, repeating a joke that was current in Feidre fifteen years ago, but which my brother had never heard.

He cocked his head. "Well, in my case, they have licensed the lungs, and the skin, and most of the rest."

Sunlight fading. He would leave me to eat and rest, see me in the morning. No need to rush the visit. Come sundown, he would get sluggish anyway, so he wanted to climb to his bed. I didn't ask where that was. As he said, we had time. I kissed him on the cheek, though. We had been affectionate and close, when we were kids, not like some brothers and sisters. He climbed up the tree, limber as anything, moving quickly into shadow.

Four

spread out my sleeping bag, pulled up the night netting over my face, lay there for a while and opened flaps some more to let the air circulate. I had chosen the far

edge of the dis, where the leaf cover grew sparse; I coul
see a piece of the night sky where the canopy had bro
ken, where the dead Dirijh lay slowly decomposing. S
close to the Cluster, all I could see were her golden stars
so many beautiful yellow suns, and if I let my eyes g
just out of focus, it was as if I were in space, starin
into the huge hollow between them, the matrix of burn
ing stars and me hanging in space, orbiting somewher
over Aramen near the white moon.

Maybe it was inevitable that I would dream abou
being a child with Binam, in the days when we lived o
the algae farm with our parents. There are many style
of family on Aramen, but ours was still one of the com
mon ones, easy and adaptable on a planet that still fe
like a frontier at times: a man and a woman with a lif
contract, having children together and raising them. Ou
parents had settled at the edge of the East Ajhevan wet
lands, a country called Asukarns, New Karns, becaus
early on it reminded somebody of a place on Senal. W
were only a couple of hours, trip by putter to the edg
of the Dirijhi preserve, and our parents used to take u
there, till Binam began to get obsessed with the trees.

I dreamed of one of those trips, when we were camp
ing on the bank of a creek, looking into the deep gree
gloom on the other side. We were within the posted lim
its of the camp ground but I wondered if the symbiont
were watching us from the closer trees, to make sure w
stayed on our side. Binam wanted to cross the creek bu

Mom repeated the story of little Inzl and Kraytl, who vanished into the forest leaving a trail of bread crumbs behind them, so they could find their way out again. But the tree roots ate the bread and the trees themselves conspired to confuse little Inzl and Kraytl, and they were imprisoned by an evil tree and almost eaten themselves before their good parents found them. We were the right age for the story at the time, and, in my dream, I was terrified all over again, and, in the way of dreams, we were no longer listening to the story but inside it, and I found myself wandering deeper into the forest with Binam's hand in mine and my parents nowhere to be seen. Binam clutched a sack of bread and looked up at the trees with terror glazing his eyes. . . .

I had never thought of myself as Kraytl when I was hearing the story on my mother's knee, my brother beside her on the bedroll. I had never thought of Binam as Inzl or the two of us as orphans, but here were we both, sleeping in a tree in Greenwood.

When I woke, something with wings was sitting on a branch looking at me, and I wondered what it found so interesting, but when I looked again, the shadow had vanished. White moonlight outlined everything, while the red moon was a thin crescent. The air was as mild as when I fell asleep, though it must have been early morning by then; the canopy holds heat in at night as efficiently as it holds heat out during the day. Some low breeze stirred.

I felt restless and got out of the bedroll, walked around the dis, listened. Choruses of insects, night birds, reptiles, a host of voices swelled in the air around me, eerie, a symphony. The Dirijhi are true to their nature as plants and have remained a part of the wild, but have at the same time learned to manipulate many parts of nature. It seemed awesome to me, now that I was here among them, these huge dark shapes in the night, listening as I was to this chorus of animal voices, wondering what part was wild and what part was the trees.

I could think to myself, these are frog songs, and grasshoppers, and crickets, and lizards, and birds, and feel as if I knew what I was hearing. But for Binam, what were these sounds to him? What news was passing all around me, my senses dull to it?

I sang a song under my breath, along with all the rest. Silly, half tuneless, something from the girls' commune. Sliding into my sleeping roll again, remembering that the tree would know what I had been thinking, that I had wakened with a winged monster hovering over me, that I had felt lost and wondered where I was.

Five

Binam knelt over me, finger to his lips. Early. He gestured, up, with a finger, would I come up?

It was plain I was to make no sound, so I nodded, slid out of the sleeping roll still wearing my clothes.

He climbed, and I followed as best I could. By watching him, I saw the handholds and toeholds he used in the places where the distance between the branches was too great, but these places were few, thankfully, and we mounted through the leafy levels of Binam's tree to the sky.

To the east was the gash in the canopy where the old tree had fallen, where the sunrise now played itself out in a thousand shades of crimson, azure, violet, against a backdrop of clouds. We could not climb higher and the tree was not yet so tall that I could see along the top of the forest, but I was close enough.

"Remember when I got lost?" Binam said.

"And the sym found you in the top of a tree, just sitting there?"

He nodded. Smiling with an expression I could recognize as peaceful. "I come here every morning. It's my favorite place."

He sat there, the picture of contentment. But I remembered the feeling of distance in his letters. "Are you still happy here?" I asked, looking him in those white eyes.

He made a sound that was supposed to be laughter, though he sounded out of practice. "You don't waste time with small talk, even in the morning, do you?"

"Small talk. What an idea."

He was peeling some layer of tissue off the back of one of his hands. Flaky bits of leaf drifting down on currents of air. For all the world like a boy on a river-bank picking at a callus, or at the dead skin on his fin-gertips. "I'm dry," he said, "I need to swim."

"Well?" I asked.

He was distant, hardly hearing my voice. His eyes so pale, the pupils so tiny, he could have been looking in any direction at all, or in none. For a moment, I thought he wanted to answer, and then it didn't seem important any more. We sat for a long time in the cool lifting breeze, the heat of the distant sun beginning to strip the clouds away. Light fell on Binam, bringing out the rich greens and softer-colored variations along his skin, and he closed his eyes and sat there. "I can't tell you what a sweet feeling this is."

"The sunlight?"

"Yes. On my chloroplasts." He licked his lips, though the moisture looked more like sap than saliva. "I can feel it in every nerve."

"It must be nice."

He nodded. "This is the best time of day for it. Later, it's too hot; I can't take so much of the sun, not like the tree."

"Is this something you need?"

He nodded again. "I don't know the science for it, I can't tell you why. But I need a certain amount of sun-light to keep my skin growing. The outer part dies off when the new inner tissue ripens, this time of year."

I had brought a calorie bar with me, my breakfast,

which I pulled out of my coveralls and unwrapped.

"Breakfast," Binam said. "That's the word. This is where I come to have breakfast."

"A nice place for it." The bar, essentially tasteless, went down quite handily.

"The tree is somewhat repulsed by that," Binam said. "Chewing and eating. It's very animal."

"I am an animal."

He had closed his eyes again, murmured, "Yes, he knows you are."

"And you?"

"Sometimes there's still too much animal in me," he answered.

"Is that your opinion, or the tree's?"

"Both."

A silence. I let the obvious questions suspend themselves. He was welcome to his opinions, after all. "You don't talk much, do you?"

"Talk? Me and the tree?"

"No. In words, like right now, I mean. You couldn't remember the word for breakfast."

He shrugged. That gesture came quite naturally. "I don't get much practice."

"What about your neighbors?"

"If we're close to our hosts, we don't really need to talk."

"You read each other's minds?"

He nodded. "I guess that's the easiest way to think of it."

"Is it better than talking?"

"It's nothing like talking. There's no way to compare it." His smile, for a moment, familiar, the way his eyes were shaped, familiar, my little brother from thirty years ago. "I like talking, as a matter of fact, right now. I forget you have to decide to do it, then you have to decide what to say. You can hide things when you talk. I'll miss it when you're gone." He stirred, reaching down with a foot, and just at that moment a cloud blanked out his moment of sunlight. "But I really want to swim."

"Can I come, too?"

He led me down to the dis and I stripped out of my coveralls. When we were on the ground he led me to a place where steps descended into the water. I followed him, taking off the rest of my clothes by the edge of the canal.

"It's clean," he said, easing into the liquid with hardly a ripple. "You don't have to worry about what's in the water."

It felt wonderful to slip into the silky liquid, to glide along the surface beside this moon-faced creature. We floated lazily in the early light, a hint of mist along the canal. Near the woody knee of one of Binam's neighbors, we stopped and headed back again. I swam close to Binam to hear the sound he was making, a low vocalization deep in the throat, like the purr of a cat. "I love to drink," he said, turning on his back to float.

"This does feel wonderful."

"You can't imagine how wonderful, if you're part leaf."

I laughed. "You do this every morning?"

"Yes." We were ashore now, seating ourselves on the lower step, still mostly immersed. "It's one of the things I can do that the tree envies. Though he shares it."

"Shares?"

"Through the link."

Silence, then. I was looking up at the Dirijh, trying to see the tree as Binam saw it, a living mind, a partner. I had been waiting to ask a certain question, and felt it was a good time. "Why did you change your mind and decide to let me visit you, this time? You always seemed so certain it was a bad idea."

He slid up from the water, dripping onto the stones. "I didn't change my mind."

"You still think it's a bad idea?"

He looked at me. Nothing recognizable, at that moment, in his face. "I don't mean to make you uncomfortable. I know you're my sister, but that was a long time ago, longer to me than it seems to you, even. Time isn't the same for me and you. So I didn't really want you to come. But now I'm glad you're here."

"Well, thanks. I guess."

He shrugged again. The gesture this time appeared less natural. "I can only tell you the truth, Kitra."

A chorus of birds, eerie calling high in the trees. Some of it sounded rehearsed, as if it were a piece of music some bird was performing.

"Are you upset?" Binam asked.

"No." I looked my brother square in the face. "I didn't simply want to come to see you, either, Binam."

"Then I expect we're approaching the same point from different places. There's an elegant way the trees have of saying that, but I can't put it in words."

"What do you mean, we're approaching the same point?"

"You came to talk to the trees about independence," Binam said. "I'm right, I know I am. Because that's why they want to talk to you."

Just then, in that eerie quiet, pandemonium of a kind. Something fell out of a tree across the canal, followed by a chorus of birds and animals, a sound as if every leaf on every tree were shaking, and Binam leapt to his feet in alarm.

"Oh, no," he said, watching something moving on the ground; he looked sickened, as if he were nauseous; then he said to me, "Stay here, please," and slipped into the water and swam across.

From other trees in the vicinity, other syms were descending, altogether invisible before, then suddenly in sight, maybe a dozen.

What had fallen from the tree was another sym, and when it stood (I could not tell what sex it had been) I was horrified; the poor creature looked flayed, as if it had been beaten, or worse, partly eaten, and the syms were picking something off it with their fingers, the injured sym shaking, a green fluid oozing down its face, chest, legs; not a sound coming out of it, or them. The healthy syms surrounded the sick one and picked what I guess were insects out of its ravaged skin, the injured one standing and shaking, some of the others helping to support it, and when they were done, they checked the injured one again head to foot and then laid it on the ground, cleaned the soles of the feet. One of the syms, not Binam, brought a large piece of vine and began to squeeze milky fluid out of it, which Binam took onto his palms and rubbed gently over the injured one.

This took a while. I watched. At first without any self-consciousness, then, noticing that some of the syms were looking my way, I began to feel as if I were intruding and drew back from the bank of the canal. When it was clear that Binam would be busy for a while, I climbed to the dis and made myself tea, using the micro-cup in my kit.

When the wait stretched beyond a full marking, I took out a portable reader and scanned some of the downloads I'd brought, items from the various nexus publications I tried to keep up with. A lot of technology is forbidden in Greenwood; for instance, I couldn't do a portable VR intract or immerse myself in one of the total-music wave stations; none of the technologies we use to feed data directly into our own neural circuitry functions in Greenwood, so I was reading for the first time in years, scanning printed words with my eyes.

The whole time, I was aware of commotion, activity on the ground across the canal. A pair of trusses arrived at a certain point, bearing more syms from farther off, I guess. Everyone sat around in a circle beneath the tree involved, and the injured sym sat with them. I suppose this was some kind of meeting. I was aware of it, trying not to spy.

When the circle dissolved and the trusses disappeared, Binam returned to his tree. He climbed to the dis, shoulders slumped, visibly distracted, shaken, though his eyes were so very difficult to read. I was sitting on one of the upraised pieces of wood on the dis, looking out over the clearing. He sat with me for a while, put his hand in mine, the same shy gesture as when he was eight, the texture of his skin tough and resinous, cool. "I'm sorry that took so long," he said.

"What happened?"

He shook his head.

"Tell me."

"I don't want to." He looked up at the canopy, the bright slivers of sky beyond the leaves. Breathless, and due to the physiological alterations, he appeared to be breathing with only the top half of his chest. "I need to climb higher for a while. When I come down, we'll talk again. Do you mind?"

"No. Whatever you need to do."

He nodded. He truly was shaken, I could see it now. He climbed into the leaves, disappearing.

Six

When I was eleven and Binam was eight, Serith and Kael took us on a picnic to wild country near Starns, the border village where the River Moses emerges from the forest. We got up early and rode the boat into Greenwood to the first Dirijhi city up the river, a treat for us, my birthday coming up, and Binam old enough to join the local scout troop, wearing his new scout hat with his first pin on it, I forget for what. I was too old for scouts now, in my opinion, but watching him in the boat with that hat, his bright face, brown hair tangled over his jug ears, I envied him a little, and wished I had not gotten to be so old. He was talking to the guide, his usual shyness gone, leaning forward to look through the plexiglass bubble at the forest around us. "Do they talk to you?" he was asking.

"No, son. What's your name?"

"Binam."

"No, Binam, the trees don't talk to me. They each have a special person who belongs to them, and that's who they talk to."

"Why don't they talk to anybody else?"

"We can't hear them," Kael threw in from her seat, nervous at Binam's need for attention. "Leave the pilot alone, dear."

The pilot turned and smiled at us. The boat was not nearly full that morning; we were awake early for the excursion. She was Erejhen, the pilot, a redhead, one of those genetic types that still recurs in their population but only rarely in the rest of us; the Erejhen can't breed with anyone else. "He's no bother. He likes the trees, that's all."

"I like them very much," Binam amended.

"Come and sit down," Serith said, his voice mild, the kind of voice that tells you you really needn't listen.

"I want to stand here."

"Well, then you can help me keep an eye on the river." The Erejhen woman looked him over. "Watch out for floating logs and branches and whatnot."

Binam nodded emphatically and folded his arms. "But I mostly need to watch the trees."

"Go ahead, that's a good thing to do, too."

"I think the trees would talk to me," he said, very seriously.

"They used to talk to me," the pilot answered, "not these trees here but the ones on my home."

"Where's that?"

"A long way from here."

"Another planet?"

She nodded. Binam's eyes got big. For a long time he had thought that every planet was somehow part of Ajhevan, he hadn't even understood the idea of Aramen, of the world we lived on; when it finally dawned on him that there were a lot of other places besides this one, he'd been very disturbed and quiet for a while. "Don't ask which one," the pilot said, "I won't tell you."

"Why not?"

"Because I won't."

"What's your name?"

"Efen," she answered, and I remembered it, because it was the first time I heard an Erejhen woman given any name other than Kirstin.

"Did you really talk to trees before?"

"Oh yes. I swear. There's nothing like it."

Serith and Kael hadn't the money for a walking tour so we rode another boat back to Starns; Efen was heading all the way up to the northernmost stop before she came back. We changed boats on one of the floating landings and Binam waved at her as she sailed away.

At the end of our picnic, we noticed that Binam was missing. He had been straying farther and farther from the spread of food Serith had brought, he being the cook in our family, Kael not very good at it. We were within sight of Greenwood, and figured that Binam had been unable to resist exploring, so Kael and I went after him while Serith packed up the food and picnic gear. Into Greenwood ourselves, along the riverbank, without a guide, shouting for Binam, who never answered. Nervous, because we were not supposed to go into the forest on foot, everyone knew it, and even though we were only on the riverbank, we were afraid. We looked for a while, then went back. Kael and Serith stood at the putter stop not knowing what to do, looking at one another oddly. I remember how frightened I was to see my parents so confused. Serith reported Binam missing to the human clerk at the park station, who grew concerned when Kael added that she thought Binam had probably strayed into Greenwood.

We stayed in a hotel in Starns overnight, when we were supposed to be traveling back to the farm. In the morning, there was still no word at first, until a putter arrived at the hotel with Binam in it, along with a human escort; one of the local syms had found him sitting in a Dirijh near the river. He had climbed nearly to the top. The Dirijh had sent word to the nearest sym to come and get him.

A long and tiring adventure. We stayed one more night in Starns; I think Serith was too nervous to travel. In bed beside Binam, I asked him what it was like to spend the night in the tree. Did it speak to him?

"Yes," he said, though we both knew he was lying, and exploded into giggles the next instant.

I have a cube taken at that picnic. Serith sits with his back to the camera, attempting to look up at the multifocus, moving restlessly instead and mostly looking at the ground; Kael is eating, pickled egg after pickled egg, along with strips of raw sea urchin, and cups of seaweed made into a puree; I am entranced in some music broadcast by whatever group I was in love with at the time, sitting with my shirt off in the sun; Binam stands behind us, looking into the forest, restlessly turning to the camera, and at the end of the cube segment he walks away altogether, so I picture that as the moment when the tree first called him, when he first felt the urge to answer.

After that, whenever he came out of a simulation with advertisements or when he saw some printed poster for the sym recruiters around Asukarns Village, he would tell Serith or Kael or both that he wanted to be a sym, he wanted to be sold to a tree. Given the size of the bounty, it was not long before our parents began to listen.

Seven

Binam rejoined me near sunset, but was distracted, not altogether present. Twice he climbed to the ground and crossed the canal, I suppose to check on his neighbor. We talked only a little. I showed him some cubes from my last visit to Serith and Kael.

"They're talking about getting out of their contract, you know. Do you ever hear from them?"

"Once in a while," Binam answered. "Serith writes. Kael sends a birthday card."

"She's very fat now. None of her doctors can figure out why. Fat blockers don't work on her. And you remember how she eats."

"You should re-engineer her."

"She's too superstitious for that."

"They're getting out of the contract? They won't be married any more?"

I nodded. "In about a year, they say. When some of their investments come to term. They're already talking to lawyers. It's very friendly; I think they're just tired of each other."

"Serith's young."

"He's only eighty. Kael's over a hundred."

"She sent me an invitation to her century party."

"I was on Paska," I said. "I haven't seen them since I got back."

He was looking off into space. As we talked, he seemed to come into focus better. "Why did you go?"

"To learn about the independence movement there. We're trying to study each other, all the groups who're trying to do the same thing we are, to share information."

Through the following exchange, at times it seemed to me that he was listening to someone else, someone speaking slowly, so that at first I simply guessed the tree was paying close attention.

"Do the Hormling know about your group?"

"Yes. Of course. It's perfectly legal to express the opinions that we do."

"So you do this work out in the open?"

"Most of it."

He absorbed this for a while. I was priming the micro-cup for tea.

"Why do you want independence? What is freedom to you?"

I laughed. "I don't know. Maybe I just don't like having my mind read by the Prin."

That might have been the wrong thing to say at the time. I studied Binam, who made no move or change of expression. "You mean, you don't like their control."

"Not just the Prin, the Hormling. Their economy. Their Conveyance, that nobody can compete with. Their billions and billions of emigrants through that damned gate."

"But it seems to us that the Prin and the Hormling make everything possible that happens in your world." Binam was nodding his head, maybe unconsciously; the movement appeared to have no meaning. "Some of these thoughts come from the link root. Some of the trees have been waiting to talk to you about your ideas."

So this was some kind of a meeting, and this being in front of me was more than Binam, at the moment. I acknowledged what he said, but answered his first statement. "The only thing the Prin and the Hormling make possible is each other. The Prin prop up the Hormling, who proceed to turn everything into a product and every place into a market."

"But this whole world is full of people who came from the Hormling world."

"That was three hundred years ago. None of us here is anything but Aramenian, any more."

He was listening again. After a while, saying, "We agree the Hormling are an intrusion. We do not care for the Prin."

I waited. Stunned, to be so close to what I had come for.

"What would independence offer the Dirijhi?" Binam asked. "Would you try to rule us? Or would you respect our authority, as the Prin do?"

"Beg pardon?"

"Aramen belongs to the Dirijhi," Binam said. "Even the Hormling admit as much. But we cannot control our world. When the Mage made the gate, we had no way to fight, we had to accept her presence. But now things are different."

Because of the syms. I began to understand.

"Do the Dirijhi want all of us to leave?"

He shook his head emphatically. "No, there would be no use in that. We can't grow in the south, we have no use for that place."

"Why not?"

Concern. A long silence. "Do you know anything about what makes us awaken?"

"As much as I could find out. The brain grows in the root crown when the roots are infected with a specific fungus, and a micorhiza is formed. The root tips swell and the interior cells begin to generate neural proteins; the root crown reacts by developing new growth cells to make a case to protect the new tissue."

He smiled. "You have studied us."

Eerie, this white-eyed creature, supposedly kin to me, speaking as if there were a hundred of him. "There's not a lot out there to read. But I looked."

"Then tell me the rest," he said.

During all the following, he seemed curiously complacent, as if it pleased him no end that I had studied the biology of the trees.

"The basal meristem grows two kinds of tissue, new xylem on one side and brain case on the other. The new xylem stays local to the base of the bole but connects to the primary xylem that runs up the bole, that forms every year in spring around the old dead tissue from previous years. The fungal brain forms hormone and protein chains in the new xylem and these start to climb up the primary xylem as water rises in the tree."

"That's good," he said. "When is the brain ripe?"

He meant when was it awake, I guessed. "When the xylem has at least one looped chain of proteins and hormones going all the way to the top and back down to the bottom, for sending and receiving messages. When the structures are all in place and the brain begins to receive energy from some of the leaves, it awakens and becomes aware. When the brain can feel the sun."

"And the water and the earth," Binam said. "The consciousness is stretched by all three of those."

"So what does this have to do with freedom?"

"The trees." For a moment, Binam only. Tired, taking

a breath. Blankness superseding, as if it were water rising through him. "Our birth is very complex, and we struggled to make every tree awaken when we had no hands. We want you to understand that life is possible for us only as a partnership with you. We cannot do without the syms, now that we have them. They are our hands and our feet." Speaking of himself and all the rest in the third person. "Also that we will never have any use for any other place than this one, this continent, because the fungus that helps us awaken grows only here."

"Did the Dirijhi try to colonize the south themselves at some point?"

"Many, many times," Binam said. "The Hormling have tried to propagate us in the southern country, too, through experimentation that we allowed, but they failed the same as we. The fungus grows only here, on this continent. It is as dependent on this place as we are on it, and now we are dependent on the syms as well. So that on Aramen there will always be room for humans and for the Dirijhi, but not for the Prin or for the Hormling gate. If you agree and we work together."

"You want to close the gate?" I asked.

"We want to control it." Shallow, half-chested breaths. "So do you."

"But what about the Mage?"

"We believe she won't say no to us. If we're wrong, we have other means."

"But she's the only one who can make the gate."

"We aren't concerned with how it's made. We're concerned only that we are half the gate, whether we make it or not. And this fact should be respected, and our wishes on our world should be respected."

"You want to get rid of the Prin?"

"We prefer not to say all we want, this first talking." Binam shivering, licking his lips, that curious tongue, like a tender shoot. "We only want to propose that we talk, and think for a while, and talk more. Though at the moment, this one is tired and needs rest."

So Binam swooned, his head swung loosely for a moment, and some change in him, of posture or expression, told me he was only himself and the meeting was over. He gazed at me and blinked. "I can only do so much of that. We should have had more syms here."

"Maybe we talked enough," I said. "You were here, listening, weren't you?"

He nodded. "It's like being at the back of the room when a meeting goes on. Though there's the other layer of it, the fact that the trees are struggling to keep up, to digest what you say and answer as fast as they can. They take turns, answering and responding. So you're not always talking to the same tree."

I shook my head. Dappled sunlight on the dis, on my hands and legs and feet. "But, anyway, it's good news, that they want to help."

He nodded. But he was looking at the surface of the canal and said nothing else.

Eight

A few days passed, more conversations took place, the last with three other syms to do the channeling, and that one was a long conversation, in which we developed a proposal for working together that I could carry back, in memory alone, to my companions in Jarutan. The trees wished for the moment that no word of their possible support for our movement should become public. I felt more suspicious of them after they made that stipulation, realizing that the Dirijhi are cautious, will move forward only very slowly, one deliberate step at a time, and only to further their own agenda; still, it was not my place to rush them or to make a decision about them, and so I listened and agreed to the one thing they wanted to plan, that some group of people return to Greenwood at some point in the near future to continue this talking, as they called it. Though the near future to the Dirijhi could mean any time in the next decade. They had been waiting for three hundred years already. No reason to act in haste.

In all this excitement, with the pure adrenaline of the talk, the growing awareness I had of the intelligence of these beings, and a feeling of luck that it was me who was to be their delegate; in all this I forgot about the sym who had fallen from the tree that first morning, the horrible wounds on its dermis. But the morning I was to leave, as Binam and I were swimming, just before my ride was due, I saw the sym climbing down from the tree to sit with its feet in the water, and on impulse, maybe because I was feeling confident and welcome, even a bit cocky, I swam across the canal and pulled myself up beside the creature.

"Hello," I said, "are you better?"

"Better?"

It did look better—he did, the bone structure appeared vestigially male to me. The wounds on the dermis were brown-edged, new green tissue growing beneath. "I saw you the day you fell. When you were hurt."

"I never fell," he said.

Binam swam up beside us, tapped me on the knee. Not even glancing at his neighbor. "You should come home now. Your truss will be here soon. Leave Itek alone."

"I was only talking," I said.

Itek had risen from the canal and hurried away, disappearing up the tree trunk.

Binam was watching him. "I told you to come home," he said to me, and swam away.

"What did I do?" I asked, on the other shore, dripping near one of the buttress roots, being careful to stay clear of the tree's cranial vents. I was drying myself, dressing, my kit packed and leaning against the buttress.

"He was embarrassed."

"But I only asked if he was feeling better, that's all."

"Now his tree will be angry."

413

"What? Why?"

When he looked at me, for a moment there was only Binam in him, nothing else; it was as if I were seeing him as he would have been, had he never been re-engineered. He was frightened and angry, and said, in a hiss, "Freedom. What freedom do *you* need?"

"Binam. I don't understand."

Suddenly he was speaking very rapidly, his half-chest pumping. "What freedom do you promise Itek? Can you free him from his tree?"

"Why?"

"You saw him. He was nearly eaten alive."

I was suddenly stunned. What he was telling me. In a rush, I understood.

Breathless, a sound in the underbrush farther down the canal, my truss, come to take me home.

"The tree did that?"

"We're their property," he spat. "Why shouldn't they do whatever they like?"

"Binam. Baby."

"Don't—" He drew away from me. "Your truss is coming."

"I didn't know."

He was gasping now, looking up at the tree.

"Come with me." Though I knew better. He never answered.

The truss pulled up nearby, the rider astride its back for the moment, legs under the stump-wings.

"Binam—"

The truss-rider asked if I was ready to leave and Binam drew back, frightened. "Good-bye," he said, moisture leaking from his eyes.

"I'll come back."

He nodded his head.

"Binam. I swear."

"Go," he hissed, gesturing, turning away.

The truss rider, sensing disturbance, decided not to linger. I could think of nothing at all to say and only hung onto that basket as it began to bounce. I was trying to look backward, to watch him to the last moment. Instead, I saw Itek across the canal, staggering down from his tree again, and, chilled, I turned away.

Most genetic alterations can be reversed; the long process that makes a tree-sym can't be. The meld that binds a sym to a tree is for life, with no release. Both these decisions were made by the Hormling and the Dir-ijhi long ago. The sym, once sold to a tree, is unable to feed itself or even to be apart from its host tree for very long. Unable even to change hosts. These are well known facts, though the language used to describe the relationship is rarely as blunt as to call a sym a slave. I had never thought about what kind of life the trees allowed. One thinks of the sym as a fresh-faced cherub living in paradise, the image of the sym recruitment poster, as facile as that.

So I headed home. Seeing Binam's face.

Nine

Surely I was not the first person to witness this kind of event among the syms. But when I looked in the Hormling data mass, there was nothing to be found about protections for the syms, nothing about abuses on the part of the trees, nothing about the legal relationship at all. No documentation in the public domain, nothing in the harder-to-access private data, though this was easy enough to explain, in part. The Hormling stat system doesn't extend to Greenwood. Nothing from the syms has ever been uploaded. The few people who visit Greenwood either record little about the experience or else the files are purged of any references unflattering to the trees; everything in the public database supports the same myth of Greenwood as paradise.

Even in Binam's letters, when I read them again on the boat, not a hint. But I could see his face, hear the dread in his voice.

I worked part of this out on the crossing boat, heading toward the central city, though I had to wait to get to Dembut for access to the data mass. My pilot on the first leg of the trip was the usual brown-haired brown-eyed Aramenian, but when I changed boats to head south, the pilot was Erejhen, and by luck, the boat was half empty. In the night, late, I shared the remains of some whiskey in my bag, never once touched while I was with Binam, and the Erejhen grew relaxed and voluble, to the point that she leaned toward me, her big hand squeezing my shoulder. "My real name's Trisvin. You can call me that."

"Your real name's not Kristen, or whatever you told me?"

"No. We never give our real names, not at first, it's bad luck."

"Where do you come from?"

"Irion."

"No, really. Where do you come from?"

"I was born in Jarutan. But my parents come from Irion."

"Sure they did."

She laughed, grabbing the whiskey bottle from me. "Everybody has to come from somewhere. Where do you come from?"

I told her. I told her why I was visiting, that my brother was a sym; that's all I said.

She looked at me for a long time. "I'm glad nobody can do that to me."

The same genetic difference that prevents the Erejhen from cross-breeding with the Hormling makes them ineligible for most re-engineering, too. "Do what? Make you into a sym?"

She nodded. "I like the trees, don't get me wrong. But I wouldn't want to belong to one."

Language I had heard, and not heard, all my life.

Ten

In Dembut, I looked up Tira, who had given me her access for the return journey, and we met for a drink in a vid parlor. I asked her, point blank, if she had ever seen her brother mistreated.

She blinked, and looked at me. "What do you mean?"

I described Itek, and what I had seen.

She shook her head. Something vehement in it. "I never saw anything at all like that." Not a bright girl, I was taxing her. But I wanted to tell her. To ask, first, *Did you know the trees do things to punish the syms? Infest their skin with parasites, refuse to feed them, burn them in the sun, alter their chemistries to make them docile*; I had begun to imagine all sorts of possibilities. *Did you know your brother might feel like a slave?* But over us, beyond the walls of glass, was the shadow of Greenwood, and I bit my tongue, not certain whom to trust.

"Ask him if he's happy, sometime," I told her. We paid for the drinks and parted, though we'd planned to stay the night together.

It would be easy to forget the look on Binam's face, to ignore his voice, *what freedom do you need?* To let this go and continue to negotiate with the Dirijhi. It's clear to me that with their support, our movement could have the leverage to bring self-government here. But days ago in my dream, Binam held my hand and dropped the bread crumbs one by one, so maybe we would be found again, when we were children and lost; only a dream, but he's still my brother.

Tomorrow, when I wake up, after copying this recording and sending it to the organization I work with, People for a Free Aramen, I'm booking passage on public putter to Jarutan, where I'll buy a plane ticket to Byutiban. I'll decide what to do next when I get there. Knowing something now that won't let go of me. The issue is still freedom, but not mine.

I am face to face with the facts, and they frighten me, because they tell me that my whole life has been based on wrong assumptions.

We believe she won't say no to us. If we're wrong, we have other means. Something hidden in the forest, something that only begins with this issue, the way the syms are treated; something is hidden there because it's the only place in the known worlds where the Prin don't come. Maybe that's too big a thought, maybe I'm only being dramatic. Maybe it's only that I know, much as I have chafed in their presence, that the Prin would learn what was happening to the syms if they were allowed on Ajhevan. So is that the only reason to keep them out, or is there more?

Beyond the river, they are brooding, the dark shapes of trees against the night sky. I watch for a long time, remembering years ago, when my father sat me down at our kitchen table and told me that Binam was gone for good. Later, I would miss Binam, become angry about his "enrollment," as they called it; later, I would raise all kinds of questions about what my parents had done; later, I would only call my father by his name, but that night when he sat back, having explained everything, a chill ran through me. "Are you going to sell me, too?" I asked.

"It's a bounty, we didn't sell him," Kael waving her thick hand at me.

"Are you?" I asked Serith.

"No," he said, but could not meet my eye. "Why don't you go to bed?"

It was a long time before I believed him. Looking at the trees now, I feel that same chill, as if the recruiter is at the door with the contract. I lie awake long into the night, as I did that first night, as if I am still waiting for my own disappearance. When I sleep, I dream I am being lowered into the tank of liquid to begin the transformation, the virus already in my blood, my breasts vanishing, my vagina drying to a flake, but I wake up whole, if covered with sweat, since for me it is only a dream.

ON K2 WITH
KANAKAREDES

DAN SIMMONS

The south Col of Everest, 26,200 feet

IF WE HADN'T DECIDED to acclimate ourselves for
the K2 attempt by secretly climbing to the 8,000-meter
mark on Everest, a stupid mountain that no self-
respecting climber would go near anymore, they
wouldn't have caught us and we wouldn't have been
forced to make the real climb with an alien and the rest
of it might not have happened. But we did and we were
and it did.

What else is new? It's as old as Chaos theory. The
best-laid plans of mice and men and so forth and so on.
As if you have to tell *that* to a climber.

Instead of heading directly for our Concordia Base
Camp at the foot of K2, the three of us had used Gary's
nifty little stealth CMG to fly northeast into the Himalaya, straight to the *bergeschrund* of the Khumbu Glacier

at 23,000 feet. Well, fly *almost* straight to the glacier; we had to zig and zag to stay under HK Syndicate radar and to avoid seeing or being seen by that stinking prefab pile of Japanese shit called the Everest Base Camp Hotel (rooms US $4,500 a night, not counting Himalayan access fee and CMG limo fare.)

We landed without being detected (or so we thought), made sure the vehicle was safely tucked away from the Icefall, seracs, and avalanche paths, left the CMG set in conceal mode, and started our Alpine-style conditioning climb to the South Col. The weather was brilliant. The conditions were perfect. We climbed brilliantly. It was the stupidest thing the three of us had ever done.

By late on the third afternoon we had reached the South Col, that narrow, miserable, windswept notch of ice and boulders wedged high between the shoulders of Lhotse and Everest. We activated our little smart tents, merged them, anchored them hard to ice-spumed rock, and keyed them white to keep them safe from prying eyes.

Even on a beautiful late-summer Himalayan evening such as the one we enjoyed that day, weather on the South Col sucks. Wind velocities average higher than those encountered near the summit of Everest. Any high-climber knows that when you see a stretch of relatively flat rock free of snow, it means hurricane winds. These arrived on schedule just about sunset of that third day. We hunkered down in the communal tent and made soup. Our plan was to spend two nights on the South Col and acclimate ourselves to the lower edge of the Death Zone before heading down and flying on to Concordia for our legal K2 climb. We had no intention of climbing higher than the South Col on Everest. Who would?

At least the view was less tawdry since the Syndicate cleaned up Everest and the South Col, flying off more than a century's worth of expedition detritus—ancient fixed ropes, countless tent tatters, tons of frozen human excrement, about a million abandoned oxygen bottles, and a few hundred frozen corpses. Everest in the 20th Century had become the equivalent of the old Oregon Trail—everything that could be abandoned had been, including climbers' dead friends.

Actually, the view that evening was rather good. The Col drops off to the east for about 4,000 feet into what used to be Tibet and falls even more sharply—about 7,000 feet—to the Western Cwm. That evening, the high ridges of Lhotse and the entire visible west side of Everest caught the rich, golden sunset for long minutes after the Col moved into shadow and then the temperature at our campsite dropped about a hundred degrees. There was not, as we outdoors people like to say, a cloud in the sky. The high peaks glowed in all of their 8,000-meter glory, snowfields burning orange in the light. Gary and Paul lay in the open door of the tent, still wearing their thermskin uppers, and watched the stars emerge and shake to the hurricane-wind as I fiddled and fussed with the stove to make soup. Life was good.

Suddenly an incredibly amplified voice bellowed, "You there in the tent!"

I almost pissed my thermskins. I *did* spill the soup, slopping it all over Paul's sleeping bag.

"Fuck," I said.

"God damn it," said Gary, watching the black CMG—its UN markings glowing and powerful searchlights stabbing—settle gently onto small boulders not twenty feet from the tent.

"Busted," said Paul.

Hillary Room, Top of the World, 29,035 ft.

Two years in an HK floating prison wouldn't have been as degrading as being made to enter that revolving restaurant on the top of Everest. All three of us protested, Gary the loudest since he was the oldest and richest, but the four UN security guys in the CMG just cradled their standard issue Uzis and said nothing until the vehicle had docked in the restaurant airlock-garage and the pressure had been equalized. We stepped out reluctantly and followed other security guards deeper into the closed and darkened restaurant even more reluctantly. Our ears were going crazy. One minute we'd been camping at 26,000 feet and a few minutes later the pressure was the standard airline equivalent of 5,000 feet. It was painful, despite the UN CMG's attempt to match pressures while it circled the dark hulk of Everest for ten minutes.

By the time we were led into the Hillary Room to the only lighted table in the place, we were angry *and* in pain.

"Sit down," said Secretary of State Betty Willard Bright Moon.

We sat. There was no mistaking the tall, sharp-featured Blackfoot woman in the gray suit. Every pundit agreed that she was the single toughest and most interesting personality in the Cohen Administration, and the four U.S. Marines in combat garb standing in the shadows behind her only added to her already imposing sense of authority. The three of us sat, Gary closet to the dark window wall across from Secretary Bright Moon, Paul next to him, and me farthest away from the action. It was our usual climbing pattern.

On the expensive teak table in front of Secretary Bright Moon were three blue dossiers. I couldn't read the tabs on them, but I had little doubt about their contents: Dossier #1, Gary Sheridan, 49, semi-retired, former CEO of SherPath International, multiple addresses around the world, made his first millions at age seventeen during the long lost and rarely lamented dot-com gold rush of yore, divorced (four times,) a man of many passions, the greatest of which was mountain climbing; Dossier #2, Paul Ando Hiraga, 28, ski bum, professional guide, one of the world's best rock-and-ice climbers, unmarried;

Dossier #3, Jake Richard Pettigrew, 36, Boulder, Colorado, married, three children, high-school math teacher, a good-to-average climber with only two 8,000-meter peaks bagged, both thanks to Gary and Paul, who invited him to join them on international climbs for the six previous years. Mr. Pettigrew still cannot believe his good luck at having a friend and patron bankroll his climbs, especially when both Gary and Paul were far better climbers with much more experience. But perhaps the dossiers told of how Jake, Paul, and Gary had become close friends as well as climbing partners over the past few years, friends who trusted each other to the point of trespassing on the Himalayan Preserve just to get acclimated for the climb of their lives.

Or perhaps the blue folders were just some State Department busywork that had nothing to do with us.

"What's the idea of hauling us up here?" asked Gary, his voice controlled but tight. Very tight. "If the Hong Kong Syndicate wants to throw us in the slammer, fine, but you and the UN can't just drag us somewhere against our will. We're still U.S. citizens . . ."

"U.S. citizens who have broken HK Syndicate Preserve rules and UN World Historical Site laws," snapped Secretary Bright Moon.

"We have a valid permit . . ." began Gary again. His forehead looked very red just below the line of his cropped, white hair.

"To climb K2, commencing three days from now,"

said the Secretary of State. "Your climbing team won the HK lottery. We know. But that permit does not allow you to enter or overfly the Himalaya Preserve, nor to trespass on Mt. Everest."

Paul glanced at me. I shook my head. I had no idea what was going on. We could have *stolen* Mt. Everest and it wouldn't have brought Secretary Betty Willard Bright Moon flying around the world to sit in this darkened revolving restaurant just to slap our wrists.

Gary shrugged and sat back. "So what do you want?"

Secretary Bright Moon opened the closest blue dossier and slid a photo across the polished teak toward us. We huddled to look at it.

"A bug?" said Gary.

"They prefer 'Listener,'" said the Secretary of State. "But mantispid will do."

"What do the bugs have to do with us?" said Gary.

"This particular bug wants to climb K2 with you in three days," said Secretary Bright Moon. "And the government of the United States of America in cooperation with the Listener Liaison and Cooperation Council of the United Nations fully intend to have him ... or her ... do so."

Paul's jaw dropped. Gary clasped his hands behind his head and laughed. I just stared. Somehow I found my voice first.

"That's impossible," I said.

Secretary Betty Willard Bright Moon turned her flat, dark-eyed gaze on me. "Why?"

Normally the combination of that woman's personality, her position, and those eyes would have stopped me cold, but this was too absurd to ignore. I just held out my hands, palms upward. Some things are too obvious to explain. "The bugs have six legs," I said at last. "They look like they can hardly walk. We're climbing the *second tallest mountain* on earth. And the most savage."

Secretary Bright Moon did not blink. "The bu . . . the mantispids seem to get around their freehold in Antarctica quite well," she said flatly. "And sometimes they walk on two legs."

Paul snorted. Gary kept his hands clasped behind his head, his shoulders back, posture relaxed, but his eyes were flint. "I presume that if this bug climbed with us, that you'd hold us responsible for his safety and well-being," he said.

The secretary's head turned as smoothly as an owl's. "You presume correctly," she said. "That would be our first concern. The safety of the Listeners is always our first concern."

Gary lowered his hands and shook his head. "Impossible. Above eight thousand meters, no one can help anyone."

"That's why they call that altitude the Death Zone," said Paul. He sounded angry.

Bright Moon ignored Paul and kept her gaze locked with Gary's. She had spent too many decades steeped in ower, negotiation and political in-fighting not to know who our leader was. "We can make the climb safer," she said. "Phones, CMG's on immediate call, uplinks . . ."

Gary was shaking his head again. "We do this climb without phones and medevac capability from the mountain."

"That's absurd . . ." began the Secretary of State.

Gary cut her off. "That's the way it is," he said. "That's what real mountaineers *do* in this day and age. And what we don't do is come to this fucking obscenity of a restaurant." He gestured toward the darkened Hilary Room to our right, the gesture including all of the revolving Top of the World. One of the Marines blinked at Gary's obscenity.

Secretary Bright Moon did not blink. "All right, Mr. Sheridan. The phones and CMG medevacs are not negotiable. I presume everything else is."

Gary said nothing for a minute. Finally, "I presume that if we say no, that you're going to make our lives a living hell."

The Secretary of State smiled ever so slightly. "I think that all of you will find that there will be no more visas for foreign climbs," she said. "Ever. And all of you may encounter difficulties with your taxes soon. Especially you, Mr. Sheridan, since your corporate accounts are so . . complicated."

Gary returned her smile. For an instant it seemed as if he were actually enjoying this. "And if we said yes," he said slowly, almost drawling, "what's in it for us? "

Bright Moon nodded and one of the lackeys to her left opened another dossier and slid a slick color photograph across the table toward us. Again all three of us leaned forward to look. Paul frowned. It took me a minute to figure out what it was—some sort of reddish shield volcano. Hawaii?

"Mars," Gary said softly. "Olympus Mons."

Secretary Bright Moon said, "It is more than twice as tall as Mt. Everest."

Gary laughed easily. "Twice as tall? Shit, woman, Olympus Mons is more than three times the height of Everest—more than eighty-eight thousand feet high, three hundred and thirty-five miles in diameter. The caldera is fifty-three miles wide. Christ, the outward facing cliff ringing the bottom of the thing is taller than Everest—thirty-two thousand eight hundred feet, vertical with an overhang."

Bright Moon had finally blinked at the "shit, woman"—I wondered wildly when the last time had been that someone had spoken to this Secretary of State like that—but now she smiled.

Gary said, "So what? The Mars program is dead. We chickened out, just like with the Apollo Program seventy-five years ago. Don't tell me that you're offering to send us there, because we don't even have the technology to go back."

"The bugs do," said Secretary Bright Moon. "And if

you agree to let the son of the mantispid speaker climb K2 with you, the Listeners guarantee that they will transport you to Mars within twelve months—evidently the transit time will be only two weeks each direction— and they'll outfit a mountain climbing expedition up Olympus Mons for you. Pressure suits, rebreathers, the whole nine yards."

The three of us exchanged glances. We did not have to discuss this. We looked back at the photograph. Finally Gary looked up at Bright Moon. "What do we have to do other than climb with him?"

"Keep him alive if you can," she said.

Gary shook his head. "You heard Paul. Above eight thousand meters, we can't guarantee even keeping ourselves alive."

The Secretary nodded, but said softly, "Still, if we added a simple emergency calling device to one of your palmlogs—a distress beacon, as it were—this would allow us to come quickly to evacuate the mantispid if there were a problem or illness or injury to him, without interfering with the . . . integrity . . . of the rest of your climb."

"A red panic button," said Gary but the three of us exchanged glances. This idea was distasteful but reasonable in its way. Besides, once the bug was taken off the hill, for whatever reason, the three of us could get on with the climb and maybe still get a crack at Olympus Mons. "What else?" Gary asked the woman.

Secretary Bright Moon folded her hands and lowered her gaze a moment. When she looked up again, her gaze appeared to be candid. "You gentlemen know how little the mantispids have talked to us . . . how little technology they have shared with us . . ."

"They gave us CMG," interrupted Gary.

"Yes," said Bright Moon, "CMG in exchange for their Antarctic freehold. But we've only had hints of the other wonders they could share with us—generation starflight technology, a cure for cancer, free energy. The Listeners just . . . well, listen. This is the first overture they've made."

The three of us waited.

"We want you to record everything this son of the speaker says during the climb," said Secretary Bright Moon. "Ask questions. Listen to the answers. Make friends with him if you can. That's all."

Gary shook his head. "We don't want to wear a wire." Before Bright Moon could object, he went on," We have to wear thermskins—molecular heat membranes. We're not going to wear wires under or over them."

The Secretary looked as if she was ready to order the Marines to shoot Gary and probably throw Paul and me out the window, not that the window could be opened. The whole damned restaurant was pressurized.

"I'll do it," I said.

Gary and Paul looked at me in surprise. I admit that I was also surprised at the offer. I shrugged. "Why not?

My folks died of cancer. I wouldn't mind finding a cure. You guys can weave a recording wire into my over-parka. Or I can use the recorder in my palmlog. I'll record the bug when I can, but I'll summarize the other conversations on my palmlog. You know, keep a record of things."

Secretary Betty Willard Bright Moon looked as if she was swallowing gall, but she nodded, first to us and then at the Marine guards. The Marines came around the table to escort us back to the UN CMG.

"Wait," said Gary before we were led away. "Does this bug have a name?"

"Kanakaredes," said the Secretary of State, not even looking up at us.

"Sounds Greek," said Paul.

"I seriously doubt it," said Secretary Bright Moon.

K2 Base Camp, 16,500 ft.

I guess I expected a little flying saucer—a smaller version of the shuttle craft the bugs had first landed near the U.N. nine years earlier—but they all arrived in an oversized, bright red Daimler Chrysler CMG. I saw them first and shouted. Gary and Paul came out of the supply tent where they had been triple-checking our provisions.

Secretary Bright Moon wasn't there to see us off, of course—we hadn't spoken to her since the night at the Top of the World three days earlier—but the Listener Liaison guy, William Grimes, and two of his aides got out of the CMG, as did two bugs, one slightly larger than the other. The smaller mantispid had some sort of clear, bubbly backpack along his dorsal ridge, nestled in the 'V' where its main body section joined the prothorax.

The three of us crossed the boulder field until we were facing the five of them. It was the first time I had ever seen the aliens in person—I mean, who ever sees a bug *in person*?—and I admit that I was nervous. Behind us, above us, spindrift and cloud whirled from the ridges and summit of K2. If the mantispids smelled weird, I couldn't pick it up since the breeze was blowing from behind the three of us.

"Mr. Sheridan, Mr. Hiraga, Mr. Pettigrew," said the bureaucrat Grimes, "may I introduce Listener Speaker Aduradake and his .. son ... Kanakaredes."

The taller of the two bugs unfolded that weird arm or foreleg, swiveled the short forearm thing up like a praying mantis unlimbering, and offered Gary its three-fingered hand. Gary shook it. Paul shook it. I shook it. It felt boneless.

The shorter bug watched, its two primary eyes black and unreadable, its smaller side-eyes lidded and sleepy-looking. It—Kanakaredes—did not offer to shake hands.

"My people thank you for agreeing to allow Kanak-aredes to accompany you on this expedition," said Speaker Aduradake. I don't know if they used implanted voice synthesizers to speak to us—I think not—but the English came out as a carefully modulated series of clicks and sighs. Quite understandable, but strange, very strange.

"No problem," said Gary.

It looked as if the UN bureaucrats wanted to say more—make some speeches, perhaps—but Speaker Aduradake swiveled on his four rear legs and picked his way across the boulders to the CMG's ramp. The humans scurried to catch up. Half a minute later and the vehicle was nothing more than a red speck in the blue southern sky.

The four of us stood there silent for a second, listening to the wind howl around the remaining seracs of the Godwin-Austen Glacier and through niches in the wind-carved boulders. Finally Gary said, "You bring all the shit we e-mailed you about?"

"Yes," said Kanakaredes. His forearms swiveled in their high sockets, the long mantis femur moved up and back, and the third segment swiveled downward so that the soft, three-fingered hands could pat the clear pack on his back. "Brought all the shit, just as you e-mailed." His clicks and sighs sounded just like the other bug's.

Compatible North Face smart tent?" said Gary.

The bug nodded—or at least I took that movement of the broad, beaked head as a nod. Gary must also have. "Rations for two weeks?" he asked.

"Yes," said Kanakaredes.

"We have the climbing gear for you," said Gary. "Grimes said that you've practiced with it all—crampons, ropes, knots, weblines, ice axe, jumars—that you've been on a mountain before."

"Mount Erebus," said Kanakaredes. "I have practiced there for some months."

Gary sighed. "K2 is a little different than Mount Erebus."

We were all silent again for a bit. The wind howled and blew my long hair forward around my face. Finally Paul pointed up the glacier where it curved near Base Camp and rose toward the east side of K2 and beneath the back side of Broad Peak. I could just see the icefall where the glacier met the Abruzzi Ridge on K2. That ridge, path of the first attempt on the mountain and line of the first successful summit assault, was our fallback route if our attempt on the North-East Ridge and East Face fell behind schedule.

"You see, we could fly over the glacier and start the climb from the base of the Abruzzi at 18,000 feet," said Paul, "miss all the crevasse danger that way, but it's part of the climb to start from here."

Kanakaredes said nothing. His two primary eyes had clear membranes but the eyes never blinked. They stared blackly at Paul. The other two eyes were looking God knows where.

I felt that I should say something. Anything. I cleared my throat.

"Fuck it," said Gary. "We're burning daylight. Let's load 'em up and move 'em out."

ON K2 WITH KANAKAREDES

Camp One, North-East Ridge, about 18,300 ft.

They call K2 "the savage mountain" and a hundred other names—all respectful. It's a killer mountain; more men and women have died on it in terms of percentage of those attempting to climb it than on any other peak in the Himalayas or the Karakoram. It is not malevolent. It is simply the Zen-essence of *mountain*—hard, tall, pyramidal when seen from the south in the perfect child's-drawing iconic model of the Matterhorn, jagged, steep, knife-ridged, wracked by frequent avalanche and unearthly storms, its essentially airless summit almost continuously blasted by the Jet Stream. No contortion of sentiment or personification can suggest that this mountain gives the slightest shit about human hopes or human life. In a way that is impossible to articulate and politically incorrect even to suggest, K2 is profoundly masculine. It is eternally indifferent and absolutely unforgiving. Climbers have loved it and triumphed on it and died on it for more than a century.

Now it was our turn to see which way this particular prayer wheel turned.

Have you ever watched a mantispid bug walk? I mean, we've all seen them on HDTV or VirP—there's an entire satellite channel dedicated to them, for Christ's sake—but usually that's just quick cuts, long-lens images, or static shots of the bug Speaker and some political bigshots standing around somewhere. Have you ever watched them *walk* for any length of time?

In crossing the upper reaches of the Godwin-Austen Glacier under the eleven-thousand-foot vertical wall that is the east face of K2, you have two choices. You can stay near the edges of the glacier, where there are almost no crevasses, and risk serious avalanche danger. or you can stick to the center of the glacier and never know when the snow and ice underfoot is suddenly going to collapse into a hidden crevasse. Any climber worth his or her salt will choose the crevasse-route if there's even a hint of avalanche risk. Skill and experience can help you avoid crevasses; there's not a goddamn thing in the world you can do except pray when an avalanche comes your way.

To climb the glacier, we had to rope up. Gary, Paul and I had discussed this—whether or not to rope with the bug—but when we reached the part of the glacier where crevasses would be most probable, inevitable actually, we really didn't have a choice. It would have been murder to let Kanakaredes proceed unroped.

One of the first things all of us thought when the bugs landed almost ten years ago was "Are they wearing clothes?" We know now that they weren't—that their weird combination of chitinous exoskeleton on their main body section and layers of different membranes on the softer parts serve well in lieu of clothing—but that doesn't mean that they go around with their sexual parts showing. Theoretically, mantispids are sexual creatures—male or female—but I've never heard of a human being who's *seen* a bug's genitals, and I can testify that Gary, Paul, and I didn't want to be the first.

Still, the aliens rig themselves with toolbelts or harnesses or whatever when necessary—just as Kanakaredes had shown up with that weird bubble-pack on his back with all of his climbing gear in it—and as soon as we started the ascent, he removed a harness from that pack and rigged it around that chunky, almost armored upper section of himself where his arm and mid-leg sockets were. He also used a regulation-sized metal ice axe, gripping the curved metal top in those three boneless fingers. It seemed strange to see something as prosaic as a red nylon climbing harness and carabiners and an ice axe on a bug, but that's what he had.

When it came time to rope up, we clipped the spidersilk line onto our 'biners, passing the line back in our usual climbing order, except that this time—instead of Paul's ass slowly slogging up the glacier in front of me—I got to watch Kanakaredes plod along ten paces ahead of me for hour after hour.

"Plod along" really doesn't do bug locomotion justice. We've all seen the bugs balance and walk on their midlegs, standing more upright on those balancing legs, their back straightening, their head coming up until they're tall enough to stare a short human male in the eye, their forelegs suddenly looking more like real arms than praying mantis appendages—but I suspect now that they do that just for that reason—to appear more human in their rare public appearances. So far, Kanakaredes had stood on just two legs only during the formal meeting back at Base Camp. As soon as we started hiking up the glacier, his head came down and forward, that "V" between his main body section and prothorax widened, those mantis-arms stretched straight ahead like a human extending two poles ahead of him, and he fell into a seemingly effortless four-legged motion.

But, Jesus Christ, what a weird motion. All of a bug's legs have three joints, of course, but I realized after only a few minutes of following this particular bug up the Godwin-Austen Glacier that those joints never seem to bend the same way at the same time. One of those praying mantis forelegs would be bent double and down so that Kanakaredes could plant his ice axe in the slope, while the other bent forward and then back so that he could scratch that weird beak of a snout. At the same time, the midlegs would be bending rather like a horse's, only instead of a hoof, the lower, shortest section ended in those chitinous but somehow dainty, divided . . . hell, I don't know, hoof-feet. And the hind legs, the ones socketed at the base of the soft prothorax . . . those are the ones that made me dizzy as I watched the bug climbing through soft snow in front of me. Sometimes the alien's knees—those first joints about two-thirds of the way down the legs—would be higher than his back. At other times one knee would be bending forward, the other one back, while the lower joints were doing even stranger things.

ON K2 WITH KANAKAREDES

After a while, I gave up trying to figure out the engineering of the creature, and just began admiring the easy way it moved up the steep snow and ice. The three of us had worried about the small surface area of a bug's feet on snow—the V-shaped hoof-things aren't even as large as an unshod human foot—and wondered if we'd be tugging the mantispid out of every drift on our way up the mountain, but Kanakaredes managed quite well, thank you. I guess it was due to the fact that I guessed at that time that he probably only weighed about a hundred and fifty pounds, and that weight was spread out over four—and sometimes six, when he tucked the ice axe in his harness and scrambled—walking surfaces. To tell the truth, the bug had to help me slog clear of deep snow two or three times on the upper reaches of the glacier.

During the afternoon, with the sun blazing on the reflective bowl of ice that was the glacier, it got damned hot. The three of us humans damped our thermskin controls way down and shed our parka outer layers to cool off. The bug seemed comfortable enough, although he rested without complaint while we rested, drank water from his water bottle when we paused to drink, and chewed on something that looked like a shingle made of compressed dog poop while we munched our nutrient bars (which, I realize now, also looked a lot like a shingle made of compressed dog poop.) If Kanakaredes suffered from overheating or chill that first long day on the glacier, he didn't show it.

Long before sunset, the mountain shadow had moved across us and three of the four of us were raising our thermskin thresholds and tugging on the parka shells again. It had begun snowing. Suddenly a huge avalanche calved off the east face of K2 and swept down the slope behind us, boiling and rolling over a part of the glacier we had been climbing just an hour earlier.

We all froze in our tracks until the rumbling stopped. Our tracks in the shadowed snow—rising in a more-or-less straight line for a thousand-foot elevation gain over the last mile or so—looked like they had been rubbed out by a giant eraser for a swath of several hundred yards.

"Holy shit," I said.

Gary nodded, breathing a little hard since he had been breaking trail for most of the afternoon, turned, took a step, and disappeared.

For the last hours, whoever had been in the lead had probed ahead with his ice axe to make sure that the footing ahead was real and not just a skim of snow over a deep crevasse. Gary had taken two steps without doing this. And the crevasse got him.

One instant he was there, red parka glowing against the shadowed ice and the white snow on the ridge now so close ahead of us, and the next instant he was gone.

And then Paul disappeared as well.

No one screamed or reacted poorly. Kanakaredes instantly braced himself in full-belay posture, slammed his ice axe deep into the ice beneath him, and wrapped the line around it twice before the thirty feet or so of slack between him and Paul had played out. I did the same, digging crampons in as hard as I could, fully expecting the crevasse to pull the bug in and then me.

It didn't.

The line snapped taut but did not snap—genetically tailored spidersilk climbing rope almost never breaks—Kanakaredes's ice axe stayed firm, as did the bug holding it in the glacier ice, and the two of us held them. We waited a full minute in our rigid postures, making sure that we weren't also standing on a thin crust over a crevasse, but when it was obvious where the crevasse rim was, I gasped, "Keep them tight," unclipped, and crawled forward to peer down the black gap.

I have no idea how deep the crevasse was—a hundred feet ? A thousand? But both Paul and Gary were dangling there—Paul a mere fifteen feet or so down, still in the light, looking fairly comfortable as he braced his back against the blue-green ice wall and rigged his climbing jumars. That clamp and cam device, infinitely lighter and stronger but otherwise no different than the jumars our grandfathers might have used, would get him back up on his own as long as the rope held and as soon as he could get the footloops attached.

Gary did not look so comfortable. Almost forty feet down, hanging headfirst under an icy overhang so that only his crampons and butt caught the light, he looked as if he might be in trouble. If he had hit his head on the ice on the way down . . .

Then I heard him cursing—the incredible epiphets and shouts almost muffled in the crevasse, but still echoing deep as he cursed straight into the underbelly of the glacier—and I knew that he was all right.

It took only a minute or so for Paul to jumar up and over the lip, but getting Gary rightside up and then lifted up over the overhang so he could attach his own jumars, took a bit longer and involved some manhauling.

That's when I discovered how goddamned strong this bug was. I think that Kanakaredes could have hauled all three of us out of that crevasse if we'd been unconscious, almost six hundred pounds of dead weight. And I think he could have done it using only one of those skinny, almost muscleless-looking praying mantis forearms of his.

When Gary was out and untangled from his lines, harness, and jumars, we moved carefully around the crevasse, me in the lead and probing with my axe like a blind man in a vale of razorblades, and when we'd reached a good site for Camp One just at the base of the ridge, offering only a short climb in the morning to the crest of the northeast ridge that would eventually take us up onto the shoulder of K2 itself, we found a spot on the last patch of sun, unhooked the rope from our carabiners, dumped our 75-pound packs, and just gasped for a while before setting up camp.

"Fucking good beginning to the goddamned motherfucking expedition," said Gary between slugs on his water bottle. "Absolutely bastardly motherfucking brilliant—I walk into goddamned sonofabitching whoremongering crevasse like some pissant whoreson fucking day tripper."

I looked over at Kanakaredes. Who could read a bug's expression? That endless mouth with all of its jack-o-lantern bumps and ridges, wrapped two- thirds around its head from its beaky proboscis almost to the beginning of its bumpy skullcrest, *always* seemed to be smiling. Was it smiling more now? Hard to tell and I was in no mood to ask.

One thing was clear. The mantispid had a small, clear device out—something very similar to our credit card palmlogs—and was entering data with a flurry of its three fingers. *A lexicon*, I thought. Either translating or recording Gary's outburst which was, I admit, a magnificent flow of invective. He was still weaving a brilliant tapestry of obscenity that showed no sign of abating and which would probably hang over the Godwin-Austen Glacier like a blue cloud for years to come.

Good luck using this vocabulary during one of your UN cocktail parties, I thought to Kanakaredes as he finished his data entry and repacked his palmlog.

When Gary finally trailed off, I exchanged grins with Paul—who had said nothing since dropping into the crevasse—and we got busy breaking out the smart tents, the sleeping bags, and the stoves before darkness dropped Camp One into deep lunar cold.

Camp Two, between a cornice and an avalanche slope, about 20,000 ft.

I'm keeping these recordings for the State Department intelligence people and all the rest who want to learn everything about the bugs—about the mantispids' technology, about their reasons for coming to earth, about their culture and religions—all the things they've somehow neglected to tell us in the past nine and a half years.

Well, here's the sum total of my recording of human-mantispid conversation from last night at Camp One—

Gary: *Uh. . Kan . . . Kanakaredes? We were thinking of merging our three tents and cooking up some soup and hitting the sack early. You have any problem keeping your tent separate tonight? There's room on this snow slab for both tent parts.*

Kanakaredes: *I have no problem with that.*

So much for interrogating our bug.

We should be higher tonight. We had a long, strong day of climbing today, but we're still on the low part of the northeast ridge and we have to do better if we're going to get up this hill and down safely in the two weeks allotted to us.

All this "Camp One" and "Camp Two" stuff I'm putting in this palmlog diary are old terms from the last century when attempts at 8,000-meter peaks literally demanded armies of men and women—more than two hundred people hauling supplies for the first American Everest expedition in 1963. Some of the peaks were pyramid-shaped but *all* of the logistics were. By that I mean that scores of porters hauled in uncounted tons of supplies—Sherpa porters and high-climbers in the Himalayas, primarily Balti porters here in the Karakoram—and teams of men and women man-hauled these tons up the mountains, working in relays to establish camps to last the duration of the climb, breaking and marking trail, establishing fixed ropes up literally miles of slope, and moving teams of climbers up higher and higher until, after weeks, sometimes months of effort, a very few of the best and luckiest climbers—say six or four or two or even one from the scores who started—were in a position to make an attempt on the summit from a high camp—usually Camp Six, but sometimes Camp Seven or higher —starting somewhere in the Death Zone above 8,000 meters. "Assault" on a mountain was a good word then, since it took an army to mount the assault.

Gary, Paul, the bug and I are climbing alpine style. This means that we carry everything we need—starting heavy and getting lighter and lighter as we climb—essentially making a direct bid on the summit, hoping to climb it in a week or less. No series of permanent camps, just temporary slabs cut out of the snow and ice for our smart tents—at least up until whatever camp we designate as our summit-attempt jumping off point. Then we'll leave the tents and most of the gear there and go for it, hoping and praying to whatever gods we have—and who knows what gods Kanakaredes prays to, if any—praying that the weather won't turn bad while we're up there in the Death Zone, that we won't get lost coming down to our high camp in the dark, that nothing serious happens to any us of during that final attempt since we really can't help each other at that altitude—essentially just praying our asses off that we don't fuck up.

But that is *if* we can keep moving steadily up this hill. Today wasn't so steady.

We started early, breaking down Camp One in a few minutes, loading efficiently, and climbing well—me in the lead, then Paul, then the bug, then Gary. There's a bitch of a steep, razor-edge traverse starting at about the 23,300 ft. level—the hardest pitch on the northeast ridge part of our route—and we wanted to settle into a secure camp at the beginning of that scary traverse by nightfall tonight. No such luck.

I'm sure I have some of Kanakaredes comments recorded from today, but they're mostly monosyllables and they don't reveal any great bug secrets. They're more along the lines of—"Kana ... Kanaka ... hey K, did you pack the extra stove?" "Yes" Want to take a lunch

break?" "That would be fine." and Gary's "Shit, it's starting to snow." Come to think of it, I don't believe the
mantispid initiated any conversation. All the clicks and
sighs on the palmlog chip are K replying to our questions. All of the cursing was ours.

It started to snow heavily about noon.

Until then things had been going well. I was still in
the lead—burning calories at a ferocious rate as I broke
trail and kicked steps in the steep slope for the others to
follow. We were climbing independently, not roped. If
one of us slipped or caught his crampons on a rock
rather than ice, it was up to that person to stop his slide
by self-arrest with his ice axe. Otherwise one had just
bought a really great amusement-park ride of a screaming slide on ice for a thousand feet or so and then a
launch out over the edge to open space, dropping three
or four thousand feet to the glacier below.

The best idea is not to think about that, just keep
points attached to the snowslope at all times and make
damned sure that no matter how tired you were, that
you paid attention to where you kicked your crampons
into the ice. I have no idea if Kanakaredes had a fear of
heights—I made a fatigued mental note to ask him—but
his climbing style showed caution and care. His "crampons" were customized—a series of sharp, plastic-
looking spikes lashed to those weird arrow-shaped feet
of his—but he took care in their placement and used his
ice axe well. He was climbing two-legged this day, his

rear legs folded into his elevated prothorax so that you wouldn't know they were there unless you knew where to look.

By 10:30 or 11:00 a.m., we'd gained enough altitude that we could clearly see Staircase Peak—its eastern ridge looks like a stairway for some Hindu giant—on the northeast side of K2. The mountain is also called Skyang Kangri and it was beautiful, dazzling in the sunlight against the still-blue eastern sky. Far below, we could see the Godwin-Austen Glacier crawling along the base of Skyang Kangri to the 19,000-foot pass of Windy Gap. We could easily see over Windy Pass now, scores of miles to the browning hills of what used to be China and now was the mythical country of Sinkiang, fought over even as we climbed by troops from the HK and various Chinese warlords.

More pertinent to our cause right now was the view up and westward toward the beautiful but almost laughable bulk of K2, with its wild knife-edge ridge that we hoped to reach by nightfall. At this rate, I thought just before looking up at it again, it shouldn't be any problem...

That was precisely the moment when Gary called up, "Shit! It's starting to snow!"

The clouds had roiled in from the south and west when we weren't watching and within ten minutes we were enveloped by them. The wind came up. Snow blew everywhere. We had to cluster up on the increasingly steep slope just to keep track of one another. Naturally, at precisely this point in the day's climb, our steep but relatively easy snow slope turned into a forbidding wall of ice with a band of brittle rock visible above for the few minutes before the clouds shut off all of our view for the rest of the day.

"Fuck me," said Paul as we gathered at the foot of the ice slope.

Kanakaredes's bulky, beaked head turned slowly in Paul's direction, his black eyes attentive, as if he was curious as to whether such a biological improbability was possible. K asked no questions and Paul volunteered no answers.

Paul, the best ice climber among us, took the lead for the next half-hour or so, planting his axe into the near-vertical ice wall, then kicking hard with the two spike points on the front of his boot, then pulling himself up with the strength of his right arm, kicking one foot in again, pulling the axe out, slamming it in again.

This is basic ice-climbing technique, not difficult, but exhausting at almost 20,000 feet—twice the altitude where CMG's and commercial airlines are required to go to pressurized O_2—and it took time, especially since we'd roped up now and were belaying Paul as he kick-climbed.

Paul was about seventy feet above us now and was moving cautiously out onto the rockband. Suddenly a slew of small rocks came loose and hurtled down toward us.

There was no place for us to go. Each of us had hacked out a tiny platform in the ice on which we could stand, so all we could do was press ourselves against the ice wall, cover up, and wait. The rocks missed me. Gary had a fist-sized rock bounce off his pack and go hurtling out into space. Kanakaredes was hit twice by serious-sized rocks—once in his upper left leg, arm, whatever it is, and again on his bumpy dorsal ridge. I heard both rocks strike; they made a sound like stone hitting slate.

"Fuck me," K said clearly as more rocks bounced around him.

When the fusillade was over, after Paul had finished shouting down apologies and Gary had finished hurling up insults, I kick-stepped the ten or so paces to where K still huddled against the ice wall, his right mantis forearm raised, the ice axe and his toe points still dug in tight.

"You hurt?" I said. I was worried that we'd have to use the red button to evacuate the bug and that our climb would be ruined.

Kanakaredes slowly shook his head—not so much to say "no" but to check things out. It was almost painful to watch—his bulky head and smiling beak rotating almost 270 degrees in each direction. His free forearm unlimbered, bent impossibly, and those long, unjointed fingers carefully patted and probed his dorsal ridge.

Click. Sigh. Click—"I'm all right."

"Paul will be more careful on the rest of the rock and."

"That would be good."

Paul *was* more careful, but the rock was rotten and here were a few more landslides, but no more direct its. Ten minutes and sixty or seventy feet later, he had eached the crest of the ridge, found a good belay stance, nd called us up. Gary, who was still pissed—he liked ew things less than being pelted by rocks set loose by omeone else—started up next. I had Kanakaredes follow hirty feet behind Gary. The bug's ice technique was by he book—not flashy but serviceable. I came up last, try-ng to stay close enough that I could see and dodge any osened boulders when we all reached the rock band.

By the time we were all on the northeast ridge and limbing it, the visibility was close to zero, the temper-ture had dropped about fifty degrees, the snow was hick and mushy and treacherous, and we could hear ut not see avalanches roaring down both the east face f K2 and this very slope somewhere both ahead of us nd behind us in the fog. We stayed roped up.

"Welcome to K2," Gary shouted back from where he ad taken the lead. His parka and hood and goggles and are chin were a scary, icicled mass mostly obscured by orizontally blowing snow.

"Thank you," click-hissed K in what I heard as a ore formal tone. "It is a great pleasure to be here."

Camp Three—under a serac on the crest of the ridge
the beginning of the knife-edge traverse, 23, 200 feet

Stuck here three full days and nights, fourth nig
approaching. Hunkered here useless in our tents, eatin
nutrient bars and cooking soup that can't be replace
using up the heating charge in the stove to melt sno
into water, each of us getting weaker and crankier du
to the altitude and lack of exercise. The wind has bee
howling and the storm raging for three full days—fo
days if you count our climb from Camp Two. Yesterda
Gary and Paul—with Paul in the lead on the incredibl
steep ridge—tried to force the way across the stee
climbing traverse in the storm, planning to lay dow
fixed rope even if we had to make the summit bid wit
only whatever string remained in our pockets. The
failed on the traverse attempt, turning back after thre
hours in the howling weather and returning ice-cruste
and near frostbitten. It took more than four hours fo
Paul to quit shaking, even with the thermskins and reg
ulated smart clothing raising his body temperature.
we don't get across this traverse soon—storm or n
storm—we won't have to worry about what gear an
supplies will be left for the summit bid. There won't b
any summit bid.

I'm not even sure now how we managed the clim
two days ago from Camp Two to this narrow patch c
chopped out ridgecrest. Our bug was obviously at th
edge of his skill envelope, even with his extra legs an

greater strength, and we decided to rope together for the last few hours of climbing, just in case K peeled loose. It wouldn't do much good to push the red panic button on the palmlog just to tell the arriving UN CMG guys that Kanakaredes had taken a header five thousand feet straight down to the Godwin-Austen Glacier.

"Mr. Alien Speaker, sir, we sort of lost your kid. But maybe you can scrape him up off the glacier ice and clone him or something." No, we didn't want that.

As it was, we ended up working after dark, head-lamps glowing, ropes 'binered to our harnesses and attached to the slope via ice screws just to keep us from being blown into black space, using our ice axes to hack a platform big enough for the tent—there was only room for a merged cluster of the smart tents, wedged ten feet from a vertical drop, forty feet from an avalanche path and tucked directly beneath an overhanging serac the size of a three-story building—a serac that could give way any time and take us and the tent with it. Not the best spot to spend ten minutes in, much less three days and nights during a high-altitude hurricane. But we had no choice; everything else here was knife-ridge or avalanche slope.

As much as I would have preferred it otherwise, we finally had time for some conversation. Our tents were joined in the form of a squished cross, with a tiny central area, not much more than two feet or so across, for cooking and conversation and just enough room for each of us to pull back into our small nacelles when we curled up to sleep. The platform we'd hacked out of the slope under the overhanging serac wasn't big enough or flat enough to serve all of us, and I ended up in one of the downhill segments, my head higher than my feet. The angle was flat enough to allow me to doze off but still steep enough to send me frequently lurching up from sleep, fingers clawing for my ice axe to stop my slide. But my ice axe was outside with the others, sunk in the deepening snow and rock-hard ice, with about a hundred feet of spidersilk climbing rope lashed around it and over the tent and back again. I think we also used twelve ice screws to secure us to the tiny ice shelf.

Not that any of this will do us a damned bit of good if the serac decides to go or the slope shifts or the winds just make up their minds to blow the whole mass of rope, ice axes, screws, tent, humans, and bug right off the mountain.

We've slept a lot, of course. Paul had brought a soft-book loaded with a dozen or so novels and a bunch of magazines, so we handed that around occasionally—even K took his turn reading—and for the first day we didn't talk much because of the effort it took to speak up over the wind howl and the noise of snow and hail pelting the tent. But eventually we grew bored even of sleeping and tried some conversation. That first day it was mostly climbing and technical talk—reviewing the route, listing points for and against the direct attempt once we got past this traverse and up over the snow dome at the base of the summit pyramid—Gary arguing for the Direct Finish no matter what, Paul urging caution and a possible traverse to the more frequently climbed Abruzzi Ridge, Kanakaredes and me listening. But by the second and third days, we were asking the bug personal questions.

"So you guys came from Aldebaran," said Paul on the second afternoon of the storm. "How long did it take you?"

"Five hundred years," said our bug. To fit in his section of the tent, he'd had to fold every appendage he had at least twice. I couldn't help but think it was uncomfortable for him.

Gary whistled. He'd never paid much attention to all the media coverage of the mantispids. "Are you that old, K? Five hundred years?"

Kanakaredes let out a soft whistle that I was beginning to suspect was some equivalent to a laugh. "I am only twenty-three of your years old, Gary," he said. "I was born on the ship, as were my parents and their parents and so on far back. Our life span is roughly equivalent to yours. It was a . . . generation-ship, I believe is your term for it." He paused as the howling wind rose to ridiculous volume and velocity. When it died a bit, he went on, "I knew no other home than the ship until we reached Earth."

Paul and I exchanged glances. It was time for me to interrogate our captive bug for country, family, and Secretary Bright Moon. "So why did you ... the Listeners ... travel all the way to Earth?" I asked. The bugs had answered this publicly on more than one occasion, but the answer was always the same and never made much sense.

"Because you were there," said the bug. It was the same old answer. It was flattering, I guess, since we humans have always considered ourselves the center of the universe, but it still made little sense.

"But why spend centuries traveling to meet us?" asked Paul.

"To help you learn to listen," said K.

"Listen to what?" I said. "You? The mantispids? We're interested in listening. Interested in learning. We'll listen to you."

Kanakaredes slowly shook his heavy head. I realized, viewing the mantispid from this close, that his head was more saurian—dinosaur/birdlike—than buggy. "Not listen to us," *click, hiss.* "To the song of your own world."

"To the song of our world?" asked Gary almost brusquely. "You mean, just appreciate life more? Slow down and smell the roses? Stuff like that?" Gary's second wife had been into transcendental meditation. I think it was the reason he divorced her.

"No," said K. "I mean listen to the sound of your world. You have fed your seas. You have consecrated your world. But you do not listen."

It was my turn to muddle things even further. "Fed our seas and consecrated our world," I said. The entire tent thrummed as a gust hit it and then subsided. "How did we do that?"

"By dying, Jake," said the bug. It was the first time he'd used my name. "By becoming part of the seas, of the world."

"Does dying have something to do with hearing the song?" asked Paul.

Kanakaredes's eyes were perfectly round and absolutely black, but they did not seem threatening as he looked at us in the glow of one of the flashlights. "You cannot hear the song when you are dead," he whistle-clicked. "But you cannot have the song unless your species has recycled its atoms and molecules through your world for millions of years."

"Can *you* hear the song here?" I asked. "On Earth, I mean."

"No," said the bug.

I decided to try a more promising tack. "You gave us CMG technology," I said, "and that's certainly brought wonderful changes." *Bullshit*, I thought. I'd liked things better before cars could fly. At least the traffic jams along the Front Range where I lived in Colorado had been two dimensional then. "But we're sort of . . . well . . . curious about when the Listeners are going to share other secrets with us."

"We have no secrets," said Kanakaredes. "Secrets was

not even a concept to us before we arrived here on Earth."

"Not secrets then," I said hurriedly, "but more new technologies, inventions, discoveries..."

"What kind of discoveries?" said K.

I took a breath. "A cure to cancer would be good," I said.

Kanakaredes made a clicking sound. "Yes, that would be good," he breathed at last. "But this is a disease of your species. Why have you not cured it?"

"We've tried," said Gary. "It's a tough nut to crack."

"Yes," said Kanakaredes, "it is a tough nut to crack."

I decided not to be subtle. "Our species need to learn from one another," I said, my voice perhaps a shade louder than necessary to be heard over the storm. "But your people are so reticent. When are we really going to start talking to each other?"

"When your species learns to listen," said K.

"Is that why you came on this climb with us?" asked Paul.

"I hope that is not the result," said the bug, "but it is, along with the need to understand, the reason I came."

I looked at Gary. Lying on his stomach, his head only inches from the low tent roof, he shrugged slightly.

"You have mountains on your home world?" asked Paul.

"I was taught that we did not."

"So your homeworld was sort of like the south pole where you guys have your freehold?"

"Not that cold," said Kanakaredes," and never that dark in the winter. But the atmospheric pressure is similar."

"So you're acclimated to about—what?—seven or eight thousand feet altitude?"

"Yes," said the mantispid.

"And the cold doesn't bother you?" asked Gary.

"It is uncomfortable at times," said the bug. "But our species has evolved a subcutaneous layer which serves much as your thermskins in regulating temperature."

It was my turn to ask a question. "If your world didn't have mountains," I said, "why do want to climb K2 with us?"

"Why do *you* wish to climb it?" ask Kanakaredes, his head swiveling smoothly to look at each of us.

There was silence for a minute. Well, not really silence since the wind and pelting snow made it sound as if we were camped behind a jet exhaust, but at least none of us humans spoke.

Kanakaredes folded and unfolded his six legs. It was disturbing to watch. "I believe that I will try to sleep now," he said and closed the flap that separated his niche from ours.

The three of us put our heads together and whispered. "He sounds like a goddamned missionary," hissed Gary. "All this 'listen to the song' doubletalk."

"Just our luck," said Paul. "Our first contact with an extraterrestrial civilization, and they're freaking Jehovah's Witnesses."

"He hasn't handed us any tracts yet," I said.

"Just wait," whispered Gary. "The four of us are going to stagger onto the summit of this hill someday if this fucking storm ever lets up, exhausted, gasping for air that isn't there, frostbitten to shit and back, and this bug's going to haul out copies of the Mantispid Watchtower."

"Shhh," said Paul. "K'll hear us."

Just then the wind hit the tent so hard that we all tried digging our fingernails through the hyper-polymer floor to keep the tent from sliding off its precarious perch and down the mountain. If worse came to worse, we'd shout "Open!" at the top of our lungs, the smart tent fabric would fold away, and we'd roll out onto the slope in our thermskins and grab for our ice axes to self-arrest the slide. That was the theory. In fact, if the platform shifted or the spidersilk snapped, we'd almost certainly be airborn before we knew what hit us.

When we could hear again over the wind roar, Gary shouted, "If we unpeel from this platform, I'm going to cuss a fucking blue streak all the way down to impact on the glacier."

"Maybe that's the song that K's been talking about," said Paul, and sealed his flap.

Last note to the day: Mantispids snore.

* * *

On the afternoon of day three, Kanakaredes suddenly said, "My creche brother is also listening to a storm near your south pole at this very moment. But his surroundings are . . . more comfortable and secure than our tent."

I looked at the other two and we all showed raised eyebrows.

"I didn't know you brought a phone with you on this climb, K," I said.

"I did not."

"Radio?" said Paul.

"No."

"Subcutaneous intergalactic Star Trek communicator?" said Gary. His sarcasm, much as his habit of chewing the nutrient bars too slowly, was beginning to get on my nerves after three days in this tent. I thought that perhaps the next time he was sarcastic or chewed slowly, I might just kill him.

K whistled ever so slightly. "No," he said. "I understood your climbers' tradition of bringing no communication devices on this expedition."

"Then how do you know that your . . . what was it, creche brother? . . . is in a storm down there?" asked Paul.

"Because he is my creche brother," said K. "We were born in the same hour. We are, essentially, the same genetic material."

"Twins," I said.

463

"So you have telepathy?" said Paul.

Kanakaredes shook his head, his proboscis almost brushing the flapping tent fabric. "Our scientists think that there is no such thing as telepathy. For any species."

"Then how . . ." I began.

"My creche brother and I often resonate on the same frequencies to the song of the world and universe," said K in one of the longest sentences we'd heard from him. "Much as your identical twins do. We often share the same dreams."

Bugs dream. I made a mental note to record this factoid later.

"And does your creche brother know what you're feeling right now?" said Paul.

"I believe so."

"And what's that?" asked Gary, chewing far too slowly on an n-bar.

"Right now," said Kanakaredes, "it is fear."

Knife-edge ridge beyond Camp III—about 23,700 ft.

The fourth day dawned perfectly clear, perfectly calm.

We were packed and climbing across the traverse before the first rays of sunlight struck the ridgeline. It was cold as a witch's tit.

I mentioned that this part of the route was perhaps the most technically challenging of the climb—at least until we reached the actual summit pyramid—but it was also the most beautiful and exhilarating. You would have to see photos to appreciate the almost absurd steepness of this section of the ridge and even then it wouldn't allow you to *feel* the exposure. The northeast ridge just kept climbing in a series of swooping, knife-edged snow cornices, each side dropping away almost vertically.

As soon as we had moved onto the ridge, we looked back at the gigantic serac hanging above the trampled area of our Camp III perched on the edge of the ridge—the snow serac larger and more deformed and obviously unstable than ever after the heavy snows and howling winds of the last four days of storm—and we didn't have to say a word to one another to acknowledge how lucky we had been. Even Kanakaredes seemed grateful to get out of there.

Two hundred feet into the traverse and we went up and over the blade of the knife. The snowy ridgeline was so narrow here that we could—and did—straddle it for a minute as if swinging our legs over a very, very steep roofline.

Some roof. One side dropped down thousands of feet into what used to be China. Our left legs—three of Kanakaredes's—hung over what used to be Pakistan. Right around this point, climbers in the 20th Century used to joke about needing passports but seeing no border guards. In this CMG-era, a Sianking HK gunship or Indian hop-fighter could float up here anytime, hover fifty yards out, and blow us right off the ridge. None of us were worried about this. Kanakaredes's presence was insurance against that.

This was the hardest climbing yet and our bug friend was working hard to keep up. Gary and Paul and I had discussed this the night before, whispering again while K was asleep, and we decided that this section was too steep for all of us to be roped together. We'd travel in two pairs. Paul was the obvious man to rope with K, although if either of them came off on this traverse, odds were overwhelming that the other would go all the way to the bottom with him. The same was true of Gary and me, climbing ahead of them. Still, it gave a very slight measure of insurance.

The sunlight moved down the slope, warming us, as we moved from one side of the knife-edge to the other, following the best line, trying to stay off the sections so steep that snow would not stick—avoiding it not just because of the pitch there, but because the rock was almost always loose and rotten—and hoping to get as far as we could before the warming sun loosened the snow enough to make our crampons less effective.

I loved the litany of the tools we were using: deadmen, pitons, pickets, ice screws, carabiners, jumar ascenders. I loved the precision of our movments, even with the labored breathing and dull minds that were a component of any exertion at almost 8,000 meters. Gary would kick-step his way out onto the wall of ice and snow and occasional rock, one cramponed boot at a time, secure on three points before dislodging his ice axe and slamming it in a few feet further on. I stood on a tiny platform I'd hacked out of the snow, belaying Gary until he'd moved out to the end of our two-hundred foot section of line. Then he'd anchor his end of the line with a deadman, piton, picket, or ice screw, go on belay himself, and I would move off—kicking the crampon points into the snow-wall rising almost vertically to blue sky just fifty or sixty feet above me.

A hundred yards or so behind us, Paul and Kanakaredes were doing the same—Paul in the lead and K on belay, then K climbing and Paul belaying and resting until the bug caught up.

We might as well have been on different planets. There was no conversation. We used every ounce of breath to take our next gasping step, to concentrate on precise placement of our feet and ice axes.

A 20th Century climbing team might have taken days to make this traverse, establishing fixed lines, retreating to their tents at Camp III to eat and sleep, allowing other teams to break trail beyond the fixed ropes the next day. We did not have that luxury. We had to make this traverse in one try and keep moving up the ridge while the perfect weather lasted or we were screwed.

I loved it.

About five hours into the traverse, I realized that butterflies were fluttering all around me. I looked up toward

Gary on belay two hundred feet ahead and above me. He was also watching butterflies—small motes of color dancing and weaving twenty-three thousand feet above sea level. What the hell would Kanakaredes make of this? Would he think this was an everyday occurance at this altitude? Well, perhaps it was. We humans weren't up here enough to know. I shook my head and continued shuffling my boots and slamming my ice axe up the impossible ridge.

The rays of the sun were horizontal in late afternoon when all four of us came off the knife-edge at the upper end of the traverse. The ridge was still heart-stoppingly steep there, but it had widened out so that we could stand on it as we looked back at our footprints on the snowy blade of the knife-edge. Even after all these years of climbing, I still found it hard to believe that we had been able to make those tracks.

"Hey!" shouted Gary. "I'm a fucking giant!" He was flapping his arms and staring toward Sinkiang and the Godwin-Austen Glacier miles below us.

Altitude's got him, I thought. *We'll have to sedate him, tie him in his sleeping bag and drag him down the way we came like so much laundry.*

"Come on!" Gary shouted to me in the high, cold air. "Be a giant, Jake." He continued flapping his arms. I turned to look behind me and Paul and Karakaredes were also hopping up and down, carefully so as not to fall off the foot-wide ridgeline, shouting and flapping their arms. It was quite a sight to see K moving his mantisy forearms six ways at once, joints swiveling, boneless fingers waving like big grubs.

They've all lost it, I thought. *Oxygen deprivation lunacy.* Then I looked down and east.

Our shadows leaped out miles across the glacier and the neighboring mountains. I raised my arms. Lowered them. My shadow atop the dark line of ridge shadow raised and lowered shadow-arms that must have been ten miles tall.

We kept this up—jumping shouting, waving—until the sun set behind Broad Peak to the west and our giant selves disappeared forever.

Camp VI—narrow bench on snow dome below summit pyramid, 26,200 feet

No conversation or talk of listening to songs now. No jumping or shouting or waving. Not enough oxygen here to breathe or think, much less fuck around.

Almost no conversation the last three days or nights as we climbed the last of the broadening northeast ridge to where it ended at the huge snow dome, then climbed the snow dome itself. The weather stayed calm and clear—incredible for this late in the season. The snow was deep because of the storm that had pinned us down at Camp III, but we took turns breaking trail—an exhausting job at 10,000 feet, literally mind-numbing above 25,000 feet.

At night, we didn't even bother merging our tents—just using our own segments like bivvy bags. We only heated one warm meal a day—super-nutrient soup on the single stove (we'd left the other behind just beyond the knife-edge traverse, along with everything else we didn't think we'd need in the last three or four days of climbing)—and chewed on cold n-bars at night before drifting off into a half-doze for a few cold, restless hours before stirring at three or four a.m. to begin climbing again by lamplight.

All of us humans had miserable headaches and high-altitude stupidity. Paul was in the worst shape—perhaps because of the frostbite scare way down during his first attempt at the traverse—and he was coughing heavily and moving sluggishly. Even K had slowed down, climbing mostly two-legged on this high stretch, and sometimes taking a minute or more before planting his feet.

Most Himalayan mountains have ridges that go all the way to the summit. Not K2. Not this northeast ridge. It ended at a bulging snow dome some 2,000 ft. below the summit.

We climbed the snow dome—slowly, stupidly, sluggishly, separately. No ropes or belays here. If anyone fell to his death, it was going to be a solitary fall. We did not care. At and above the legendary 8,000 meter line, you move into yourself and then—often—lose even yourself.

We had not brought oxygen, not even the light osmosis booster-mask perfected in the last decade. We had one of those masks—in case any of us became critically ill from pulmonary edema or worse—but we'd left the mask cached with the stove, most of the rope, and other extra supplies above Camp IV. It had seemed like a good idea at the time.

Now all I could think about was breathing. Every move—every step—took more breath than I had, more oxygen than my system owned. Paul seemed in even worse shape, although somehow he kept up. Gary was moving steadily, but sometimes he betrayed his headaches and confusion by movement or pause. He had vomited twice this morning before we moved out from Camp VI. At night, we startled awake after only a minute or two of half-sleep—gasping for air, clawing at our own chests, feeling as if something heavy was lying on us and someone was actively trying to suffocate us.

Something *was* trying to kill us here. Everything was. We were high in the Death Zone and K2 did not care one way or the other if we lived or died.

The good weather had held, but high wind and storms were overdue. It was the end of August. Any day or night now we could be pinned down up here for weeks of unrelenting storm—unable to climb, unable to retreat. We could starve to death up here. I thought of the red panic button on the palmlog.

We had told Kanakaredes about the panic button while we heated soup at Camp V. The mantispid had asked to see the extra palmlog with the emergency beacon. Then he had thrown the palmlog out the tent entrance, into the night, over the edge.

Gary had looked at our bug for a long minute then and then grinned, extending his hand. K's foreleg had unfolded, the mantis part swiveling, and those three fingers had encircled Gary's hand and shaken it.

I had thought this was rather cool and heroic at the time. Now I just wished we had the goddamned panic button back.

We stirred, got dressed, and started heating water for our last meal shortly after 1:30 a.m. None of us could sleep anyway and every extra hour we spent up here in the Death Zone meant more chance to die, more chance to fail. But we were moving so slowly that tugging our boots on seemed to take hours, adjusting our crampons took forever. We moved away from the tents sometime after three a.m. We left the tents behind at Camp VI. If we survived the summit attempt, we'd be back.

It was unbelievably cold. Even the thermskins and smart outer parkas failed to make up the difference. If there had been a wind, we could not have continued.

We were now on what we called Direct Finish—the top or bust—although our original fallback plan had been to traverse across the face of K2 to the oldest route up the northwest Abruzzi Ridge if Direct Finish proved unfeasible. I think that all three of us had suspected we'd end up on the Abruzzi—most of our predecessors climbing the northeast ridge had ended up doing so, even the legendary Reinhold Messner, perhaps the greatest climber of the 20th Century, had been forced to change his route to the easier Abruzzi Ridge rather than suffer failure on the Direct Finish.

Well, by early afternoon of what was supposed to have been our summit day, Direct Finish now seems impossible and so does the traverse to the Abruzzi. The snow on the face of K2 is so deep that there is no hope of traversing through it to the Abruzzi Ridge. Avalanches hurtle down the face several times an hour. And above us—even deeper snow. We're fucked.

The day had started well. Above the almost vertical snowdome on which we'd hacked out a wide enough bench to lodge Camp VI, rose a huge snowfield that snaked up and up toward the black, starfilled sky until it became a wall. We climbed slowly, agonizingly, up the snowfield, leaving separate tracks, thinking separate thoughts. It was getting light by the time we reached the end of the snow ramp.

Where the snowfield ended a vertical ice cliff began and rose at least a hundred and fifty feet straight up. Literally fucking vertical. The four of us stood there in the morning light, three of us rubbing our goggles, looking stupidly at the cliff. We'd known it was there. We'd had no idea what a bitch it was going to be.

"I'll do the lead," gasped Paul. He could barely walk. He free-climbed the fucker in less than an hour, slamming in pitons and screws and tying on the last of our rope. When the three of us climbed slowly, stupidly up to join him, me bringing up the rear just behind K, Paul was only semi-conscious.

Above the ice cliff rose a steep rock band. It was so steep that snow couldn't cling there. The rock looked rotten—treacherous—the kind of fragile crap that any sane climber would traverse half a day to avoid.

There would be no traverse today. Any attempt to shift laterally on the face here would almost certainly trigger an avalanche in the soft slabs of snow overlaying old ice.

"I'll lead," said Gary, still looking up at the rock band. He was holding his head with both hands. I knew that Gary always suffered the worst of the Death Zone headaches that afflicted all three of us. For four or five days and nights now, I knew, every word and breath had been punctuated by slivers of steel pain behind the eyes for Gary.

I nodded and helped Paul to his feet. Gary began to climb the lower strata of crumbling rock.

We reach the end of the rock by mid-afternoon. The wind is rising. A spume of spindrift blows off the near-vertical snow and ice above us. We cannot see the summit. Above a narrow coloir that rises like a chimney to frigid hell, the summit-pyramid snowfield begins. We're somewhere above 27,000 feet.

K2 is 28,250 feet high.

That last twelve hundred feet might as well be measured in light years.

"I'll break trail up the coloir," I hear myself say. The others don't even nod, merely wait for me to begin. Kanakaredes is leaning on his ice axe in a posture I've not seen before.

My first step up the coloir sends me into snow above my knees. This is impossible. I would weep now, except that the tears would freeze to the inside of my goggles and blind me. It is impossible to take another step up this steep fucking gully. I can't even breathe. My head pounds so terribly that my vision dances and blurs and no amount of wiping my goggles will clear it.

I lift my ice axe, slam it three feet higher, and lift my right leg. Again. Again.

Summit pyramid snowfield above the coloir, somewhere around 27,800 ft.

Late afternoon. It will be almost dark when we reach the summit. *If* we reach the summit.

Everything depends upon the snow that rises above us toward the impossibly dark blue sky. If the snow is firm—nowhere as mushy and deep as the thigh-high soup I broke trail through all the way up the coloir—then we have a chance, although we'll be descending in the dark.

But if it's deep snow . . .

"I'll lead," said Gary, shifting his small summit-pack

on his back and slogging slowly up to replace me in the lead. There is a rockband here at the top of the narrow coloir and he will be stepping off it either into or onto the snow. If the surface is firm, we'll move *onto* it, using our crampons to kick step our way up the last couple of hours of climb to the summit—although we still cannot see the summit from here.

I try to look around me. Literally beneath my feet is a drop to the impossibly distant knife-edge, far below that the ridge where we put Camp II, miles and miles lower the curving, rippled river of Godwin-Austen and a dim memory of base camp and of living things—lichen, crows, a clump of grass where the glacier was melting. On either side stretches the Karakoram, white peaks thrusting up like fangs, distant summits merging into the Himalayan peaks, and one lone peak—I'm too stupid to even guess which one—standing high and solitary against the sky. The red hills of China burn in the thick haze of breathable atmosphere a hundred miles to the north.

"OK," says Gary, stepping off the rock onto the snowfield.

He plunges in soft snow up to his waist.

Somehow Gary finds enough breath to hurl curses at the snow, at any and all gods who would put such deep snow here. He lunges another step up and forward.

The snow is even deeper. Gary founders almost up to his armpits. He slashes at the snowfield with his ice axe, batters it with his overmittens. The snowfield and K2 ignore him.

I go to both knees on the pitched rock band and lean on my ice axe, not caring if my sobs can be heard by the others or if my tears will freeze my eyelids open. The expedition is over.

Kanakaredes slowly pulls his segmented body up the last ten feet of the coloir, past Paul where Paul is retching against a boulder, past me where I am kneeling, onto the last of the solid surface before Gary's sliding snow-pit.

"I will lead for a while," says Kanakaredes. He sets his ice axe into his harness. His prothorax shifts lower. His hind legs come down and out. His arms—forelegs—rotate down and forward.

Kanakaredes thrusts himself into the steep snowfield like an Olympic swimmer diving off the starting block. He passes Gary where Gary lies armpit deep in the soft snow.

The bug—*our* bug—flails and batters the snow with his forearms, parts it with his cupped fingers, smashes it down with his armored upper body segment, swims through the snow with all six legs paddling.

He can't possibly keep this up. It's impossible. Nothing living has that much energy and will. It is seven or eight hundred near-vertical feet to the summit.

K swims-kicks-fights his way fifteen feet up the slope. Twenty-five. Thirty.

Getting to my feet, feeling my temples pounding in agony, sensing invisible climbers around me, ghosts hovering in the Death Zone fog of pain and confusion, I step past Gary and start postholing upward, following K's lead, struggling and swimming up and through the now-broken barrier of snow.

Summit of K2, 28, 250 ft.

We step onto the summit together, arm in arm. All four of us. The final summit ridge is just wide enough to allow this.

Many 8,000-meter-peak summits have overhanging cornices. After all this effort, the climber sometimes takes his or her final step to triumph and falls for a mile or so. We don't know if K2 is corniced. Like many of these other climbers, we're too exhausted to care. Kanakaredes can no longer stand or walk after breaking trail through the snowfield for more than six hundred feet. Gary and I carry him the last hundred feet or so, our arms under his mantis arms. I am shocked to discover that he weighs almost nothing. All that energy, all that spirit, and K probably weighs no more than a hundred pounds.

The summit is not corniced. We do not fall.

The weather has held, although the sun is setting. Its last rays warm us through our parkas and thermskins. The sky is a blue deeper than cerulean, much deeper than topaz, incomparably deeper than aquamarine. Perhaps this shade of blue has no word to describe it.

We can see to the curve of the earth and beyond. Two peaks are visible above that curving horizon, their summit icefields glowing orange in the sunset, a great distance to the northeast, probably somewhere in Chinese Turkestan. To the south lies the entire tumble of overlapping peaks and winding glaciers that is the Karakoram. I make out the perfect peak that is Nanga Parbat—Gary, Paul, and I climbed that six years ago—and closer, the Gasherbrums. At our feet, literally at our feet, Broad Peak. Who would have thought that its summit looked so wide and flat from above?

The four of us are all sprawled on the narrow summit, two feet from the sheer dropoff on the north. My arms are still around Kanakaredes, ostensibly propping him up but actually propping both of us up.

The mantispid clicks, hisses, and squeeks. He shakes his beak and tries again. "I am . . . sorry," he gasps, the air audibly hissing in and out of his beak nostrils. "I ask . . . traditionally, what do we do now? Is there a ceremony for this moment? A ritual required?"

I look at Paul, who seems to be recovering from his earlier inertia. We both look at Gary.

"Try not to fuck up and die," says Gary between breaths. "More climbers die during the descent than on the way up."

Karakaredes seems to be considering this. After a minute he says, "Yes, but here on the summit, there must be some ritual . . ."

"Hero photos," gasps Paul. "Gotta . . . have . . . hero photos."

Our alien nods. "Did . . . anyone . . . bring an imaging device? A camera? I did not."

Gary, Paul and I look at each other, pat our parka pockets, and then start laughing. At this altitude, our laughter sounds like three sick seals coughing.

"Well, no hero photos," says Gary. "Then we have to haul the flags out. Always bring a flag to the summit, that's our human motto." This extended speech makes Gary so light headed that he has to put his head between his raised knees for a minute.

"I have no flag," says Kanakaredes. "The Listeners have never had a flag." The sun is setting in earnest now, the last rays shining between a line of peaks to the west, but the reddish-orange light glows brightly on our stupid, smiling faces and mittons and goggles and ice-crusted parkas.

"We didn't bring a flag either," I say.

"This is good," says K. "So there is nothing else we need to do?"

"Just get down alive," says Paul.

We rise together, weaving a bit, propping one another up, retrieve our ice axes from where we had thrust them into the glowing summit snow, and begin retracing our steps down the long snowfield into shadow.

Godwin-Austin Glacier, about 17,300 ft.

It took us only four and a half days to get down, and that included a day of rest at our old Camp III on the low side of the knife-edge traverse.

The weather held the whole time. We did not get back to our high camp—Camp VI below the ice wall— until after three a.m. after our successful summit day, but the lack of wind had kept our tracks clear even in lamplight and no one slipped or fell or suffered frostbite.

We moved quickly after that, leaving just after dawn the next day to get to Camp IV on the upper end of the knife-edge before nightfall . . . and before the gods of K2 changed their minds and blew up a storm to trap us in the Death Zone.

The only incident on the lower slopes of the mountain happened—oddly enough—on a relatively easy stretch of snowslope below Camp II. The four of us were picking our way down the slope, unroped, lost in our own thoughts and in the not-unpleasant haze of exhaustion so common near the end of a climb, when K just came loose—perhaps he tripped over one of his own hindlegs, although he denied that later—and ended up on his stomach—or at least the bottom of his upper shell, all six legs spraddled, ice axe flying free, starting a slide that would have been harmless enough for the first hundred yards or so if it had not been for the drop off that fell away to the glacier still a thousand feet directly below.

Luckily, Gary was about a hundred feet ahead of the rest of us and he dug in his axe, looped a line once around himself and twice around the axe, timed K's slide perfectly, and then threw himself on his belly out onto the ice slope, his reaching hand grabbing Kanakaredes's three fingers as slick as a pair of aerial trapeze partners. The rope snapped taut, the axe held its place, man and mantispid swung two and a half times like the working end of a pendulum, and that was the end of that drama. K had to make it the rest of the way to the glacier without an ice axe the next day, but he managed all right. And we now know how a bug shows embarrassment—his occipital ridges blush a dark orange.

Off the ridge at last, we roped up for the glacier but voted unanimously to descend it by staying close to the east face of K2. The earlier snowstorm had hidden all the crevasses and we had heard or seen no avalanches in the past seventy-two hours. There were far fewer crevasses near the face but an avalanche could catch us anywhere on the glacier. Staying near the face carried its own risks, but it would also get us down the ice and out of avalanche danger in half the time it would take to probe for crevasses down the center of the glacier.

We were two-thirds of the way down—the bright red tents of Base Camp clearly in sight out on the rock beyond the ice—when Gary said, "Maybe we should talk about this Olympus Mons deal, K."

"Yes," click-hissed our bug, "I have been looking forward to discussing this plan and I hope that perhaps . . . "

We heard it then before we saw it. Several freight trains seemed to be bearing down on us from above, from the face of K2.

All of us froze, trying to see the snowplume trail of the avalanche, hoping against hope that it would come out onto the glacier far behind us. It came off the face and across the *bergeschrund* a quarter of a mile directly above us and picked up speed, coming directly at us. It looked like a white tsunami. The roar was deafening.

"Run!" shouted Gary and we all took off downhill, not worrying if there were bottomless crevasses directly in front of us, not caring at that point, just trying against all logic to outrun a wall of snow and ice and boulders roiling toward us at sixty miles per hour.

I remember now that we were roped with the last of our spidersilk—sixty-foot intervals—the lines clipped to our climbing harnesses. It made no difference to Gary, Paul and me since we were running flat out and in the same direction and at about the same speed, but I have seen mantispids move at full speed since that day—using all six legs, their hands forming into an extra pair of flat feet—and I know now that K could have shifted into high gear and run four times as fast as the rest of us. Perhaps he could have beaten the avalanche since just the south edge of its wave caught us. Perhaps.

He did not try. He did not cut the rope. He ran with us.

The south edge of the avalanche caught us and lifted us and pulled us under and snapped the unbreakable spidersilk climbing rope and tossed us up and then submerged us again and swept us all down into the crevasse field at the bottom of the glacier and separated us forever.

Washington, D.C.

Sitting here in the Secretary of State's waiting room three months after that day, I've had time to think about it.

All of us—everyone on the planet, even the bugs—have been preoccupied in the past couple of months as the Song has begun and increased in complexity and beauty. Oddly enough, it's not that distracting, the Song. We go about our business. We work and talk and eat and watch HDTV and make love and sleep, but always there now—always in the background whenever one wants to listen—is the Song.

It's unbelievable that we've never heard it before this.

No one calls them bugs or mantispids or the Listeners any more. Everyone, in every language, calls them the Bringers of the Song.

Meanwhile, the Bringers keep reminding us that they did not *bring* the Song, only taught us how to listen to it.

*   *   *

I don't know how or why I survived when none of the others did. The theory is that one can swim along the surface of a snow avalanche, but the reality was that none of us had the slightest chance to try. That half-mile-wide wall of snow and rock just washed over us and pulled us down and spat out only me, for reasons known, perhaps, only to K2 and most probably not even to it.

They found me naked and battered more than three-quarters of a mile from where we had started running from the avalanche. They never found Gary, Paul, or Kanakaredes.

The emergency CMG's were there within three minutes—they must have been poised to intervene all that time—but after twenty hours of deep-probing and sonar searching, just when the Marines and the bureaucrats were ready to lase away the whole lower third of the glacier if necessary to recover my friends' bodies, it was Speaker Aduradake-Kanakaredes's father *and* mother, it turned out—who forbade it.

"Leave them wherever they are," he instructed the fluttering U.N. bureaucrats and frowning Marine colonels. "They died together on your world and should remain together within the embrace of your world. Their part of the song is joined now."

And the Song began—or at least was first heard—about one week later.

* * *

A male secretary to the Secretary comes out, apologizes profusely for my having to wait—Secretary Bright Moon was with the President—and shows me into the Secretary of State's office. The secretary and I stand there waiting.

I've seen football games played in smaller areas than this office.

The Secretary comes in through a different door a minute later and leads me over to two couches facing each other rather than to the uncomfortable chair near her huge desk. She seats me across from her, makes sure that I don't want any coffee or other refreshment, nods away her secretary, commiserates with me again on the death of my dear friends (she had been there at the Memorial Service at which the President had spoken), chats with me for another minute about how amazing life is now with the Song connecting all of us, and then questions me for a few minutes, sensitively, solicitously, about my physical recovery (complete), my state of mind (shaken but improving), my generous stipend from the government (already invested), and my plans for the future.

"That's the reason I asked for this meeting," I say. "There was that promise of climbing Olympus Mons."

She stares at me.

"On Mars," I add needlessly.

Secretary Betty Willard Bright Moon nods and sits back in the cushions. She brushes some invisible lint from her navy blue skirt. "Ah, yes," she says, her voice still pleasant but holding some hint of that flintiness I remember so well from our Top of the World meeting. "The Bringers have confirmed that they intend to honor that promise."

I wait.

"Have you decided who your next climbing partners will be?" she asked, taking out an obscenely expensive and micron-thin platinum palmlog as if she is going to take notes herself to help facilitate this whim of mine.

"Yeah," I said.

Now it was the Secretary's turn to wait.

"I want Kanakaredes's brother," I say. "His ... creche brother."

Betty Willard Bright Moon jaw almost drops open. I doubt very much if she's reacted this visibly to a statement in her last thirty years of professional negotiating, first as a take-no-prisoners Harvard academic and most recently as Secretary of State. "You're serious," she says.

"Yes."

"Anyone else other than this particular bu ... Bringer?"

"No one else."

"And you're sure he even exists?"

"I'm sure."

"How do you know if he wants to risk his life on a Martian volcano?" she asks, her poker face back in place. "Olympus Mons is taller than K2, you know. And it's probably more dangerous."

I almost, not quite, smile at this newsflash. "He'll go," I say.

Secretary Bright Moon makes a quick note in her palmlog and then hesitates. Even though her expression is perfectly neutral now, I know that she is trying to decide whether to ask a question that she might not get the chance to ask later.

Hell, knowing that question was coming and trying to decide how to answer it is the reason I didn't come to visit her a month ago, when I decided to do this thing. But then I remembered Kanakaredes's answer when we asked him why the bugs had come all this way to visit us. He had read his Mallory and he had understood Gary, Paul, and me—and something about the human race—that this woman never would.

She makes up her mind to ask her question.

"Why . . ." she begins. "Why do you want to climb it?"

Despite everything that's happened, despite knowing that she'll never understand, despite knowing what an asshole she'll always consider me after this moment, I have to smile.

"Because it's there."

ABOUT THE AUTHORS

James Patrick Kelly has had an eclectic writing career. He has written novels, short stories, essays, reviews, poetry, plays and planetarium shows. His books include *Think Like A Dinosaur* and other stories (1997), *Wildlife* (1994), *Heroines* (1990), *Look Into The Sun* (1989), *Freedom Beach* (1986) and *Planet of Whispers* (1984). His fiction has been translated into fourteen languages. He has won two Hugos: in 1996, for his novelette "Think Like A Dinosaur" and in 2000, for his novelette, "10^16 to 1." He writes a column on the internet for *Isaac Asimov's Science Fiction Magazine* and his audio plays are a regular feature on Scifi.com's Seeing Ear Theater. He is currently one of fourteen councilors appointed by Governor Jeanne Shaheen to the New Hampshire State Council on the Arts.

Michael Blumlein is the author of the World Fantasy Award-nominated story collection, *The Brains of Rats*, and two novels, *The Movement of Mountains* and *X,Y*. The latter book is being made into a movie. His many

489

stories have been translated and reprinted widely. He plans a second collection in the near future.

Richard Wadholm is a recent Clarion graduate who has sold several fiction pieces to *Asimov's Science Fiction*, most notably the story "Green Tea," which won the Theodore Sturgeon award for Short Fiction and was reprinted in *The Year's Best Science Fiction: Seventeenth Annual Edition*. His first novel, *Astronomy*, was published electronically in 2001.

Robin Wayne Bailey is the author of a dozen novels, including the *Brothers of the Dragon* series, *Shadowdance*, and *Swords Against The Shadowland*, which continues the adventures of Fritz Leiber's famous characters, Fafhrd and the Gray Mouser. His short science fiction has appeared in numerous anthologies, including *Silicon Dreams*, *Past Imperfect*, *Guardsmen of Tomorrow*, and *Far Frontiers*. His next book, *Night's Angel*, will be published by Meisha Merlin Books in May. He lives in North Kansas City, Missouri.

Gregory Benford is a working scientist who has written some 23 critically-acclaimed novels. He has received two Nebula Awards, principally in 1981 for *Timescape*, a novel which sold over a million copies and won the John W. Campbell Memorial Award, the Australian Ditmar Award, and the British Science Fiction Award. In

1992, Dr. Benford received the United Nations Medal in Literature. He is also a professor of physics at the University of California, Irvine since 1971. He specializes in astrophysics and plasma physics theory and was presented with the Lord Prize in 1995 for achievements in the sciences. He is a Woodrow Wilson Fellow and Phi Beta Kappa. He has been an advisor to the National Aeronautics and Space Administration, the United States Department of Energy, and the White House Council on Space Policy, and has served as a visiting fellow at Cambridge University. Recent work includes his first book-length work of nonfiction, *Deep Time*, which examines his work in long duration messages from a broad humanistic and scientific perspective.

Born in 1943, Ian Watson taught literature in Tanzania and Japan and Futures Studies in Birmingham England before becoming a full-time writer in 1976. His first novel, *The Embedding*, was a winner of the John W. Campbell Memorial Award and of the French Prix Apollo. Many novels followed, as well as enough short fiction to fill eight collections. The ninth, *The Great Escape*, is due in Spring 2002 from Golden Gryphon Press, which will also publish his novel *Mockymen* in 2003. His first poetry collection, *The Lexicographer's Love Song*, appeared from DNA Publications in Fall 2001. He wrote the screen story for Spielberg's film *A.I.* and he lives in the heart of rural England with a black cat.

Michael Swanwick is one of the most prolific and inventive writers in science fiction today. His works have been honored with the Hugo, Nebula, Theodore Sturgeon, and World Fantasy Awards, and have been translated and published throughout the world. Recent collections of his short work include *Tales of Old Earth* (Frog, Ltd.), *Moon Dogs* (NESFA Press), and the reissued *Gravity's Angels* (Frog, Ltd.). His novels include *Jack Faust*, *The Iron Dragon's Daughter*, and the Nebula award-winning *Stations Of The Tide*. A weekly series of short-short stories, "Michael Swanwick's Periodic Table of Science Fiction," one story for every element in the periodic table, is currently running online at Sci Fiction (www.scifi.com/scifiction). He lives in Philadelphia with his wife, Marianne Porter. His next novel, *Bones of the Earth*, will be published in February of 2002 by HarperCollins.

Nancy Kress is the author of eighteen books. She is perhaps best known for the science fiction "Sleepless" trilogy (*Beggars in Spain*, *Beggars and Choosers*, *Beggars Ride*). Her most recent book is *Probability Sun* (Tor), a 2001 sequel to the previous year's *Probability Moon*. Kress's short fiction has won three Nebulas: in 1985 for "Out Of All Them Bright Stars," in 1991 for the novella version of "Beggars In Spain" (which also won a Hugo), and in 1998 for "The Flowers of Aulit Prison." She has also lost over a dozen of these awards. Kress is the monthly "Fiction" columnist for *Writer's Digest Magazine*. She lives in Silver Spring, Maryland, with husband and fellow SF writer Charles Sheffield.

Stephen Baxter writes, "I was born in Liverpool, England, in 1957. I have degrees in mathematics, from Cambridge University, and engineering, from Southampton University. I worked as a teacher of math and physics, and for several years in information technology. I applied to become a cosmonaut in 1991—aiming for the guest slot on Mir eventually taken by Helen Sharman—but fell at an early hurdle. My first professionally published short story was in 1987. I have been a full-time author since 1995.

"My science fiction novels have been published in the UK, the US, and in many other countries including Germany, Japan, France. My books have won several awards including the Philip K Dick Award, the John Campbell Memorial Award, the British Science Fiction Association Award, the Kurd Lasswitz Award (Germany) and the Seiun Award (Japan) and have been nominated for several others, including the Arthur C Clarke Award, the Hugo Award and Locus awards. I have published over 200 sf short stories, several of which have won prizes. My novel *Voyage* was dramatized by Audio Movies for BBC Radio in 1999. My novel *Timelike Infinity* and my short story 'Pilot' are both currently under development for feature films. My TV and movie work includes development work on the BBC's *Invasion: Earth* and the script for Episode 3 of *Space Island One*, broadcast on Sky One in January 1998. My non-fiction includes the books *Deep Future* and *Omegatropic*. My next publication will be the novel *Evolution* (Gollancz, Nov 2002)."

Jim Grimsley is a playwright and novelist who was born in Rocky Mount, North Carolina. He attended the University of North Carolina at Chapel Hill and currently lives in Atlanta, Georgia. His first novel, *Winter Birds*, was published by Algonquin Books in 1994, and won the 1995 Sue Kaufman Prize for First Fiction given by the American Academy of Arts and Letters, as well as a special citation from the Ernest Hemingway Foundation as one of three finalists for the PEN/Hemingway Award. Jim's second novel, *Dream Boy*, was published by Algonquin in September, 1995, and won the 1996 Award for Gay, Lesbian and Bisexual Literature for the American Library Association; the novel was also one of five finalists for the Lambda Literary Award. His third novel, *My Drowning*, was published in 1997 and for this book Jim was named Georgia Author of the Year. His fourth novel, *Comfort & Joy* was a Lambda Literary Award finalist, and his fifth mainstream novel, *Boulevard*, will be published in April 2002. His first fantasy novel, *Kirith Kirin*, was published by Meisha Merlin Press in June

2000 and won the Lambda Literary Award in the Science Fiction/Horror category. His short fiction has been anthologized in *The Year's Best Science Fiction: Sixteenth Annual Collection*, edited by Gardner Dozois, in *Best New Stories from the South*, 2001 edition, edited by Shannon Ravenel, and in other anthologies. He is a member of PEN, Dramatists Guild, Alternate ROOTS, and the Science Fiction & Fantasy Writers of America.

Born in East Peoria in 1948, Dan Simmons became an elementary teacher after earning a master's degree from Washington University in St. Louis, in 1971, and worked in the field of education for the next ten years. His fiction career began in earnest in 1981, when Harlan Ellison entered Simmons' short story, "The River Styx Runs Upstream," in a contest for beginning writers, where the story won the contest and publication in 1982. Three years later, his first novel, *Song of Kali*, won the World Fantasy Award. Since then, he has published more than a dozen novels in several different genres, including *Phases of Gravity*, *Hyperion* and *The Fall of Hyperion*, and *Endymion* and *The Rise of Endymion*. He has also produced four collections of short stories, including *Prayers to Broken Stones* and *Lovedeath: Five Stories about Love and Death*, and two nonfiction books about writing. Along the way, he has earned a Hugo Award, two World Fantasy Awards, a Theodore Stur-

ABOUT THE AUTHORS

geon Award for short fiction, eight Locus Awards, the British Fantasy and Science Fiction Awards, and four Bram Stoker Awards from the Horror Writers of America. Recent novels include *Darwin's Blade*, *Hardcase*, and *A Winter Haunting*.